American Challenge

1770-1819

4 Stories in 1

BARBOUR
PUBLISHING

Lydia the Patriot © 2004 by Barbour Publishing, Inc.
Kate and the Spies © 2004 by JoAnn A. Grote
Betsy's River Adventure © 2004 by Barbour Publishing, Inc.
Grace and the Bully © 2006 by Barbour Publishing, Inc.

ISBN 978-1-61626-463-5

All scripture quotations are taken from the King James Version of the Bible.

Cover design © Greg Jackson, Thinkpen Design

Published by Barbour Publishing, Inc., P.O. Box 719, Uhrichsville, Ohio 44683, www.barbourbooks.com

Our mission is to publish and distribute inspirational products offering exceptional value and biblical encouragement to the masses.

ecpa Member of the
Evangelical Christian
Publishers Association

Printed in the United States of America.
Bethany Press International, Bloomington, MN 55438; October 2012; D10003566

Lydia
the Patriot

Susan Martins Miller

A NOTE TO READERS

In *Lydia the Patriot* we meet Stephen and Lydia Lankford. While the Lankfords are a fictional family, the Boston Massacre actually did take place, and this story of the shootings and the trial that followed are based on the many firsthand accounts that still exist.

It may strike you as odd that the baby born at the beginning of this book doesn't get named for eight months. While we usually name our babies right away, it was common for parents in the eighteenth century to wait several months, and sometimes years, before they named their children. More than one in six babies died before they reached their second birthday, and usually parents waited until they were sure their child would live before they decided on a name.

Contents

CHAPTER 1

Unwelcome Soldiers

Lydia was doing it again. Ten-year-old Stephen Lankford closed his brown eyes and let his head hang down to his chest.

Lydia's green eyes flashed as she bobbed her brown-haired head around the corner and shouted, "Lobsterback!"

"This is great!" Lydia said gleefully. She rested against the brick of the customs building to catch her breath. "He doesn't even see us!" She leaned around the corner again. "Bloodyback!"

"It doesn't matter if he doesn't see you," said Stephen, who was much more sensible than his fiery twelve-year-old sister. "He's a British soldier on duty. He doesn't care what you are doing."

"Uncle Cuyler says the soldiers are human beings like the rest of us," Lydia asserted. "If he's human, then he has to notice when someone is bothering him. It's just a question of how long it takes." She stepped out farther this time. Cupping her hands around her mouth, she called, "Lobsterback! Go home!"

"Why do you do this, Lydia?" Stephen asked, his irritation

growing. He shifted the bucket of food he carried from one hand to the other. "He's a soldier. He gets his orders from a general or the king or somebody. You're just a silly little girl. He's not going to go home to England just because you scream at him in the street."

"I am not a silly little girl!" Lydia declared. "I'm twelve years old, and my father is a leading citizen in Boston."

"That doesn't matter to a soldier."

Lydia stepped away from the wall more brazenly. "Be a man! Do what is right!" She stood there, her feet planted in the snow and her hands on her hips, glaring at the soldier.

The British soldier blinked in the early March snow flurry that fell gently from the sky. The tall egg-shaped bearskin hat made him look taller than he really was. His red woolen jacket and white breeches were splattered with the mud of dirty snow. Nevertheless, he stood with his feet solidly apart, his musket leaning over his shoulder. He was on duty. He paid no attention to Lydia. She certainly was not the first child who had pestered him while he was on duty.

"This is silly, Lydia," Stephen insisted. He stepped forward. "Let's keep going."

"No!" she cried indignantly. "I'm not finished." Lydia nearly knocked the breath out of him when she swung her arm around into his stomach.

Stephen grimaced and leaned against the building, holding his stomach. Lydia was acting the way she always did. She had to have her own way, and she refused to listen to logic. When she did not get what she wanted, she flailed around in such a fit that nearly everyone gave in to her just to calm her down.

Even their mother let Lydia have her way most of the time. In contrast, Stephen preferred to keep to himself and not disturb anyone else.

Stephen looked forward to the day when he would be allowed to move around Boston on his own. As it was, he always had to be with one of his older siblings. And considering the condition of Boston, his day of freedom was a long way off. Even Lydia usually had to have either their older sister, Kathleen, or their brother, William, with her. But on this day, she had nagged her mother into allowing her to cross Boston from the Lankford home to the home of Aunt Dancy and Uncle Ethan without supervision. Thinking that two were better than one, Mother had sent Stephen along. She could rely on him for an accurate report of any mishaps.

Stephen did not want to face any mishaps. He wanted Lydia to leave the soldier alone and move on to Aunt Dancy's house. He shifted his load once more.

Stephen knew he would most likely grow into manhood before peace came to Boston. Since Massachusetts was a British colony, Stephen had always accepted that it was logical for British soldiers to be there. But it seemed as if fewer and fewer people felt that way. Since the Townshend Acts took effect in 1767 and Boston became the headquarters for collecting customs fees, the people of Boston had started rioting the same way they had during the Stamp Act when Stephen was younger. Mobs broke into houses of British officials or anyone associated with the British government. They threw furniture around and made vicious threats, forcing some of the officials to leave Boston in fear of their lives. Even lifelong neighbors who showed a small amount of sympathy for British officials faced the fury of street gangs.

Stephen did not remember much about the Stamp Act. He had been only five then. In those days, his sister Kathleen had tried to protect him from what was happening. But William had told him the stories as he grew up. And now William made sure Stephen understood the Townshend Acts and why so many British troops were in Boston.

William Lankford, Stephen's brother, was nineteen now. He still lived in the Lankford family home and shared an attic room with Stephen, but William was a man. He worked all day alongside their father, Richard Lankford, putting out a newspaper and extra flyers about special events. Will was hardly ever home after supper.

When Stephen was younger, Will used to tell him simply that he had meetings to go to in the evenings. Now Stephen was old enough to know that most of Will's friends were in the Sons of Liberty. He also knew that many people in Boston believed that the Sons of Liberty were responsible for many of the wild activities that happened. Some even said that the Sons of Liberty were the ones who truly ruled Boston.

With Sam Adams and the other members of the Sons of Liberty, Will spent all his spare time planning how America, as he called the colonies, would someday be free of the British. America would make its own decisions about taxes and how to spend money. Each colony would be able to give its opinion about what was best for its citizens. And King George of England would mind his own business and concern himself with England.

When Stephen was eight, a single day had forced him to grow up in a hurry. He had been visiting his uncle Ethan, who owned Foy Shipping, down near the harbor. Suddenly the crew of one of the idle ships had scrambled through the streets around Boston Harbor with the news: British troops were coming. Holding his uncle's hand tightly, Stephen had run down to the harbor to see for himself.

The large British fleet had maneuvered its way in from the sea, past the green islands of Boston Harbor. The decks of the ships were solid red, covered with British soldiers who stood shoulder to shoulder. Their muskets were ready for action if needed. Anchors plunged from the ships and lodged in the mud beneath the harbor. The crowd watched from the docks as rowing boats were lowered from the ships and four thousand British soldiers rowed to shore.

That was a year and a half ago, and life in Boston had not been the same since. Stephen had always accepted the presence of British soldiers as normal. A few hundred were needed to conduct the king's business. But four thousand! It was as if England had decided to take its own colony captive.

The soldiers had no place to stay once they arrived. Citizens of Boston had already been forced to take British soldiers into their homes. Uncle Ethan and Aunt Dancy had had two soldiers with them for a while a few years ago. Stephen remembered because his cousins, David and Charles, had come to stay with the Lankford family for a few months while the soldiers were in their house. Uncle Ethan and Aunt Dancy did not want their sons sitting at the same table where British soldiers ate.

But four thousand soldiers could not find beds to sleep in

or tables to eat at. They soon resorted to seizing the private property of Boston's citizens. One regiment even pitched its tents on Boston Common. Another took over Faneuil Hall, a public meeting place. Soldiers filled the State House also. The citizens of Boston lost the privacy of their homes as well as the freedom of their public places.

William had explained it all to Stephen again and again. One of the reasons the troops had come to Boston was to help enforce the taxes of the Townshend Acts. Paper, lead, glass, paint, and tea were taxed. The money was used to pay the salaries of royal officials in the colonies. Since they were now paid by the king rather than the residents of the colonies, the officials paid attention to what Parliament in England wanted instead of listening to the colonists. Frustration with taxes that most people thought were unfair led people to take their feelings out on the soldiers.

Lydia did not pay taxes, so Stephen doubted that she could truly be frustrated with them. He thought she just liked to stir up trouble.

Lydia was still busy taunting the British soldier. Stephen was tired and cold, and he did not hold it against the soldier that he was British. No doubt the soldier was tired and cold, too.

"Lydia," Stephen said sternly, "if you don't stop this nonsense, I'm going to turn around and go home and tell Mama."

Lydia rolled her eyes. "You sound like Uncle Cuyler. You should pay more attention to William instead. Taking a stand against the British is not nonsense."

"Calling that soldier names is not accomplishing anything. You're just pestering him."

"It's all I can do," Lydia said, pouting. "Everyone thinks I am too young to do anything important."

"I'm serious, Lydia. You know Mama would not approve of this."

"She doesn't always approve of what William does, but she lets him."

"That's different."

Stephen glared at his sister, turned around, and took three steps in the direction they had come from. He was prepared to follow through with his threat.

"All right, all right," Lydia said. She grabbed Stephen's arm and made him stop. "I give up."

"I'm glad you've come to your senses. Now just keep walking and leave him alone."

Lydia did not answer, but she began to walk casually toward the soldier. Stephen followed, suspicious of Lydia's sudden change of mind. They were directly in front of the soldier now. Stephen kept his eyes straight ahead.

Suddenly Lydia ducked down and scooped up a handful of snow.

"What are you doing?" Stephen hissed. He pulled on her arm as hard as he could.

Lydia broke from his grip easily. She pressed the snow between her hands into an icy ball. Then she hurled it at the soldier.

"Lydia!" Stephen cried.

The snowball hit the soldier squarely on the forehead.

His musket came off his shoulder and swung around toward Lydia. Stephen lurched forward and grabbed her again.

"You little troublemaker!" the soldier shouted.

Lydia laughed loudly while Stephen pulled on her arm.

"If you dare try such a stunt again, I'll not be so easy on you the next time!" The soldier wiped the snow from his face and glared at Lydia.

"You wouldn't hurt me!" She was not afraid to defy him. "You would get into too much trouble."

"Just try me!"

Stephen's heart was pounding. He was not interested in finding out whether Lydia or the soldier was right.

"Lydia," he whispered harshly, "if you don't come with me this instant, I will tell Papa, not Mama!"

Lydia scrambled up the street, giggling, while Stephen trudged behind her, infuriated.

CHAPTER 2

Unknown Dangers

When they were out of shouting distance, Lydia stopped to catch her breath and laughed again.

"That was great!"

"You could have gotten hurt, Lydia," Stephen said. Frustrated, he pushed on her elbow to nudge her along. His stomach was still flipping rapidly.

"You are such a fraidycat," Lydia said.

"I am not!" Stephen said indignantly. "But this is why Mama does not want you out by yourself."

"Just because Mama is frightened does not mean that I am."

Stephen did not want to talk about it anymore. "It's cold out here, Lydia. Let's keep moving." He stepped ahead of her and gestured that she should follow. When she seemed to resist, Stephen added, "Aunt Dancy is waiting for us, and we don't want her going out in this cold because she's worried about where we are. If we don't hurry up, we'll be late."

Aunt Dancy was the reason they were making this trip across town. She was going to have a baby. Charles and David were excited about having a new baby in the house, even though they were twelve and fourteen years old. Stephen was the youngest of all the cousins in the Turner and Lankford families. Everyone was excited about a new member of the family after ten years.

"Aunt Dancy is not a fraidycat," Lydia declared. "She's going to have a baby in a month, but she's not afraid to be alone in her house."

"That may be true," Stephen argued, "but she will be afraid if we don't show up on time when there's so much danger on the streets. Now let's go!"

Uncle Ethan had needed to make a business trip from Boston to New York City. He hated the thought of leaving Aunt Dancy in her condition, but the business was pressing, and he felt he must go.

Charles and David had been nagging to go to New York for months. Aunt Dancy had insisted that Uncle Ethan take their sons with him. After all, the baby was not going to be born for at least a month. It was better if everyone kept busy while they waited, she had pointed out. It was good for the boys' education to see New York and learn more about their father's business. Uncle Ethan had resisted at first, but not for long. He had learned many years earlier that there was little point in arguing with his wife once she had made up her mind.

As a compromise, Aunt Dancy had agreed to let the other relatives take turns spending the nights with her. Uncle Ethan did not want her to be alone, just in case something unexpected should happen—which Dancy was sure would not happen. She agreed to her husband's plan simply to keep him happy.

So Stephen and Lydia's older sister, Kathleen, had spent

several nights with Aunt Dancy, as had their mother. Uncle Cuyler's wife, Aunt Abigail, had taken several turns. Then Lydia had pleaded for a turn. She'd insisted that twelve years of age was old enough to be trusted with something as simple as sleeping in the same house with her aunt. After days of listening to her daughter's relentless insistence that she was ready for grown-up responsibility, Mama had given in. But she'd sent Stephen along as well. Lydia had objected furiously, but Mama had held firm this time.

As they walked, Stephen checked the tin bucket of food he carried. This was their supper. The biscuits wrapped in a cloth had survived the excitement, but some of the gravy had spilled during the frenzy of getting away from the soldier. Stephen's fingers were getting sticky. He decided that if there was not enough to go around, he would simply say that he did not care for any gravy with his biscuits that night.

Uncle Ethan had been gone ten days now. In only two more days, he would return to look after Aunt Dancy himself. In the meantime, she spent her days at the Foy Shipping office, making sure the accounts were kept current. Both Stephen's mother and Aunt Abigail found a series of excuses to drop in at the office of Foy Shipping. Aunt Dancy spent her evenings chatting with whatever relative had been assigned to bring her supper and sit with her for that night. Now it was Lydia and Stephen. Aunt Dancy kept insisting that there was plenty of time before the baby would come and that they were all fussing over nothing, but she accepted the attention anyway.

"Do you think Aunt Dancy will have a boy or a girl?" asked Lydia.

Stephen shrugged. "I'm sure they would like a girl, since they have two boys."

"Charles and David want a little brother."

"I'm sure Aunt Dancy and Uncle Ethan would be happy with another boy, too."

"Don't you ever have an opinion about anything?" Lydia taunted.

"Why should I have an opinion about whether Aunt Dancy should have a boy or a girl?" Stephen defended himself. "The baby is already a boy or a girl. No one can change that now."

"Stephen Lankford, you're hopeless. You have no imagination." Lydia skipped ahead of her brother.

Lydia stopped abruptly a few yards ahead of Stephen. "Look," she said as she pointed. "There's William."

Stephen looked across the street and saw William standing under the elm tree that all of Boston called the Liberty Tree. His height and his sleek, thick brown hair made him easy to spot. Sam Adams, the leader of the group, was there, along with a dozen or so other young men.

"William!" Lydia cupped her hands around her mouth and shouted across the street. "William Richard Lankford!"

William turned around and grinned at his younger siblings. He gave a friendly wave and turned back to the meeting.

"Why don't they find a warm place to meet?" Stephen wondered aloud.

"Because the British have taken over all the buildings, silly."

"Not every building," Stephen countered. "They must be getting cold out here."

"They don't mind. They are talking about important matters,

so they don't notice the cold."

"Well, I do. Let's get moving again."

Lydia's green eyes flashed. "Let's go see him!"

Before Stephen could protest, Lydia had dashed out into the street between horse carriages. He had no choice but to follow. Mama had given him firm instructions to stay close to Lydia. Weaving through the horses and people who crowded the street, Stephen was trapped several steps behind his sister.

"Watch where you're going!" A man shouted gruffly from a carriage Stephen had nearly stepped in front of.

Stephen searched the road for Lydia. She had already made it across and caught William's attention.

William met them at the edge of the street. "What are you two doing out and about this afternoon?" he asked lightly.

Lydia drew herself up tall. "It's my turn to stay with Aunt Dancy tonight."

William glanced at his brother. "And Mama wanted Stephen to go, too?"

Lydia folded her arms across her chest and pouted. "She doesn't want to treat me like a grown-up. She makes Stephen go everywhere with me so she can find out everything that happens."

William looked at her seriously. "You listen to Mama, do you hear me? She is doing the best thing for you." He moved his gaze to Stephen. "What do you have there?"

Stephen held up the bucket. "Biscuits and gravy for supper."

"Good. Aunt Dancy should just rest and let people take care of her."

"You would never do that," Lydia challenged.

William laughed. "I'm not about to have a baby!"

Stephen liked it when William laughed. The brothers looked very much alike. Everyone thought so. Their dark hair and dark eyes and their tall, slender frames made people know immediately that they were brothers. But the resemblance ended there. In temperament and personality, Lydia was more like William, and Stephen was more like their quiet sister, Kathleen.

"What are you doing here?" Lydia asked eagerly. "Shouldn't you be at the print shop?"

"I finished my work early. Papa said he would stay and clean up."

"Does he know you're here?" Stephen asked.

Stephen knew that although Papa could not stop his grown son from making his own political choices, he still worried about Will and wanted to know where he was as much as possible. Stephen had seen his father sit up late many nights beside the fire, waiting for Will to come home. Sometimes the wait lasted all night.

Will was nodding. "I tell Papa as much as I can," he said. "Even though we don't agree on everything, he is still my father, and I respect him."

"Do you think Papa will ever let you print what you want to print in the newspaper?" Lydia asked exuberantly.

Will's eyes twinkled. "The newspaper belongs to Papa, but I keep asking. I haven't given up hope." He nodded back toward the tree. "I need to go back to my meeting. Give Aunt Dancy my love."

"Can we stay and listen?" Lydia begged. Stephen cringed inwardly.

"I don't think that is a good idea," Will said.

"But it's a public place," Lydia argued. "Sam Adams doesn't own this tree."

"It's cold, Lydia, and it will be dark soon. Go on to Aunt Dancy's."

Stephen saw the look of firmness in his brother's eyes and breathed a sigh of relief. Lydia was not going to get her way this time.

Stephen heard the bolt slide from the inside of the door. Everyone kept their doors bolted, even during the daytime. He was glad to see that despite Aunt Dancy's insistence that she would be fine on her own, she was being careful. *Lydia,* Stephen thought, *would leave the front door wide open and dare British soldiers passing by to cross the threshold.*

"Hello, you two," Aunt Dancy said. "You're late. I was just about to come looking for you. Now that would certainly defeat the purpose of your coming, wouldn't it?"

Stephen gave Lydia a knowing look and then turned away from her glare. He was relieved. Aunt Dancy was in a good mood. The evening would pass pleasantly; he would sleep in David's bed, and then in the morning, he'd go home for a big breakfast. He smiled at his aunt.

"We brought supper," he said, holding up the bucket.

"Good. I'm starved." Aunt Dancy snatched the bucket with one finger and took it to the kitchen, where she hung it in the fireplace to warm. She noticed the pasty remains of the gravy that had slopped over the rim.

"Did you sling this over your head, Stephen?" she teased.

"It's quite a mess."

"No, ma'am," he said simply. "We just. . . Well, we. . .we had to hurry, that's all."

"He doesn't want you to know," interrupted Lydia.

"Know what?"

Lydia grinned. "I threw a snowball at a soldier outside the Customs House."

Aunt Dancy looked at Lydia sharply. "Lydia! Why on earth would you do that?"

"But, Aunt Dancy, you hate the soldiers."

Aunt Dancy pressed her lips together for a moment. "I don't hate anyone," she said. "God is not a God of hate, but of love."

"I'm not sure even God could love the British," Lydia said haughtily.

"Lydia, don't be flippant," warned Aunt Dancy. "You are both too young to remember what Boston used to be like. The soldiers have been here almost all your lives." She turned to stir the gravy.

"Don't you want the British to go away," Lydia pressed, "so life can be the way it was again?"

"Of course I do," Aunt Dancy answered. "I hate the thought that my baby is being born into a city that is virtually occupied by soldiers and with so many freedoms stripped away from the citizens." She shook a pewter spoon at Lydia. "But that is no justification for your behavior. Provoking a British soldier could have serious consequences."

"He's not going to hurt a child," Lydia said smugly.

"I thought you did not like to be called a child," Aunt Dancy challenged.

"I don't. But the soldier would think I'm a child, and he wouldn't dare hurt me."

"But you will not always be a child. You will not always be able to hide behind your age, and you may regret the habits you have formed."

"I haven't formed any habits, Aunt Dancy. I just threw one snowball."

Lydia makes her actions sound so casual, so accidental, Stephen thought. She had not even mentioned how she had teased the soldier for so long before she ever threw that snowball.

Stephen took three plates down from a shelf as he watched Aunt Dancy turn back to the gravy. She was concentrating on it far more than necessary. He wondered what she was thinking. Was danger closer than he or Lydia realized?

CHAPTER 3

Emergency at Midnight

Stephen sat bolt upright. His eyes instantly widened to alertness. A chorus of church bells shattered the black night and rushed him to consciousness. From the time he was a toddler, Stephen's parents, and then his sister Kathleen, had drummed into him one response to the clatter of the town's bells—fire!

Stephen leaped out of bed and threw open the second-story window. His nightshirt fluttered in the chilly night air as he leaned out and scanned the neighborhood. It was not Aunt Dancy's house that was on fire. In fact, Stephen saw no flaming towers lighting the black sky—only torches carried by people in the street. Dozens of people, perhaps more than a hundred, scurried in the street to a destination Stephen could not see.

Not stopping to close the window, Stephen darted across the room and out into the hall. Aunt Dancy's bedroom door was open, as was the door to the new baby's room, where Lydia had slept.

"Aunt Dancy!" Stephen called urgently, "Lydia! Where are you?" In his haste he had not thought to bring the candle from the night table in his room. The blackness in the hall was broken only by an occasional flicker from the torches outside.

"I'm here, Stephen," came Aunt Dancy's comforting voice. As she turned toward Stephen, her candle lit her face. She was just starting down the broad front stairs. Stephen quickened his steps to catch up.

"What's going on?" Stephen asked, taking the hand his aunt offered.

"I don't know, but we'll find out soon enough."

By the time they reached the bottom of the stairs, Lydia had flung the front door wide open. The cold air rushing into the house made Stephen gasp, and he wrapped his arms around himself. Outside, men and boys hurtled down the cobblestone street.

"It's a mob!" Aunt Dancy said. The disappointment in her voice was obvious. Boston had seen so much violence in the last few years. Many wondered if the streets would ever be safe again.

"An angry mob," Stephen emphasized.

"But what happened?" Lydia questioned. She started to move out the open door, but Aunt Dancy pulled her back. "Stay back, Lydia. Stephen, close the door, please. And bolt it."

"But I want to see what's going on," Lydia protested, twisting free of her aunt's hold.

"Lydia Lankford! Do you honestly think that your mother would ever forgive me if I let you out in the street in the middle of this madness? I am responsible for you tonight. You will stay indoors!"

Lydia pushed out her bottom lip in a pout. Aunt Dancy

stood between her and the door.

"The door, Stephen," Aunt Dancy reminded the boy, who seemed frozen in his spot.

"I just saw William!" Stephen said.

"William? Where?" Lydia once again lurched toward the door.

And once again, Aunt Dancy firmly pulled Lydia back. This time she closed the door herself and leaned against it, scowling at her two charges. "Both of you know better than to think of going out," she said. Looking at Lydia, she added sternly, "I would like to hear the explanation you would give your mother if you did go out."

"But William is out there!" Lydia cried.

"I don't know what is happening out there," Aunt Dancy said evenly, "or how William is involved. But Will is nineteen. He makes his own choices. You will not go out there under any circumstances."

"May we at least look out the window?" Lydia begged.

"All right, but if there is any further sign of danger, we will go to the kitchen, away from any windows."

Stephen and Lydia huddled at the window and watched the action in the street. The torches lit up the furious faces of the people who carried them. Their shouts were muffled by the wind, but the expressions on their faces were a picture of the words they spoke. Some beat the air violently with clubs.

"Something terrible must have happened to make those people this mad," Stephen said mournfully.

"Everything that happens in Boston is terrible," Lydia pronounced. "And things will not get better until the Redcoats are driven out. That's what Will always says."

"Now, Lydia," cautioned Aunt Dancy. With one hand she rubbed her enlarged belly as she looked anxiously out the window.

Stephen watched his aunt. He had seen her rub her belly that way before, he reminded himself. It was an unconscious habit that meant nothing. He looked back out the window.

Lydia's eyes grew wide, and she poked Stephen with an elbow. "Maybe they're driving the Redcoats out tonight!" she exclaimed. "That's why William is out there. Oh, this is exciting!"

"You can't be sure of that," Stephen said. "It would take more than a few torches and sticks to make soldiers of the Crown desert their posts."

Stephen glanced over at Aunt Dancy, expecting her to reinforce his argument. The expression on her face alarmed him. He watched as she wrapped both her arms around her stomach and pressed her lips together.

"Aunt Dancy! Are you all right?" Stephen asked. He was no longer interested in what was happening in the street.

"I'm sure it's nothing," she replied as she let out her breath. "Just the excitement."

Lydia had not stopped looking out the window. "I wish we could see where they are going. Maybe it's the Customs House. I know they keep guards there all night. Those are probably the first soldiers that the Sons of Liberty will drive out."

"Yes, perhaps so." Aunt Dancy politely agreed with Lydia as she lowered herself into a nearby chair. She took a deep breath and exhaled slowly.

"Aunt Dancy, are you sure you are all right?" Stephen queried. He went to stand beside her.

Lydia finally turned away from the window, puzzled. "The baby is not supposed to come for at least a month," she said. "Mama says your babies are always stubborn and late."

Aunt Dancy chuckled. "She said that, did she? As I recall, you put up quite a fight at your birth, too. No doubt it's just the tension making me feel this way. But perhaps you should help me back upstairs just the same."

"Here, Aunt Dancy, you can lean on me." Stephen offered his arm to his aunt. Next to her bulging body, his thin, ten-year-old frame looked very small, but he was quite earnest. Aunt Dancy smiled at him and allowed him to help her out of the chair. Lydia slipped an arm around Aunt Dancy's waist from the other side, and together they began to climb the stairs. Lydia looked over her shoulder out the window one more time.

As Stephen tucked the quilt around his aunt's shoulders a few minutes later, he saw the shadow of pain cross her face. Their eyes met, and his heart beat faster.

"Stephen," Aunt Dancy said softly, "I'm going to ask you to do something very important."

"Whatever you need, Aunt Dancy, I'll do."

"Stephen, Lydia, the baby is coming."

"Now? Tonight?" Lydia cried. "You said it was just the excitement."

"I was wrong," Aunt Dancy said with certainty. "The baby is coming tonight, and I'm going to need help. Stephen will have to go for the midwife. She warned me not to be alone for this birth. Do you know where Mistress Payne lives, Stephen?"

Stephen nodded mutely.

Lydia pushed in closer to her aunt. "I should go," she said indignantly. "I'm older."

Aunt Dancy winced and started sweating. "Lydia, listen to me. Stephen will go, but he might not make it back in time. You might have to birth this baby for me. That's why I want you here."

"What?" Lydia cried. "But I've never done that before."

"The baby will do most of the work, and I'll tell you what you have to do. Right now I want you to get some things ready. Hot water, extra cloths, some string. The baby blankets are in the trunk at the foot of my bed. Can you do this, Lydia?"

"Yes, yes. Water. Cloths. String." Lydia flew into action.

Aunt Dancy took Stephen's hand. "You know I wouldn't ask you to face the danger outside for anything else."

"I'm not afraid." Stephen's voice was faint but confident.

"Take the backstreets. Stay away from the Customs House."

"I know all the shortcuts."

"Get your coat and go. Tell Mistress Payne to come quickly."

Outside, Stephen chose his route carefully. He was usually not allowed out so late in the evening—certainly never alone. He paid extra attention to every step he took. Avoiding the street in front of the Customs House would mean circling wide and approaching the Paynes' street from the other direction. Stephen carried no torch to brighten the night. Buildings that were familiar in the daylight loomed ominously in the night's shadows. But his heart was steady and determined. He was not going to let Aunt Dancy down when she needed him. He ran as fast as the darkness would allow.

When he reached Mistress Payne's street, he was far away from the commotion they had heard from Aunt Dancy's house. The neighborhood was dark, but he knew which house the Paynes lived in. With quick steps, he traveled the cobblestone walk and approached the house. Not a single candle burned within. He rapped on the red wooden door and listened. No sounds came from inside. He rapped again, harder this time. A knot of fear formed in his chest.

"Mistress Payne," he called out. Still there was no answer. Five times, Stephen knocked on the door and called out, more loudly each time. Clearly, no one was home at the Payne house.

Stephen heard footsteps in the street behind him and wheeled around. He set his feet solidly apart, ready for what might come.

"If you're looking for the Paynes," a voice said in the darkness, "you'll find them down by the Customs House." Stephen peered into the street and recognized the father of a classmate.

"My aunt's baby is coming," Stephen explained. "I must find Mistress Payne."

The neighbor shook his head. "Half of Boston is at the Customs House. You'll not find her easily."

"I have to try." Stephen wheeled around and started running toward the place where he had been forbidden to go.

He ran for blocks. Stumbling over loose cobblestones, he nearly collided with a lamppost as he whizzed past. The blackness was blinding in some places. He ran from memory of where the streets turned and intersected. Picturing Aunt Dancy in her bed, with her face tense from fighting the pain, Stephen ran harder. For Aunt Dancy's sake and for the baby not yet born, he ran even when he thought he would collapse with the next step.

As he got closer to the center of town, Stephen was engulfed in a swelling crowd. Gasping for air, he finally allowed himself to stop and look around. He could not see the reason why the crowd had gathered, and he did not care. He cared only about Aunt Dancy. Everyone was bundled up against the frigid temperature. Viewed from behind, every person in the crowd looked alike. Stephen began to bump up against people so he could look into their faces one by one. He pulled on elbows and tugged on coats. "Have you seen Mistress Payne?" he asked urgently of anyone who would listen to his thin voice in the middle of the mob.

Then he bumped up against a coat he recognized. "Uncle Cuyler!"

"Stephen! What in the world are you doing here?" Uncle Cuyler grabbed Stephen by the shoulders and tried to steer him out of the throbbing mob.

"It's Aunt Dancy. I came to look for Mistress Payne, but she wasn't home."

Uncle Cuyler looked down at Stephen in alarm. "Stephen, is Aunt Dancy all right?"

Stephen nodded. "She's fine. At least she was when I left. But she said the baby is coming. I have to find Mistress Payne."

Uncle Cuyler shook his head. "There is no time to waste. I will come with you."

Uncle Cuyler and Stephen swung open the front door and started running up the stairs.

"Lydia! Aunt Dancy!" Stephen called out. "Uncle Cuyler is here."

Lydia appeared at the top of the stairs and fell into Uncle Cuyler's arms just as he reached her.

"I'm so glad you're here. When the baby started coming, I didn't know what to do!"

CHAPTER 4

The Baby

W here is she?" Uncle Cuyler released Lydia and glanced around.

"She's in her bed." Lydia pointed down the hall. "She looks terrible, Uncle Cuyler. Is she going to die?"

"She's having a baby, Lydia. But most likely she'll be just fine."

Lydia and Stephen scampered down the hall after their uncle.

"But it's too early," said Stephen. "Will the baby be all right?"

"If there is anything to worry about, I'll tell you both."

Aunt Dancy's door stood open.

"Cuyler!" she said. "What are you doing here?"

"I couldn't find Mistress Payne," Stephen explained. "Nobody was home. Everybody was down on King Street. I know you told me not to go there, but I had to find someone to help you."

Aunt Dancy smiled faintly. "Under the circumstances, it's understandable." She grimaced in pain, then glanced at Uncle Cuyler. "I'm not used to having a man help me birth a baby."

Uncle Cuyler grinned. "Well, if you would rather have Lydia stay. . ."

"No!" Lydia shouted. She backed away from the bed with her palms held up. "Uncle Cuyler is a doctor. He can help you."

Uncle Cuyler turned to Lydia and Stephen. "As Aunt Dancy said, under the circumstances, it's understandable. Now why don't the two of you go downstairs. I'll call you if I need anything."

Lydia shot out of the room. Stephen backed through the doorway reluctantly. He was glad Uncle Cuyler was there, but he wanted to be completely sure that Aunt Dancy would be all right.

When he had joined his sister downstairs, he said, "I hope nothing happens to Aunt Dancy. I don't think it's good for a baby to be born too early. Something must be wrong."

Lydia threw her hair over her shoulder haughtily. "You find too many things to worry about."

"I do not!" Stephen picked up a poker and tried to stir the embers in the fireplace into flame. He added three new logs. Having a baby was a natural thing, but it was also danger-ous. His own grandmother had died giving birth to Uncle Cuy-ler. Stephen thought he had good reason to feel nervous about Aunt Dancy no matter what Lydia said.

Lydia moved to the window. "Was it really exciting out there? Did you really go to King Street?"

"Yes, I went to King Street. But it was not exciting. It was frightening."

"You're exaggerating," Lydia accused. "It couldn't have been too bad out there. Otherwise, why was Uncle Cuyler there? He always tries to stay out of trouble."

"I don't know," Stephen mumbled. "Maybe he went because he's a doctor and he thought somebody might get hurt." He glanced toward the stairs. It was quiet. Was it supposed to be so quiet when a baby was being born?

Outside, the streets throbbed with the action of the crowd. The people scurrying down the street now were curious on-lookers who had been lured from their beds by the tumult.

"Half of Boston must be out there," Lydia observed. She could not tear herself away from the window. "How many people did you see?"

Stephen shrugged. "I don't know." He was satisfied that the fire was going to catch. He held his hands over its heat to warm them. His feet felt like blocks of ice. He had not been aware of how cold and wet he had gotten during his trek into the night.

"What's the matter—haven't you learned your figures in school? Even a six-year-old can count."

"It was dark, and I was looking for Mistress Payne, not counting heads." Stephen sank, exhausted, into a wing chair. He bent over to pull off his wet boots. Under his coat, his nightshirt had stayed dry. Scooting the chair closer to the fire, he drew comfort from its warmth and light.

"Did you at least see what was happening?" Lydia's questions persisted. "Why is everyone out there?"

"I don't know that either," Stephen confessed. "Some men were shouting. That's all I know."

"How could you be out there for so long and not find out what is going on?" Lydia was disgusted at her brother's incompetence.

Stephen just shrugged. He was too tired to argue with Lydia.

"You're not much good for anything, are you?" Lydia snapped.

Stephen glared at his sister but did not respond.

Lydia turned away from Stephen. "I think I'll step outside for a bit of fresh air," she said casually. She took her cloak off the hook next to the door.

Stephen sprang from his chair. "You can't go out there!"

"I simply must have some fresh air, or I will never be able to get any rest tonight." Lydia tossed her cloak around her shoulders.

Stephen threw himself against the door and checked the bolt.

"Don't be silly," Lydia scoffed. "I'm older than you are, so you can't tell me what to do."

"I can when you are doing something foolish."

"I'm also bigger than you are, so you can't stop me."

To prove her point, Lydia hurled herself at Stephen and knocked him off balance. He landed on his knees. Laughing, Lydia unbolted the door and opened it. Proud of her accomplishment, she stepped outside.

Stephen scrambled to his feet and planted himself in the doorway. "Lydia Lankford! You get back inside!"

"Are you going to make me?" She took two more steps and craned her neck to look down the street. "Oooh, everybody is coming back this way now."

"Lydia, I insist that you come back inside!"

Lydia laughed. "Are you going to tattle to Aunt Dancy? I think she has more important things on her mind right now."

Stephen wheeled around and looked up the stairs. Only

empty, quiet space looked back. He hoped that was a good sign. If something were wrong, surely Uncle Cuyler would have called for help. In the meantime, Lydia was right. She had made up her mind, and he could do nothing to stop her. He spun around once more and stood facing the street, but he did not step across the threshold. He was helpless. He could do nothing for his aunt or her baby, and he could not even protect his sister from the danger in the street. He groaned, wondering how he would ever explain this night to his parents.

Lydia's observation about the movements of the crowd was accurate. The throng did seem to be moving in the direction of Aunt Dancy's house instead of away from it. But what that meant, Stephen did not know.

Now he was glued to a sentry post of his own. He did not plan to follow Lydia out into the night, but he would stand in the doorway and watch her as far as possible. But Lydia was not moving. At least her feet were not. Her head wagged from side to side as she tried to make sense of what she was seeing.

"I don't see any soldiers," she called over her shoulder to Stephen. "They probably carried them off to the harbor and pushed them off in rowboats."

Stephen shook his head. Even Lydia had to recognize how silly that sounded.

Suddenly Lydia began to run up the street against the press of the crowd. Stephen's heart sank. He could do nothing for her now.

"William!" Lydia shouted.

Stephen jerked his head up and peered into the dark. He saw Lydia fling herself into William's startled embrace. He could not hear what William said, but he could see his brother turn Lydia around and point back toward the house. Stephen breathed a sigh of relief. Lydia was more likely to listen to William than to anyone else. William and Lydia approached the house together. Lydia had her arms crossed and her lower lip stuck out as far as it would go.

"Thank goodness you're being sensible," William said to Stephen. "Keep Lydia here, in the house."

"That's easier for you to say than for me to do," Stephen replied.

William chuckled briefly. "Right you are. But try." Even in the cold air of a March night, Will was sweating. He wiped the back of his hand across his forehead. Stephen noticed how worried William looked.

Lydia stamped one foot. "At least tell us what's going on."

"I don't have time right now. Besides, what are the two of you doing out here in your nightclothes? Where's Aunt Dancy?"

"Upstairs," Stephen explained. "The baby is coming." He saw the look of alarm in William's eyes. "But don't worry. Uncle Cuyler is taking care of her."

"I'm glad for that," Will said. He glanced over his shoulder into the street. Then he put his hands squarely on Lydia's shoulders and stooped slightly to look her in the eyes. "I have to go. Promise me you will stay here. In the house. With the door bolted."

Lydia pouted, but she finally agreed.

In a few more minutes, the streets were quiet. Whatever had brought the crowd out of their beds was over, and everyone had gone home. For a long time, Lydia adamantly refused to believe it was over and resisted sleep. She kept her vigil at the window and waited for the next round of activity. Stephen gave up trying to persuade her of anything and let his exhaustion overtake him. He fell asleep on the rug in front of the fireplace with a quilt his grandmother had made pulled around his shoulders.

In his dream, Stephen heard a cat. Actually, it was just a kitten, and it sounded frightened and cold. It stood in the middle of King Street and shivered. Stephen tried to reach the kitten before the crowd trampled it, but his feet were stuck in mud, and he couldn't move. Just as the crowd was about to press down on the cat, Stephen woke.

"It's the baby!" Lydia was shaking his shoulder. "Did you hear it cry?"

Stephen rubbed his eyes and sighed in relief. There was no kitten on King Street. There was a baby upstairs.

"It sounds like a boy to me," Lydia said authoritatively.

The cry came again.

"You can't tell if it's a boy or a girl by the way it cries." Stephen rolled his eyes. Lydia said the most ridiculous things. "I just hope the baby is all right."

"It's crying, isn't it? That's exactly what a new baby is supposed to do."

Stephen stood up. The fire had grown cold again. Lydia must have fallen asleep, too. He added more logs and wondered if he should carry some wood up for the fire in Aunt Dancy's room. The baby should not get cold.

"Let's go upstairs!" Lydia said.

"Don't you think we should wait for Uncle Cuyler to call us?"

"He'll think we're asleep and not bother us for hours. I'm going even if you aren't." Lydia pranced toward the stairs.

"I'm coming; I'm coming." Stephen shed his quilt and grabbed an armful of logs.

Upstairs, they knocked gently until they were given permission to enter. Aunt Dancy was sitting up in bed looking exhausted but joyous. She held a tiny bundle in her arms. "Come see your new cousin."

Stephen surrendered his load of wood to Uncle Cuyler, who was tending the fire. "Is he all right?"

Uncle Cuyler chuckled. "He is a she. And she is just fine."

Putting their differences aside for the moment, Stephen and Lydia sat on the edge of the bed and peeked into the blanket their aunt held. Tiny little arms flailed in their faces.

"She's so small!" Lydia exclaimed.

"Yes, she's small because she came early," Aunt Dancy said. "But Uncle Cuyler assures me that she is perfectly healthy."

"And you?" Stephen asked. "Are you all right?"

Aunt Dancy smiled and reached for his hand. "I'm just fine, thanks to you. You found me the best help anyone could have."

"I would have gone, you know," Lydia said emphatically. "You should have sent me."

"I needed you here. Everything you did to prepare for the birth was important."

Satisfied, Lydia turned her attention back to the baby. "What is her name going to be?"

Aunt Dancy gave a quick laugh. "Your uncle Ethan and I have not agreed on a name for a girl yet. We thought we had at least another month to think about it, and we wanted to be sure the baby was healthy."

"So she doesn't have a name?" Stephen asked.

"Not yet. There's no hurry. We want her to have just the right name."

Stephen pressed a finger against his new cousin's palm, and the baby with no name gripped it tightly.

That's right, little girl, Stephen thought. *You can depend on me.*

CHAPTER 5

The Attack

It's a girl!" Lydia pushed open the front door of the Lankford home and bellowed as loudly as she could.

Seventeen-year-old Kathleen was not impressed with the announcement. "Of course you're a girl. We've known that for over twelve years."

"Not me," Lydia said, stamping one foot. "Aunt Dancy's baby. It's a girl."

"You can't tell that until it's born," Kathleen retorted.

Stephen finally tumbled through the front door. Breathless, he said, "She's right. It's a girl. She was born about three hours ago."

Kathleen's eyes widened, and her jaw dropped open. "Mama!" she called out. She spun around on one foot and ran to the kitchen. Lydia and Stephen followed, grinning with their news.

Margaret Lankford set down the pan she was warming and wiped her hands on her apron. "But what are both of you doing here? Surely you didn't leave your aunt Dancy alone!"

"Uncle Cuyler is there," Stephen said assuringly. "He took

very good care of her all night."

"Cuyler?" Mama said, puzzled. "What about Mistress Payne?"

"I couldn't find her. But I found Uncle Cuyler in King Street."

Mama's shoulders jerked slightly, and her fists tightened. "You were in King Street? Last night?"

Stephen nodded. "I had to go, Mama. The baby was coming. Aunt Dancy needed help."

"And I'm not ready to birth any babies!" Lydia exclaimed. "When Uncle Cuyler got there, I was never so glad to see anyone in my whole life."

"And he's still there?" Kathleen asked.

Stephen nodded. "Yes, but he wants Mama to come."

"I want to go with you," Kathleen said to her mother.

"Certainly." Mama turned to her younger daughter. "Lydia, run upstairs and tell your father to come down immediately. You'll have to fend for yourselves for breakfast." She reached for a basket on a high shelf and began filling it with food.

"Is William home?" Stephen asked, although he could guess the answer.

Mama shook her head.

"He didn't come home all night?"

Again she shook her head.

Stephen wanted to ask more questions, but he could see the double concern his mother already bore for her patriotic son who had been out all night during a riot, and for her sister-in-law and dear friend who had given birth prematurely. So Stephen said nothing more. When he allowed himself to sit down and rest for a few minutes, he realized how truly tired he still was.

In a few minutes, Lydia was back with her father in tow, and Mama and Kathleen hurriedly bundled up the things they thought they would need and left for Aunt Dancy's house.

Richard Lankford rubbed his hands together energetically. "Why don't I mix up some batter for pancakes to celebrate your new cousin?"

Lydia grimaced. "Because your pancakes are always lumpy!"

Stephen flashed a disapproving look at his sister. To his father, he said, "I would love some pancakes, Papa."

"You don't mind the lumps?"

Stephen shook his head. "The lumps are the best part."

Papa threw his head back and laughed. "Stephen, you are too kind. I can always depend on you to say something more generous than I deserve."

"That's our boy!" said a tired but fiery voice. All heads turned to see William leaning against the door frame. His face was grimy and his clothes disheveled. His hat was cocked to one side. Stephen thought he looked so tired that he could hardly stand.

"William!" Lydia shot out of her chair and hurled herself at her brother. "If you tell me absolutely everything now, I will forgive you for not talking to me in the street this morning."

Will backed away from his demanding little sister. "I'm filthy. Don't touch me, or you'll get dirt all over your frock."

"Lydia," Papa said as he cracked an egg into a bowl of batter, "get your brother something to clean up with."

Lydia pouted, but she obeyed.

"Are you all right, William?" Stephen asked quietly.

Will mustered up the energy to smile at his brother with his big brown eyes. "I am just fine," he said, "and grateful to be home."

"You must tell us what happened!" Lydia insisted as she handed him a damp towel.

Will began wiping grit from his face and glanced at his father.

Papa cracked another egg and stirred. "Yes, I suppose you must give us an account," Papa said. Stephen thought his father sounded unsure whether he really wanted to know what had been going on all night. But Lydia would certainly not give up until she had heard every last detail, so William began.

"I'm sure you all heard the fire alarm," he said.

"No fire!" declared Lydia.

"That's right. It was a false alarm. But it seemed to make folks edgy, and they stayed out in the streets. The moonlight was nice, I suppose. Some of the men went into the taverns. But for some reason, a group of men formed in front of the Customs House and started bothering the sentry on duty."

Stephen, remembering Lydia's actions on the previous afternoon, glared at his sister. She stuck her tongue out at him.

"Was it a mob?" Lydia asked. "A riot?"

Will had moved on to cleaning his hands and arms. "No one is sure what happened. Someone said that some boys had been throwing snowballs at the soldier. Or it might be that the soldier threatened the boys. Someone else said that a man passing by had insulted the soldier and angered him. Then there was a story about a barber's boy trying to collect payment for a haircut his master had given, and the soldier was refusing to pay. And someone else said that the soldier was defending his captain and whacked a boy with the butt of his musket for insulting the captain."

"This is exciting!" Lydia squealed.

Stephen tilted his head to one side. "So you don't really know what happened?"

"Well, no, I don't," William answered.

"How can we know what to believe?"

"That's a difficult question, Stephen. I don't know the answer."

"Didn't you see what happened?" Lydia asked.

"I was not there when it all started. I was down at the docks. But I heard there was some commotion and went to see what it was all about."

"With the Sons of Liberty?" Lydia asked eagerly.

William said simply, "I was with some friends. When we got to the Customs House, there were about a hundred men surrounding the poor soldier. Maybe there were even two hundred. It was hard to tell in the dark."

"Don't tell me you feel sorry for that soldier," Lydia said, hardly believing that her patriotic brother could stoop so low as to have sympathy for a British soldier.

"That's enough, Lydia." Papa's tone was sharp, and Lydia shrank back in her chair.

Will continued, "By the time I got there, they were shouting, 'Kill the soldier! Kill the coward!' It is possible that his life truly was in danger. But I doubt that they would have harmed him. He should have known that."

"What did he do then?" Stephen asked.

"He backed up the steps of the Customs House. They were throwing things at him—wood, chunks of ice, stones. So he was backing away. But he was priming his musket as he moved. He banged on the door of the building with the butt of his musket, but he couldn't get in. At least I don't think he could get in. I talked to Josiah Simpson, and he insists that he saw someone open the door and talk to the soldier. But he did not go in. Instead, he yelled for help. He shouted, 'Turn out, Main Guard.' "

Papa sighed and stopped stirring the batter. "This is far worse than I had imagined. You're telling me it was one man against a hundred, perhaps two hundred? That's hardly a fair fight."

Lydia opened her mouth to comment, but a warning look from her father silenced her.

"When he called for help, seven more soldiers came running from the barracks across the square."

"All with muskets, I assume," Papa said.

William nodded. "Yes, now there were eight muskets. The soldiers were shoving people in all directions. I think all that the Boston residents had were sticks and cobblestones they pried out of the street. They could hardly defend themselves if the soldiers should start firing. But they refused to break up. They just kept screaming insults at the soldiers."

"Such foolishness," Papa said emphatically. "All for nothing. No one can even say for sure how it started. Where was the commander of the guard?"

"Captain Preston? He showed up a few minutes later. He

saw the state of the crowd and ordered his men to prime their muskets and load."

"He what!" Papa was stunned. "Did he not even try to determine what had happened up until then?"

"The British are not as reasonable as you and I, Papa," William said.

"Weren't the people afraid of the muskets, Will?" Stephen asked.

"I guess not, Stephen," William answered. "They didn't stop. They just kept calling out: 'Let's see you fire! Lobsterback! Bloody-back! You won't dare fire!'"

"Dare I ask what you were doing during all of this?" Papa asked.

"William's no coward," Lydia asserted.

Papa shot her another warning look.

"Papa, I tell you the truth, I was not mixed up in this. I had nothing to do with it. I was just there."

"Why didn't you leave?" Stephen asked.

William shrugged. "I don't know. I guess I thought I would be able to help somehow." He hung his tired head in his hands. "I did try. I tried to pull some of the loudest men out of the crowd. They just pushed me down in the street."

"Go on," Papa prodded.

"One of the soldiers got hit by something—ice, perhaps—and he slipped and fell. He lost his grip on his musket. The mob started screaming, and I guess the other soldiers thought they heard an order to fire."

"They fired!"

William nodded.

"And?"

"Four are dead. More are wounded, and one probably will not live."

No one in the room spoke for several minutes. Even Lydia was stunned by the drama of the story. Stephen felt a lump forming in his throat. While Aunt Dancy gave birth to a new cousin, four men lost their lives.

Papa finally broke the silence. "Who?"

"Crispus Attucks. Samuel Gray. James Caldwell. Samuel Maverick. And Patrick Carr is seriously hurt."

"Did the captain order them to fire?" Stephen asked quietly.

"He says he did not, Stephen, but there were a dozen witnesses who said they heard him give the order."

"Who do you believe?"

Will met Stephen's questioning eyes. "The witnesses are not the sort of people who go around telling lies."

"Does Captain Preston tell lies?" Stephen asked.

Will looked away and did not answer.

"What happened next?" Papa prodded.

Will sighed deeply and continued. "Preston called for reinforcements, and three companies of soldiers surrounded the crowd and dropped to a firing position. Then the bells started going off again."

Papa nodded. "Yes, I heard them."

"Those are the ones that woke us up in the middle of the night," Lydia said.

"There were hundreds of people in the square, people with clubs, knives, anything they had been able to grab. They lined up as if they were actually going to fight the British troops."

"That would be sheer madness. Surely they wouldn't!" Papa furiously cracked another egg, causing Stephen to jump in his seat.

"I believe they would have if Governor Hutchinson had not shown up just then. He came with Colonel Dalrymple, who is in charge of all the troops in Boston. They took charge. I was amazed that the people listened, but they did. Governor Hutchinson talked the crowd into disbanding by promising that justice would be served. He promised that Preston and his men will be tried in a court of law."

"For what crime?" Papa asked.

"Murder, of course. What else could it be?"

Again the room was silent.

"By three o'clock," Will said, "everything was over. Hutchinson sent everyone home. He said a terrible tragedy had occurred and asked everyone to go home quietly. He promised to do everything in his power to see that justice would be done."

Stephen said, "That's when the baby was born. About three o'clock."

What kind of city has this precious new life come into? Stephen wondered.

Argument in the Print Shop

Stephen welcomed the sleep that his father insisted on. After filling his stomach with his father's lumpy pancakes, he had tumbled into bed gratefully.

School would be canceled for several days. The leaders of Boston needed time to decide how to handle the turmoil in the city. As merchants passed each other in the streets, they exchanged whatever information they had about the events of the previous night. Horses clip-clopped on the cobblestones as Boston came to life for a new day. Before long, anyone who had not already heard the news would learn of the tragedy, and Boston would rally against the British once again.

Stephen, however, had no strength left. He slept deeply. William was sound asleep next to him. Lydia was in the next room pretending that she was not tired, but in only a few minutes, the sounds of her thrashing stopped. They slept for several hours.

Stephen dreamed of mewing cats and the red tongues of angry wolves anxious for their prey. He awoke when he heard

Will moving about their room. The cabinet door creaked as Will opened it to rummage for clean breeches. Stephen rolled over and rubbed his eyes, blinking at his older brother.

"Where are you going?" Stephen asked sleepily. He put his hand over his mouth to cover a yawn.

"To the print shop." Will's voice was almost a whisper. "I didn't mean to wake you. But I promised Papa I would not miss work because of my. . .activities."

"You mean, because you've been with the Sons of Liberty."

William grinned sheepishly. "I should stop treating you like an infant. You know as well as anyone else in the family what I'm involved in, don't you?"

Stephen sat up and smiled. "You're the only one who doesn't treat me like a baby."

"Well, you are the youngest in the family." Will stepped into his breeches.

"Lydia is only two years older than I am, but she acts like she's a grown-up and I'm a child."

Will chuckled. "Lydia certainly has a mind of her own. You are far more patient with her than I would be."

"She just doesn't think about things before she says them." Stephen swung his legs over the side of the bed. His toes scrunched up when they hit the cold wooden planks of the floor.

Will snatched a shirt off a hook and pulled it over his head.

"Can I come with you?" Stephen asked.

"To the shop? I thought you didn't like the shop. You always seem to head for Uncle Cuyler's clinic."

Stephen shrugged. "There's no school. I don't feel like staying in the house all day when so much is happening."

"Are you sure you don't want to go back to sleep?"

Stephen shook his head. "I'm not sleepy anymore." He did not mention the wolves in his dream. He was afraid that if he tried to go back to sleep, the wolves would howl through the darkness behind his eyes.

"You know, of course, that we'll have to wake Lydia and take her with us," Will said.

Stephen grimaced. "I know. Papa won't want her to be home alone. She won't want to stay put anyway, once she wakes up. She would make me go somewhere with her."

"She's good at getting her way, of that I am certain."

"Mostly, she wants to be like you."

William stopped and looked thoughtfully at Stephen. "Do you really think so?"

Stephen nodded. "All she ever talks about is what William thinks and what William is doing."

"She should stick to working on her posture."

Stephen laughed.

William threw a shirt at Stephen. "Get dressed, young man. We leave in ten minutes."

When the trio reached the print shop, their father was hard at work at his great walnut desk. To Stephen's delight, Uncle Cuyler and his daughter Anna were in the shop. Anna was busy spinning a top on the wooden counter. Stephen joined her. Lydia perched on a stool and pretended to be bored, while William struck up a conversation with their father.

"What are you working on, Papa?"

"I'm finishing up a story about the events of last night."

"I could have done that for you," William offered. "I was there. I saw as much as anyone did."

Papa shook his head and sighed. "It seems that even the eyewitnesses cannot agree on what they saw." He gestured at the pile of papers on his desk, his notes from several interviews. "You yourself said that people had many different ideas about what started the riot in King Street."

"I told you everything I know this morning," William said. "I know I did not hear every word that was spoken, but I have given you an accurate account of what happened."

Papa glanced up at his brother-in-law. "Your uncle has a slightly different version."

William turned to his uncle, puzzled. "You were there? I didn't see you."

"Nor I you. But I was there—at least until I stumbled upon Stephen searching for Mistress Payne."

"Then you left. You did not see everything."

"No," Uncle Cuyler admitted. "I did not see everything. But I saw enough."

Something about Uncle Cuyler's tone of voice made Stephen stop the top and glance at his cousin. This would not be the first time that William had argued with Uncle Cuyler about political events. Uncle Cuyler usually tried not to argue, but William could not help trying to convince people to agree with him. William could persuade many people of many things. But Uncle Cuyler was not so easy to convince.

Uncle Cuyler was sympathetic to the British Parliament's need for more income. As long as the colonies were receiving the protection of the British Empire, he felt it was reasonable for the colonies to contribute to the cost of running the empire. He certainly did not want the colonies to break off their relationship with England. Life would become far more difficult. The colonies simply were not able to manufacture everything they needed for themselves. Their lives would not be as organized and comfortable without the support and protection of England.

In many ways, life in the colonies was no different than life in England—at least, it hadn't been until people had started to boycott British goods. They were already finding out that life was harder and the products much less pleasing when they tried to make do with what they could manufacture themselves. When Anna needed a new dress, Aunt Abigail sewed one from coarse cloth that she had woven herself instead of the fine fabrics of Europe. It was difficult to buy fabric from Europe, and if Aunt Abigail had dared use European fabric, she would have been ridiculed in the streets. Many people had also learned to drink coffee rather than buy British tea and pay a tax for it.

England provided many things that the colonies could not provide for themselves. Uncle Cuyler was firmly convinced that being part of the British Empire was the best thing for Massachusetts.

William, on the other hand, thought that British goods were only an excuse for Parliament to interfere in the lives of the colonists at every opportunity. The reason the colonies could not manufacture the things they needed was because Parliament had forbidden it. The British troops were not in Boston to protect the city, but to control it. If Boston accepted the taxes that the king had signed into law, money that belonged in Massachusetts would go to fatten someone's bank account in England. William had no doubt that it was time for the colonies to break free. Sooner or later, he was convinced, it would happen.

"I'm telling you, Papa," William said insistently. "I can write that story. You need no other witnesses."

"You said the shooting last night was murder," Papa said slowly. "In Cuyler's opinion, it was rightful self-defense—or maybe even an accident."

"Self-defense!" William slammed an open hand down on the counter. "No man in that crowd had a musket."

"A gun is not the only thing that can kill a man," Uncle Cuyler retorted. "They were pressing in on the soldier in great numbers. They refused to disperse. If only one man had chosen to swing a club—and I saw many who would have done so gladly—the soldier could have been mortally wounded. Yes, it was self-defense."

"It was murder!" William insisted. "Even if one sentry was in danger, when the rest of the troop came, the crowd was clearly overpowered. Captain Preston had no right to order his men to fire."

"Are you sure that he did?" Uncle Cuyler asked. "Did you hear the words come out of his mouth?"

"It was impossible to hear anything in the middle of a riot."

"That is exactly my point," Uncle Cuyler said evenly. "How could you have known whether the captain gave the order?"

"And how can you be sure he did not?" William retorted. "You were gone by then to birth Aunt Dancy's baby."

Stephen listened to his brother and then his uncle, back and forth. He did not know what to believe. Neither William nor Uncle Cuyler was someone who would tell an outright lie. But they could not both be right, not in this situation.

Lydia slid off her stool and kicked the side of Anna's shoe. "Your father was not there," she whispered ferociously. "Why doesn't he stop trying to tell everyone what to think?"

"Lydia!" Stephen protested as loudly as he dared. "Leave Anna alone. She has nothing to do with this argument. It's between William and Uncle Cuyler."

Anna looked at him with grateful eyes. Stephen and Anna understood each other. In many ways, he was closer to Anna than he was to his own sisters. They were the same age, and they got along well, no matter what they were doing. He could not remember ever having an argument with Anna.

"You're just defending her because you agree with Uncle Cuyler!" Lydia snapped. "You should try paying attention to your own brother once in a while. Then you might understand politics a little better."

"I understand politics as well as you do."

"If you understood politics, you would know William is right."

"Stop it, Lydia," Anna warned.

Lydia folded her arms across her chest and stared spitefully at her little brother. "You were there last night in front of the Customs House, and you couldn't even figure out what was going on."

"I was worried about Aunt Dancy. I was trying to find help!"

"Ha! You cannot tell a Loyalist from a Patriot from a Lobsterback!"

"Lydia Lankford, you take that back!" Without realizing it,

Stephen had raised his voice. Stephen had had a long night and not enough sleep. Not more than an hour ago, William had commented on his patience with Lydia. But his patience was wearing thin now. His brown eyes narrowed as he glared at his sister.

"What's going on over there?" Papa took a step toward his two youngest children.

Lydia and Stephen continued to glare at each other.

"I'll not have all this bickering in my shop," Papa declared. "First it is Uncle Cuyler and William, and then Lydia and Stephen. This is a print shop. I am a businessman, not an assemblyman. I have a story to write for today's edition of the newspaper. I have several sources to draw on—all of them reliable—and I will write the story as fairly as possible."

No one spoke for a moment.

"Richard, I am very sorry for my behavior," Uncle Cuyler said contritely. "I should have exercised more self-control."

"I'm sorry, too, Papa," Will muttered.

Papa's eyes flashed at the children.

Stephen swallowed the lump in his throat. "Please forgive me, Papa. I did not mean to lose my temper."

All eyes turned on Lydia. She huffed haughtily and looked the other way.

"Lydia," warned Papa.

"I'm sorry, Papa," she said reluctantly.

"I think you owe Stephen an apology as well."

Lydia clamped her teeth together and grunted, "I'm sorry."

"Thank you, all," Papa said. "And from now on, keep your brawling in the streets, please." He turned back to his desk.

"William, we have work to do."

"Yes, Papa." William reached for the leather apron he wore when he worked the press.

"I'll be on my way," Uncle Cuyler said. "Patrick Carr is in my clinic. Abigail is tending him, but I promised I would be back soon."

"Patrick Carr!" Lydia burst out. "He was one of the men who was shot."

Stephen studied the concern in his uncle's face. "Is he going to be all right, Uncle Cuyler?"

Uncle Cuyler sighed and shook his head. "He was wounded very badly. Four men have already died. I hope that he will not be the fifth."

"Can I go with you, Uncle Cuyler?" Stephen asked.

"To the clinic?"

Stephen nodded.

"Certainly. I can always use another assistant."

"I'm going to stay here and help William," Lydia declared.

Stephen looked at Anna and gave a weak smile. No doubt the clinic would be a more peaceful place to spend the day.

CHAPTER 7

The Patient

Walking a few steps ahead of Uncle Cuyler and Anna, Stephen pushed open the clinic door and peeked in. Aunt Abigail moved around the clinic quietly and efficiently. As she straightened supplies and swept the floor, she often glanced at the patient lying on the cot in the center of the room. He lay still, his breathing fast and shallow.

After Patrick Carr had been shot—while Uncle Cuyler was delivering his new niece—men had carried him to the clinic. Several doctors spent the rest of the night with him. Aunt Abigail often helped Uncle Cuyler in the clinic, but taking care of someone as ill as Patrick Carr made her nervous. Gently, she lifted the quilt to check his bandage and tucked the quilt around his neck again.

Uncle Cuyler and Anna nudged Stephen from behind, and the threesome entered. Uncle Cuyler hung his coat on a hook and motioned that the children should sit on two three-legged wooden stools near the wall. Stephen was content to watch from that distance.

He liked coming to the clinic to visit Uncle Cuyler even when Anna was not there. Uncle Cuyler often remarked that there was a great deal about the human body that doctors did not yet understand. Even so, Stephen was impressed with Uncle Cuyler's knowledge. Occasionally he was allowed to hand his uncle a bandage or something to clean a wound. Today, though, he knew he would only watch from his stool. Before him was the evidence of last night's horror.

Stephen wished he could remember only the joyous birth cry of his new cousin. Instead, his memory of her birth would always be mingled with the scenes he had witnessed as he ran through the streets of Boston in the dark. And now this image of a man lying wounded and bleeding in a doctor's office would haunt him. For a split second, he tried to imagine the four men who had fallen dead in King Street during the previous night's chaos. But the image was too horrible, and he chased it away before the wolves could come.

Stephen looked over at Anna and smiled slightly.

"Mr. Carr looks very sick," Stephen whispered. "I hope your papa can help him."

"If anyone can help him, my father can," Anna answered confidently. She pushed her hood back and let her yellow curls frame her face. Stephen was glad to have Anna with him. She was so different from Lydia. When he was with Anna, he did not have to be careful about everything he said. She would never fling his words back in his face.

Stephen watched as Aunt Abigail approached her husband.

"I'm glad you're here," Aunt Abigail said quietly. "The other doctor had to leave to see his own patients, and I believe there is little I can do to help Patrick Carr. You're the doctor, not I."

Uncle Cuyler looked at his wife gratefully, tenderly. "You have done your best to keep him comfortable. That is a great deal."

Uncle Cuyler felt for Patrick Carr's pulse and laid his hand against the pale forehead to judge the fever. He murmured something to Aunt Abigail, who nodded in response and opened a cabinet for a fresh bandage.

While Uncle Cuyler changed the dressing on the wound, Stephen observed his uncle. The haggard lines of his face announced that he had not been to bed during the night for even a few hours. Uncle Cuyler had gone straight from Aunt Dancy's house to the crisis of Patrick Carr. Mr. Carr would need constant attention, so the team of doctors who had cared for him during the night had set up a schedule to make sure a doctor was always available for him. It was Uncle Cuyler's turn. Sleep would have to wait. Uncle Cuyler blinked back the fatigue from his eyes.

Stephen leaned over and whispered to Anna, "Do you know Mr. Carr?"

Anna nodded. "He came to see my father a few times. We would greet each other in the street."

"He looks like a nice man."

"He is. I'm sorry he got hurt."

"I'm sorry anyone got hurt," Stephen said.

They were silent again as they watched Uncle Cuyler and Aunt Abigail work.

Finally, Aunt Abigail walked toward them, wiping her hands on her apron.

"Anna, perhaps we should be going home. Stephen, you are welcome to come and spend the day if you'd like."

"Thank you, Aunt Abigail, but I think I'd like to stay here."

"Uncle Cuyler will be working very hard. Mr. Carr is quite ill."

"That's all right. I like to watch."

"Does your father know where you are?"

"Yes, ma'am."

"All right, then. Come, Anna, let's go home and clean up. Then we'll go see the new baby."

Stephen smiled at the thought of his new cousin. "She's very beautiful."

"I can't wait to see her," Anna said, clearly excited.

"I do hope they give her a name soon," Aunt Abigail said, chuckling. "But so many times parents wait for months before they decide on a name."

They left, and Stephen was alone with his thoughts while Uncle Cuyler tended his patient. The clinic took up several rooms on the first floor of a building near the center of Boston. Stephen was sitting in the main room, where Uncle Cuyler kept his supplies and examined patients. The walls were lined with cupboards filled with bandages, bedding, alcohol, herbs, and other potions that Uncle Cuyler mixed up for his patients. Uncle Cuyler had once let Stephen watch a bloodletting procedure on a man with malaria. Stephen was not sure he understood how bloodletting would help cure the illness, but still he was fascinated by medicine.

Behind the main room were two rooms. One was a small room where Uncle Cuyler kept a supply of wood for the fire he always kept burning, and the other room, more finely finished, was where he studied. Bookshelves lined the walls.

Uncle Cuyler liked to read just about any kind of book: Shakespeare's plays, the Bible, science textbooks. Of course, he especially enjoyed anything that had to do with medicine. He kept every medical book he had ever studied. It seemed like a lot of books to Stephen, but Uncle Cuyler insisted there could never be too many medical books.

Recently he had begun loaning books to Stephen. Many of them were too difficult for Stephen to understand. But he wanted to learn, so he studied them for hours, reading each paragraph over and over until he began to understand it. The volumes that illustrated human anatomy interested him the most. Stephen often thought that he might like to learn to be a doctor someday. Uncle Cuyler could teach him everything he knew, and then they could work together.

Uncle Cuyler sank down on the stool next to Stephen and sighed heavily. Stephen turned his eyes to his uncle's face and studied it. Uncle Cuyler looked more worried than tired.

"Will he be all right, Uncle Cuyler?" Stephen asked. His voice was hardly more than a whisper.

"I don't know for sure, but right now I would say that probably he will not recover."

"Oh, Uncle Cuyler, can't you do anything else for him?"

"The other doctors were with him all night. We have done everything we can. The wounds are extensive."

"I don't want anyone else to die," Stephen said mournfully.

"I don't either. But we are living in a time of madness, Stephen. I fear that many more people will lie in my clinic wounded by British muskets before this is all over."

"Lydia doesn't think it's madness. She think it's exciting."

"Lydia has always been an excitable child."

"She doesn't think she's a child either."

Uncle Cuyler chuckled. "Twelve years old is such an in-between age. But I don't think Lydia realizes the seriousness of what is happening in Boston—and all over the colonies. Perhaps if she were here and saw Patrick Carr herself, she would think differently."

Stephen shook his head. "Lydia would never come here to see Patrick Carr. She thinks William knows everything. Whatever he says, she thinks it's right. Like last night. She wasn't there. And even though you were there for part of the time, she believes everything William says and nothing you say."

"Don't forget that you were there yourself for a few minutes."

Stephen hung his head. "Lydia says I'm good for nothing because I didn't try to see what was happening. But I was worried about Aunt Dancy."

Uncle Cuyler put one arm around Stephen's thin shoulders. "You did the right thing, Stephen. I know Lydia is older than you are and she likes to tell you what to do, but you have a mind of your own. And it's a very fine mind, I think."

Stephen smiled shyly. "Do you really think so?"

"Yes, I do."

A moan from the cot drew Uncle Cuyler's attention away from their conversation. He jumped off the stool and ran across the room as Patrick Carr began to thrash around on the cot.

"Stephen!" Uncle Cuyler called. "Help me keep him still. He'll tear open his wound."

Stephen knew what to do. He had done this before with his uncle. He placed his hands firmly on the shoulders of the patient and let all his weight bear down. Uncle Cuyler held Patrick Carr's ankles, and in a few moments, the patient was quiet again. Uncle Cuyler pulled back the quilt to inspect the wound once more.

"He's bleeding again, Stephen. I'll need fresh bandages—lots of them."

Without hesitation, Stephen went to the correct cupboard and pulled out a handful of bandages. He rushed back to the cot. Uncle Cuyler began trying to soak up the leaking blood.

"He's lost far too much blood," Uncle Cuyler said somberly.

"He looks hot," Stephen observed.

"His fever is raging again. We don't seem to be able to stop it."

A lump rose in Stephen's throat. Uncle Cuyler finally stopped the flow of blood and rebandaged the wound.

"Uncle Cuyler, if he dies. . .will it be. . .murder?"

"What do you think, Stephen?"

"William would say it is, but you say it isn't."

"And what do you think?" Uncle Cuyler repeated.

Stephen backed away from the cot toward his stool. "I don't know what to think. I know William wouldn't lie to me, and neither would you."

Satisfied that his patient was calm for the time being, Uncle Cuyler sat next to Stephen again. "William and I often disagree. It has been that way for several years—ever since the Stamp Act. But I respect William."

"You do?"

"Yes, and you should, too."

"But if you don't agree with him, how can you respect him?"

"William is a man who thinks for himself. And that is what I respect. He does what he believes is right before God. He is a man of integrity."

"But what if what William thinks is right really is wrong?"

Cuyler raised his eyes to the cot across the room and pondered the question. "No matter what any of us thinks, we all have to face that question. If a deadly deed is done in the name of patriotism or loyalty, is it noble? If a good deed is done out of fear, does it lack all virtue?"

"I'm not sure I understand, Uncle Cuyler."

"I'm not sure I do either, Stephen. But this is my point: You can listen to me, you can listen to William, and you can even listen to Lydia. But in the end, you must find your own answers. And only God can give you the answers."

"But you and William both believe in God. You both go to church; you both pray. Why doesn't God tell you the same thing?"

Cuyler nodded. "That is one of the great mysteries of our time, Stephen. And I struggle with that question every day."

CHAPTER 8

The Funeral

The relentless March wind whipped through the crowd and chapped Stephen's cheeks. His nose started to run. He sniffled and tried to ignore the slow drip. He clenched his fists and pulled them up into his coat sleeves to keep them from the cold, raw air. Stephen stood with his parents and his sisters on the side of King Street, watching but not participating in what was happening. Uncle Ethan, back from New York at last, was with them.

Three days had passed since the shooting in King Street. William had hardly been home at all during those three days. Stephen went to bed in their room alone, and when he woke, William's bed would be rumpled but empty.

The streets had been strangely quiet, even during the hours when merchants usually did most of their business. Governor Hutchinson, who had finally dispersed the crowd on the night of the shooting, stayed hidden from sight much of the time. Sam Adams, however, walked the streets with the Sons of Liberty.

Stephen's sister Kathleen had said that Samuel Adams

looked like he had worn his clothes to bed every night for a week. His wig was never on straight, and he seemed to have trouble keeping a job. Often he did not know where his next meal was coming from. Still, he committed himself to the one cause he believed in: overthrowing British oppression. He wrote so many letters to the newspapers in Boston that Richard Lankford would groan aloud when he saw the handwriting that had become familiar to every editor in town.

After the shootings, Sam Adams made no threats and gave no hints that he was planning any action that would stir up the people more. Yet Governor Hutchinson and the other British officials watched him carefully. Even when he seemed to be doing nothing, Sam Adams could make people think he was stirring up trouble. The Sons of Liberty could fly into action at a moment's notice.

Stephen felt Kathleen's hand on his shoulder and looked up at her.

"Are you warm enough?" she asked.

Stephen shivered but nodded. He was as warm as anyone could expect to be, so he would not complain. He turned his back to the street and raised his arm to block the glare of the winter sun.

Patrick Carr was still critically ill. Uncle Cuyler and the other doctors worked to keep him stable and comfortable, but he was worse every day. Stephen had visited the clinic every day during Uncle Cuyler's shift to see for himself. Patrick's face was gray, and his breathing heavy. Every day Stephen hoped for a turnaround. But every day Patrick Carr was closer to death.

The four who had already died were to be buried today. All

activity in Boston had shut down in the late afternoon. The schools remained closed. Merchants left their shops. Mothers bundled up their children against the March temperatures. Even the Lankfords had come out to watch respectfully as four caskets were carried through the streets to the cemetery.

When it was over, Papa would go back to the print shop to write a story about it for the next edition of the newspaper. It seemed to Stephen that everyone would have seen the funeral for themselves. Who would be left to read about it in the paper?

"Why can't we march?" Lydia whined. "I want to march in the funeral procession."

"It is unbecoming to make a spectacle out of the deaths of these men," Papa told his squirming daughter. He put a hand firmly on her shoulder to make sure she could go nowhere.

"But everyone else is marching. There must be five thousand people in the street."

"I would guess more like ten thousand," Papa said. "Maybe even twelve."

Sam Adams had organized the funeral. He had been quiet since the "massacre," as he called the shootings. But he was not wasting his time. The funeral was a chance for the Sons of Liberty to let the people of Boston know that everything was under control. Sam had enlisted members of the Sons of Liberty to carry the coffins ceremonially through the streets of Boston, one by one.

The route included a symbolic turn around the Liberty Tree. Whether or not the four men had belonged to the Sons of Liberty did not matter. Sam Adams presented them as a visible reminder that the British were oppressing the colonies.

The elm stood solidly as a reminder to all of Boston of the zeal of Sam Adams and the Sons of Liberty. After circling the tree, the men proceeded up the hill to the burying ground.

Stephen studied the thousands of people who marched behind the coffin. He had never before seen so many people together in one place. He was curious.

"Did all these people really know the men who were killed?" Stephen asked his father. "I can't imagine having twelve thousand friends."

"That's because you're not a hero," Lydia snapped.

"Lydia!" Papa warned his daughter with his tone. To Stephen he said, "No, all these people did not know them. But they have come out of respect, as we have."

"Are they heroes, Papa?" Stephen asked.

"Some people believe they are," his father answered.

"I believe they are!" Uncle Ethan burst into the quiet conversation. "They were willing to give their lives for the freedom of Boston. I think that makes them heroes."

"We're not at all sure that is what happened," Papa said. "Cuyler and dozens of other men tell a different story."

"Cuyler is becoming more of a Loyalist every day," Uncle Ethan said. "His perspective on the facts is colored by his leanings."

"Don't you think your Patriot leanings influence your perspective?" Papa challenged.

"Please," Mama pleaded, "let's not have an argument standing out on a street corner during a funeral."

Her husband and her brother quieted, and they all continued watching. The funeral procession plodded past them with the second casket. The six men who carried it on their shoulders, dressed in their finest black clothes, wore somber expressions and looked only ahead of them. Behind them came several thousand mourners. Some were sincere; others were there out of curiosity. The crowd buzzed with opinions and comments. Stephen turned his head from one conversation to another.

"We will always remember the Boston Massacre, and it will strengthen us to defy the British so that these men did not die in vain."

"We must not allow them to die for nothing."

Stephen pondered the phrase "Boston Massacre." That sounded like the troops had killed the men on purpose. But had they? Another fragment of conversation drifted toward him.

"Crispus Attucks was black. Can he still be a hero?"

"Any man who gives his life for this cause is a hero."

"If only Patrick Carr were here. I'm sure he would have a few words to say to the British officials."

But Patrick Carr could not be there. Stephen wondered how many people were even thinking about Patrick Carr right now. Did they know how sick he was?

"Those soldiers should be hung as soon as possible."

"Governor Hutchinson promises that there will be a fair trial."

"Only one verdict is fair. Guilty!" The man who said this spoke gruffly and loudly and stood only a few feet away from the Lankfords. Stephen checked to see if his father was listening. Papa turned to the man and started to say something. The touch of his wife's hand on his arm held him back.

"He's right, you know," Uncle Ethan whispered. "For British

troops to fire into an unarmed assembly of citizens and kill four of them is illegal and unforgivable. If we let this go by, the British can come in and massacre all of us whenever they want."

"That is not going to happen," Papa said. "We are subjects of the Crown. We have the king's protection."

"Don't be too sure of that."

"Hey, look!" Lydia shouted as she pointed at the procession. "There's William. Please, may I go walk beside William?"

"No, you may not," Mama said sharply. "You will stay exactly where you are standing."

"Mama, please."

"Mind your mother, Lydia," Papa said.

Stephen searched the procession until he had spotted his older brother. William was tall and easy to find. His brown eyes met Stephen's. William's eyes burned with belief in what he was doing. The sleepless nights he sat up writing flyers for the Sons of Liberty, the long meetings under the Liberty Tree in the middle of winter, the missed meals—William did not seem to mind any of that. It was as if he had no choice but to devote his energy to resisting British oppression.

Stephen's eyes were wide with questions about what he was watching. Why had all these people come to the funeral? The four men who died were ordinary men who would not have been known by twelve thousand people. If one of them had been struck down by a runaway horse, not more than a hundred people would have come to see him buried. Yet Papa thought there were twelve thousand people marching in the procession, and there were thousands more watching from the sidelines.

"You should be proud of William," Uncle Ethan said to

Papa and Mama. "He has grown into a fine young man. I hope my own boys learn to act with as much conviction as he has."

"I want all my children to do what they know is right," Papa said.

Stephen looked into his father's eyes. He couldn't tell if Papa was really proud of William or not. But that was the way Papa was. He wanted to be fair. It did not matter if people could tell what he was thinking. Papa did not always agree with what William did. Was he proud of him anyway? Would he ever be proud of Stephen?

William moved down the street and was lost in the crowd again. The third coffin was coming into view from the other direction. When the funeral had begun late that March afternoon, no one had known how many people would come to pay their respects. But after watching and listening, Stephen decided that most of the people had come to pay their respects to the Patriots' cause, not to the four men who were being buried. He felt sad about that.

"Ethan," Mama said, as they were waiting for the next coffin to pass them, "have you and Dancy given that child a name yet?"

Uncle Ethan laughed. "I'm afraid we can't seem to agree on anything except that she is a beautiful little creature."

"I don't understand why the task is so difficult."

"I only got home yesterday," Uncle Ethan reminded his sister. "We have not really had time to discuss names."

"Is the baby all right?" Stephen asked. He knew from talking to Uncle Cuyler how many babies died within a few weeks after being born. Several of his friends had lost little brothers or sisters. He shivered in the March chill and thought of the tiny baby being held in her mother's arms at home next to the warm fire.

"The child is fine," Uncle Ethan said confidently. "She is so small that I can almost hold her in one hand. But her cry is every bit as loud and demanding as the boys' when they were babies."

Mama laughed. Stephen felt better. How badly he wanted the baby to thrive and grow strong. If only he could protect her from the sorrow of the night of her birth.

The fourth casket came into view. Stephen did not want to watch anymore.

CHAPTER 9

Important News

S tephen! Over here!"

Stephen blinked into the bright sunlight outside the schoolhouse a few days later. William was waiting for him with the horse and cart that he used for delivering newspapers in the afternoon.

"What are you doing here?" Stephen asked. He walked toward William, glancing over his shoulder for Lydia. His usual afternoon routine was to wait for Lydia, who liked to dillydally after school, and the two of them would walk home together. Sometimes they would stop by their father's print shop.

"Where's Lydia?" Will asked. His eyes scanned the school yard. He was in a hurry.

"She's still inside," Stephen said. "She likes to talk to her friends after school. What's happening?"

"She doesn't have time for gossiping today," Will said. "We've got to get going."

"Why? What's going on?" Will was not answering his questions, and Stephen was getting more anxious by the moment.

"Go back in and get Lydia," Will said, "and tell her to hurry."

"William! Tell me what's happening. Is Mama all right? Papa?"

Lydia appeared in the doorway. At the sight of William, she forgot all about her friends and dashed toward him.

"William!" Stephen was certain his sister's screech could be heard for blocks.

"Quickly, get in the cart. Both of you." William gestured that they should hurry.

"You mean we don't have to walk home today?" Lydia clambered up into the seat in front of the cart, while Stephen jumped into the open back. William took the reins and immediately started the horse in a quick trot.

"William, you're scaring me," Stephen called from the back.

"I'm sorry, Stephen. Everybody is fine. No one is ill."

"Then why have you come for us?" The cart rumbled along. Stephen held tight to the side to keep from falling over.

"While you were in school today, the grand jury met."

"What does that mean?"

"It means that Captain Preston and eight soldiers will stand trial for the massacre last week. The prosecuting attorney believes he has enough evidence to convict them of murder."

"Oh," Stephen said, and he leaned back against the side of the cart.

Lydia was thrilled with the news. "This is what you wanted, isn't it, William?"

"It's the first step toward justice," William said. He slapped the mare's rump to make her go even faster.

"I still don't understand," Stephen said. "Why would you

come all the way over to the school to tell us that?"

"I need the two of you to do the deliveries this afternoon."

Lydia groaned. "I hate delivering newspapers. They're so dirty and heavy. And they smell funny."

"That's the ink," Stephen said matter-of-factly.

"You can do this," William said. "Kathleen and I used to do this when we were your age. Use the map that I drew for you a few months ago. This is the kind of emergency the map is for. I marked an X on all the corners where you need to leave papers."

"But where will you be?" Lydia asked.

"I have some important business to take care of."

Lydia's eyes widened with excitement. "Sons of Liberty business?"

"Never mind what the business is. Just deliver the papers."

They pulled up in front of the print shop. William jumped down and flew through the door. Stephen and Lydia followed him in.

"Papa, Stephen and Lydia are here." He stopped abruptly. "Oh, hello, Uncle Cuyler."

"Hello, William."

Stephen furrowed his brow thoughtfully. William and Uncle Cuyler had become very cool toward one another in the last few days.

Papa set a jumbled tray of metal letters on the counter and began putting them back in their proper places. "Uncle Cuyler just heard the news about the grand jury," he said. "He wanted to read our story."

"I'm glad to see that the course of justice will be followed," Uncle Cuyler said to William. "I heard some rumors that the

Sons of Liberty were threatening to take matters into their own hands."

"We all want justice," William said. He took a rag from the counter and wiped the press in random places. "It's only a matter of time before those men will hang."

"I'm disappointed to hear you say that," Uncle Cuyler said. "I was hoping you would have an open mind toward justice. The men have not yet been tried. How can you know they deserve to hang?"

"Under the law, hanging is the penalty for murder."

"True enough—but only men who have committed murder deserve the penalty."

"The jury will confirm what we already know."

"I trust that your own personal opinions will not influence your work on the paper," Uncle Cuyler said evenly.

"My father does not complain about my work." William locked his eyes onto his uncle's.

"Nor should he." Uncle Cuyler met William's gaze evenly. "He has a reputation for being fair-minded. I'm sure you appreciate the importance of that quality in Boston right now. I know you would do nothing to compromise your father's reputation."

Stephen suddenly realized he had been holding his breath while he listened to this exchange between his brother and his uncle. He gasped for air.

William turned to Stephen. "I'll help you load the papers. Then I have to go."

"I don't want to deliver papers," protested Lydia. "I want to go with William."

"You will do as you are told," Papa said. "We tied the papers in smaller bundles so you will have no difficulty lifting them."

Lydia groaned, but she returned to the cart. "At least I get to drive the cart. Stephen is much too young for that!"

"Slow down!" Stephen called from the back of the cart. "You're going past the marks on the map."

Lydia yanked on the reins and brought the cart to an awkward stop. Stephen slammed into the side of the cart. She looked at him with eyes full of mischief. "Is that slow enough for you?"

Stephen sighed, then jumped off the back of the cart and ran with a bundle of papers to the shop they had passed. Word had already spread around town about the indictments. People were eager to see the paper.

"It won't be long now," the merchant said as he scanned the headline. "We'll have us a public hanging of nine lobsterbacks."

"That will teach the rest of them not to push around the people of Boston," a customer added.

Stephen walked back to the cart, wondering why everyone—except Uncle Cuyler—was so sure the men would be found guilty.

"Did you hear? Did you hear?" a schoolmate ran alongside Stephen the next afternoon. Stephen had been walking very slowly, hoping that Lydia would soon realize how late it was getting and leave her friends so they could go home.

"About the indictments?" Stephen answered his schoolmate. "Of course I heard. My father publishes a newspaper."

"No, not that. That's yesterday's news."

"What are you talking about?"

"Patrick Carr. He died today."

Stephen hardly glanced over his shoulder at Lydia. It took him only a fraction of a second to decide what he would do. Without another word to his friend or a thought about Lydia, he sped off toward Uncle Cuyler's clinic. Yesterday Patrick had opened his eyes for a few minutes while Stephen visited. Stephen had wanted very much to believe that this was a good sign. And now the news of his death!

As he ran through the commons, past the Customs House, and down King Street, he saw people talking in little groups. Even though he did not stop, portions of their conversations wafted to his ears.

"The British will pay for this!"

"Patrick Carr's death will be added to the indictments! He was murdered just as surely as the others."

"We will have our revenge when those men hang!"

"Tomorrow would not be soon enough for me."

Stephen burst breathless through the doors of Uncle Cuyler's clinic.

"Is it true? Is he. . . ?" He looked toward the cot. It was empty and freshly made up. "I thought he was better. Yesterday he looked at me."

"He was very badly wounded, Stephen. You knew that." Uncle Cuyler caught his nephew up in a hug. "We did everything we could for him. It wasn't enough."

"Were you here?"

"No. Dr. Jeffries was with him."

"Now everyone wants the soldiers to be tried for murdering

Patrick Carr, too. I heard people talking in the streets."

"Yes, I know. I expected that." Uncle Cuyler led Stephen to a chair.

"The Sons of Liberty will have another funeral, and everyone will come and watch. They'll say horrible things about the British soldiers all over again."

Uncle Cuyler nodded. "But Dr. Jeffries told me something interesting about Patrick Carr's last moments."

"What was that?"

"Patrick said that he bore the soldiers no malice."

Stephen was puzzled. "What does that mean?"

Uncle Cuyler leaned back in his chair and spoke thoughtfully. "I think Patrick knew that the soldiers were in a difficult situation and responded as any of us would. He did not hold their actions against them."

"So it is not their fault?"

"Patrick Carr did not think so."

"But everyone else in Boston does."

"Not everyone."

"Everyone except you."

Uncle Cuyler shook his head adamantly. "I am not alone in my opinion. Those of us who disagree with the Sons of Liberty are not as visible as they are. But we have great confidence that the justice system will treat these men properly."

"Will Dr. Jeffries tell the judge what Patrick said? Will it make a difference?"

Uncle Cuyler shrugged. "The decision will be in the hands of the jury." He looked at Stephen with raised eyebrows. "Does your father know you are here?"

Stephen shook his head. "I came straight from school. Lydia's going to be really mad, too. I didn't wait for her."

"Come on. I'll walk you over to the print shop, and we'll make sure everything is all right."

Stephen was right. Lydia was annoyed that Stephen had left her to walk alone. But his father was simply relieved that Stephen was safe. His older sister Kathleen was there too, working on typesetting some flyers.

"Where is William?" Stephen asked.

"With the Sons of Liberty, of course," Lydia said. "Where would you expect him to be on a day like this?"

"What about the papers? Is he coming to deliver them?"

Papa shrugged. "If he does not get here in a few minutes, you and Lydia will have to do it again."

Lydia moaned.

The print shop door opened, and in came William.

"Just in time!" Lydia said gleefully.

"We've done it!" William announced. "We have beaten the British."

"William!" Uncle Cuyler said harshly. "Another man died today. I hardly think that is cause for rejoicing."

"No, of course not." William sobered for a moment. "I'm as sorry about Patrick Carr as you are, Uncle Cuyler. That's not what I'm talking about."

With puzzled eyes, everyone looked at William.

"The troops are being withdrawn," William announced.

"The troops are being withdrawn?" his father echoed.

"Yippee!" shouted Lydia. She threw a stack of flyers into the air.

Stephen glanced at Uncle Cuyler for his response.

"When?" Uncle Cuyler asked quietly.

"Immediately." The sound of victory in William's voice was unmistakable. "This is the beginning of the end of British oppression."

Kathleen leaned across the counter. "How do you know the troops won't be back when Boston has quieted down?" she asked.

William shrugged carelessly. "We won't let them back this time. We are much more organized than we were two years ago when they first arrived in such numbers. Sam Adams has a wide following—and not just in the Sons of Liberty. We simply would not allow them to row ashore."

"Britain has a much larger army than Boston can muster," Uncle Cuyler said.

"But don't you see, Uncle Cuyler? It's not just Boston. It's all the colonies. Ever since the Stamp Act, leaders in all the colonies have been thinking alike. The British are only beginning to realize what they are up against."

"The British Parliament is a powerful institution, William. It will not be as easy as you think."

"The Patriots are quite serious, Uncle Cuyler. Do not take us lightly."

Kathleen turned back to her typesetting. Papa took the rag from William and continued wiping off the press.

"I'd better get back to the clinic," Uncle Cuyler said. He stepped toward the door.

"I'll get the cart loaded," William mumbled. "Then I have to leave."

Stephen watched as everyone turned back to the work that gave structure to their days in times of great change.

Was William right? Was this really the beginning of the end?

CHAPTER 10

Family Feud

Captain Preston and the other twelve men accused of crimes were jailed.

Stephen had seen the inside of the jail once. What he remembered most about it were the strong walls. There was one tiny window high in the wall with bars across the glass. A bundle of straw served as the bed. The heavy wooden door had a slot in it, through which the prisoner received his food. If the prisoner had any energy for resisting imprisonment, he was put in iron chains. Jail was a dismal place.

Stephen thought of Thomas Preston, captain in the king's army, wearing his fine red coat. Thinking of a man like that sitting in a dark cell on a damp pile of straw was an ugly picture. Whenever it came into Stephen's mind, he blinked his eyes until it went away.

Despite the ugliness of prison, Uncle Cuyler thought it was the safest place for the accused men to be. Many people in Boston were ready to take the law into their own hands and hang the men at the first chance they got. If the men were walking around free, their lives would be in danger, and a jury would never get the chance to decide their guilt or innocence. If justice was to be served, Uncle Cuyler kept saying, the men should stay in prison until their innocence was proven. Even then it might not be safe for them to walk the streets.

Boston thrived under the management of Sam Adams and the Sons of Liberty. The thousands of British troops were gone, and Boston felt freer than it had for years. Technically, the governor and officials appointed by Parliament were in charge, but anyone who lived in Boston knew that it was the Sons of Liberty who were running the city.

More and more often, William recruited Stephen and Lydia to deliver papers because he had other things to do—things that he felt were of utmost importance. With the soldiers gone, Bostonians were left to quarrel among themselves. It was becoming more and more difficult to remain neutral on political questions. To be a Loyalist meant to support the king and Parliament and accept their right to govern the colonies any way they saw fit. On the other hand, to be a Patriot meant to detest anything British and do everything possible to throw out the British. There was very little ground in between the two extremes.

William and Uncle Cuyler had learned to hold their tongues with each other—most of the time. Uncle Ethan just shook his head at the path his younger brother had chosen. Stephen hated to see squabbling in the family.

The trials of the accused men did not happen as quickly as everyone expected. The judge who was to preside over the case became ill, and Preston and the others needed time to find lawyers who were willing to defend them. Spring stretched into early summer as the men languished in their cells and all of Boston waited for justice.

Stephen was enjoying a new sense of freedom. School was not in session in June, and the troops were gone. He could walk from home to the print shop or Uncle Cuyler's clinic whenever he wanted.

When he arrived at the print shop one afternoon in late June, Stephen's heart sank. As soon as he pushed open the door, he could hear William's raised voice. His whole family was there. Kathleen had come in to work on a typesetting project, Lydia had been tagging along after William every chance she got, and Mama had just brought a basket of lunch. When Stephen arrived, the Lankford family was all in one place—but not exactly enjoying one another's company.

"Papa, you cannot possibly print this!" William was red-faced and serious.

"I have an obligation to my readers." Papa dampened the paper in the press, preparing to print on it.

"Have you no sense of patriotism, Papa?" William had lowered his voice, but he had not changed his tone.

Richard Lankford glared at his oldest son until William shamefully turned his eyes to the floor.

Stephen had no idea what they were talking about, but it must have been very serious to make William speak to his father in such a tone. Circling around the edge of the room, Stephen decided he would ask Kathleen what the argument was about.

"If you feel this work is beyond your conscience, you may be excused for the afternoon," Papa said. He straightened the paper in the tray. "I am not a member of the Sons of Liberty. Sam Adams has not earned my undivided, unthinking loyalty."

"My loyalty is not unthinking," William retorted. "My loyalty to Sam comes from a deep conviction that he is the leader who will bring fairness and freedom to the colonies. I am honored to be associated with him."

Stephen reached Kathleen and tugged on her sleeve. "What are they fighting about?" he asked quietly.

Kathleen set down a tray of letters and sighed. "Captain Preston wrote a letter to the king. Papa wants to print it, and William does not think he should."

"Why not?"

"Because Captain Preston is defending himself in the letter."

"If he didn't think he did anything wrong, why shouldn't he defend himself?"

"William thinks Captain Preston went too far. In the letter, he did not just defend himself. He almost came right out and accused several men of starting a fight with the sentry that night on purpose. William does not want Papa to print that part of the letter."

"Captain Preston really does think somebody planned the massacre?"

"Not exactly. Captain Preston believes that there was a group of men determined to break into the Customs House and steal money."

"The Customs House is where they put the money for the king."

"Right," Kathleen said. "Captain Preston said the men wanted to take that money back. If they would have to kill the sentry on duty to get into the building, then they were willing to do that."

"Ow!" Stephen wheeled around to see that Lydia had snuck up on him and poked him in the back. "Stop that, Lydia."

"Oh, don't be such a baby."

"I'm not a baby."

"Maybe not, but you're a Loyalist, aren't you?"

"Don't be silly," Kathleen said. "Stephen is far too young to get involved on either side of a political question—as are you."

Lydia stamped her foot. "I'm old enough to think for myself, and I agree with William. Papa should not let the paper be used to defend Captain Preston's outrageous order to fire on an innocent crowd."

"It's Papa's job as owner of the newspaper to keep people informed. This is news. Everyone will be interested in the letter whether they agree with it or not."

Stephen nodded his emphatic agreement with what Kathleen had said. Lydia rolled her eyes.

At the sound of a chair scraping across the floor, they turned their attention back to William and their father. William sat heavily in the wooden chair.

"If you have any respect for me at all, you will not print that letter," William said.

"William, you will gain nothing by putting me in a difficult position. Your mother and I have raised you well. You know what you believe, and you have the courage to act on your convictions. You must allow me to do the same." Papa raised his eyes to Kathleen. "We don't have time for a rest, Kathleen. Keep working on the type."

Kathleen's hands flew into action again. Stephen could see the letter she was copying from. It had already been printed in the newspapers in England and read by the king and the members of Parliament. Only recently had a ship brought a copy of it back across the ocean to the city where the letter had been written weeks ago.

William was silent. Papa continued preparing the press. Stephen held his breath, waiting to see what William would say next. At last William spoke.

"At least let Sam Adams write a companion article. He spoke to Preston and challenged the contents of the letter. Preston did not deny that someone may have tampered with his words."

"There is no time for that today. We must begin printing in the next few minutes."

"Please, take time for a bit of lunch." Mama had spread a cloth across the counter and laid out bread, cheese, and coffee.

"What about tomorrow?" William pressed his father further, without responding to the invitation to lunch. "We could print Sam's article tomorrow. Give him a chance to get to the truth behind Preston's accusations."

Papa paused to consider William's proposal. "The article must be on my desk first thing in the morning."

"That is fair."

"And I reserve the right to approve it before we print."

"I understand."

"So be it." Papa turned to Kathleen. "Is the first page of type almost ready?"

"Yes, Papa, just a few more words."

"Richard, please, eat some lunch." Mama gestured again to

the lunch. "Children, come and eat. There is plenty for all of you."

William stood up, walked over to his mother, and kissed her cheek. "I'm sorry, Mama. The lunch looks lovely. But I have no time to eat it now."

"Will you be home for supper?"

"I'm not sure. Don't wait for me."

"Can I come with you?" Lydia linked her arm through William's.

Mama threw a sharp look at Lydia. "You know the answer to that."

William released his arm from Lydia's hold. "We'll talk about all this later."

William left then, and Lydia scowled. Papa and Kathleen went back to work. Stephen watched his mother nibble at a piece of bread. Her face was drawn and her shoulders rigid.

Stephen stepped up to the counter. "I would like some lunch, Mama."

Mama smiled through her strain at her youngest child. "Have as much as you like, Stephen. It appears that I brought more than we need." She glanced hopefully at her husband. He glanced back, but he made no move to come and eat.

"Lydia, come and eat," Mama said.

Lydia had her face pressed against the window in the front of the shop, watching William disappear from sight.

"He went to the Liberty Tree," she said. "I just know that's where he went."

"Pay no mind to William's whereabouts," Mama said. "Come and eat."

"I'm not hungry."

"You must eat properly, or you'll fall ill."

"I'm not hungry!" Lydia insisted, not moving from the window.

"Do as your mother says," Papa commanded. But he did not stop working.

Dragging her feet noisily, Lydia crossed over to the counter and picked up a piece of cheese. "Kathleen," she said, "William told me that when you were my age you actually wanted to help a British soldier."

Stephen stopped chewing and looked up at Kathleen. A wave of pain crossed her face before she answered. He forced the lump in his throat down. Kathleen spoke calmly, but her voice quivered ever so slightly.

"That's right, Lydia. I did. He was hungry and cold. He had been shot during a Stamp Act riot. I helped Uncle Cuyler nurse him back to health. I'm only sorry that I could not have done more for him."

"But he was a British soldier!" Lydia protested with disgust.

"He was a human being," Kathleen said simply. "He died a few months later. He was only sixteen." She turned away to put the last letter of type in place.

"You and Stephen are just alike." Lydia tossed her un-manageable hair over her shoulder and picked up a piece of cheese. "You sympathize with the British so much that you are almost lobsterbacks yourselves. It's because you spend too much time with Uncle Cuyler."

"Lydia, hold your tongue!" Papa's voice meant what he said.

Stephen threw down a half-eaten piece of bread and wheeled around at Lydia.

"And you are too much like William!" he shouted. "Nothing matters to you except the Patriot cause."

"It is the most important thing!" Lydia retorted.

"What about truth?" Stephen challenged. "Doesn't that matter?"

Stephen ran to the door and yanked it open. Both his parents were calling to him, but he ignored them and ran out into the street. He had to get away from Lydia.

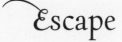Escape

Stephen tumbled out into the street, hardly able to see through the tears welling up in his eyes. He heard the print shop door open behind him and his mother's voice pleading for him to come back. But he did not want to face her just then. He did not want to see the lines in her face that deepened with every political quarrel that erupted in the family.

It was bad enough that her two brothers, Uncle Ethan and Uncle Cuyler, held opposing views. And even though Papa and William agreed on many things, they quarreled about the best way to bring change to the colonies. Lydia never missed a chance to side with William, no matter whose feelings she hurt. Stephen was tired of it all. So he kept running.

He kicked at the cobblestones with his boot. All he accomplished was to hurt his toe. With the back of his hand, he wiped the tears from his eyes. He was hurt by the spiteful way Lydia spoke to him. But even more than that, he was angry at himself for letting her upset him.

His feet took him where they most naturally wanted to

go—across the town square to Uncle Cuyler's medical clinic. Whenever he needed refuge, he went to the clinic. The building itself, with its warm wood tones, comforted him. The clinic was a place where anyone could come for help, Patriot or Loyalist. Uncle Cuyler had worked hard to make sure the clinic was neutral territory, no matter what his own political opinions were.

And if his uncle was there, Stephen knew that he could stay as long as he liked. He only had to stay out of the way while Uncle Cuyler was with a patient. Sometimes Anna was there, too. Anna had told him she would be there all that morning. It was barely lunchtime. Stephen hoped she would still be there.

As he rounded the last corner, Stephen forced himself to slow down and catch his breath. He made sure his cheeks were dry of tears. Anna and Uncle Cuyler were sitting on a bench in front of the clinic munching on lunch. Uncle Cuyler was leaning back comfortably with his long legs stretched out in front of him, crossed at the ankles. Anna swung her short legs in the wide space beneath the bench. They looked content to be together.

Stephen smiled weakly at them.

"Do you feel all right, Stephen?" Uncle Cuyler asked. "You look a little red in the face."

"I'm all right," Stephen said. "I've just been running—that's all." He hoped that they would not be able to tell he had been crying—almost.

"What is the hurry?" Anna asked.

Stephen shrugged. How could he explain the scene that had driven him from the print shop?

"Have you had lunch?" Uncle Cuyler asked. He offered Stephen a piece of dried meat.

Stephen thought of the half-eaten chunk of bread he had left on his father's counter. He felt guilty about running out on his mother's lunch. She would ask him later if he had eaten anything.

Stephen accepted the meat. "Thanks," he said. With the knot in his stomach, he did not know if there would be any space for food.

Anna scooted over. "There's room for you here."

Stephen squeezed in between Anna and Uncle Cuyler. He felt calmer immediately. Settling back against the bench, he looked absently out into the street, in the direction he had just come from. He wondered why was it so easy for him to be with Uncle Cuyler and Anna.

"I saw your mother carrying a basket to the print shop awhile ago," Uncle Cuyler said.

"I know." Stephen nibbled politely on the meat.

"You are welcome to share our lunch," Uncle Cuyler said. "But if you are still hungry, I'm sure your mother has plenty."

"I know. I was just there."

"Oh?" Uncle Cuyler raised an eyebrow and questioned Stephen with his eyes.

Stephen looked away. If he confided in Uncle Cuyler, he would have to repeat what Lydia had said. And he did not want to hurt Uncle Cuyler. He did not want Uncle Cuyler to know Lydia had said something mean about him. He did not want to explain why he was there and not at the print shop eating lunch with his own family.

The three sat in silence for several minutes. Anna crunched on a carrot. Uncle Cuyler uncrossed his long legs and stretched one arm across the back of the bench. Stephen tried to swallow a bite, but he was having a hard time.

Uncle Cuyler scanned the sky. Occasional fluffs of white drifted across the peaceful blue expanse. "Looks like a good day for fishing, don't you think?"

"I suppose so," Stephen agreed reluctantly. He had not really noticed the weather before that point in the day.

"Can we go? Can we go?" Anna loved to fish.

"I'll tell you what," Uncle Cuyler said. "I have to stay here and see patients this afternoon. But I don't see why you two shouldn't go. I happen to have two poles propped up behind my office door. And the widow Spencer said we could fish in the pond at the back of her property on any day of our choosing."

"Let's do it, Stephen!" Anna cried.

"Can we go alone?" Stephen asked. He was still not used to the freedom of Boston without British troops, and he'd always thought the widow Spencer was a scary person.

"I don't see why not. It's not very far away."

"I don't know." Stephen seemed hesitant.

"Don't worry about your folks," Uncle Cuyler said. "I'll send a message about where you are."

"Come on, Stephen; it'll be fun!"

Anna's enthusiasm won him over. "All right, I'd like to go fishing."

They packed up the rest of the lunch, slung Uncle Cuyler's poles over their shoulders, and headed for the widow Spencer's property. They left the cobblestones of downtown Boston and followed the dirt road that led to the outskirts of town.

"All right, Stephen," Anna said, "we're alone now, so you can tell me what is bothering you."

Stephen smiled at his cousin gratefully.

"It's Lydia, isn't it?" Anna said.

"How did you know?" Somehow Anna always knew what he was thinking.

"Because she is the only person who bothers you so."

Stephen kicked a loose rock in the dirt. "She makes me angry. I get frustrated with the way she talks about the British. She thinks the British do everything wrong and the Sons of Liberty do everything right."

"You pay too much attention to Lydia," Anna said. "You should not let her bother you."

"That's easy for you to say. But she's my sister. She lives in the same house. And my parents think we should do everything together."

"And she likes to talk," added Anna.

Stephen laughed. "Yes, most of all, she likes to talk."

"She just says the things she hears. She doesn't really understand everything she hears. Lots of people in Boston are that way. That's what my father says."

"Lydia doesn't care what your father says." Stephen shifted his fishing pole to the other shoulder.

"Well, she ought to care. My parents are Loyalists. Uncle Ethan and Aunt Dancy are Patriots. So is William. But we're all in the same family."

"Deep down, my parents are Patriots, too," Stephen said.

"But they all want the same thing," Anna insisted.

"No, they don't," objected Stephen. "Your parents want the colonies to be part of England, and William and Uncle Ethan think the colonies are ready to be a separate country."

"But don't you see? They all want what they think is best for the colonies."

"But they don't agree on what is best." Stephen kicked at the ground in frustration. Dry dirt sprayed up in front of them.

"That's not the important part," Anna said. "What matters is that everyone wants what is good for Boston and all the colonies."

"That's the part that Lydia forgets."

"And that's why you have to remember it."

Stephen did not respond. What Anna said made sense. But how was that going to help him get along with Lydia?

They arrived at the widow Spencer's pond and cast their lines. To Stephen's relief, the widow was nowhere to be seen. Anna took off her socks and shoes and wiggled her toes into the dirt. Giggling, Stephen did the same. The damp black earth at the edge of the pond oozed between his toes. He squished his feet down deeper. It felt cool.

"Do you think this dirt was ever part of England?" Anna asked.

"What do you mean?" Stephen looked at the ground. It was ordinary dirt.

"We're on one side of the ocean, and England is on the other side. The tide washes back and forth on both sides. Maybe this very dirt used to be on the shores of England."

Stephen tilted his head. "I suppose that's possible. But it's Boston dirt now."

"That's what the Patriots would say," Anna observed.

"And the Loyalists would say that if this dirt was ever part of England, it still is."

They laughed at the strange comparison.

Anna pulled in her line and cast it out farther. "Do you think Aunt Dancy and Uncle Ethan are ever going to name their baby?"

Stephen laughed. The baby was more than three months old, and still she had no name. Aunt Dancy and Uncle Ethan's inability to agree on a name had become a family joke. Various members of the family made suggestions, which Uncle Ethan and Aunt Dancy promised to consider. But the longer the process went on, the more ridiculous the suggestions became.

"They could call her Indecisive," Anna suggested.

"Or Patience, because she waited so long for a name."

"Or Hope, because she has to hope she'll have a name someday."

"Or Tiny, because she is so small."

"Or Wakeful, because she won't sleep through the night."

"Or Quarrel, because Uncle Ethan and Aunt Dancy quarrel about her name."

Stephen dropped his pole and plopped back in the grass laughing. "Can you imagine such a name!"

"Right now they just call her Sister. I'm afraid they might decide to stay with that."

"That would be awful—not to have a real name of her own."

"Maybe we'll have to choose a name and sneak her off to the minister to be christened," Anna said, giggling.

"We'll have to try to look very tall to make him think we are the parents."

"I'll use stilts and wear one of my mother's longest dresses."

Stephen laughed at the mental image of Anna on stilts in an oversized dress.

"I just want the baby to grow up happy and to have a good life no matter what happens to Massachusetts."

After that, they did not speak. The fish were not biting, but they sat with their poles stuck in the ground and watched the pond anyway.

Stephen was glad he had escaped with Anna for the afternoon. When the two of them were together, they were just Stephen and Anna, ten-year-old cousins who enjoyed being together. They were neither British nor American, neither Loyalist nor Patriot. Just Stephen and Anna. And he liked that feeling.

Stephen stared at the pond and tossed an occasional pebble. He watched as even the tiniest pebble disturbed the smoothness of the pond. From one shore to the other, the entire pond rippled from the gentle plink of each pebble. Stephen picked up a handful of pebbles and some larger stones. He threw them in the pond, one after the other, rapidly. One ripple followed closely after the one before it.

As Stephen watched the ripples and the small waves he had created, he saw a collage of images. He saw the strain in his mother's face as she tried to keep the family together in a time of turmoil. He saw Kathleen's guarded expression as she gave the factual answers to his questions. He saw his father's determination to be fair at all times. Lydia's face rose in his mind with self-assured green eyes, and William's face burned with the fire of change. The only face missing in Stephen's mind was his own. He could not see himself, could not make out his features in the greenish background of the pond. Why wasn't he in the picture?

CHAPTER 12

The Trial

Stephen went fishing with Anna many times that summer. The Lankfords and the Turners feasted when they caught something, and their mothers were happy to have them bring home something that the British could not tax.

But it did not really matter if they caught any fish or not. They simply loved walking down the dirt road together, confiding their secrets to each other, and wading in the pond on the hottest days to cool themselves. They stretched out on the grassy slope beside the pond and daydreamed about a time when Boston would be at rest. The British troops would stay away, and Boston's citizens would stop quarreling.

The widow Spencer was not nearly as scary as Stephen had thought. It turned out that she was only sad, not mean. Mr. Spencer had been killed accidentally when Stephen and Anna were little. He had been at the wrong place at the wrong time when a street riot broke out during the Stamp Act. The Spencers did not have very strong political opinions. He was not a part of the riot. But he got knocked over, hit his head on a post, and died the next day.

The widow Spencer had never gotten over feeling angry and frustrated that her innocent husband had died for someone else's cause. She hardly talked to anyone anymore. She had stopped going to church, and she never chatted with people in the town commons. But she did seem to enjoy having Stephen and Anna come to fish. Sometimes she even brought them a snack or a cold drink.

During the summer, Boston grew restless for the trials to take place. The citizens waited impatiently for the presiding judge to regain his health, and they stormed through the streets when they heard that John Adams had agreed to defend Thomas Preston. Only two lawyers in Boston were not afraid to defend the British soldiers. Josiah Quincy Jr. was eager to assist John Adams. All of Boston respected John Adams.

Stephen remembered how surprised William was that John Adams, a distant cousin of Sam's, would take the case. John had always supported the views of the Patriots when they opposed the British. He was well known as a person who defended the rights of people living in American colonies. He believed England had been wrong to send thousands of troops to Boston. For all these ideas, William admired John Adams. But John Adams also believed that any person living in the colonies deserved a fair trial and a strong defense. So he took the case, and with the help of Josiah Quincy Jr., he put together the best defense possible.

Captain Preston's trial date kept getting pushed back later and later, until finally it was set for Wednesday, October 24. As the summer of 1770 gave way to autumn, and the farmers gathered their crops, and school resumed for the children, Stephen grew more and more nervous. Uncle Cuyler was confident that Captain Preston would have a fair trial and be found innocent. William was certain Captain Preston would have a fair trial and be found guilty.

On the morning of October 24, Mama handed Lydia and Stephen their lunch buckets and made sure they were dressed warmly enough for the day. The two children set out on their usual route to school. Lydia put a book on her head to prove that she had practiced her posture well. Stephen giggled at the ridiculous sight. He was glad he was a boy and did not have to do that. Lydia marched ahead of Stephen. That was fine with him. They were supposed to stay together on the way to school. Stephen figured that as long as he could see Lydia ahead of him, they were together. They had plenty of time. They would not be late for school. He could not imagine what her hurry was that morning.

Then suddenly Lydia veered to the left, down a street that did not lead to school.

"Lydia!" Stephen started pumping his legs. His lunch bucket knocked against his knees. "Where are you going?"

Lydia did not slow down. Stephen ran faster, till he caught up with her and grabbed her elbow. The book on her head tumbled to the ground.

"Look what you did!" she cried.

"Where are you going?" Stephen demanded. "This is not the way to school."

"No, but it is the way to the courthouse."

"The courthouse!"

"You can go to school if you want to," she said, "but I'm going to the trial."

"Don't be silly, Lydia. You'll never be allowed inside the building."

"That doesn't matter. I know a good place outside, in the back of the building. If I sit under the window, I'll be able to hear what people are saying."

"Mama and Papa will be very angry," Stephen said.

"Mama and Papa do not have to know," Lydia answered, glaring at her brother with a dare in her eyes.

"Do you want me to lie for you?" Stephen could not believe what Lydia was asking of him.

"If they ask you if I went to the courthouse, then I suppose you'll have to tell the truth," Lydia conceded. "But they won't ask that question as long as they think I was in school as usual."

"Lydia, you could get in a lot of trouble."

Lydia scowled. "Is that all you ever think about—staying out of trouble? Stephen, there is more to life than obeying the rules all the time. You ought to try to be adventuresome once in a while."

"I can be adventuresome!"

"Oh, yes? Then prove it."

"What do you mean?"

"Skip school. Come to the courthouse with me."

Stephen scraped the toe of his boot around in the dirt. "I don't know, Lydia."

"Fraidycat!"

"I am not a fraidycat!"

"Then come with me."

"All right," Stephen decided. "I will."

Lydia led the way around to the back of the brick courthouse while a crowd of adults gathered in the front.

"Nobody will pay any attention to us back here," Lydia assured Stephen.

Stephen did not feel comfortable. His stomach had turned sour during the walk to the courthouse. His eyes darted around to see who might be watching them.

Lydia pointed up above their heads. "See those windows? All we have to do is figure out how to get up there, and we'll hear everything."

Stephen scowled. "I thought you had this all figured out. How are we going to get way up there?"

"Uncle Cuyler keeps saying you have a good brain," Lydia said. "Use it. Help me figure something out."

They looked around. The space behind the courthouse was littered with forgotten items.

"See that barrel over there?" Lydia said, pointing about twenty feet away. "Roll it over here."

"Why don't you roll it?"

"If I muss up my frock, Mama will know something's up."

Frowning, Stephen went to inspect the barrel. It was empty, and he easily tipped it over. He heard one of the slats splinter as it hit the ground. As he awkwardly rolled it toward Lydia, he said, "This barrel is half rotted. I don't think this is a good idea."

"It's the only idea we've got. Stand the barrel up over here, right under the window. Climb up on it."

"It might break," Stephen protested.

"It might not," Lydia countered.

Sighing, Stephen did as Lydia instructed. The barrel, frail as it was, held his weight.

"Now help me up."

Stephen squatted and linked his hands together. Lydia put one foot in his hands and grabbed the top of the barrel. As she hoisted herself up, the barrel creaked.

"Lydia, I don't think—"

The barrel gave way, and Lydia tumbled to the ground, knocking Stephen over. Lydia scrambled to her feet and began brushing the telltale dust off her dress. Stephen glanced around. No one seemed to notice them.

"Let's just forget this and go to school," Stephen said.

"You can if you want to," Lydia answered. "I'm staying here." She surveyed the rubble behind the courthouse again. "Look, there are some crates. We could stack them and climb up."

"Those crates won't even be as strong as that old barrel, and look where the barrel landed us."

"We'll figure something out." Lifting her skirt out of the dust with one hand, Lydia picked up a crate with the other and set it next to the brick wall.

"Maybe if we make a wide base," Stephen pondered. He picked up two more crates and set them next to the first one.

Soon they had a pyramid of crates that he was certain would be sturdy enough to hold them. They climbed the makeshift stairs and perched side by side on the top crate next to the window.

The window was closed.

"See if you can get the window open," Lydia directed.

Stephen rolled his eyes. But it was too late to back out now, he thought. So he shoved on the window frame. To his surprise, it lifted several inches.

"See?" Lydia said. "I told you this would be easy."

Lydia peered inside.

"What's happening?" Stephen asked.

"The attorney for the prosecution is saying something. I can't hear him very well. And he is using a bunch of big words. Why can't lawyers talk in plain language?"

"Do you think we're really going to be able to see what's going on from here?" Stephen was doubtful that all their effort would bring any reward.

"Maybe it's like studying French," Lydia said. "If we listen long enough, we'll start to understand the words."

They listened all day. Sometimes they could understand what was happening. When the witnesses were talking, they understood. It was when the lawyers spoke that it seemed like a foreign language. Stephen watched the movement of the sun carefully, and when it was time for school to be out, they scrambled down from the crates and took a direct route to the print shop.

William was in court. Stephen and Lydia offered to deliver newspapers without complaining and then went home for supper. Lydia even volunteered to set the table, which she hated to do.

Conversation around the table focused on the trial. Now Stephen and Lydia could figure out some of the missing pieces.

"That was quite an impressive line of witnesses the prosecution brought forth," William said. "One after the other, they seemed quite certain that Captain Preston gave the order to fire."

Papa broke off a piece of bread and put it in his mouth. He nodded, then said, "But I understand that John Adams has some impressive witnesses of his own. When time comes for the defense to present its case, he may be able to refute the statements given today."

"These men were eyewitnesses," William insisted. "They are men of honor."

"They are sailors," Papa said, "who are tired of being forced to remain in Boston to testify."

"I have confidence in the prosecuting attorney. He has worked hard to gather the evidence."

"You should not dismiss John Adams lightly," Papa said. "I have seen him in court before. He does not lose very often."

After supper, Lydia pulled Stephen aside. "I'm going back tomorrow. I want to hear the witnesses for the defense. Are you coming?"

Stephen hesitated for only a moment before nodding his head. It was exciting to watch the trial, even through a cracked window.

So they went back to their stack of crates the next day, and again the day after that. Stephen had stopped worrying about who might see them and easily settled into a familiar position on the crates. He was absorbed in the activities of the courtroom.

"Stephen and Lydia Lankford! Come down from there immediately!"

Stephen jerked around so hard that he almost upset the delicate balance of the crates. His mother stood below them, and he knew they were in trouble. Mama was furious.

Lydia groaned and began the climb down.

"How did you find out?" Lydia asked.

"I saw Mistress Sommers in the square this morning. Imagine my surprise," Mama said, "when she asked after your health. Her daughter mentioned last night that you had not been in school for several days."

"But, Mama," Lydia protested, "we wanted to see the trial."

"Obviously," Mama said, "but you did not have permission to miss school." She turned to Stephen. "I'm surprised at you, Stephen. This is not like you at all."

Stephen looked away. How could he face his mother? He had known better than to get involved in Lydia's scheme, but he had done so anyway.

Mama sent them straight home and upstairs to their rooms. They would have no supper that night. And the next day, Saturday, when they could have attended the trial, they were forbidden to leave the house.

CHAPTER 13

The Verdict

Saturday was a very long day, the longest that Stephen could remember. He was alone in the house with Lydia. The rest of the family had gone to the courthouse to watch the trial. The prosecution and defense were supposed to give their closing arguments that day. Then it would be up to the jury to decide if Thomas Preston was guilty or innocent of murder. Papa was prepared to spend all night at the print shop, if necessary, to publish the results of the trial.

But Lydia and Stephen were left to ramble around the house on their own, with strict instructions that they must not leave. Stephen made up his mind early in the day that no matter what Lydia said to him, he would not disobey his parents' direct instructions to stay in the house.

To his surprise, Lydia made no suggestions about sneaking out of the house. She pouted all day long, claiming that the punishment was more severe than the crime, but she made no effort to rebel. In fact, she hardly left the window. She could not see much from their front room. In the morning, it seemed that hundreds of people passed by, headed for the courthouse. After that, the streets were quiet while court was in session. Still Lydia watched the window. She wanted to see the first sign of the jury's verdict that afternoon.

But when the people finally began to stream down the street in the opposite direction, she saw no sign of victory on either side. Everyone simply made his or her way home as if this were a day like any other.

"I don't understand," she said to Stephen as they stood together in front of the window. "William was sure that the trial would end today."

"William can be wrong sometimes," Stephen commented.

"That was a mean thing to say!"

"But it's true. William is not in charge of the trial. He can't promise you when it will be over."

Even Lydia saw Stephen's logic this time. When Papa, Mama, William, and Kathleen finally came home at suppertime, they could talk of nothing else but the trial. Lydia pressed them with dozens of questions about every detail that had transpired.

"It is difficult to know what to believe," Kathleen said. "Two men swore that Captain Preston gave the order to fire, but others swore that he did not."

"He gave the order all right," William said confidently.

"I'm not so sure," Kathleen said. "I think the sentry fired first, after he had his musket knocked out of his hand. Then the others started shooting at random. I'm no soldier, but I would think that if the captain gave the order to fire, all the shots would have come at one time."

"You have a point," her father said. "That is exactly one of the points the defense is trying to make."

"It was hard to hear anything," William said. "Perhaps they did not all hear him give the order to fire at the same moment."

"My sources tell me that many people were daring the soldiers to fire, just as many of the witnesses said," Papa commented. "If the soldiers thought they heard the command and acted upon it, that does not mean that the captain actually gave the command. He cannot be held responsible for the actions of his men if they disobeyed his orders."

"Captain Preston said that the guns were not even loaded when the troops arrived," Mama said. She stoked the kitchen fire to start cooking the evening meal.

"Sam Adams believes differently," William countered. "He is positive the guns were loaded and the bayonets fixed on the ends of them. Sam has plenty of witnesses who would testify to that."

"All the testimony is over now," Mama said. "The responsibility is now on the jury."

Stephen entered the conversation. "If the testimony is finished, why did the trial not end?"

"The lawyers did not give their closing arguments," Papa explained. "The trial will break for the Sabbath, and then the jury will consider the matter on Monday."

Sunday was an even longer day than Saturday. At church, hardly anyone paid attention to the sermon. Instead, they pondered the trial and whispered their opinions discreetly in the pews. The minister preached about God's justice and rewards in the afterlife. Stephen did not think anyone cared about that. They wanted justice right now, not after they were dead.

The Sabbath was a day of rest. Mama had strict rules about observing the Sabbath. The family ate lightly and did nothing that Mama considered to be unnecessary work. She forbade anyone to discuss the trial, which was the only thing they were all thinking about. It was difficult for Stephen to pass the time when he was not allowed to do anything but sit in the front room and read. The day dragged endlessly, and Stephen went to bed early. It was a relief to be able to get up and go to school on Monday morning.

Stephen was sharing a table with Wesley Mason and figuring sums when the word came. The jury took only a few hours to decide the fate of Captain Thomas Preston. They believed he was innocent of the charge. Students all over the classroom jumped out of their seats. Some were ecstatic. Others were furious. The teacher dismissed the class, and the students poured out of the little building to join the throngs in the streets of Boston.

"The Sons of Liberty will never stand for this!" Lydia declared. "How could twelve intelligent men come up with such a verdict?"

"Whether the Sons of Liberty like it or not," someone commented, "the jury's verdict is final."

"Sam Adams is a brilliant man—every bit as brilliant as his cousin John," Lydia insisted. "The Sons of Liberty will think of something."

Stephen knew only one place he wanted to be at such a moment. He found his cousin Anna in the schoolyard, and together they ran to Uncle Cuyler's clinic.

"Did you hear? Did you hear?" Anna burst through the door.

Uncle Cuyler cleared his throat loudly. He was behind a screen examining a patient.

"Oops." Anna giggled. "I'll get a lecture tonight!"

Stephen and Anna managed to contain their enthusiasm while Uncle Cuyler finished the examination and dismissed the patient.

"It's wonderful news, isn't it?" Uncle Cuyler said, grinning.

Stephen could not help but agree. From the scraps of testimony he had heard through the window during the trial and the mealtime discussions with his family, he had come to the silent conclusion that Thomas Preston was not trying to hurt anyone. In fact, he was trying to make sure no one fired a gun.

"What will happen now, Papa?" Anna asked.

"I hope that the intelligent men of Boston will realize that Thomas Preston was given a fair trial. They must honor our system of justice and disgrace him no further."

Stephen was not convinced. "You think there will be more trouble, don't you, Uncle Cuyler?"

The smile faded from Uncle Cuyler's face. He sighed heavily. "I'm afraid the men of Boston are not as intelligent as I give them credit for. Yes, I think there will be trouble."

The clinic door swung open, startling them all. Uncle Ethan stood there, out of breath.

"Cuyler, I need to speak with you."

"Not now, Ethan. I'm sure you are disappointed with the verdict, but the jury has spoken. There is no need for us to quarrel about it any longer."

Ethan was shaking his head vigorously. "It's not the trial. It's the baby."

"The baby?" Stephen's alarm echoed Uncle Cuyler's.

"She's not breathing well, Cuyler. She's been sickly for a couple days."

"Why did you wait until now to call me?" Uncle Cuyler thrust his arms into his coat and snatched up his bag of medical supplies.

"Dancy thought it was no more than a bit of a chill. She did not want to disturb your Sabbath. But we can't calm the baby today. I'm afraid she's going to turn blue."

"Let me come with you," Stephen pleaded. "I was there when she was born. I want to be there to make sure she is all right."

Uncle Cuyler shook his head. "No, Stephen. Not this time. I want you both to run and find your mothers. Tell them to meet me at your aunt Dancy's house immediately."

Uncle Cuyler left. For an instant, Anna and Stephen looked at each other with wide, fearful eyes. Then they started to run in opposite directions.

Stephen burst into the print shop. Mama, Kathleen, and Lydia were all there.

"Mama, Uncle Cuyler needs you right away!"

Stephen gave his breathless explanation, and his mother flew out of the shop.

"I want the two of you to stay indoors now," Papa said sternly. "People are angry about the verdict. I've heard rumblings of trouble already. I don't want you out in it."

"Where's William?" Lydia wanted to know.

Papa shook his head and looked absently out the window. "I wish I knew, Lydia. I wish I knew."

"What about the papers?" Stephen asked.

"I'll do them myself this afternoon." He turned back to the press. Kathleen laid more paper in the tray, and Papa brought the great bar down to print the next copy.

Lydia pressed her face to the window. "It doesn't look so bad out there to me," she commented. "After all, it's not as if there are any British troops to worry about."

A crash outside the door, followed by the sound of scuffling feet, brought Papa to the window.

"Stay back!" he ordered. He looked out the window himself. "There will surely be a riot any minute now. We will all stay inside the shop until it is over. Is that understood?"

Lydia, Stephen, and Kathleen nodded mutely.

"Perhaps the riot will be brief this time," Papa said. "It's difficult to argue with the verdict of a court of law. People will come to their senses and go home for supper."

Papa went back to the press, with Kathleen helping him.

"Lydia, Stephen," he said. "The two of you can start folding the papers and bundling them up. I'll take them out when this is all over."

"Yes, sir," Lydia and Stephen both mumbled. They crouched side by side on the floor and folded the large press sheets into a size that was easier to handle.

At first they worked without speaking. More sounds of struggling came through the walls.

"Aren't you curious about what is happening out there?" Lydia whispered to Stephen.

"I know what is happening. It's a riot, just like all the others."

"I'm disappointed," Lydia said. "When you came to the

courthouse with me, I thought you had finally gotten a sense of patriotism."

"I have plenty of patriotism," Stephen hissed back. "I love Boston as much as you do, maybe even more."

"Nobody loves Boston as much as I do," Lydia declared, still keeping her voice low. "If I were a boy and a little older, I would join the Sons of Liberty, just like William."

Stephen did not answer.

"You're lucky you're a boy," Lydia said. "You could go out and do something. You could fight for all the colonies. But you don't care about the colonies, do you?"

"Of course I do!"

"Then why don't you prove it?"

"What are you talking about?"

"Go and find out what's happening, who is fighting whom."

"You heard what Papa said."

Lydia scowled. "Papa understands why William does what he does. He would understand you, too. It's me he keeps an eye on."

Once again, Stephen did not answer.

"Are you afraid, Stephen? Is that it?" Lydia prodded.

"I'm not afraid." Stephen glanced over his shoulder at his father. Bent over the press making adjustments, Papa and Kathleen had their backs to Stephen and Lydia.

"He won't even hear you leave," Lydia said. "Just go out for a few minutes, find out what is going on, and come back and tell me."

Stephen's heart started to thunder. Why was he even considering this? He looked into Lydia's green eyes. They dared him to prove his fearless patriotism.

"All right, but I'm coming right back."

Folding a paper as he walked, Stephen moved across the room. Papa never turned around. Stephen put his hand on the latch. The sound of the press in action covered the creak of the hinge as he pulled the door open.

Stephen was outside.

CHAPTER 14

Unconscious!

Stephen ran to the tailor's shop, three doors down, and pressed himself against the brick wall. After a long while, he let out his breath. Was this a dream, he wondered, or had he really snuck out of the print shop on Lydia's dare?

He could not go back this soon without looking like a coward. Lydia expected him to return with some information about what was happening in the streets. He was not quite sure what she wanted to know or how he was supposed to learn anything. It was not as if he could walk up to John Adams and demand a report of the jury's discussions. But he would have to try whatever methods he could think of. When he returned to the print shop having completed his mission successfully, Lydia would have to stop accusing him of being afraid, and she would have to stop doubting his patriotism.

Stephen surveyed the street before him. Everyone seemed in a hurry. Many of the shops had closed early. Sensing that the evening might bring danger, the owners had locked the doors and headed for their homes. Even though the evening newspaper had not hit the streets yet, everyone seemed to know the verdict. Stephen's father often said that word of mouth was the fastest method of communication he had ever seen, but people needed to read a newspaper so they could hear both sides of the story.

William was no doubt disappointed by the verdict. *No,* Stephen corrected himself, *William is certain to be downright angry about the verdict, along with Sam Adams and the rest of the Sons of Liberty.* Suddenly Stephen knew what he needed to do to impress Lydia. If he could find William and take back a message to Lydia, she would never call him a mean name again. That was it! He would find William.

But where would William be? He had never shown up at the print shop after the jury's verdict was announced. He had to be somewhere with the Sons of Liberty. Stephen took stock of his location and mentally mapped a route to the Liberty Tree. He could take the back streets. He would stay out of the way of any mobs that might form spontaneously.

One advantage of Stephen's smallish size and quiet nature was that people did not always realize he was nearby. He discovered that he could walk without running down the street. If he stayed close to the buildings, he blended into the background. Anyone with a temper to vent tended to walk down the middle of the street. When he came upon a cluster of men at one corner, Stephen pretended to adjust his boot and stopped for a few minutes to listen.

"The prosecution should never have let John Adams change the charge from murder to manslaughter."

"I know most of the people on the jury, even if they aren't

from Boston. They are Loyalists, I tell you. The jury was stacked with Loyalists."

"All that talk about self-defense! A soldier ought to have more control than to get spooked and fire a gun."

"That sentry's life was never in danger. The defense never proved that anyone in the crowd had a gun."

"Anybody with an ounce of common sense would have found Preston guilty. But what do you expect from a bunch of Loyalists? If they had any common sense, they wouldn't be Loyalists in the first place."

"They had their minds made up before they ever left the jurors' box. The jury did not stay out long enough to give thorough consideration to the evidence presented by the prosecution."

"The Sons of Liberty will not let this end here, I am sure of that."

The group of men moved along down the street. Stephen stood up and straightened his jacket. He had been successful at finding one piece of the puzzle. The jurors were not from Boston, and many of them were Loyalists. Or at least that is what one person said. Stephen had no idea who any of those men were or whether he could believe them. So maybe he had not discovered anything helpful after all.

Stephen continued on toward the Liberty Tree. The light was starting to fail now. In the gray haze of dusk, every shape around him took on an eeriness and shadowy quality. Twice he got disoriented in the back streets, but only briefly. Soon he came out in the center of town with a good view of the Liberty Tree.

Dozens of people were milling about the Liberty Tree, but not the sort of people he expected. He saw only ordinary citizens. Granted, they were more irate than usual, but they were ordinary citizens. There was no sign of Sam Adams, William Lankford, or any of the other Sons of Liberty.

Stephen slapped the side of his own head for his foolishness. Why had he thought the Sons of Liberty might be meeting at a time like this? This was no time to stand around exchanging ideas under an elm tree. This was a time for action.

Darkness had fallen fully by now. Stephen was suddenly frightened. He would never be able to find William in the dark. Sneaking out of the print shop had been a stupid idea, and he had been foolish to let Lydia talk him into it. Surely his father would have missed him by now, and Stephen would have to face the consequences of his foolishness later. He looked back in the direction he had come from. The streets seemed fuller every minute. Turning around, he looked in the other direction—toward Uncle Ethan and Aunt Dancy's house. Actually, he was closer to their home than to the print shop.

Stephen's mind flashed back to the night of the massacre, the night the baby had been born almost eight months earlier. The streets had been just as full that night and tempers just as high. But somehow none of that had concerned him as he ran through the streets searching for help. All that mattered was the baby. The mission of finding help for Aunt Dancy and the baby had kept his feet pumping long after his own strength would have given out. Stephen had never taken time that night to question why so many folks were out.

Tonight was much the same. Stephen did not care about

the results of Captain Preston's trial nearly as much as he cared about his baby cousin. If he was going to risk his safety for any cause, it would be for one he believed in, not one Lydia smothered him with.

Stephen made a decisive turn, quickened his step, and headed for Aunt Dancy and Uncle Ethan's house. The closer he got, the steadier his breathing became. Once he was inside, he would face a severe scolding, but he would be safe. And he would know whether the baby was all right. He was almost there.

A sudden thud against the back of his head brought darkness.

The cat was meowing. It was a loud sound, almost screeching. As Stephen listened, he realized the loud meowing was not angry. The cat was distressed. It gave a painful, mournful cry.

"What's wrong with the cat?" Stephen murmured, as his brown eyes fluttered open. Gradually, they focused on the face of Uncle Cuyler.

Uncle Cuyler furrowed his brow. "What cat?"

"Oh," said Stephen, breathing heavily, "it's the baby crying." He was lying on a pallet of quilts in front of the fire at Aunt Dancy's house. As he realized where he was, he understood what the sound was.

"Yes, she's been crying most of the evening."

"What's wrong?"

"She has a fever."

"Will she be all right?" Stephen tried to prop himself up. "Ow!" He moved his hand to where a sharp pain pierced him in the side.

"Take it easy," Uncle Cuyler said, helping him lie back. "I think you have a couple of broken ribs."

"The baby. . . Is she all right?"

"It's been a long night, but yes, I think she will improve."

Stephen breathed a sigh of relief. "I'm glad."

"Stephen," Uncle Cuyler said, "your concern for the baby is touching, but I must ask you what you were doing out."

Stephen turned his head away. "I know it was dumb," he said, "but Lydia dared me. She said it was the only way to prove my patriotism."

Uncle Cuyler nodded and pressed his lips together. "And did you?"

"I guess not. And when Lydia finds out I came here, she will really think I'm stupid."

Uncle Cuyler smiled faintly. "You know, Stephen, your mother is my older sister. I know what it's like to have an older sister. I understand how it feels to be the youngest one in the family."

"You do?"

"Sure. I was the baby, and for a long time no one trusted me to do anything. Your mother made me walk home from school with her long after my friends were free to roam around on their own."

"Then you do understand." Stephen laughed, then grabbed his side again. "That really hurts!"

"Do you remember what happened?"

Stephen shook his head. "After I realized what a dumb idea it was to try to find Will, I decided to come straight here. Something hit me in the back of the head."

"My guess is that you got in someone's way. I had to go to the clinic for a potion for the baby, and I found you outside. But I don't know how long you were there."

"Did you get the medicine. . .for the baby?"

"Yes, I gave her a dose, and we'll wait to see what happens."

"You have to take care of her, Uncle Cuyler. Don't worry about me."

"Just lie back and rest, Stephen. I'll send your mother in."

A knock on the front door startled them both. Mama and Aunt Abigail both appeared from the next room, staring at the door with worried frowns. The knocking persisted.

"Step back," Uncle Cuyler said, and he went to the door.

"Who is there?" he called.

"Cuyler? It's me, Richard. Stephen is missing."

Quickly Uncle Cuyler undid the bolt on the door and let his brother-in-law in.

Papa spotted Stephen by the fire immediately. "Stephen, are you all right?" He rushed to his son and knelt next to him. Mama, too, knelt next to Stephen and laid her cool hand on his cheek.

"Uncle Cuyler says my ribs are broken. I'm sorry, Papa. I disobeyed you, and I know it was foolish."

"We'll discuss that later," Papa said. "I'm just glad you're safe."

"I should have known you would miss me. I'm sorry to make you come out when there is so much happening in the streets."

"Actually, it was Lydia who told me that you were gone."

"Lydia?"

Papa nodded. "She told me everything—how she goaded you

into going out. We had quite a bit of activity outside the shop this afternoon. So when you didn't come back, she panicked and told me what had happened. I looked all over town for you. I even saw William and started him looking. Then it came to me that this is where you would go—to check on the baby."

"I don't really care about the trial," Stephen said, grimacing with the effort. "Even William cannot convince me that politics are important at a time like this. But the baby—I wanted to be sure she is all right." He looked hopefully at Uncle Cuyler.

"Your uncle will take good care of her," Papa said. "He's a good doctor. And remember, she's strong—like you, Stephen."

Stephen moved to embrace his father and stopped suddenly. "Ow!"

Papa smiled at him in sympathy. "I think this is one lesson you'll be painfully reminded of for a long time."

CHAPTER 15

Family Reunion

In the morning, the baby's cry was a soft coo. Stephen awoke smiling. But when he tried to sit up, he was forced to surrender to the throbbing headache and the slicing pain in his side. He lay back and listened to the baby's coo and Aunt Dancy's soothing tones, as she hummed and rocked the child across the room from Stephen.

Last night's events were like a bad dream. If he had not found himself sleeping in Aunt Dancy's front room with a knifelike pain cutting through his torso every time he tried to move, Stephen might have thought he had imagined everything. But the pain was real, and the gurgling baby was real.

Stephen knew that the trial of Thomas Preston was only the beginning of Boston's dealings with the men who had been involved that dreadful night more than seven months earlier. The other eight soldiers and the four civilians who had been charged with crimes still awaited trial. The jury agreed that the captain had not given the order for his soldiers to fire. But they had fired, and five men had died. Boston was still determined to hold those who had shot responsible for their actions. William had told his family many things about Samuel Adams. So Stephen knew that the Sons of Liberty were not finished with this case.

It was still very early in the morning. His parents had been persuaded to go home and get some rest with the promise that Uncle Cuyler and Aunt Abigail would look after him. Stephen brightened at the thought that Uncle Cuyler, Aunt Abigail, and Anna had all spent the night at Uncle Ethan and Aunt Dancy's house. They would all be together to celebrate the baby's recovery.

Without moving his body, Stephen turned his head toward his aunt and baby cousin. Aunt Dancy looked calm and content. Her daughter was on the road to recovery. She probably had not paid any attention to the jury's verdict, Stephen decided. Aunt Dancy knew what was important. Her child mattered more than the trial.

Stephen sighed contentedly and dozed once again.

"Stephen? Stephen? Are you awake?"

Without opening his eyes, Stephen turned toward the voice and moaned softly. He had been sleeping deeply and did not want to awaken.

"Stephen, wake up. I have to talk to you."

He forced his eyes open and looked into Lydia's familiar green eyes.

"Papa and Mama said you were hurt. I didn't sleep all night, worrying about you."

"You were worrying about me?" Stephen had not expected

that Lydia would be concerned.

"Of course. You're my little brother."

"Oh." He did not know what else to say.

"This is all my fault, Stephen," Lydia said humbly. "I should never have let you leave the shop."

"You practically pushed me out the door," Stephen reminded her.

"But I didn't think you would really go!" Lydia retorted. "I was sure you would be back in three minutes. You have far too much common sense than to stay in the streets during a riot."

Stephen was puzzled. "I thought you wanted me to be more adventuresome."

"That's what I thought, too." Lydia drew her knees to her chest and wrapped her arms around them. "I guess I was counting on you to draw the line between adventuresome and foolish. I'm sorry."

"So you didn't really want me to go out last night?"

"Well," Lydia said thoughtfully, "I did want to know what was going on out there. When you didn't come back right away, I thought maybe you really were going to find something out. But then. . ."

"What happened?"

"There was a street fight right outside the print shop. Some Patriots were lining up against a group of Loyalists. They said awful things to each other! These were people who have been neighbors for years—Sarah Parkenson's father and Agatha Fleming's older brother. Then someone starting swinging a stick. If his friends hadn't had sense enough to stop him, someone would certainly have been hurt. And then I thought about you—how it could be you who got hurt. Then I started to pray."

Tears welled up in Lydia's eyes. She pushed them back with her open palms.

"And I told Papa you were gone. He thought you were in the back room, but you had been gone for almost an hour by then."

Stephen smiled mischievously. "So you were right about one thing. Papa didn't notice when I left."

"I wish I had been wrong about that. Then he would have made you come back immediately, and you...you...you wouldn't have been hurt at all. I would understand if you said you could never forgive me."

"Of course I'll forgive you. It's really my own fault that I went out. Besides, I'll be all right. Uncle Cuyler says my ribs will heal quickly because I'm young."

"I'm glad for that. I suppose I'll have to deliver papers by myself until then."

Stephen smiled inwardly at that thought. "And I can just rest at the clinic until I am fully recovered—which could be a very, very long time."

"Don't get any crazy ideas in your head. You can recover at home, and Uncle Cuyler will surely tell us when you are well enough to go back to work."

"You know," Stephen said, "I was at the clinic yesterday when Uncle Ethan came in. At first Uncle Cuyler thought he was there to argue about the jury's verdict. But he was there about the baby. Uncle Cuyler and Uncle Ethan never agree about anything, but when the baby got sick, Uncle Ethan knew where to come. He knew Uncle Cuyler would help."

Lydia laughed. "They actually spent the night under the same roof, and the house is still standing."

Stephen smiled as much as his sore ribs would allow him. "I thought about that a lot during the night. I know that everything William is working for is important—taxes and freedom and everything else he talks about."

"I haven't given up on that," Lydia said.

"I know. It is important. When Mama and Papa talk about how things were when they were growing up, I realize that Boston has been changing my whole life. I don't know when the change will be finished."

"William says the change is only beginning," Lydia said. "He says the Sons of Liberty are willing to go to war against the British if necessary."

"If that happens, I hope that Uncle Cuyler and Uncle Ethan will remember this night," Stephen said, "the night when they forgot about politics because they needed each other."

"It was the baby who brought them together," Lydia said. "An innocent baby who knows nothing of politics or Parliament or the king or colonial assemblies."

Stephen was getting excited. Painfully, he propped himself up on one elbow.

"You're right, Lydia," he said. "It looks like you and I found something to agree on, too."

Aunt Dancy entered the room holding the baby.

"Is she better?" Lydia asked.

"I heard you singing to her earlier," Stephen said. "She wasn't crying."

"She is much better, thanks to your uncle Cuyler." Aunt

Dancy smiled at the babe sleeping in her arms.

Lydia reached out and stroked the top of the infant's head. "She's a beautiful baby. I don't think I ever told you that I thought she was beautiful."

Aunt Dancy smiled proudly.

"Does anyone want breakfast?" Aunt Abigail and Anna joined the group in the front room.

"I'm starving," said Lydia most dramatically. "Let's have a huge breakfast."

"Somebody get the boys up to milk the cow," Aunt Dancy said. Anna scurried up the stairs to do her aunt's bidding.

At the sound of a friendly knock on the door, Aunt Abigail opened it. The rest of the Lankford family entered.

"Stephen, you're awake. Good!" Mama went immediately to her son.

"You gave us quite a scare," William said. He shook his finger at Lydia. "I'll talk to you about this later."

"Have you had breakfast?" Aunt Abigail asked.

"No, we came right over here to check on things," Papa said. "I wanted to make sure Stephen and the baby were all right before going to work."

"You'll join us then," Aunt Dancy announced.

Anna was back with the boys. "What is everybody doing here? It's like a holiday family dinner but no holiday," Charles said, rubbing the sleep out of his eyes.

"I think it's wonderful," Anna said. "I'll set the table."

"I would like to offer our patient some toast and tea," Aunt Abigail said, "but I suppose coffee will have to do."

Stephen scowled. He did not like coffee. He missed the tea that his family used to drink before the boycotts.

"I'll put a lot of milk in it," Aunt Abigail assured him.

Aunt Dancy smiled wryly. "I believe that if you look on the top shelf of my pantry, in the back left corner, you will find a tin of tea."

"Really? Tea?" Stephen could hardly believe his good fortune.

"Did someone say tea, or am I still dreaming?" Uncle Cuyler ruffled his uncombed hair with his fingers. Uncle Ethan was right behind him.

"The tea can wait," Lydia announced, rising to her feet. "Stephen and I have something to propose first."

She looked at Stephen, who nodded his agreement.

"I would have thought that the two of you would have learned your lessons about scheming," warned Aunt Abigail, "considering what you have been through in the last few days."

Lydia shook her head vigorously. "This is different. This is not a scheme." She looked around the room, meeting everyone's eyes. When she had their complete attention, she turned to Aunt Dancy and put out her arms. "May I hold Margaret?"

"Margaret?" Aunt Dancy questioned. She glanced at Margaret Lankford.

"The baby," Lydia insisted. "Her name must be Margaret." She took the baby from Aunt Dancy's arms.

Uncle Ethan and Aunt Dancy chuckled. "You have decided the baby's name?"

"Yes, and I'll take her to the minister to christen her myself if I must."

"It's thoughtful of you to want to name her after your grandmother," Margaret Lankford said, "but I do think Uncle Ethan and Aunt Dancy should choose the name for their own daughter."

"But isn't it obvious?" Lydia asked her mother. "Her name must be Margaret. The original Margaret Turner—Kathleen Margaret Turner, your mother and my grandmother—brought this family into being when she had you and Uncle Ethan and Uncle Cuyler. She wanted our family to love each other. Now her little granddaughter was born on the night of the massacre, and she has brought the family together in spite of our differences—just like Grandma would have wanted."

"I agree with Lydia," Stephen said, grimacing as he pulled himself to a full sitting position. "The baby's name should be Margaret. And she is not named only for our grandmother, but for all the family that came before her."

"Stephen and Lydia have my vote." Will stepped forward and took the baby from Lydia. He studied the infant's face.

"I haven't paid enough attention to you, little one," he said tenderly. "But whatever is ahead for Boston and the rest of the colonies, you will be among those who face the future. It is only right that you should have a name that reminds you of your past."

Aunt Dancy and Uncle Ethan looked at each other and laughed. "Margaret it is," Uncle Ethan said.

"Your grandmother would be proud," said Mama.

Stephen lay back contentedly. Everyone he loved best in the world was in that room right then—even Lydia. War could rage through the streets of Boston, but what mattered most were the people around him right then, no matter what their politics.

But for the moment, he was going to enjoy the benefits that came with being a patient. "I'm ready for that tea and toast now."

Kate and the Spies

JoAnn A. Grote

A NOTE TO READERS

While the Miltons and Langs are fictional, the turmoil in Boston leading up to the Revolutionary War is not. By the time war broke out, one in every four people in Boston was a British soldier. These soldiers were everywhere—in people's homes, businesses, and public meetinghouses. Whether citizens were Loyalists or Patriots, most of them wished there were far fewer in their town. In spite of all the soldiers, Patriots continued to work secretly for American rights.

CONTENTS

CHAPTER 1

Mysterious Visitors

Boston, December 16, 1773

O*of!"*
Eleven-year-old Kate Milton braced against the crowd that dragged her and her cousin Colin Lang along. Whistles and yells from merchants, craftsmen, and seamen filled the early night air.

"A Boston tea party tonight!" called a large man beside her. From the smell of him, Kate guessed he was one of Boston's many fishermen.

Kate struggled to keep her footing on the slippery wet stones of Boston's Milk Street. She hung on tightly to Colin's arm, clinging to him for support. Thousands of people filled the streets. She had never seen such a crowd in Boston. She and her cousin had no choice but to go the same way as everyone else. Her heart beat like crazy beneath her wool bodice. She and Colin had wondered for weeks what would happen tonight, and now they were about to find out!

"Where's everyone going?" Kate had to yell to be heard. She tipped her head back, trying to see Colin's face, but he was taller than she was, and his face was turned away as he scanned the crowd. Kate stood on tiptoes and pushed back the gray wool cloak from her blond curls, but she could still only see the backs of the people ahead of them.

"We're headed toward Griffin Wharf at Boston Harbor," Colin shouted. "The tea ships are there."

Kate felt fear settle in her chest like a rock. "Are the people going to hurt the crews? Will they sink the ships?"

"I don't think so," her cousin answered. "People aren't carrying weapons or sticks or stones."

When they reached Griffin Wharf, Kate had to step carefully to keep from tripping on the slippery wooden planks and huge coils of rope. Beneath them, water lapped at the tall wooden poles that held up the dock.

The people filled the wharf to the very end. Judging by the light from tin and wooden lanterns on long wooden torches that people carried, Kate guessed the next wharf was just as crowded.

The *Dartmouth*, one of three ships carrying tea, rose high above them. It tugged at the thick ropes tying it to the pier. The other two tea ships were anchored nearby.

Kate looked at the three ships, dark outlines against the darker sky of early evening. With their sails rolled up, the ships' straight pine masts stood like tall, leafless trees, but the ships themselves were like great winged beasts, poised to swoop into the air. "The ships look like dragons, don't they?" Kate whispered.

Will the ships still be here in the morning? she wondered. *Will the tea?*

At least the rain had stopped. The December chill crept through Griffin Wharf's wet wooden planks, up through the soles of Kate's leather shoes, through the three layers of itchy wool stockings, through the woolen petticoats beneath her gown, and right into her bones. She shivered, yanked her hood over her head again, and wrapped her cloak more tightly around her shoulders.

It's not only the cold that makes me shiver, she thought. *It's fear.* Fear for Boston. Fear of the unknown. Fear for her older cousin Harrison's life.

The fear had been crawling inside her ever since that day two weeks ago at her uncle's print shop. That was when Harry had told Colin and Kate what might happen and had asked them to help.

They'd been printing handbills, or posters, for the Sons of Liberty. Kate didn't mind helping, but she liked helping her father better. Her father was Dr. Firth Milton, and Kate was fascinated with the thought that he could actually do something to help sick people heal.

As he had talked to them, Harry's eyes, as brown as Colin's, had flashed with excitement. He'd leaned across the huge printing press and told them the plan in a loud whisper. "The law says the *Dartmouth* has to either leave Boston on December sixteenth or unload its tea by then."

"I know." Colin and Kate were hanging up copies of the paper, fresh from the press, to dry. "They've only fourteen days left."

"Mark my words, the tea won't be unloaded or sold here."

Kate frowned. She always felt so powerless in the face of all the events that swirled around her, but Harry sounded as confident as if he had some control over what happened. Harrison was twenty-two, nine years older than Colin. He was an adult, and a man besides, while Kate was only a little girl. Still, what could he or the other men do? "I don't understand," Kate said.

Harry spoke quickly, excitedly. "If the ships are unloaded here, we Patriots will do it ourselves. It will take lots of hands. We need men and boys to help who aren't well known in town." He glanced at Kate. "You'd pass for a boy if you tucked your hair up inside a hat and wore some of Colin's old clothes. We need people to help us who can be trusted not to tell what they do that night—not before and not after. You're Patriots, the both of you, and I'd trust you with my life."

Pride flooded Kate at her cousin's words, but she still felt uneasy.

"I'm a Patriot, all right," Colin said proudly, "and I'll keep your secret. You can count on us."

Kate nodded silently. What else could she do? She couldn't let Harry down.

Kate knew her father referred to people like Harry as rebels, but she had to admit she liked the word "Patriot" better. Rebel sounded like an enemy of King George III. Patriot sounded like a loyal British citizen, and that's what both Colin and Harry were. And so was she, she supposed.

Harry grinned at the two children. "Then you'll help?"

"I don't know." Kate still wasn't certain about this. "How are you going to unload the tea?"

"We're going to throw the tea into the harbor."

Kate's heart thumped like a drum. "You're going to ruin it?" Her voice rose in a squeak, and Harry waved his hand to shush her. He nodded once, sharply.

"But. . .but that's like stealing!" Kate's chest hurt from the deep breaths she was taking. Surely her cousin wouldn't steal, even to keep the tea out of Boston!

"We'll only do it if we have to. We're trying to get the governor to send the ships away with the tea. If he does, we won't have to toss the tea overboard."

"What if the governor has you arrested for dumping the tea?" Colin asked.

"That's why we need boys that most adults in town won't know. Lots of boys your age are helping. Are you with us?" Harry looked from Colin to Kate.

Kate swallowed. "I can't. It's too much like stealing."

She was relieved when Colin nodded his agreement. Would Harry think they were cowards? Colin and Harry looked alike, and they were both Patriots, but in many ways the two brothers were very different. Harry was always doing exciting things, while Colin was quiet, serious. He thought things through carefully before making decisions. Still, Kate knew how much Colin looked up to his older brother.

"You have to do what you believe is right," Harry said.

Colin let out his breath with relief. Kate knew he had been scared Harry would be angry with him.

"But," Harry continued, "I have to do what I believe is right, too. I know you won't tell anyone what I've told you."

Neither of them had told anyone Harry's secret. Kate would have liked to talk things over with her father, but she knew she couldn't. Her parents were Loyalists, who believed the Patriots should do as Parliament and the king said, even if what they said was wrong. He wouldn't want to get Harry in trouble, but if her father knew Harry's secret, he might think it was his duty to tell the British admiral. Then Harry's friends would be in trouble.

Kate just wanted to go home. She tugged at her cousin's coat sleeve. "Let's go."

"We'll never make it through this crowd." Colin's teeth were chattering so hard that Kate could barely understand him. "If only the governor had let the *Dartmouth* leave tonight with her tea, everything would have been fine."

"Why are people making such a fuss about the tea?" Kate asked. "The tax on it is small, and people like tea." She had heard people talk about the tea in her uncle's print shop many times, but she still couldn't really understand why everyone was so upset. When she was with Colin, she called herself a Patriot because he was one—but when she was with her own family, she couldn't help but think that their point of view made sense, too.

"In Britain," Colin explained, "Parliament passed the tea tax law. Older laws say only people who serve us can pass laws taxing us. No one in Parliament serves the Americas."

Kate's gray wool cloak lifted as she shrugged her shoulders. " 'Taxation without representation.' People say that all the time. But the king chose representatives for the American colonies."

"Those men vote the way the king wants, or they lose their

jobs. If we elected them, they'd have to vote the way we want."

"Parliament has a right to make laws, even if Americans don't like them." Kate's pointed chin jutted out. Sometimes out of sheer stubbornness, she liked to argue with Colin, trying to make him see the Loyalists' perspective.

As she spoke, the crowd grew suddenly still. Kate looked around, hoping no one had heard her. What was happening? She stretched onto her tiptoes, trying to see above the people. "I hate being short!"

The crowd opened to let a few raggedly dressed boys and men through.

Kate grabbed Colin's arm. "Indians!"

The newcomers were only pretending to be Indians, she realized as they drew closer. Anyone could tell they weren't genuine natives. She could smell the grease and soot they'd used to darken their faces. Swipes of paint brightened some noses. Knit caps hid hair. Feathers were stuck in a few caps. Blankets draped over shoulders.

But it was what they carried that made Kate's heart beat faster: metal things that glittered in the light from the torches and lanterns. "Axes!" she whispered. "What are they going to do with them?"

No one answered her.

As more "Indians" came, people pressed even closer together to give them room. Kate thought there must be over one hundred of them.

One of the ragged, smelly young men bumped against Kate. The man winked at her and then passed on to join the others.

Kate stared after him, then nudged Colin. Harrison!

CHAPTER 2

A Wild Tea Party

Harry was helping the "Indians" pull one of the other two tea ships up to the wharf. Fear made Kate's stomach feel like it was wrapped around itself as tightly as the thick ropes tying the ships to the wharf were coiled. What was going to happen? Would Harry and the other Patriots dare go through with their plan?

In the moonlight, she could see the harbor was filled with every size and kind of ship and boat, just as it had been all her life. Somewhere out there in the dark harbor, British soldiers were stationed at the fort on Castle Island. Warships were in the harbor, too. She could see the lanterns on the British man-of-war that bobbed only a quarter-mile away. All of Boston knew that the governor had ordered the ships and fort to fire their cannons on the tea ships if they left the harbor with the tea on board.

She yanked on Colin's sleeve again. "Do you think the men-of-war will fire their cannons at these Indians?"

"Of course not. They might hurt innocent people."

Kate crossed her arms. "Those Sons of Liberty," she hissed. "Sons of Trouble, Papa calls them. He says they're nothing but troublemakers, always stirring people up. There must be other ways to get Britain to listen to what people want."

Colin didn't answer. She knew he wouldn't criticize the Sons of Liberty, even if he might secretly agree with her. After all, his brother, Harry, was a Son of Liberty.

Kate studied the "Indians." Many looked like they might be about her age or a little older. Were any of them Colin's friends?

Five more joined the group. A man who acted like a leader greeted them by saying, "Me know you." The voice sounded familiar. The five repeated the three words. Kate guessed it was a sign, a way the "Indians" would know there wasn't a spy in the group. They didn't sound like Indians, though, and her lip curled. They were like little boys playing a game of make-believe. But she knew there could be serious consequences to this game.

The moonlight rested on the man's face. Kate squinted at him. Was that Paul Revere, the silversmith who stopped at the printing shop to talk with Harry so often? Surely not. Harry had said they wanted people who wouldn't be recognized, and lots of people knew Mr. Revere. Still, the man's voice had sounded like Mr. Revere's.

The "Indians" quietly boarded the three tea ships. Standing close to the *Dartmouth*, Kate heard someone on deck say, "We no hurt your ship, Captain, only the tea. Please bring lanterns."

Was the speaker afraid someone would recognize his voice if he spoke normally? Kate wondered.

In a few minutes, lanterns shone on the three ships' decks.

Then came *whack! whack! whack!*—the sound of axes chopping open wooden chests. In the light from the lanterns and the moon, Kate and the crowd watched smashed boxes drop over the ships' sides.

Kate gasped. "They're really doing it! They are throwing the tea into the water! Where are the constables, or the night watchmen, or the marines?"

"I guess they can't get through the crowd," Colin answered. "Maybe they don't know what's happening."

"We were right, Colin," Kate whispered. "I don't care what Harry said. These people are no better than thieves! Why doesn't someone stop them?"

"No one wants trouble, Kate. They just want the tea unloaded tonight like the law says it must be."

"The law doesn't mean it's to be unloaded this way, and you know it!"

Colin shifted his feet uncomfortably. Kate knew that what was happening was illegal. Still, she had to admit that the Patriots had tried to have it sent legally away from Boston first.

She was surprised to see both Loyalists and Patriots watching quietly. Did the Loyalists think, like the Patriots, that destroying the tea was the only thing left to do?

She didn't see any of the Patriot leaders in the crowd. She and Colin had seen Sam Adams, John Hancock, Josiah Quincy, and Dr. Warren earlier at the town meeting at Old South. Was it too dangerous for them to be seen here?

The terrible "game" went on for three hours. The children stood frozen, trapped by the crowd, listening to the whack of axes, the sound of canvas tearing—Kate guessed that was the bags inside the wooden chests, bags meant to keep the tea dry if the chests got wet. The bags wouldn't help now.

Splintered chests splashed as they landed alongside the ships, and the wooden chests bobbed in the moonlight. Spilled tea drifted like seaweed on top of the dark water. She could smell the tea over the strong smell of sea and fish.

Her legs had long ago grown tired, and her feet ached. She leaned on Colin, though she knew he must be tired, too. But she had forgotten about leaving. Something kept her there, as though she needed to bear witness to something important that was unfolding out there in the harbor. No one else left, either.

For a while, she watched nervously for boats of marines to come from the men-of-war. They never came.

When all the tea had been dumped, the "Indians" finally left the ships. They lined up, four in a row. *Just like soldiers,* Kate thought, so tired now that she felt like collapsing. They rested their axes on their shoulders the same way soldiers rested their rifles. Someone played a tune on a fife.

The tea destroyers marched down the wharf toward town. Kate spotted Harry again, and Colin must have seen him, too, because he lunged toward his brother, keeping a tight hold on Kate's hand so they wouldn't lose each other. Colin grinned as he kept up with the "Indians," who were now humming the cheerful tune the fife played, and Kate found that she couldn't help but smile as well. Now that everything was over, she almost wished she and Colin had joined Harry. It couldn't have been so bad after all, since even the Loyalists and British marines hadn't tried to stop it. Surely no one would be arrested. It would have been exciting to be part of it.

The marching men reached the head of Griffin Wharf, where buildings lined the street at the edge of the harbor. Wood squeaked against wood as a window opened. Kate looked up just in time to see a man shove his head out the window above them. Admiral Montague of the British marines! He'd watched the whole thing!

Kate stopped in her tracks so fast that the man behind her ran right into her. She didn't even notice.

"Well, boys," the admiral said, "you've had a nice night for your Indian caper, haven't you? But mind, you've got to pay the fiddler yet."

One of the "Indians" made a cocky reply. The admiral slammed the window closed.

The men started marching again. Kate's thoughts spun as she followed. She wasn't smiling now. The admiral's words made her sick to her stomach with fear. How would the admiral make Harry and the tea raiders "pay the fiddler"?

"We'd best get home, Colin," she said with a sigh. She was suddenly so exhausted that she thought her legs might give out beneath her.

"I didn't realize it was so late," Colin said as they threaded their way through the crowded streets toward Kate's house. "It must be after nine o'clock. I'll walk you home. You shouldn't be on the streets alone this late."

"Mama will be furious I'm still out." Kate sighed again. All she wanted to do was crawl into her bed. She didn't want to have to face an angry mother.

But they were barely through the front door when her mother met them in the hallway. Like Kate, Mama was short with blond hair and blue eyes, but she wasn't slender like her daughter. Usually, Kate felt comforted by her mother's soft shape, but tonight even Mama's white apron and crisp skirts seemed to crackle with rage.

"Where have you been, young lady?" Her eyes flashed as she faced the children.

"We were at the meeting at Old South Meetinghouse. You said I could go, remember?"

"That was early this afternoon. You know you're to be home before dark. Your father is out searching the streets for you."

"But Mama, you can't imagine what happened!"

"I've been imagining all kinds of dreadful things happening to you!"

"I've been with her the whole time, Aunt Rosemary," Colin spoke up.

"Humph! There are things a boy of thirteen like yourself can't protect her from." Mama wrapped her shawl closer about her shoulders. "I shouldn't have allowed you out of the house today at all, Kate. With the Patriots in such a vile mood over the tea ships and the crowds in the streets—why, I wouldn't be surprised if we ended up with another Boston Massacre."

"Oh, no, Mama!" Kate said eagerly. "The British marines didn't do anything to stop the Indians!"

"Indians?" Mama's hand flew to her throat.

"Not true Indians," Kate assured her quickly.

Mrs. Milton shook her head. "I don't know what you are talking about, child. Colin, you'd best get home. Take a lantern with you. Honestly, out on the streets without even a lantern, among the angry crowds. You both should have known better."

"Yes, Aunt Rosemary," Colin murmured, moving past her into the parlor to light a candle for the lantern at the fireplace.

"Don't think you're going to get by without being punished for this," Mama was saying to Kate as Colin slipped out the door.

"But let me tell you about the tea and the Indians," Kate said as the door closed behind Colin.

She knew Mama had been worried, but she didn't understand why being worried always made parents angry. As she listened to her mother scold, Kate wondered how things were going for Colin. At least she didn't have a room full of people listening to her mother reprimand her. Colin would have his older sisters, Isabel, age fifteen, and Susanna, age twenty, as well as Harrison's wife, Eliza, all pretending not to listen to Aunt Jane's shrill voice while they worked on their fancy needlework. Harrison and Eliza's six-month-old baby, Paul, would be asleep in a wooden cradle beside the hearth, and Kate wished she could be there, if only so she could scoop up the round little baby boy and cuddle him in her arms.

Somehow, it helped to imagine Colin's family now, instead of paying too much attention to the anger in her mother's voice. Colin's mother was tall and lean like her brother, Kate's father. She had red hair like her Irish mother. Right now, Kate was pretty sure her aunt's green eyes were stormy.

"I'm sorry, Mama," Kate said, pulling her mind back to her own home, "but we just forgot about the time. We wanted to see what happened, and the crowd was so thick—"

"Go to your room, Katherine Milton," her mother snapped. "I don't want to hear your excuses."

With tears burning her eyes, Kate made her way up to her room. At least she could go to bed now. But she would have liked some supper first.

The next day when she saw Colin, she asked him how things had gone at his house the night before. "Was your mother as angry as mine was?"

Colin grimaced. "More. But she was interrupted before she could really get going."

Kate raised her eyebrows, waiting for her cousin to explain, and Colin grinned. "You see, this strange 'Indian' suddenly came through our back door."

"You mean Harry?. . ."

Colin nodded. "Mother didn't even recognize him until he said, 'It's me, Mother.' And then she wanted to know why he was dressed like that—and why he smelled like tea leaves!"

"Was she upset?" If Aunt Jane had been angry with Colin for being out late, it seemed to Kate that her aunt should have been even angrier with her older son. But Colin shook his head.

"Father came home then—and everyone forgot about me because Harry was telling about the tea party. Ever since the Boston Massacre, you know how my parents have been more sympathetic toward the Patriot cause. Everyone clapped and laughed at Harry's story."

Kate tried to imagine it. She was fairly certain that even if Mama weren't a Loyalist, she would never laugh and clap if Kate broke the law the way Harry had. But Colin's family was different from hers. That was part of the reason why her cousins fascinated her so much, she supposed.

"And then," Colin continued, "Harry took off his shoe and shook it. He had tea inside it. And Mother laughed even harder and said how your mother would hate to see good tea going to waste like that." Colin smiled at the memory. "Mama said she was proud that Harry had stood up for Englishmen's rights." He sighed and his smile faded. "But then she said how glad she was that I hadn't been involved. She'll never think of me as anything but a little boy." His voice was resentful.

Kate gave him a sympathetic smile. "Well, you are the baby of the family."

Colin made a face. "At least Harry doesn't think I'm a baby. But it's a good thing Mother doesn't know he asked us to help with the tea party. She would have been fuming angry then."

"What did your father say?" Kate asked.

"He warned us all not to tell anyone that Harry was involved." Colin's face puckered with worry. "The marines and constables didn't arrest anyone last night, but we don't know what might happen later."

Kate gave a little shiver. She couldn't help but remember the admiral's warning: *You've got to pay the fiddler yet.*

What Happened to Liberty?

King George is making Boston 'pay the fiddler' now," Colin said to Kate early in June.

"He's making all Boston pay, not just those men who threw the tea overboard." Kate's mouth bent in a pout.

The peal of bells drifted over the water. All of the churches in Boston had been ringing their bells for hours. Everyone said it was the worst day in Boston's history.

So many months had passed since the tea party that Kate had hoped the king had forgotten about it. He hadn't. Finally a ship came from England carrying the Boston Port Bill, a law passed by Parliament. It said that until Boston paid for the tea it dumped into the harbor, Boston's port would be closed.

From where they stood on Long Wharf, which ran half a mile into Boston Harbor, Kate could see the British man-of-war that was anchored between Long Wharf and Hancock's Wharf. In all, nine men-of-war were now guarding the harbor from entering ships. No other ships were in the harbor. The warships wouldn't let small boats, barges, or ferries approach

Boston by harbor or river. A boat couldn't be rowed from one dock to another.

Boston was built on a peninsula that was almost an island. Only a narrow piece of land, called the Neck, connected it to the rest of Massachusetts. With the harbor closed, the Neck was the only way in or out of town.

At least no one had been arrested for the tea party. No one knew for certain who most of the "Indians" were—and no one would tell even if they did know—so no one had been arrested. The day after, Paul Revere had left for Philadelphia and New York to let people there know what had happened. Sons of Liberty in those cities had sent word that they thought Boston had done the right thing.

Hardly anyone was working. People wandered about town, angry and unable to believe what was happening. A soft salt breeze cooled the summer day but did nothing to cool people's tempers.

Colin and Kate had joined their families in a prayer service at church before coming to the wharf. Loyalists, Patriots, and people who hadn't chosen sides had been there. Everyone was afraid the port's closing would leave people without jobs.

Kate shoved a blond curl behind her ear, out of the breeze's way. "I've never seen the wharf so quiet. There's none of the usual bustle of unloading and loading ships and clerks running about with their ledgers. And none of Uncle Thomas's merchant ships are in the harbor."

The king thought that when Boston's port closed, the other towns would jump at the chance to take business away from Boston. Instead they'd offered to help Boston. Uncle Thomas was in Salem arranging for his ships to land at Salem's port. His merchandise would have to be shipped over land, which would cost more money and make business more difficult, but it would keep business from stopping altogether.

"Only our enemies' ships are in our harbor," Colin's father had said after the prayer service this morning.

Sparks flew from Dr. Milton's eyes. "The British fleet isn't our enemy. Boston is part of England."

Uncle Jack's brown eyes grew cold. "Since when does England point cannons at its own people?"

"Since Boston's people threw someone else's tea into the harbor." Kate's father stared at his brother-in-law, his mouth hard. "Even Ben Franklin sent word from London that the tea party was illegal. He thinks Boston should pay for the tea."

"Boston's citizens would sooner starve."

"I don't think so. There are lots of Loyalists in town. We don't want to lose business because of what those involved with the tea party did. With the port closed, it won't take long for the rest of Boston to come to its senses and pay for the tea."

"Never!"

Dr. Milton waved an arm toward the shops, countinghouses, and warehouses on the wharf. "Can't you see that these buildings are closed and their windows shuttered? The men are without work. People won't be able to buy food or clothing or your newspapers. How are you going to run your print shop?"

"I've bought a good supply of paper and ink," Uncle Jack answered. "I agree things will be rough if people don't have money to buy newspapers or place advertisements. But there will be news the people need to know, and I aim to print it. I'll say things with fewer words and use less paper."

"And when you run out of ink?" Father asked. Kate waited for her uncle's answer. British law said people in America had to buy all their ink from England.

Uncle Jack crossed his arms. "Then Harry and I will learn to make it ourselves."

Kate stared at her uncle. Could they really do that?

"Boston will get by," Uncle Jack continued. "Sons of Liberty in New York and Philadelphia have promised to help us."

"How?" Kate's father waved a hand scornfully. "With brave words? The other colonies don't care about us. Do you think they'll give Boston fuel, food, and other supplies?"

Kate remembered the picture of the snake her uncle had printed in the newspaper the previous week. Ben Franklin had drawn it many years ago. The snake was in pieces, each piece representing a different colony. The pieces weren't joined together because the colonies always argued among themselves instead of working together. Beneath the picture, Mr. Franklin had written "Join or Die." He'd said that if the colonies didn't work together, they would be like a snake that was cut up into pieces. They would die.

Was Father right? Kate wondered. Wouldn't the other colonies help Boston?

"Remember what I printed in yesterday's paper?" Uncle Jack asked. "Colonel George Washington threatened to raise one thousand men and force the British troops from Boston."

"You wish to see fighting in our streets?" Her father's face was red from fury.

"No, but I don't wish to give up our rights as English citizens, either, just to keep peace."

Kate leaned close to Colin's ear and whispered, "Our fathers haven't stopped fighting in years. Why can't they be friendly like us? You and I don't always agree, but we don't argue about it."

Her father turned to Colin and Kate. "We'd best get back to the apothecary. A doctor's work doesn't stop because people can't pay him. There may be more work than ever for you, Colin. My other apprentice, Johnny, left Boston with his family. You'll have to take over his duties, too. You can start by weeding the medicine herb garden."

Father's long legs set a brisk pace. In her long skirt and petticoat, Kate couldn't keep up. She was grateful that Colin matched his steps to hers. "I didn't know Johnny was leaving," Colin remarked.

Kate lifted her skirts so they wouldn't be soiled by the puddle they were passing. "He and his family went to Salem. Johnny's father is looking for a job there." Kate's forehead puckered with worry. Johnny's father was a carpenter who worked in the shipyards. The Port Bill had put him out of work. She would miss Johnny, and she knew Colin would, too. Johnny wanted to be a doctor more than anything. What if he never had the chance again? Kate's chest ached for him. She couldn't bear it if Uncle Jack made Colin give up his chance to be a doctor. If only she could have the chance to be a healer, too—but Mama said that midwives could only make a living these days in small villages where no doctor came. No daughter of hers, Mama insisted, was going to end up in the backwoods.

Kate sighed. When Kate was much younger, her mother had taught her to read and write—but now that Kate was older,

Mama couldn't understand why Kate would want to continue to study and learn. After all, Mama said, a girl only needed to be able to read the Bible and do enough writing and arithmetic to keep house. The big medical books in Father's library fascinated Kate, but Mama said it was a waste of time for Kate to be always poking her nose into the thick books. Mama didn't understand how Kate felt about healing. All Mama wanted was for Kate to grow up and get married to some well-off young man.

Kate noticed that many of the houses they passed were empty. Shops were empty and dark, too. They gave her an eerie feeling. Families leaving town passed them with carts and arms piled high with belongings.

Kate's eyebrows scrunched together. "Johnny's father said the people who stay in Boston are going to starve. Do you think we're going to st–starve?"

"Of course not," Colin said stoutly. "Didn't you hear Father say the other colonies will help us?"

But would they? Goose bumps ran up Kate's arms. Who was right—Father or Uncle Jack?

Hours later at the apothecary, Kate watched while Colin held a small marble bowl in one hand and a marble pestle in the other, grinding soft yellow primrose flower petals into powder. Father wanted them for a patient, and Kate knew the primrose would help the woman's painful hands. The flower's gentle smell filled the air.

The woman had barely left before off-key singing came through the open door:

"Rally, Mohawks! Bring out your axes,
and tell King George we'll pay no taxes
on his foreign tea!"

Father grunted. "You'd think people would be sick of that song about the tea party."

Kate grinned. She kind of liked the song's cheery tune, but she knew it got under the skin of Loyalists like her father.

Kate watched as Colin took his journal from the open shelves, where he always kept it handy. The shelves were filled with white jars. Blue letters told what herbs each held. Kate liked the way the apothecary always smelled of dried flowers and herbs. Drawers below the shelves held roots and barks for medicines and curved saws for surgery.

Colin's quill pen tip scratched across the page as he wrote down what his uncle had told the woman about the primrose. Colin had been an apprentice for almost three years now, and Kate tried hard not to be too jealous of him.

Her father smiled down at his nephew. "I'm glad you like to learn. You're the best apprentice I've ever had."

She watched Colin's cheeks turn pink with pride. "I don't want to forget how to treat all the different sicknesses when I'm a doctor."

"You'll have books to help you remember, like this new one you bought at Henry Knox's bookshop down the street." Her father lifted a thick book bound in brown leather with gold letters.

"I—I want to get a degree from a medical school, too." Colin held his breath. Kate knew it was his greatest dream to get a university degree. He'd never told anyone but her.

Her father shook his head. "You don't need to go to a university to be a doctor. Most doctors learn only through apprenticeship and reading, as you're learning."

"I know, sir, but I want to be the best doctor possible. I want to know everything I can to help my patients."

Father smiled. "Have you decided which university you want to go to?" The tone of his voice told Kate he wasn't taking Colin seriously.

"Either Philadelphia or King's College in New York. They're the only medical schools in the American colonies." Colin's voice was determined.

"Well—"

Crash!

All three of them spun toward the door. Kate's friend, Sarah, leaned against it. Wrapped in her apron, she carried a small tan dog with a black nose and a black tip on its long, skinny tail.

"Liberty!" Kate cried. "What happened to my dog?"

ᕫᐧ CHAPTER 4 ᐧᕬ

Will Boston Starve?

The lilac dress Sarah wore was covered with dirt. The ties of her white linen scarf had slid up under one ear. She sounded as though she had been running.

"Put Liberty on the counter," Father said.

Kate could see that Sarah was handling the dog gently, but Liberty still whimpered. She ran a hand lightly over the dog's short fur, and her heart ached for her little friend. "It's okay, boy," she soothed.

"It's his right front leg." Sarah was still trying to catch her breath. "He can't walk on it."

Kate's father took the leg carefully between his hands. Liberty yelped and tried to sit up. Kate put her hands on both sides of Liberty's head. "Shh, Liberty."

While her father ran his fingers lightly over the rest of Liberty's body, looking for other injuries, Kate looked at Sarah. "What happened? Was he hit by a carriage?"

Tears pooled in Sarah's blue eyes, but they couldn't hide the anger that flashed there. "No. It was some mean Loyalist boys.

When the boys heard me call him Liberty, they said he was a nasty Patriot dog. They threw stones at him!"

Anger flashed through Kate. How could anyone be so cruel?

"His leg is broken," her father said.

"I'll set it." Colin glanced up at the doctor. "I mean, if you don't mind, sir."

"You certainly know how to handle a broken leg by now. I'll get some bandages and wood for a splint." Kate's father started for the small room at the back where wood was stored.

Sarah's blue eyes sparkled above her freckled nose, and her dark brown hair waved over her shoulders. "I yelled at the boys to stop. They called me awful names and kept throwing stones at poor Liberty."

"How did you get Liberty away?" Kate asked.

Sarah shrugged. "I ran into the middle of them and picked up Liberty in my apron."

Colin looked impressed. "Did you get hit by any stones?"

"A couple."

Dr. Milton gently grasped Sarah's shoulders. "Were you hurt?"

Sarah winced. "Not much." She rubbed a dirty spot at the top of one arm. "I think I might have a black and blue spot here." Her hand went to her head and gingerly explored a spot there.

Dr. Milton pushed her scarf back. "Sarah, there's a lump here as large as a goose egg!"

Sarah shrugged again. "Well, I haven't a broken leg like Liberty."

"You could have been hurt badly," Dr. Milton said. "What if

a rock had hit you in the face?"

"It didn't. Anyway, I couldn't let them keep hurting Liberty!" She looked up at Dr. Milton. "Please don't tell my parents, though," she pleaded. "I'm really fine."

Dr. Milton shook his head. "I don't know, Sarah. You seem to be all right, but your mother should probably keep an eye on you this evening. I'd hate to see you punished, though, for protecting our dog."

"It's those stupid Loyalist boys who should be punished," Sarah stormed. "Just shows how awful Loyalists are."

Kate laughed and propped her hands on her hips. "My family is Loyalist, remember?"

"I forgot."

Kate giggled when Sarah blushed.

Kate's father started back toward the wood room. "We'd best set Liberty's leg. Go and clean up, Sarah, before you go home. Maybe your mother won't be as upset if you don't look as though you just came through a battle."

Kate remembered the way Mama had been the night she came home late after the tea party. She realized her father must understand that the more worried a mother felt, the angrier she was apt to be.

Kate put her hand on her friend's arm. "Sarah, thank you. You're a good friend and a brave one."

Sarah grinned. "So are you. Even if your family is Loyalist."

Kate knew Sarah and her family were strong Patriots. Her father was even more outspoken about Englishmen's rights than Uncle Jack and Harrison were. She was glad that Father never seemed to hold that against Sarah.

Kate smiled and stroked Liberty's head. "I'm just glad Liberty wasn't hurt any worse."

Liberty tried to lick her hand. Kate didn't know what she would have done if Sarah hadn't saved the little dog from the cruel boys. How could people act so mean? She hated the angry feelings that were swirling through Boston these days, driving people apart.

A month later, shades of pink and orange cast by the rising sun were fading from the sky over Boston's streets and harbor as Colin, Susanna, and Kate hurried down the cobbled, narrow street toward the common. Two- and three-story brick houses hugged the street's edge on either side of them. The homes and shops were built so close their walls touched. Smoke from breakfast fires and craftsmen's fires filled the air.

The young people leaped into a nearby doorway to let a farmer and his creaking, two-wheeled cart pass. Colin grinned and pointed. "Look at the turkey." The bird sat in the cart atop a basket of turnips. It turned its head this way and that and gobbled constantly. "At least farmers can still get into Boston over the Neck to sell their food, even if nothing can come by boat or ferry."

Kate's smile died. "Farmers come to the market, but people aren't buying much. People don't have much money. Sarah's father is a carpenter. He hasn't had any work since the harbor closed."

Many of her father's patients hadn't paid the doctor, either. These days, some people made less money in a month than they used to make in a day.

"Many farmers sell most of their vegetables, flour, and meat to the soldiers and marines," Susanna said. "The redcoats won't starve. Britain sends ships with food for them."

Kate sighed. "Father says things will get worse after harvest is over."

"Harvest is months away," Colin said. "Surely the blockade will be over by then."

Kate's blue eyes sparkled with hope. "Do you think so?"

"I haven't heard anyone say so," he admitted. "Still, I can't believe the British troops would let people starve. Even some of the Patriots are friendly with the soldiers. Some of the soldiers are courting Boston girls. Why, I've even heard that Lieutenant Colonel Percy breakfasts every day with John Hancock. There's no stronger Patriot than Mr. Hancock! Could the soldiers hurt the townspeople when they are so friendly with us?"

"I hope you're right." Kate sighed.

Susanna rested her arm along Kate's shoulders and smiled. "Our heavenly Father will look out for us, you'll see."

"I hope He looks out for us better than the other colonies have," Kate said. "They promised to help us, but they haven't yet." Fear squiggled down her spine. Maybe Father was right and the other colonies weren't going to help Boston.

Before they reached the common, they heard the silver bugles calling the redcoats to drill. The day after the harbor was closed, a regiment of British troops had set up camp on the common. Now four regiments were camped there and two groups of artillery with cannons. Cannons on the common, threatening Boston's own people! In the harbor, men-of-war pointed more cannons at the town. A year ago, Kate would never have thought such a thing could happen.

Still, part of her couldn't help but find it exciting to have the streets, shops, and common filled with soldiers in the bright red uniforms that made people call them "lobsterbacks" and "redcoats." When she watched them drill, a thrill ran through her. She didn't tell anyone, though. She was ashamed to feel that way, no matter what her family believed about the soldiers. Lately, Kate felt torn between Patriots and Loyalists. When she was with Mama and Father, she felt like a Loyalist—but when she was with Sarah or Colin and his family, she felt like a Patriot. Which side was right? Was God on one side and not the other? Or could both sides possibly be right? It was all so confusing that it made her head ache sometimes.

Tents and red-and-white uniforms splashed color across the common's grassy slopes. Soldiers were smothering the fires where they'd cooked their breakfast. Kate could still smell the meat and eggs they'd cooked. Some soldiers were readying horses for the officers. Others were grabbing muskets from where they'd been stacked in a circle and rushing to line up for drill. Men and boys from Boston stood in groups, watching. With the port closed, many had time to watch instead of work.

Kate stopped near a bay-colored horse with a black mane and tail. She ran a hand over the horse's shoulder. It turned its head and sniffed Kate's hand.

"What are you looking at, lass?"

Kate's head jerked toward the tall officer beside the horse. Like all officers, he wore a powdered white wig that curled tightly at his ears and tied in a club in back. His black eyebrows showed his hair's true color.

Kate swallowed the lump in her throat. "I–I was just looking at the fine horse, sir."

"Maybe you were thinking of stealing her. You and your young friends here." He scowled at Colin and Susanna.

"No, sir! We wouldn't!"

The officer crossed his arms and looked up and down at the three young people. "I suppose you're all Patriot rebel brats."

Colin's hand balled into a fist. "I'm a—" He stopped short. Kate knew he wanted to say he was a Patriot and proud of it. But Uncle Jack and Harrison had warned all the family to be careful what they said around the soldiers. The Patriot leaders didn't want to anger the troops. "I'm an English citizen," Colin finished lamely.

The officer snorted. "Not a loyal one, I'll bet."

Susanna's fists perched on her hips. Long red curls slipped over the shoulder of her yellow muslin gown. "You needn't speak to him that way. Have British officers no manners?"

"It isn't wise for the town's children to be fooling with an officer's horse, miss." The officer stared boldly at her.

"Is there a problem here, Lieutenant Rand?" Kate turned toward the calm, sure voice. Another officer had stepped up beside them.

Lieutenant Rand straightened. "Just speaking with some of the locals."

"I'm Lieutenant John Andrews." The new officer's friendly, blue-eyed gaze swept over them. "I'm honored to make your acquaintance." Removing his two-cornered black hat, he bowed from the waist. "Have you come to see the troops?"

"No, sir," Colin answered. "We brought medicine for the regiment's doctor."

A frown settled above the blue eyes. "That's a strange delivery, isn't it?"

"I'm Colin Lang, Dr. Firth Milton's apprentice. This is my sister, Susanna, and Dr. Milton's daughter, Kate. Your regiment's doctor sent a soldier to Dr. Milton saying he needed certain herbs. I've brought them for him, but I don't know where to find him."

"The doctor's tent is over there." Lieutenant Andrews pointed to the top of a grassy knoll where a tent was pitched beneath a tall oak. "If I might suggest, it would be best if you young ladies didn't come near the soldiers' camps without a male escort."

Colin stepped between the officer and Susanna. "That's why I'm with them."

Surprise widened Lieutenant Andrews's eyes. Kate waited for him to say that Colin was only a boy. Instead he nodded and shook hands with Colin. "Of course. How wise of you." With another bow to Susanna and Kate, he left.

"He's awfully nice, isn't he?" Kate stared after him.

"He's a British officer. The reason he's in Boston isn't nice at all," Colin reminded her.

Kate smiled hopefully. "Maybe all these soldiers will make Boston pay for the tea, and then everything will go back to the way it used to be."

"Girls!" Colin exclaimed in disgust. "You think there's an easy answer for everything." He stalked toward the doctor's tent, and Kate hurried to catch up with him. She didn't care what Colin said. She was certain that Lieutenant Andrews could make things right again in Boston if he only had the chance.

But then Kate thought of Harry and Uncle Jack and Sarah's father. Men like them were so angry. She sighed. Colin was right after all. There was no easy answer.

When the young people headed back toward town, the streets were filled with more families piling carts with everything they owned and leaving Boston. Kate knew they were afraid there'd be fighting with troops in Boston. Many more troops were on their way.

"Colin! Susanna! Kate!"

They turned to see Harrison running toward them, his tricorn hat in one hand. "Great news!" He stopped beside them, panting and grinning.

"What is it?" Colin asked.

"Rice! South Carolina's sent two hundred barrels of rice. The rice is coming across the Neck now. And Carolina's promised to send eight hundred more barrels." Harry whipped his hat in the air. "They're uniting! The colonies are uniting for Boston!"

⁓ CHAPTER 5 ⁓

Signs of War

To the surprise of the Loyalists and redcoats, gifts poured in over the Neck. The other colonies sent rice, meal, flour, rye, bread, codfish, cattle, and money. A farmer from Connecticut brought an entire flock of sheep.

Colin and Kate's uncle Thomas was on the town's Gifts Committee, along with some of the colonies' strongest Patriots, Sam and John Adams and Josiah Quincy.

When Uncle Thomas asked Kate to help deliver gifts, she eagerly said yes. It didn't matter whether the people she took the gifts to were Patriots or Loyalists. "No one should go hungry, no matter what he believes," she told Colin.

"Thanks to the other towns and colonies, no one in Boston has gone hungry," Colin said.

Kate's shoulders sagged beneath her yellow and blue calico gown. "If the Patriots would pay for the tea, people wouldn't have to beg the committee for food."

"It's not the Patriots' fault King George is punishing everyone in Boston for what the tea partyers did," Colin said quietly.

Kate sighed. Here it was again, the same old confusion that made her head ache. When she was with Colin, sometimes she thought of herself as a Patriot—and other times, like now, she felt as though she had to defend the Loyalists. Lately, she and her cousin argued more and more, just like their fathers did.

Things were tense all over Boston. The men who were out of work were growing angrier every day. They couldn't buy what their families needed, and since they weren't working, they had nothing to do with their time but gripe about their troubles. The men fished off the empty, quiet wharves and complained about the king. They were certain the king was wrong and the Patriots were right. Many people who didn't know whether to be Loyalists or Patriots before the tea party were now becoming Patriots. But not Kate's parents. They were still loyal to England.

Not everything was bleak, though. In order to receive the food that the other colonies had donated, Bostonians had to volunteer for various projects. Streets were paved, buildings were fixed, docks were cleaned, wharves were repaired, and hundreds worked at the brickyard on the Neck.

"It's like the town is having a housecleaning!" Kate joked to Colin when she came home from making deliveries one day.

On a day in late August, Kate whistled as she walked home from making her deliveries. She knew Mama wouldn't approve of her whistling—"It's not ladylike!" she'd say—but Kate was feeling happy for a change. She liked the bustle and sounds of the street: a boy beating a drum while calling out his master's wares, wooden cart and wagon wheels rumbling along the pebbles, horses' hooves marking a lazy beat, the creak of the wooden signs above every shop swinging in the breeze.

If only there weren't redcoats everywhere, reminding her that everything had changed.

She stopped in the open door of her uncle's printing shop. Lieutenant Rand was waving a sheet of freshly printed paper and yelling at Uncle Jack, Colin, and Harry. "This is treason!" His face was almost as red as his uniform.

Uncle Jack leaned a hip against the tall, wooden printing press and swung his wire-rimmed spectacles in one hand. Kate wondered how he could be so calm with a British officer screaming at him only a couple feet away. "The handbill only tells what our county leaders said today at their meeting."

Lieutenant Rand threw the handbill down and ground it into the wooden floor planks with the heel of his shiny black boot. "They've all but declared war on England!"

"Lieutenant Rand, what they said is not my problem. With the harbor closed, I'll gladly print items for either Patriots or Loyalists in order to feed my family."

Kate watched wide-eyed as Lieutenant Rand clutched the hilt of the sword that hung at his side. Surely the lieutenant wouldn't draw his sword on her uncle! Kate's heart beat so hard it made her chest hurt.

Lieutenant Rand let go of his sword. His eyes glittered with anger. "Mr. Lang, be very careful what you print from now on."

Kate stepped quickly from the doorway to get out of Lieutenant Rand's way as the officer left. "Why is he so mad?" Her voice sounded very small.

Harry grinned. "The Suffolk County leaders drew up this list because of the Port Bill and Intolerable Acts." He handed Kate a copy of the handbill.

The Intolerable Acts were Boston's latest punishment for the tea party. Parliament called them Regulatory Acts. Patriots called them Intolerable Acts, because they said no Englishman would tolerate or stand for them.

The Intolerable Acts changed the way Massachusetts was run. Instead of elections, the king and his friends chose people for all the important jobs. Juries were even appointed by the king's friends, so it would be hard for people to get fair trials.

Kate stood in the doorway where there was enough light to read the list. "Suffolk Resolves" was printed in large letters at the top. The most dangerous thing it said was just what had made Lieutenant Rand so angry: that Massachusetts army should train and be ready to fight to keep the rights the king and Parliament wanted to take away.

Fear slid through Kate in an icy wave. "Are the Patriots declaring war on England?"

"No." Harry's brown eyes were serious. "But we need to be ready to protect ourselves."

"We could use your help, children," Uncle Jack said to Kate and Colin. "Paul Revere is waiting for us to finish these handbills. He'll take them to the Continental Congress meeting in Philadelphia."

Kate knew the colonies had decided to hold a meeting called the Continental Congress. People from every colony were invited. They wanted to make a plan to convince the king and Parliament to leave Boston alone and give people in America the rights they used to have.

It's like Harry said months ago, Kate thought. The king meant to hurt Boston by closing the harbor. Instead the Lord was using Boston's trouble for something good, to get the colonies to work together. *Maybe,* she thought, *things will turn out all right in the end after all.*

She watched while Colin put on a leather apron to protect his linen shirt and brown cotton breeches. Kate wet the big pieces of paper, and Colin inked the type with ink-soaked balls of wool and leather. Uncle Jack and Harry took turns swinging the large wooden handle to work the press, and Kate hung up the paper to dry when it came off the press. Before they finished, they had to light candles and lanterns to see.

Kate was thinking as she worked, trying to decide if she was really a Patriot or a Loyalist. It felt good to work hard with her uncle and her cousins. She was glad she could help. Did that mean she was a Patriot?

Mr. Revere arrived as Harry hung up the last handbill. His dark eyes twinkled in his ruddy face. "It looks like you've been helping with the handbills, Colin. We shall make a Son of Liberty of you yet."

Colin grinned, and Kate knew how proud he must feel. She wished Mr. Revere would notice her, too, but men never seemed to pay much attention to little girls.

"I wish I could be with you in Philadelphia, Paul, to hear what the Continental Congress thinks of the handbill," Uncle Jack said, removing his apron.

Harry agreed eagerly. "I wonder if they'll dare say they feel as we do about the army."

"You may be sure I'll let you know." Mr. Revere held out a sheet of copper to Colin's father. "Here's the engraving I promised you."

Uncle Jack put on his wire glasses. He held the metal near a tin and glass lantern to check the picture the silversmith had carved into the copper. "Perfect. I'll use it in the next copy of the *Boston Observer.*"

Mr. Revere picked up some handbills and started for the door. His boots jingled. Kate saw his spurs made the sound.

"Are you leaving tonight?" Harry asked.

Kate knew Sam Adams had set up a system of post riders to carry news between towns and colonies. It was called the Committee of Correspondence. Paul Revere often rode for them.

Mr. Revere said, "The congress begins in only nine days. The trip to Philadelphia often takes twice that long. I've a strong horse, but I'll have a hard ride."

Kate, Colin, and Harry watched from the doorway while Uncle Jack walked with Paul Revere to his horse, which was tied to a post in front of the shop. Kate remembered Mr. Revere's copper engraving. "What is the picture he made, Harry?"

"It shows how to make saltpeter. If war comes, the Patriots will need saltpeter to make ammunition. We won't be able to buy it from England."

War! The word never went away. A shiver ran through Kate. "I thought the Patriots didn't want war. I thought we just wanted things back the way they were."

Harry nodded. "So we do. But we can't always have what we want without a fight. We need to be ready, just in case."

Kate remembered how angry Lieutenant Rand had been earlier that day, how quickly he'd grabbed for his sword. It wouldn't take very much for a few angry men on either side to start a fight like the Boston Massacre four years ago.

But after the massacre, the people of Boston had been able to make peace again. This time if there was a riot and one side began shooting, would the people be able to keep peace—or would there be war?

 A Spy

Colin, Kate, and Liberty hurried along the road to the Neck on a cool September day. Sarah's father was helping build a wall there for General Gage, and they wanted to see it. With the harbor closed, there wasn't much else to watch in Boston these days, except soldiers.

A family that looked tired after walking a long way scuffed along carrying bundles and leaning on walking sticks. They were headed toward Boston.

"Another Loyalist family," Kate said. "If we didn't live in Boston, my family might have been forced to leave our home as well."

She couldn't keep the anger and pain from her voice. Patriots in towns other than Boston were mad at the Loyalists for the punishments King George and Parliament were forcing on Boston. Patriots were threatening Loyalists, chasing them from their homes. The Loyalists had nowhere to go but Boston.

"I guess the Loyalists know the redcoats here will keep them safe," Colin said. "How are things going with the Loyalist family from Concord that moved into your house last week?"

"I hate sharing our home with them." Kate kicked at a stone and almost tripped over the petticoat beneath her pink skirt. "Esther—she's my age—shares my bed. She won't play with Sarah because Sarah is a Patriot. Sarah is furious."

"Maybe she thinks you feel the same way as Esther. Sometimes I don't know what you believe, Kate."

"Why does it have to matter?" Kate stamped her foot in frustration. "Sarah's my best friend. She's much nicer than Esther. And you're my cousin. Why should anything like Patriots and Loyalists come between us?" She stuck out her lip, tired with the way everything had changed lately. "There's lots more work with Esther's family, too," she complained.

"Doesn't Esther's mother tell her to help with the chores?"

"Esther and her mother spend all their time saying how terrible the Patriots are and eating our food. Today Esther complained that we hadn't more sweets. With the price of sugar and molasses, we can't afford many sweets."

"She sounds spoiled."

"Mama says not to speak badly of her." Kate sighed. "It must have been awful to be forced out of their home. They only had time to pack a few clothes. I truly am sorry for her."

Life was so confusing lately. Yesterday, she had asked her father why he continued to treat patients who he knew were Patriots, when he didn't believe in their cause. He had looked upset that she would even ask the question.

"A doctor treats everyone, Kate. Regardless of what people believe or what they've done or how much money they have. . . or anything else. You should know that." He sighed. "Besides, each man has to make up his mind for himself about whether to be a Loyalist or a Patriot. I can't force my beliefs on anyone."

Then why do you always argue so much with Uncle Jack? Kate wanted to ask.

But she kept thinking about what Father had said: *Each man has to make up his mind for himself.* She wasn't a man, of course—and how could she make up her mind when she felt so confused?

They reached a small rise in the road, and she saw that soldiers and workmen covered the Neck in front of them. Some were working, others watched. A few days after Paul Revere left for Philadelphia, General Gage had ordered a wall built all the way across the Neck. He called it a fortification because the wall protected the town like the wall of a fort.

It was a cool day, but sweat trickled down Kate's spine beneath her cotton gown. The townspeople couldn't leave Boston by water because of the warships. Now they wouldn't be able to leave by the only road out of Boston if General Gage decided they shouldn't. Seeing the wall and cannons made Kate feel like a prisoner in her own town.

Townsmen were teasing the soldiers. "Can't ye build any better than that?" called one man. "Your wall is no stronger than a beaver dam!" yelled another. "That wall won't protect you. A group of Patriots could blow it down!" called a boy about Colin's age.

Some soldiers ignored them. Others yelled nasty comments back at them. But the townspeople knew the officers wouldn't let the soldiers harm them.

Colin and Kate sat down beneath an oak tree to watch.

Workers hauled bricks in two-wheeled wooden carts. Others laid the bricks to make the wall. Sweat glistened off the men's faces. Their shirts were wet with sweat. Officers yelled orders. In the middle of it all, people and carts and donations filed over the Neck along the road into and out of Boston.

Kate's stomach growled. She put a hand over the apron that protected her dress and laughed, embarrassed.

Colin smiled. "Seems everyone's always hungry these days. Thanks to the gifts, at least no one's starving." He pulled two small green apples from his breeches pockets and handed her one. Kate knew the breeches used to belong to Harrison, as had his patched white shirt. Colin had grown so much during the last year that his own clothes no longer fit. "These are from our apple tree."

The children watched a boy a couple years older than Colin push a cart filled with bricks. The boy's red hair was tied back in a club with a piece of leather. He wore a blue farmer's smock that came almost to his knees over his homespun breeches and a black hat with a floppy brim. While they watched, one of the wheels struck a large rock and started to tip.

"Watch out!" Colin jumped up and darted forward.

The boy struggled with the cart's wooden handles, trying to keep the load upright. Before Colin could reach him, the bricks shifted to one side. The cart tipped. Hard clay bricks poured out on top of the boy.

Colin dropped to his knees and frantically pushed bricks off the boy. The lad groaned, trying to sit up.

Other men hurried to help Colin free him. Kate ran and crouched by his side. As the bricks were cleared, Kate fought back a wave of panic at the sight of the boy's leg. The bricks had torn away the knee-high stocking. She could see how badly the leg was hurt.

"We'll have to stop the bleeding," Kate said to Colin.

He nodded and glanced about quickly, then turned to one of the men beside him. "I'm a doctor's apprentice. Is there any drinking water about?"

"I'll get some." The man scurried to get the bucket.

Colin looked up at Kate. "We need something to clean the wound."

She hesitated only a moment, then unpinned the part of the apron that covered the top of her dress and untied the bow in back. Next, she ripped off the square that made up the top of the apron. She tore the apron's ties off and then tore the rest of the apron in half, handing everything to Colin.

The workman returned with the leather water bucket, panting slightly and sloshing water onto the ground in his haste.

The boy clutched Colin's arm. "What—what are yuh goin' to do?" His face was pale as a clamshell and covered with sweat. His hat had fallen off, and his red hair was as damp as his face. Green eyes, huge and frightened, stared up at Colin.

Colin smiled, and Kate knew he was trying to look brave. "I'm going to clean your leg and stop the bleeding so I can see how badly you're hurt."

"It—it hurts somethin' fierce."

Colin nodded. "I know. I'll be as careful as I can, but cleaning it will hurt some more. Can you stand it?"

"I guess I don't have a choice."

"What's your name?"

"Larry. Lawrence Crews. From out Lexington way."

"Well, Larry Crews, if it gets to hurting too much, you just yell at me."

Liberty stuck his nose next to Larry's face and sniffed. Then the dog licked Larry's cheek and laid down beside him, resting his chin on Larry's shoulder. Larry reached out one shaking hand and rested it on Liberty's back. "That's my dog," Kate said. "His leg was hurt awhile back. He understands how you feel."

"Did it heal up good?" Larry asked between clenched teeth as Colin dabbed at his leg with a damp piece of Kate's apron.

"Yes, indeed. He limps a bit, but it doesn't stop him from going wherever he's a mind to."

Kate knelt beside Liberty and started telling Larry about the boys who'd attacked the dog. She was trying to keep Larry's mind off his pain.

The workman who'd fetched the bucket of water held Larry's ankle to keep his leg still while Colin worked. Kate was aware that most of the workmen in the area were standing about, watching.

A minute later, she heard horses' hooves thud against the ground behind her. "What's the problem?" a man's voice asked, and Kate turned her head to see a redcoat officer looming on horseback behind her.

A babble of voices answered him as a number of men all spoke at once. Kate was the one who finally explained. The officer knelt down and laid a hand on Larry's shoulder. "Keep courage, lad. Thank God there was a doctor's apprentice near."

Kate glanced again at the officer. "Lieutenant Andrews!" It

was the kind officer they'd met at the common.

The lieutenant nodded. "What can I do to help?" he asked Colin.

"Is there a wagon we could use? I haven't any instruments or medicine with me. We can take him to Dr. Firth Milton's."

Lieutenant Andrews gave sharp orders. Kate admired the way the man quickly arranged for a wagon pulled by two strong horses. The lieutenant ordered hay put in the back of the wagon to make the ride easier for Larry. While the wagon was made ready, Colin tied a clean piece of Kate's apron over the wounded leg with the apron's ties.

Watching Lieutenant Andrews and one of the workmen lift Larry into the wagon, Kate frowned and exchanged glances with Colin. She didn't like the look of that leg. "It will need to be stitched up," Colin muttered in her ear. "I'm afraid some of the nerves and muscles might have been cut by the bricks' sharp edges."

Half an hour later, Larry lay on the counter in the apothecary shop while Kate and Colin watched Dr. Milton examine the leg. "You're right," Kate's father said to Colin with an approving nod, "we'll have to sew it up. One of the muscles is torn but not badly."

Dr. Milton let Colin sew up the badly wounded leg. The doctor held Larry's leg while Colin bent over the leg, concentrating as he used the curved needle. He was sweating from trying so hard to do his work right. Every few minutes he rubbed his forehead against his shoulder so the sweat wouldn't run into his eyes. Kate wished her father would let her help, too. After all, she knew how to sew fine stitches!

Colin was almost through when the bells over the door tinkled cheerfully and Harry entered. He came and stood beside Colin, careful not to block the sunlight, but he didn't say anything.

Taking a deep breath, Colin made the last stitch, tied a knot, and cut the thread.

The doctor smiled. "I couldn't have done better myself."

Larry groaned and opened his eyes. "Is it over?" Dr. Milton had given Larry laudanum to help him endure the pain, but like most patients, Larry had been awake through the stitching. Kate saw Larry was sweating as much as Colin had.

Larry squinted at Harry. "What are you doin' here?"

"Heard about your accident and came to see how you are."

"I'm fine." He nodded toward Colin. "Thanks to this lad." He looked from Colin to Harry and back again. "You two look a lot alike."

They both laughed. People always said Colin and Harry looked alike. It was truer as Colin grew older.

While Dr. Milton, Kate, and Harry talked with Larry, Colin wiped his hands on a rag, then dipped water from a bucket into a basin and washed up.

Dr. Milton wanted Larry to stay in Boston for a couple days so he could keep a watch on Larry's leg. Patients usually stayed at home, but Dr. Milton sometimes let patients from out of town stay on a small bed in his library. He suggested Larry use it.

"You won't be able to do hard labor at the Neck for a while. When the swelling goes down a bit, Colin can use my carriage to take you back to your father's farm," Dr. Milton said.

Kate ran to fetch a blanket and a warm meal for Larry. She often had to help care for patients who stayed in the library, and she was glad for the chance to use her healing skills.

After Kate's father went back to his apothecary's shop, Harry grinned at Larry. "Took your patriotic duty a bit seriously, didn't you?"

Larry managed a small smile, though his lips were still pale from pain. "My load of bricks wasn't dumped on purpose. It was a true accident." Kate thought he looked ashamed. "A British officer was barkin' at some workers, callin' them lazy good-for-nothin's. I was laughin' inside and thinkin' if he only knew what we have in mind for the Neck, he'd be sayin' somethin' worse. Should have been watchin' where I was goin'."

Kate frowned. "What are you two talking about?"

Harry chuckled. "When General Gage needed people to help his soldiers build the wall, the Patriots made sure he got the kind of help we think he needs. The Patriots don't want the wall built. The Patriot workmen work slowly, do sloppy work, and tip over carts filled with supplies, but they make it all look like accidents. They even sunk a barge of bricks."

Kate couldn't believe her ears. "I thought the bargeman ran into an unexpected reef and lost the bricks."

Harrison grinned. "That's what we want people to think. We don't want Gage finding workers who might truly help him."

"Of course," Colin muttered, wiping clean his needle. Kate just pinched her lips together tight. She wasn't sure what she wanted to say, but she knew that whatever it was probably wouldn't have been the right thing.

Lieutenant Andrews stopped by then to check on Larry's leg. Kate thought it was a nice thing for a busy officer to do. She wondered what Lieutenant Andrews would think if he knew why Larry had taken the job on the Neck!

Later, Kate walked with Harry and Colin to the printing shop through the narrow streets. As always, they had to make their way between redcoats. When they reached the shop, Paul Revere was waiting for them.

Harry shook Paul's hand heartily. "Welcome back! Have you brought news of the Continental Congress?"

"That I have." He stepped past Harry, Kate, and Colin, closed the heavy wooden door, and leaned against it. "There are serious things we must talk about."

"Yes." Harry leaned back against the printing press and crossed his arms over his long brown vest. "General Gage didn't like the Suffolk Resolves you took to the Continental Congress. He believes they come too close to declaring war on Britain. On September first, he sent redcoats across the river. They took Charlestown's ammunition."

That had changed everything in Boston, Kate thought. It had made everything worse between the redcoats and Patriots. People in all thirteen colonies were mad as hornets that the redcoats had stolen a town's arms. From the time the first English came to America, towns always had to be ready to protect themselves. No one should take their guns and ammunition! The Patriots were right about that much. Kate settled down on a three-legged stool in the corner of the room. As always, Mr. Revere seemed to barely notice she was there. At least that meant she could listen and think. . .and try to make up her mind whether

Harry and Mr. Revere were right.

Harry told Paul Revere about the Charlestown raid. Thousands of Massachusetts men had grabbed their guns and rushed from their villages and farms to help Charlestown. They were too late. The redcoats were already back in Boston.

General Gage was afraid the angry men would take the Neck road into Boston and attack the redcoats. His men had taken four cannons to the Neck to keep them out. Then his men had ruined Boston's cannons so they couldn't be used against the redcoats. He even sent a letter on a ship to England asking the king to send more redcoats to Boston. General Gage was building the wall on the Neck because he was afraid.

"Gage started the wall to keep armed citizens out, but it will also keep redcoats and townspeople in Boston." Paul Revere turned his three-cornered hat in his hands. "People are upset about Charlestown, but maybe it's a blessing to the Patriots."

"How?" Harry asked.

"It showed us that we need to warn the other towns when the troops are getting ready to leave Boston."

"How can we do that?" Colin asked. "The redcoats won't tell Patriots the army's plans."

"That's why we need a group of watchers. Men to watch the army and see when they're getting ready to leave town, men to listen to everything redcoats say for a hint of their plans. Next time Gage plans a raid on a town's gunpowder, we want to get the news to the town first."

Colin shifted uncomfortably. "Can we do that?"

"We must. We'll need a small band of trusted Patriots, about thirty men. Everyone will be sworn to secrecy."

Harry nodded eagerly. "That's a good plan. We can call the group the *Observers.*"

"We'll need a place to meet. What about this shop?"

"No." Harry shook his head. "Redcoat officers are already suspicious about us. They'll be watching the shop."

Colin cleared his throat. "Thirty men meeting in a home or shop would look suspicious, wouldn't they? What if they met at the Green Dragon Tavern? Harry goes there all the time."

Paul Revere rubbed his thumb across his chin. "You're right. No one would think anything of men going to the tavern." He grinned at Colin. "Are you ready to be a Son of Liberty?"

Colin blinked. Kate knew he wasn't sure how to answer. Sometimes Kate suspected her cousin was almost as confused as she was. "I–I already help Harry and Father print things for the Sons of Liberty."

"You can be a far greater help to us if you're willing."

Colin gulped. "I wouldn't hurt anyone or their property. I want to be a doctor. I want to help people, not hurt them."

The silversmith nodded. "I respect you for that. You won't be asked to hurt anyone."

"Then. . ." Colin straightened his shoulders as though he had reached a decision. "I'll be glad to help."

Paul Revere rested a hand on Colin's shoulder. "As a doctor's apprentice, you have good reason to be about Boston. Dr. Milton is a well-known Loyalist. British officers like and trust him. No one would suspect a boy in his shop of spying for the Patriots." For the first time he glanced over at Kate. "You're Dr. Milton's daughter, aren't you, lass? Can we count on your help?"

"S–spying?" Kate's voice was a squeak.

"If you don't want to, you needn't." Revere's calm voice reassured her.

Kate's eyes met Colin's. He nodded, as though he were answering a question she had asked without speaking, and she tried to ignore the painful way her heart was thumping. Maybe it was time for her to make up her mind for herself, once and for all, the way Father had said.

"All right," she whispered. "I'll be a Patriot spy."

Harry moved closer. "You'll need to keep your wits about you all the time. Never breathe a word about what you're asked to do to anyone but Paul and me."

"Harry is right," Mr. Revere said. "With General Gage and his army getting so jumpy, there's no telling what might happen if you're caught."

"We'll be careful."

Kate swallowed the lump that suddenly formed in her throat, but she still couldn't find her voice. She let Colin speak for her.

"Tell us what you want us to do."

"Nothing right away, but be prepared. I've plans for you. Until then, keep your ears open around the redcoats. Pass along anything you see or hear to Harry."

"Yes, sir."

Kate felt like she'd just stepped off a cliff and could never again get back to safety.

CHAPTER 7

The Warning

Colin and Kate waited, frightened and excited, for their first orders as spies. A month passed, and they still hadn't been asked to do anything scary for the Patriots. They hadn't heard the redcoats whisper any secrets, either.

Sitting in her aunt and uncle's parlor, she glanced across the room at Colin. They had always been close, but now their secret was pulling them closer than ever.

The room was filled with family tonight. Kate's family and Harry's family were here. Shadows danced and darted over the families while they worked.

Colin and Harry sat close to the fireplace. They needed the light to repair the wool carders, pulling out broken wires and putting new ones in their place.

The soft whir of the great wheel as Colin's mother spun the balls into yarn was a pleasant background to the family talk.

The family used to buy much of its yarn and material, but the harbor's closing had changed all that. Most Patriots had agreed to make their own yarn and material, called homespun, instead of buying it from Britain.

Kate and Colin's sister, Isabel, were carding wool into soft balls. The wool cards were wooden paddles with hundreds of short wire teeth. The wool was placed between two cards and combed to remove dirt and tangles. The cards' teeth made a scratching sound, like Liberty's claws when he pawed at a door to get out.

"It's so nice to spend an evening with family instead of strangers!" Kate said, pulling a fluff of wool from between her cards.

"I think it was wonderful of you to take that family into your home," Eliza said, looking up from her mending.

"Yes," Susanna agreed. She was making a pair of breeches for Colin, which he badly needed. "But it must be difficult having strangers living with you."

"It certainly is!" Kate said.

"Remember, Kate, it could have been our family chased from our home," her mother reminded her. Mama sat at the small clock wheel, winding the yarn from the great wheel onto small wooden reels.

No one said anything for a minute. Everyone knew Mama meant if the Patriots were chasing Loyalists from their homes in other towns, it could happen in Boston, too. And everyone in the room except Mama was a Patriot.

"The Patriots are wrong to chase people from their homes," Colin's mother said quietly. "We can all agree on that."

Everyone nodded.

Raised voices came from the hallway.

"It sounds like our fathers are arguing again," Kate said. She sighed and her eyes met Colin's. She saw the same pain and fright in his eyes that she felt when their fathers fought. She wasn't sure why it frightened her, but it did.

She took a deep breath. It had been such a pleasant evening, with everyone working together and visiting. Now the day would end unhappily.

Uncle Jack and her father entered the parlor, still arguing. They stopped nose-to-nose and toe-to-toe. Dr. Milton waved a copy of the *Boston Observer* in one hand. "How can you print such things?"

Uncle Jack crossed his arms. "We only printed what the Continental Congress in Philadelphia said."

Dr. Milton's eyes sparked. "You printed that Americans should not buy anything from Britain until Parliament gives up the tea tax, reopens Boston Harbor, and lets Massachusetts be run by its old charter."

"It's a peaceful way to try to get Parliament to change its mind," Uncle Jack observed. "What's wrong with that?"

Dr. Milton shook the paper right in his brother-in-law's face. "It's what you printed next that's wrong! The congress said if the redcoats attack people here, the other colonies will send troops to help Boston."

Uncle Jack grabbed the paper, crumpling it with one hand. "You think that is wrong?"

"They've almost declared war on Britain, on our own government!" Dr. Milton pushed his wig back from his forehead.

Kate choked back a giggle when she saw how funny Father looked with his wig sliding off the back of his head, but at the same time she was feeling sick to her stomach at the word "war." Everyone seemed to be using that word these days.

"John Hancock is the leader of the congress," Colin's father said. "He says we should ask God to forgive the sins that have caused our trouble with Old England. And to ask God's help in becoming friendly with England again."

Kate took a deep breath. "That sounds like the Patriots want peace, not war, Father."

Dr. Milton snorted. "Don't be fooled, Kate. The congress also said it's a Christian's duty to fight bad leaders. But the Bible says we are to obey our leaders."

"The Bible also says that rulers must be just and rule in the fear of God," Uncle Jack argued. "God wants kings to treat people well so they can live in peace and have good lives."

Harry stepped into the argument now. "Until King George rules the way the Bible says he should, we will serve no king but King Jesus."

That's the Patriots' slogan, Kate remembered. The words always sent a shiver of awe and pride through her. It seemed a great thing to choose to serve Jesus. But she knew the words only angered Loyalists like Father and Mama. After all, they served Jesus, too. They just disagreed on the way to go about doing that.

Father's fists bunched at his sides. "The congress called the king a tyrant."

Uncle Jack's face grew red. "When a king uses his power to hurt people instead of help them, he is a tyrant."

"Bah!" Dr. Milton waved both hands at him. "You make your living with words. You can make anything sound true. It's treason to declare war against the king. Treason! Until you admit as much, we're no longer friends!"

"That's fine with me!" Uncle Jack roared.

Father grabbed Kate's hand. "Come, Kate, Rosemary. We're leaving."

Kate tried to keep up with her father as she stared back over her shoulder, her wide eyes meeting Colin's. She tripped over her skirt and petticoat, and her stomach jolted. Colin's stomach clenched. What she and Colin had feared had happened—their fathers' arguments had broken their friendship.

Before the Miltons could reach the door, a loud pounding sounded outside, as though someone was insisting on entering. Kate saw that Colin had grabbed the candlestick, and now he pushed past them to answer the knocking. When he opened the door, the breeze blew the flame sideways.

Kate peered past her cousin's shoulder. There was no one on the door stoop. Only a house away, though, she saw two redcoats walking swiftly. One looked back over his shoulder with a wicked grin. Lieutenant Rand!

Why had he pounded on the door if he didn't want to come inside? A flutter caught Kate's eye. A handbill nailed to the door! Colin yanked it off and turned around.

"Who was it?" his uncle asked.

Colin didn't say anything. His face was very white. Kate looked down at the paper in his hands and saw a skull and crossbones. It made her skin crawl. She looked up at her father. "What does it mean?" she whispered.

Father's face was grim, but he didn't answer. He hesitated in the doorway, as though uncertain whether they should go or stay. Uncle Jack and Harry had come into the hallway from the parlor, and now they pressed closer to see the paper Colin held in his hand. Colin set the candlestick on a small, round piecrust table beside the door. Kate suspected he didn't want anyone to notice how badly his hands were shaking.

Colin read the paper aloud. When he got to the end, his voice was shaking as badly as his hands. "'If fighting breaks out between the Patriots and the British troops, the Patriots' leaders will be destroyed,'" he finished.

Uncle Jack grunted. "Destroyed is a nice way to say they'll be tried in England and hung as traitors."

"Unfortunately, they are traitors." Kate thought Father's voice sounded more sad than angry now.

The paper listed Sam Adams, John Hancock, and a few others.

"Is that all it says?" Harry leaned over his younger brother's shoulder.

Colin shook his head. "There's a little bit more. 'Those trumpeters of evil, the printers, will not be forgotten.'" Kate leaned over his arm and saw that a list of Patriot printers followed. Uncle Jack's and Harry's names were at the top of the list.

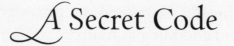A Secret Code

Destroyed! Hung! Threats against her own uncle and cousin! Fear swept through Kate like a wildfire. The skull and crossbones seemed to laugh at them in the candlelight.

Uncle Jack picked up the paper, holding it so the candle's light fell on it. "So, Harrison, it's come." His voice was heavy.

"Yes."

Kate stared at them. How could they sound so calm? Hadn't they heard what the paper said? "Father," Colin said, his voice cracking in the way Kate knew he hated, "they've threatened your life and Harrison's."

His father, still bent over the paper, glanced at him from beneath thick black-and-gray eyebrows. "Before we can be hung, we must be brought to trial and found guilty of treason against Britain and the king. We have only printed what the congress and others said. We haven't said we agreed with them."

"That's why you've been so careful," Colin said slowly. "Sarah said you were a coward, that after General Gage brought so many troops, you didn't dare say what you thought."

"I hope we haven't been cowards. I like to think we've been wise. I've always believed that if we printed the truth, people would be smart enough to decide for themselves whether the king and Parliament were right or whether the Patriots were right. A few years back, you'll remember I hadn't decided what I felt was the right course of action." Uncle Jack glanced at his brother-in-law, who still lingered by the doorway. "The Loyalists have several reasonable arguments, and I wanted to be sure I was not making a commitment out of emotion." He shot his oldest son a rueful smile. "Your older brother was quite impatient with me, if I remember correctly."

Harry grinned sheepishly.

"As England repeatedly infringed on our rights," Uncle Jack continued, "I came to believe in the Patriot cause. But I still was careful to print all sides of an issue in the paper. If we printed our own opinions, Harry and I could be found guilty of treason. It might come to that yet, but I hope not."

The air coming through the doorway was cold, but Kate felt suddenly damp with sweat all over. "Will you be arrested?" she asked in a small, scared voice.

Her uncle smiled at her. "We can only wait and see."

Harrison patted her shoulder. "I'm sure whoever wrote this is only trying to frighten us."

Uncle Jack nodded. "General Gage has tried to buy us— to pay us—to print only things the British government liked. Lieutenant Rand threatened us the other day. Now this."

Colin stood up a little straighter. "I think Lieutenant Rand nailed this to our door. I saw him on the street."

His father sighed. "It would be like him to use his position to try to bully us. Thank God all the British officers aren't like him." He folded the paper in half and turned to look at his wife through the parlor's open doorway. Kate saw that her aunt and the other women were sitting frozen, their faces very white. "Don't fret over this," Uncle Jack said, his voice strong and calm. "We are in the Lord's hands."

Kate watched as Harry went back into the parlor and took down the old musket that hung over the fireplace. He ran a hand along the barrel. The musket had been there for as long as Kate could remember.

"Do you think it works?" Colin asked.

"I don't know. I'm not sure we can get ammunition for it. It's awfully old. Our great-grandfather, Robert, carried it to war against the French in 1710. He fought alongside the British soldiers then. Now if we fight with it, we'll be fighting against the British."

Kate saw Colin's Adam's apple jerk, as though he were fighting back a lump in his throat. "He was killed in that war. Our grandfather, his only child, was born while he was fighting, remember? He never even saw his son."

Harrison nodded, his eyes grave.

Colin stuck his hands in his breeches' deep pockets. "Do you think that might happen to your son, Paul, if you fight? If you were. . .if you were killed—"

Kate gulped and fought back the tears that burned her eyes.

"You'd never see Paul again," Colin finished, his voice cracking. "He's only six months old. He might not even remember you when he grows up."

"I know." Harry's words were so low that Kate almost didn't

hear them. Harry carefully hung the musket back in place. "I've joined the minutemen." He turned and looked at his wife. "I have to do what I believe is right."

"I thought you would." Colin's voice was barely more than a whisper.

"I talked it over with Eliza first," Harry said. "I do think about Paul. I worry what will happen to him and Eliza if we go to war. But Eliza and I agreed that when Paul grows up, we want him to have the rights Englishmen have had for more than five hundred years—even if that means I have to fight."

Kate's father moved as if to go out the door. She knew he didn't want to hear any of this, that he did not want to be associated with what he considered treason. But she could tell by the look on his face that he also hated to leave. After all, Colin's mother was his sister. They were family. No matter how much Father and Uncle Jack argued, Kate knew her father loved his family.

"What about you?" Harry asked Colin.

Colin frowned. "What do you mean?"

"If war comes, will you fight with the Patriots?"

Colin shrugged and kicked at a bit of ash on the floor with the toe of his shoe. "I won't fight against them."

Harry grinned. "I didn't think you would, but that's no answer. You're thirteen, almost a man."

Colin squared his shoulders. "I don't know if I can try to kill anyone. I want to be a doctor and save lives." He turned and looked at his uncle, then looked back at his brother. "Have you ever seen anyone die?"

Harrison shook his head. "No."

"I have, lots of times. It's terrible. Uncle Firth and I do everything we can sometimes—and yet people still die." He pressed his lips together hard and spread his hands. "Do you understand? Life is precious. When I know how hard it is to save a life, how can I choose to kill? It's much easier to take a life than save one."

Kate knew her father was proud of his nephew's words. But would Harrison understand? She held her breath, waiting for Harry's reply. Colin put so much stock in his brother's good opinion. He would be crushed if this war came between him and his brother.

Harrison sighed. "You have a good head on your shoulders, Colin. You don't let anyone push you into anything you don't believe in. That's good." He, too, glanced at his uncle. "I've heard Uncle Firth say more than once that each man has to make up his mind for himself. I respect that. But what if everyone refused to fight and let King George take away all our rights? What would our children and grandchildren say when they found out we'd let our rights be taken away without a fight? If war comes, you may not have a choice but to fight. The only choice left will be which side you fight for."

Kate's gaze slid to the musket, almost hidden now in the room's dark shadows. The dull gray metal on the musket's barrel looked cold in the firelight—and a chill that was just as icy wrapped itself tight around her heart.

"Come along, Kate," her mother whispered. "It's time for us to go."

The next morning, Kate looked out the apothecary window and saw Colin standing outside beneath the creaking sign with the mortar and pestle. His hands were bunched into fists at his sides.

Kate pulled a cloak around her shoulders and ran out into the street. "What are you doing?"

He shrugged, his face worried. "Does your father still want me to be his apprentice? After what happened yesterday. . .will he even want you and I to be friends?"

"Well, you won't find out standing in the street," Kate replied. "Come inside and find out."

Colin took a deep breath and went inside.

Kate's father looked up from his account book. "Colin, I'm glad you're here! I was afraid your father might not let you come after last night."

Kate heard Colin let out a long breath of relief. "He didn't tell me I couldn't come, but I was afraid you might not want me."

Dr. Milton laid down his quill. His gaze met Colin's. "My argument is with your father, not with you. I count you not only my apprentice and nephew, but my friend."

"Thank you, sir, but I—I'm a Patriot, too, like Father."

"Do you think King George is a tyrant?"

"I'm not sure. When I hear you talk about what you believe about the king and our rights, what you say sounds right. But I think what Father believes is more right, and I believe what Father believes."

"At least you listen to both sides. You aren't encouraging anyone to fight like your father is."

"No, sir." Colin frowned, and Kate knew he was uneasy with her father's words. What would Father say if he knew she had promised to help spy for the Patriots?

"Your father is a stubborn man." Her father grinned. "But your aunt Rosemary says I'm one, too. Don't worry yourself over your father and me. We've been angry at each other before. We'll work things out eventually. Now, let's get to work, you two. There are some plants in the medical garden that need to be picked and dried."

In spite of her father's assurances, Kate wasn't convinced the men would work things out. The two had quarreled a lot through the years, but Kate had never seen them as angry at each other as they were now. At least Father still wanted Colin to be his apprentice. She was glad this one thing in life was the same. She couldn't imagine life without Colin.

At eleven o'clock, Kate ran home and brought back lunch for her father and Larry.

"I know you brought your own lunch," she said to Colin, "but I brought you a piece of apple pie."

"Great!"

She wrinkled her nose. "Not too great. It's Boston Tea Party apple pie. We're out of sugar and good flour, so I sweetened it with honey, and the crust is of cornmeal." All the women in town were using substitutes in their cooking. With the port closed, many of the foods they were used to using couldn't be found in Boston or were too expensive to buy.

"Mother and I try to make a game of it, figuring out how to make our favorite dishes using different foods. Some things turn out better than others." Kate sighed.

Two days later, when Kate stopped at Colin's house, she noticed the musket was gone from over the fireplace. She didn't ask where it went. Patriots were collecting weapons in case of war. But the thought of Harry with a gun in his hand made her shiver.

But something else pushed all thought of the musket from her mind. She and Colin were given a spy assignment!

Kate's father had asked Colin to take Larry home to his farm near Lexington, and Kate was going to ride along. When Harry and Paul Revere heard, they told Colin to take some copies of the *Boston Observer* to Buckman's Tavern in Lexington.

"There's a hidden message in the newspaper," Harrison had said, stacking the single sheets into a pile.

Colin laughed. "You can't hide anything in a newspaper!"

"The best place to hide anything is right in plain sight." Harry's eyes twinkled with fun. "The message becomes clear when the reader uses a mask to read it."

"You're funning us," Kate giggled. "How can wearing a mask help?"

"Maybe the mask has spectacles with magic glass," Colin teased.

"It's not that kind of mask. The reader doesn't wear the mask. He lays the mask over the newspaper. Like this." Harry showed Kate and Colin a cutout of the picture that was always printed at the top of the *Boston Observer*. It was a man looking through a telescope. The inside of the picture had been cut out. Harry laid the mask over the covered page. "See for yourself."

Colin grinned. "You're just waiting for me to make a fool of myself and try to find a secret message where there is none. Like the time I was six and you told me there were fish in Mill

Pond that could walk. I fished and watched for those walking fish for weeks before Susanna told me you were only teasing!"

Harry crossed his arms over his vest and chuckled. "This is no walking fish, I promise. Look."

Kate and Colin looked. The mask was small. The opening only covered ten lines of the tiny type, and two of the six narrow columns. The message inside the cutout included words from more than one column. Kate's mouth dropped open as she read them. "Why, this says—"

Harry clapped a hand that smelled strongly of ink and leather over Kate's mouth. "Never repeat a message aloud, even when you think you're alone or with someone you can trust, like now. You only need to be wrong one time to get in a lot of trouble."

Kate and Colin both nodded, their smiles fading.

Harry took away his hand. "Now that redcoats are checking everyone who comes into and leaves Boston, the Patriots are trying new ways to get messages to each other safely. Sometimes the messages will be true. Sometimes they will be false, used only to test whether people can be trusted or are spies for the British. You're never to tell anyone you're carrying a message or what it says."

"We won't," Colin promised.

Harry glanced at Kate, and she nodded. "I give my word." It was hard to speak past the lump in her throat.

Harry grinned. "Your word is always good enough for me."

Colin was studying the mask. "How does the person who gets the message know what part of the paper to put the mask over so he reads the right words?"

"That's a secret you'll never know."

∽ CHAPTER 9 ∽

Escape from Boston

A few days later, Larry, Colin, Kate, and Liberty sat together in Dr. Milton's carriage. Every once in a while, Larry's leg bounced against the side when a wooden wheel rolled over a rock or rut. Larry would grunt and dig his teeth into his bottom lip, but he never complained. Kate admired him for that. She knew Larry's leg was still mighty sore and would be for weeks.

"Whoa." Colin pulled on the reins, bringing Dr. Milton's small bay mare to a stop at the town gate on the Neck. Redcoats were checking everyone who left town now. In front of them, a farmer with an empty cart waited patiently behind another farmer with an empty wagon.

One of the redcoats knelt down and looked beneath the wagon, then stood and felt beneath the hard wooden seat the farmer sat upon. A moment later he waved the farmer on.

"They're lookin' for guns," Larry said in a low voice. "They've heard Patriots are sneakin' guns out of Boston."

Goose bumps ran up and down Kate's arms. Had Harry slipped the musket past the guards somehow?

Woof! Liberty's bark startled Kate. In a flash, the skinny dog scrambled across her lap and leaped from the carriage after a squirrel.

"Liberty, stop!"

Liberty ignored his mistress's cry. The squirrel darted under the farmer's moving wagon, and Liberty headed after him.

Kate leaped to her feet. Liberty was going to be run over! "Stop, Liberty!"

A farmer with a cart in front of them dove for Liberty. He caught his skinny tail and held tight. Liberty yelped a complaint, but the farmer yanked him back, saving him from the wagon's rumbling wheels. He handed Liberty up to Kate with a friendly grin.

"Thank you, sir. Guess you saved his life."

"A life worth saving, I'm sure. Have a dog of me own I wouldn't trade for King George's palace."

The soldiers were searching the farmer's cart. It didn't take long. When they waved the farmer on, he gave them a jaunty salute before starting.

"Halt!" One of the soldiers pointed his musket at the farmer. "I know you! Deserter!"

Kate's heart seemed to leap to her throat. She watched, stunned, as the soldiers arrested the man who had cheerfully saved Liberty's life.

Kate and Colin looked at each other. A deserter! Larry shrugged nervously. "We've nothin' to worry 'bout. We're not sneakin' anyone or anything out of town."

Kate's foot touched the pile of newspapers on the floor. Larry didn't know they carried a Patriot secret.

The redcoat who had checked the cart waved for Colin to move forward, and Colin clicked his tongue at the horse. The soldier looked underneath the carriage. Then he ordered Kate, Colin, and Larry to get out.

Kate forced herself to not look at the newspapers as she climbed down.

"Larry has a bad leg," Colin told the soldier. "He hurt it working on the wall here on the Neck. Can he stay in the carriage? It still hurts him a lot to walk on it."

The soldier looked into the carriage and reached for Larry's leg. His hand stopped above the bandages. Larry had no stocking on that leg. It was still too swollen and too heavily wrapped for a stocking to fit. "Stay where you are, then," he told Larry.

The soldier pointed to the pile. "Are those rebel Patriot newspapers or Loyalist newspapers?"

"Just newspapers, sir."

Pretend everything is normal, Kate commanded him silently.

"The editor prints facts, not opinions."

The redcoat grunted. "I'll be deciding that for myself. Let me see one of them rags."

Larry untied the twine that held the papers together and handed him one off the top. The soldier glanced over it. "Why, this tells all about that rebel Patriot congress in Philadelphia!" His eyes looked like small black beads as he glared over the top of the page at Colin. "Says the colonies should train their armies in case we attack them! What do you mean saying this isn't a rebel paper?"

"Only tells what the congress said, sir. Doesn't tell the readers to do as the congress asks. Besides, there's a Loyalist handbill we're carrying as well."

Colin pulled out a handbill topped by a skull and crossbones and handed it to the soldier. It was the same handbill that threatened his father's and Harry's lives. "You see, the editor prints news for both Patriots and Loyalists."

"You the printer's apprentice?" The soldier raised one black eyebrow and eyed Colin suspiciously.

"Oh, no, sir! I'm Dr. Milton's apprentice. This is his carriage. I'm taking his patient home to his farm."

The soldier grunted again. "Dr. Milton's a good Loyalist."

"Yes, sir. Can't find a man more loyal to the king."

"Sure wish I hadn't hurt this leg." Larry rubbed his knee and shook his head. "Wanted to keep helpin' build that wall for General Gage. Lot more excitin' than farmin'."

The redcoat handed Larry back the paper and handbill. "Have any good fishing streams on that farm?"

"The best in Massachusetts, sir. I plan to take the children here fishin' there today."

"Maybe you'll bring a few fish back for me?" The soldier grinned, showing three of his teeth were missing on one side of his mouth.

"Be glad to, sir." Colin climbed back into the carriage.

He and Kate waved and smiled at the soldier as they drove off. When they'd gone about one hundred feet, Colin let his breath out in a whoosh. "I didn't think he was going to let us take those papers with us."

"Me, either. Redcoats have good guns and cannons, but it's words that scare them."

They both laughed at that.

Kate hadn't been out of Boston in months. She felt suddenly free out on the road.

Once they reached Lexington, it was easy to find Buckman's Tavern, a two-story wooden building with two chimneys. It stood by the town common, called Lexington Green. The road ran right past the green.

The tavern master gave no hint that he knew the papers held a secret message. Kate wondered if he was the man who knew how to read the message. Or maybe it was one of the tavern workers or a stable boy who watched the guests' horses. Could it be the craftsman who walked in and bought a copy almost right away?

A spy could be anyone, Kate realized. She giggled. Who, for instance, would think she was a spy?

"What's so funny?" Larry asked her.

"Just glad to be out of Boston for a change." She exchanged glances with Colin, and they both grinned.

The tavern keeper gave them each a mug of cold apple cider. They took their drinks outside and sat on the edge of the green beneath a large oak tree. The ground was covered with brown, musty-smelling leaves that crackled beneath Kate's skirts when she sat down. The dampness from the earth seeped through the leaves and through her petticoat and skirt, but she hardly noticed.

The Lexington minutemen were practicing on the green. Back home, the minutemen couldn't practice on Boston Common, what with the redcoats living and training there.

Watching the men, Kate's good spirits suddenly deserted her, and her heart sank as fast as a rock to the bottom of one of

Boston's ponds. Lexington's army looked like a ragtag group of boys playing at war compared to the redcoats. The minutemen were dressed in their everyday work clothes: craftsmen in leather breeches and rough shirts, farmers in frocks, storekeepers and town leaders in fancy greatcoats and long vests. No one wore a uniform. Not one carried a musket as fine as the redcoats' muskets. Instead they held squirrel and duck rifles or old muskets like the one that had hung over the Lang fireplace. A few men who'd fought in the French and Indian Wars years ago had swords at their sides. No one had a bayonet like the redcoats had on the ends of their muskets.

The minutemen didn't snap to orders with sharp attention like the redcoats on Boston Common. They didn't move as one person to the officers' orders. Kate wondered whether they even knew how poorly they compared to the redcoats. The men tramping through the crisp leaves beneath the bright blue sky were eagerly trying to follow commands, their eyes shining, their faces excited.

"Why don't they practice shooting?" Colin asked Larry.

"Savin' their bullets. With General Gage and his men raidin' towns' ammunition, we don't dare waste any."

The longer Colin and Larry watched, the sadder Kate grew. Harry was part of Boston's minutemen. Were they as poorly furnished and trained as these men? If a war started, what chance did Harry and the minutemen have against the redcoats?

"I'm goin' to join the minutemen," Larry said, "soon's my leg's better."

"Do you have a gun?" Colin asked.

"Only an old squirrel gun, but I can shoot with it." Larry

leaned back against the tree. "Shot lots of squirrels and rabbits and such. A man should be easy to hit."

Kate's stomach turned over at the thought of shooting a man like he was wild game.

When the practice was over, a boy carrying a large drum and a handful of men with fifes started playing "Yankee Doodle" and started across the green. The minutemen fell in behind them. They headed toward a large wooden building beside Buckman's Tavern.

Colin jumped up. "Where are they going?"

"To the meeting house," Larry said. "A Patriot minister will give them a sermon tellin' them to fight bravely for God and their country." He got slowly to his feet. "I'd like to be getting home, if you don't mind."

Larry kept his word and took the cousins fishing at a stream that ran through his father's property. It was the most fun Kate had had in a long time. When she and Colin headed back to Boston later that afternoon, a huge basket with sixty smelly perch sat between them on the floor of the carriage. Larry's father and mother had also sent back pumpkins, corn, and flour for the doctor. "There's barely room left for me," Kate had told Larry with a grin.

Colin didn't forget the soldier at the gate. When they arrived there late that evening, he gave him a dozen fish. The soldier grinned from ear to ear as he piled the fish on the ground beside the gate, where they would lie until the soldier was off duty.

"Remember that deserter we caught this afternoon?" the soldier asked, taking the last fish Colin handed him.

Kate's heart thumped so hard she could barely hear herself

think. Why would the redcoat ask Colin about the deserter? Had he somehow learned Colin had slipped a secret message out of town right beneath his nose?

Beside her, Colin gulped and wiped his hand on his breeches. "Sure, I remember. He was dressed like a farmer."

"They shot him this afternoon on the common." The soldier grinned. "General Gage came out personally to tell me and the other guard here how well we'd done in capturing him."

"Congratulations," Colin said in a shaky voice. "Good night, sir. Enjoy your fish." He reached for the reins and slapped them lightly against the horse's rump.

Kate's eyes were too blurry with tears for her to see the road ahead. Other redcoat deserters had been shot, but she hadn't known who they were. She hadn't seen them captured only a few feet from freedom. They hadn't smiled at her and saved her dog.

Suddenly, Kate pulled desperately on Colin's arm. She was going to be sick.

CHAPTER 10

A Dangerous Mission

Six weeks later, Kate gritted her teeth as she came through the door of Colin's house. The first thing she heard was a voice she'd grown to dislike: Lieutenant Rand's. She wondered for the hundredth time how Lieutenant Rand had been assigned to live in her uncle's house!

Winter was coming, and many British officers were staying in townspeople's houses. Quartering, it was called. But why Lieutenant Rand of all people?

Kate stepped softly past the parlor, where the officers were visiting, toward the kitchen. She caught a glimpse of the firelight and candlelight that gave the parlor a mellow glow, but the hallway was dark and shadowed. Until the officers had moved in, the family had saved scarce wood and candles by keeping the parlor closed. They visited by the kitchen fireplace instead. There the wood could be used for three things at once: It heated the room, heated food, and heated water for washing and chores. Now, though, they were forced to waste expensive fuel and light on the redcoats.

"You there, lass!" Lieutenant Rand's voice stopped her before she could reach the kitchen.

Kate sighed and walked into the warm parlor. "Yes, sir?"

"See that someone polishes my boots."

Kate's cheeks grew hot. She pressed her lips hard together to keep from telling the officer to polish his own boots. Her uncle had warned them all to treat the officers like guests. "Yes, Lieutenant Rand," she managed to say meekly. "I'll tell my cousin."

"See he does a better job than he did last week."

"Yes, sir." Kate looked at the other officer, who stood before the fireplace with his elbow on the mantel, frowning at Lieutenant Rand. "Shall I have Colin polish your boots, too, Lieutenant Andrews?"

The senior officer smiled at her. "No, but it was kind of you to offer."

Kate nodded at both men and made her way back to the kitchen. At least Lieutenant Andrews acted kindly toward the family. Still, she liked having the officers in Colin's home even less than she liked having them in her own. What if they found reason to arrest Uncle Jack or Harry?

She knew the officers had taken over the bedchamber Harrison shared with his wife, Eliza, and their son, Paul. Now Harrison's family used Colin's bedchamber, and Colin slept on the high-backed wooden settle beside the kitchen fireplace.

He tried not to complain about it. Officers were quartered all over town. Uncle Thomas had officers staying with him, and so did Kate's family. But Kate knew how much it galled Colin to have to give up his room because of the redcoats.

As Kate slipped into the warm kitchen, her aunt greeted her with a warm smile. "Ah, Kate, it's always good to see you." Kate knew the disagreement between her father and uncle pained her aunt. "Colin was just saying he was hoping you'd come by."

Kate glanced at her cousin where he sat whittling by the fire. "Want to take a stroll with me?" he asked, setting aside the knife.

She nodded, wondering why Colin felt a sudden urge to walk around the chilly streets. But as soon as they were outside the kitchen door, Harry stepped out of a doorway across the street, as though he'd been standing there waiting for them.

"Are you staying for supper, Kate?" Harry asked in a low voice.

She nodded, wondering why he looked so serious.

"I need to talk with you two." Harry glanced at the house. "Make an excuse after the meal to slip out to the print shop."

Kate looked at the empty street and frowned. "Why not talk here?"

"Walls have ears these days. And windows have eyes."

Colin nodded. And Kate realized that with the officers here, it wasn't safe for them to talk about Patriot matters even in the street. She wondered what could be so important that they had to go somewhere tonight to talk. Could the Sons of Liberty have another spying assignment for them?

A little later when she joined her aunt and uncle and cousins for the evening meal, she noticed that Susanna and Lieutenant Andrews were in the doorway between the parlor and hallway. Kate wondered why Susanna was smiling up at the British officer in that funny, sugary-sweet way with her cheeks all pink.

Could Susanna like Lieutenant Andrews? Not just friendly-like, but as a woman likes a man? Could Susanna be falling in love with someone who wasn't a Patriot?

When they finished dinner, Lieutenant Rand pushed back his chair. "I'll have a cup of tea in the parlor, Miss Susanna. See that it's good English tea—none of your rebel Patriot brew."

Everyone stopped talking and stared at him. Finally Susanna stood. Her long red curls reflected the light from the few candles that burned on the table. "I'll be glad to bring you tea, sir." Her voice trembled. "But I'm afraid it will be raspberry leaf tea. We don't serve English tea in this house. English tea has brought too much trouble to our town."

Lieutenant Rand threw down his napkin. "No lady in England would treat a guest like this!"

"Lieutenant Rand!" Lieutenant Andrews sounded shocked.

Uncle Jack leaped up. "Apologize to my daughter!"

Lieutenant Rand snorted and ignored Uncle Jack's demand.

Susanna paid no attention. "Lieutenant Rand, in Boston, no gentleman asks for anything he knows his host is not able or willing to give."

Good for her! Kate thought, her hands clenched into fists beneath the table.

Red color started at Lieutenant Rand's neck and rushed up over his face to his wig. He turned to Lieutenant Andrews. "If anyone asks for me this evening, I'll be at Dr. Milton's." He glared over his shoulder at Susanna. "The Miltons know how to treat their guests." He stomped toward the door, his boots thunking against the floor.

Harry gave Kate a strange look. "I didn't know Lieutenant

Rand knew your father."

Kate nodded. "Officers are quartered at my house, too. They use my father's library in the evenings instead of going to the taverns like most soldiers." She wrinkled her nose. "They expect us to wait on them, just like Lieutenant Rand."

"I apologize for our officers," Lieutenant Andrews said. "I know it's hard for people to have us living in their homes. Please remember that it's hard for the officers, too. They'd rather be in their own homes with their own families back in England."

Susanna smiled at him. "Of course they would."

Kate wondered again how Susanna felt about the kind, good-looking young officer.

A few minutes later, Kate, Colin, and Harry were headed toward the print shop, their cloaks wrapped tightly against the cold November wind whipping through Boston's narrow streets. They had to watch where they were going, as the streetlights weren't lit. The town had only had streetlights for a year and a half, and Kate had thought they were the most wonderful invention she'd ever seen. She liked watching the men climb their ladders each night with their oil cans to light the lamps. Now, though, the town couldn't even use them. People couldn't buy lamp oil when money was so tight.

Kate wondered all the way to the printing shop what Harry would tell them. The redcoats they passed in the street reminded her why they had to be so cautious. A fourth of the people in Boston now were British soldiers. Many of the other people were Loyalists. Patriots had to be careful what they said everywhere.

"Brrr! It's almost as cold inside as out!" Colin rubbed his

mittened hands together after entering the shop.

Harry reached in his pocket for a flint to light a candle. The flint sparked and the candlewick flared. Its yellow flame gave a small circle of light but left most of the room with its press and piles of paper in dark shadows.

"What do you have to tell us?" Kate couldn't wait any longer.

Harry hiked himself onto the wooden worktable beside the candle. "The Observers have another assignment for you two."

Kate's heartbeat quickened, but Colin sounded calm as he said, "Do they want us to sneak more newspapers out of town?"

"No. This is far more dangerous."

"What. . .what is it?"

"A redcoat wants to desert. He needs help getting out of Boston."

Kate shivered. She remembered the deserter arrested at the Neck. "Deserters are killed if they're caught." Her voice trembled.

"Yes."

"What happens to people who help them?" Colin asked, and his voice sounded shaky, too.

"Prison. Still want to help us?"

Kate took a deep breath. This was scarier than she'd thought it would be.

"Yes," Colin said. "But I don't see how we can get anyone past the guards on the Neck in Uncle Firth's carriage."

"You won't need to. You just need to hide him for one night, give him different clothes to wear, and hide his uniform."

"Where can we hide him?" Kate asked. "Officers are living with both of us! Do you mean to hide him here in the print shop?"

"No. The redcoats are watching this place too closely. We want you to hide him at the apothecary shop for a few hours."

Kate frowned. "The apothecary is full of officers and Loyalists. How could we hide him there? Father would never let us."

Harry smiled. "It's like the hidden message in the newspaper. The best place to hide something or someone is in plain sight. No one will think it strange to see a soldier go into a Loyalist doctor's place. Your father need never know. Now, here's the plan."

CHAPTER 11

The Deserter

Kate was so excited she didn't fall asleep until very late. She tossed and turned, trying to think where she could hide the deserter in the apothecary shop. How could she keep Father from finding out?

When she finally did fall asleep, she dreamed she and Colin were standing in front of a redcoats' firing squad! She woke up sweating.

The next morning, Colin met her outside the apothecary shop with a burlap sack under his arm. "Is that your lunch?" she asked him, though she was pretty sure it wasn't. She clutched her ankle-length cape over her warm quilted skirt to keep away the November chill.

"That's right," he said. "I have an enormous hunger today. Comes from all those stingy meals we've been having. Want to see what I've got?"

He held the top of the sack open so she could see the folded petticoats and woman's gown and wig. Kate knew they were for the deserter. "Mmm," she said, her eyes dancing. "It looks delicious."

All day, as Kate and Colin worked inside the apothecary, Harry's plan was all Kate could think about. They didn't know when the deserter would show up. He would have to watch closely for a chance to get away from the other redcoats without raising suspicion.

Kate watched for the deserter all day. And all the next day. By the third day, she was beginning to wonder if the soldier would ever show up. But she forgot about him for hours at a time while she worked. Putting together the different medicines fascinated her.

She tried to remember everything her father said about which plants healed what ailments. Someday, when she was grown up and all this Patriot and Loyalist business was somehow behind them, she was determined that she would be a healer. Even if she had to leave Boston and go live in some wilderness community far to the west. Maybe when she was older, she could find a midwife who would take her as a sort of apprentice.

Her daydreams made the day go faster. By the time she and Colin were closing up the shop, it was long past candle-lighting time. Before they finished, the officers quartered with the Miltons came through the shop on their way to the house. Colin carried wood and started a fire for them in the library fireplace while one of the officers lit what seemed to Kate to be a wasteful number of candles.

Kate had just gone back into the apothecary to bar the door when she heard a knock outside. She swung the door open. A redcoat with brown curly hair stood there. He wasn't an officer. "Are you looking for the officers, sir?" Kate asked him.

"No, I'm looking for a doctor. I've cut my hand."

"The doctor's visiting patients. I'm his daughter. Come in. I'll fetch my father's apprentice." She called Colin to come in from the library. Her cousin placed a tin lantern on a table and unwrapped the bloody cloth from the redcoat's hand. Colin studied the wound in the light.

"I was polishing my bayonet," the redcoat said, "and it slipped. How bad is the cut?"

"Not as bad as it looks," Colin said. "Even though it bled a lot, it will be fine when the wound heals."

The man gave a large sigh of relief. "Good." He set his hat on the table. "What are your names?"

"Colin Lang. And this is my cousin, Kate Milton." Colin started to go get clean bandages, but the soldier's good hand clamped Colin's shoulder and stopped him. Colin's head jerked up in surprise.

"God bless the Liberty Boys," the man whispered.

Kate blinked. That was the code Harry had said the deserter would use!

The door into the Milton home swung open and Captain Ingles came in. He was a large, kind man, but Kate's heart was beating so loudly in her ears that she could hardly think. Had the captain heard the code? No, he couldn't have heard them from behind the thick door! The soldier had only whispered.

Seeing the captain, the injured redcoat snapped to his feet in attention. The captain waved a pudgy hand. "Sit down. Heard the bells on the shop door ring when you came in." He studied the soldier's hand. "Nasty wound there."

"I looked for the troop's doctor. When I couldn't find him, I came here."

Colin stood up. "I can take care of it, sir."

The captain looked down his thick nose into Colin's eyes. "I shouldn't be surprised if you can. The doctor speaks highly of you, lad."

Colin grinned with pride. "Thank you, sir."

"Show the other officers to the library when they arrive, will you, miss? There's a good lass."

When the library door shut behind the captain, Colin looked at Kate. She wondered what they should do next. Should she repeat the code, so the deserter would know he'd found the right place?

But what if he wasn't the deserter? What if the redcoats had found out about the plan and this man was here to trap them? Kate raised her eyebrows at Colin, trying to ask him silently what they should do next.

Colin seemed as lost as she was. He rubbed his hands down the thighs of his homespun breeches. "Thread me a needle, Kate," he said. "I'm going to take a couple stitches so the wound will heal faster."

While Kate threaded the curved needle, her mind raced. They could play it safe. They could pretend the man's words meant nothing to them. But if he *were* the deserter and Colin and Kate didn't help him, would he ever have another chance to get away?

The man held his wounded hand in the candlelight while Colin bent his head over the wound and made his stitches. When he was done, while their heads were still close together above the tin lantern, Kate heard her cousin whisper, "God bless the Liberty Boys."

Liberty, who had been sleeping in a ball beneath the table, heard his name and sat up. He thudded his skinny tail against the floor and whined.

Kate giggled. "Not you, boy." She explained to the soldier about Liberty's name.

The soldier's face lit up in a smile. He patted Liberty's head. "Thought I'd made a mistake when you didn't repeat the code." He spoke in a whisper.

"Are you going to come back after the officers go to bed?" Colin asked.

The soldier shook his head. "I'm not leaving. When it's discovered I'm missing, the officers will remember I was here. The officer saw my wound, so they'll know I was hurt. I'm hoping they won't think you or this place have anything to do with my escape."

Colin led the soldier over to the waist-high wooden counter and opened two doors beneath the counter. Then he looked the soldier up and down. He wasn't a tall man, and he wasn't large or fat, either, but he had broad shoulders.

"I thought this would be the perfect place to hide you," Colin whispered. "Some doctors' apprentices sleep on shelves in doctors' apothecaries. But I'm not sure you'll fit."

Kate had emptied the cupboard earlier. She'd even taken out the middle shelf to make more room.

The soldier squatted down and held the lantern by the tin handle at the top so it shone into the cupboard. "A bit of a tight squeeze, perhaps, but I think I can make it." He stood, set the lantern down, and held out his good hand. "Thank you, Colin Lang." He gave Kate a little bow. "I'll never forget the chance you two are taking for me. My name is George Lambert. I hope we'll meet again someday, when the redcoats have left Boston."

George Lambert turned toward the cupboard. "Go open the door, Kate. Pretend I'm leaving, Colin."

Kate did as she was told. She glanced up and down the street to see whether there was anyone that might see. She saw only a couple lantern flickers too far away for the people carrying them to tell whether anyone stood before the apothecary. In a loud voice, Colin wished Mr. Lambert Godspeed and told him to come back in a couple days to have the doctor look at his wound.

Then Colin hurried back to the counter. He pointed to a cloth bag in the cupboard. "Your new clothes are in there."

"Daren't change now. I'd better try out my new home before the officers come out here." Lambert grinned.

Laughing voices outside the door startled them. Lambert scuttled into the cupboard, drawing his knees up beneath his chin. Colin closed the doors just as Lieutenant Rand and another officer entered.

Kate bit her bottom lip hard. If there was anyone they didn't want to see, it was Lieutenant Rand! No one would rather catch a Lang with a deserter than that man.

Lieutenant Rand was carrying a tray with pewter mugs and a tall bottle. "We were hoping to have some hot punch. Make us some, lass." He glanced at Colin as he set the tray down on the countertop. "Working late, lad?"

Colin nodded and continued to put away the various medicines he had used that day. Kate hurried to fetch from the kitchen a large silver bowl with oranges, lemons, and spices in it. She could have made the punch over the kitchen fire, but she decided to use the stove in the apothecary instead. She wanted to keep an eye on Lieutenant Rand.

As she came back into the shop, a movement across the room caught her attention. Liberty was playing with Mr. Lambert's hat! Her feet seemed to freeze to the floor. She glanced at Colin, but he seemed not to have noticed. What if Rand saw that hat? He mustn't!

Liberty and the hat were in the shadows. Rand might not recognize the hat if he didn't get close to it. But what if Liberty dragged it closer? The best thing to do would be to go right over and pick up the hat, like nothing was wrong, she decided.

She almost had to pick up her feet with her hands to make them move, she was so scared. As she walked, she untied her white apron. When she reached Liberty, the dog thumped his tail, thinking Kate was going to play. Kate dropped her apron on top of the hat, then stooped and picked up both hat and apron together. Liberty caught one of the apron's ties in his teeth and growled playfully. "No! Down!" Kate ordered.

Liberty tucked his head.

"You hurt his feelings," Colin said as he put the last bottle away. "He just wants to play."

"Stupid mutt." Lieutenant Rand started toward the library. Liberty darted under a chair. The dog had learned that Lieutenant Rand's boots had a way of kicking him if he wasn't careful.

As Lieutenant Rand passed him, Kate bundled the apron closer around the hat. "Always cloths and aprons to wash out when you work in a doctor's apothecary," she complained.

Lieutenant Rand made a face and quickly left the room.

Kate breathed a sigh of relief. She'd never have gotten away with it if it had been daylight! At the counter, she opened the door, threw in the hat and apron, and slammed the door shut.

Colin looked at her as though she had lost her mind. "Lambert's hat," Kate said under her breath as she leaned close to her cousin. "It was on the floor."

Colin turned pale as he realized the close call they had had. Silently, they worked together making the punch. Kate's mouth watered at the wonderful smells of the oranges and lemons when she sliced them.

"Well, that's one advantage of having the officers quartered with us," Kate said. "They can get the best food. We can't afford fruit like this anymore."

Colin didn't look as though he had heard her. "What are we going to do?" he whispered. "How are we going to get Lambert on his way without the officers seeing?"

Kate frowned. Then she remembered something she had just learned. She smiled. "I have an idea."

CHAPTER 12

A Safely Delivered "Package"

Captain Ingles came into the shop. "Bring us more firewood, lad. We plan to be here awhile."

Colin hurried to get the wood, while Kate watched him with her heart in her mouth. Every minute the soldiers spent in the library was another minute of danger for the deserting soldier—and for her and Colin! Would her idea work?

She scraped the hard brown nutmeg against the tin grater, then handed it to Colin when he came from the library. While he sprinkled the spice into the punch, she ground some of her father's herbs in a mortar.

"What's that?" Colin asked as she poured the crushed herbs into the punch.

Kate smiled. "Just something new." She held up the herbs so he could see what she was using.

Colin's eyes widened. "What if it makes the punch taste funny?"

Kate shook her head. "The officers will like it fine." She knew the taste of the fruit and spices would be stronger than

236

the herb's. And the herb made people sleepy. They would have to use a lot of it in the punch to be sure it had the effect she wanted. She only hoped it would work and send the men to their beds early.

Kate and Colin carried the bowl and mugs into the library. Kate used a dipper to fill the mugs. Captain Ingles smacked his lips and reached for a poker heating in the fireplace. The poker sizzled when he stuck it in his mug to warm the spiced punch.

Lieutenant Rand picked up a mug. "At least there's one family in Boston that knows how to give an Englishman good food."

Kate clenched her teeth and shot a warning glance at Colin. She knew Lieutenant Rand was reminding them that Susanna wouldn't serve him English tea.

Kate started rearranging books on a shelf near the library door. It was a good place to stand to try to overhear the officers, so she often pretended to be busy there.

Woof! Woof!

Kate whirled around at Liberty's yelp. Liberty was usually too well behaved to bark inside!

Liberty was in front of the cupboard door. His nose was almost on the floor. His rear end, with its tail going a mile a minute, was stuck up in the air.

Something red on the floor in front of Liberty moved. A piece of Mr. Lambert's uniform! Lambert was trying to pull it back inside without opening the door. Liberty jumped on the moving cloth with another yelp. He growled playfully, tugging the cloth back and forth.

"What's all the noise?" Lieutenant Rand bellowed from

the doorway. Kate's heart leaped right into her throat at his unexpected voice.

"I'm sorry, sir. My dog must have seen a mouse!" Kate said loudly.

"Can't you keep that mutt quiet?"

"We're trying, sir," Colin said. He knelt beside Liberty, hiding the piece of red cloth. If Lieutenant Rand saw the cloth, he'd be sure to know it was part of a redcoat's uniform!

"Dogs don't belong inside anyway," Rand muttered, closing the library door.

It wasn't easy to make Liberty let go of the cloth, but Colin finally did. "We'd better put Liberty outside."

Kate scrunched up her face. "But it's cold out! And what if those rough boys find him again?"

Colin glared at her. "He's endangering a man's life!" He scooped Liberty up in his arms and put him outside the door in the street.

Kate quickly opened the cupboard door and pushed the piece of uniform at Mr. Lambert.

"Sorry," the soldier mouthed.

Kate took the dirty apron she'd put away in there earlier and closed the door. Her heart still hadn't slowed down! And now she could hear Liberty whimpering outside the apothecary door. She hated to have her dog shut out in the street—but she knew Colin was right. Without meaning to, Liberty could give them all away.

Suddenly, she was tired of the whole thing. She wished there was no deserter in the cupboard, no redcoats in the library, and that everything was the way it had always been. Being a spy no longer seemed exciting or brave.

When will all this be over? she wondered. *Will things ever go back to normal?*

Her mother stuck her head in the door of the apothecary, and both Kate and Colin jumped.

Mama laughed. "My, you two are as nervous as cats tonight." She looked down at the dirty apron Kate still clutched in her arms. "Take care of that, Kate, and put on a clean apron so you can help me put the food on the table. Supper is almost ready, and the officers are eager for their meal." Mama smiled at Colin. "You'll stay and eat with us, won't you, Colin?"

Colin hesitated. Kate was sure that he must be trying to keep his eyes from wandering toward the cupboard, just like she was. "Yes, ma'am," he said finally, and Kate was grateful that he wasn't going to leave her.

"Goodness," Mama said, cocking her head at the door. "Why is that dog shut out in the street? Let him in, Kate, and come along."

Mama disappeared again, and Kate looked at Colin. "You take care of Liberty," she whispered. "I have to help Mama. Maybe I can find a bone in the kitchen. If I can, I'll get it to you somehow. And then you can shut Liberty up in my room. He'll be quiet if he has a bone to gnaw on."

Smuggling a bone out from under Mama's eyes did not prove to be easy, though. Meanwhile, Kate could hear Liberty woofing and whining as he tried to figure out why such an interesting and unusual scent was coming from the apothecary cupboard.

"What ails that dog?" Mama asked as she dished up the potatoes.

"Can't you quiet that dog?" Lieutenant Rand bellowed from the library.

In desperation, Kate held up the old stew bone she had found in the larder. "Can't I give this to Liberty, Mama? Then he'll be quiet and won't bother the officers."

Mama pushed a wisp of hair out of her face. She looked tired and worried, Kate noticed. "That's a good idea, Kate," Mama said absently. Kate gave a sigh of relief and hurried to take the bone to Colin.

At least the herbs must have worked, she thought an hour later. The officers ended their evening far earlier than usual. Stretching and yawning, they said good night. Those who boarded elsewhere headed out into the dark streets, while the others climbed the stairs to their rooms.

"Everyone seems tired today," Mama said with a long weary sigh. "I hope your father will be able to come home soon. He must be tired as well."

"Let me clean up," Kate said. "You go on up to bed."

Her mother gave a small, surprised smile. "Why, thank you, Kate. If you don't mind, I think perhaps I will retire early. If your father comes home before you go to bed, please tell him his supper is in the kettle over the fire." She smiled at both children. "Good night, Colin. Good night, Kate."

Kate and Colin looked at each other. At the same time, they both let out a long breath, as though they had each been trying not to breathe all evening. They stood for a moment listening to the silent house, then tiptoed into the apothecary. Now they had to get Mr. Lambert on his way before Father came home.

Colin shuttered the apothecary windows and barred the door so no one could surprise them. Then he opened the cupboard door. Kate turned her back so Mr. Lambert could slip quickly out of his uniform to change into his "new" clothes.

Colin chuckled. "Hope you don't mind looking like a woman."

Mr. Lambert grinned. "Not if it gets me out of Boston safely."

Colin helped Mr. Lambert into an old dress and petticoat of his mother's. A wig hid the man's brown curls. A lace-edged mobcap topped it all off. Kate bit back her giggles as she stuffed the uniform into the cloth bag and hid it behind some pottery in another cupboard.

Mr. Lambert shaved carefully with Harry's razor. He put on an old hooded cloak, slid a market basket Colin had brought over his arm, and slipped into the dark street.

Kate knew Mr. Lambert was to meet a Patriot farmer who would be driving a cart a few streets over on his way home. Would Mr. Lambert make it? Or would the redcoats stop the funny-looking woman?

The next day, Kate heard Captain Ingles ask Colin about Mr. Lambert. "Did Lambert say where he was going when he left the apothecary?"

Colin shrugged. "Maybe he went to one of the taverns that are so popular with soldiers."

Kate grinned. At least she knew the man was still free! She was glad she'd buried the uniform in the herb garden early that morning.

Days later Harry said to Kate and Colin, "The post rider says the package you sent arrived safely."

Colin frowned. "The package?"

Harrison grinned, nodded, and walked away.

"Oh!" Kate's eyes met Colin's and they both grinned. The package was Mr. Lambert. If he "arrived safely," he must have made it out of Boston.

Kate wondered where he was living. Would he stay in another town in Massachusetts or on a farm, or would he live in another colony, far away from the redcoats that might recognize him? Would they ever see each other again?

CHAPTER 13

Fighting Friends and a Late-Night Secret

Colin and Kate spent fall days in the medical garden, removing plants before they were killed by early winter frosts. In the apothecary, they tied the plants together in bunches and hung them upside down from the ceiling to dry. Soon the ceiling was covered with fragrant purple, yellow, and white flowers.

One morning while Colin and Kate were tying up bunches of lavender thistle, the bell above the door jingled cheerfully, and Kate's friend Sarah entered.

Kate's face brightened. "Hello! I haven't seen you in days!"

"I've been busy." Sarah fumbled with the red-and-white-checked material covering the basket on her arm.

Kate nodded. "Me, too. We've been cleaning the garden. Tomorrow I'm delivering food baskets to some invalids and older ladies for the Gifts Committee. Will you help me?"

Sarah shook her head, her brown curls bouncing on the white linen scarf tied over the top of her blue dress. "I don't think so."

"But it would be fun! It would give us time to be together."

Sarah lifted her head with a jerk. Her blue eyes flashed. "I said no!"

Kate gasped and stepped back.

Sarah hurried to the counter and set down her basket. "I need some medicine. Mother's teeth are hurting." Her chin lifted and she glared at Colin. "We can't pay for it right now, but Father says to tell the doctor he'll pay for it as soon as the port opens again."

Colin nodded, pretending it was normal for Sarah's father to ask for credit. "Of course."

"I'll get the herbs." Kate took down a white china jar from a shelf.

"Is that the right medicine?" Sarah asked Colin.

"Yes," Colin assured her. "Kate's learned a lot about herbs from her father. If women could be doctors, she'd make a good doctor one day."

Kate spooned a bit of herb onto a piece of paper. Then she folded the paper so none of the herb could fall out and tied a bit of string about it. She handed the packet to Sarah. "Pour hot water over these herbs, the same as if you were making tea. Then have your mother put the wet leaves on her teeth."

"Thank you," Sarah mumbled, dropping the package into her basket. She hurried toward the door.

Kate shot Colin a worried glance. "Wait, Sarah, please." Kate bit her bottom lip, not sure what she should say next. "I don't know what I've done to make you mad," she said finally, "but I'm sorry."

Sarah started to walk around her without saying anything.

Kate grabbed her arm. "Please, Sarah, tell me what's wrong."

"It's the Gifts Committee you help with. My family is using some of the food and firewood people have donated. I'm so. . . ashamed." Tears ran down Sarah's freckled cheeks.

Kate stared at her, openmouthed.

Colin cleared his throat. "It's not your father's fault the king took away his job when the harbor closed. All the Patriots have to stick together and help each other through these hard times."

"Right now your family needs things other people can give them," Kate said. "Another time, your family will be helping someone. That's the way it works."

Sarah blinked at her tears. "When the tea was thrown into the harbor and later when the port was closed and the Patriots were all saying they'd starve before they'd pay for the tea, it felt so brave to be a Patriot." She brushed a hand over her eyes and sniffed. "It doesn't feel brave when you're begging for food."

Kate rubbed a hand on Sarah's arm. She wished she could make her friend feel better.

Sarah jerked away from Kate's touch. "It's Loyalists like your family who have made so much trouble for Boston."

"But Mama and Father didn't throw the tea in the harbor!"

"They didn't stand up with us, either." Sarah's voice jerked angrily. "If the Loyalists had stood by the Patriots, everything would have been fine. The king wouldn't have shut the harbor if everyone stood up to him together."

Kate stared at her. "Sarah, that's silly. You can't know what would have happened. No one can. Everyone has to do whatever they believe is right. That's what Father says."

Sarah sniffed. "I don't care what your father says. He's a

Loyalist, and it's his fault everything is so terrible!" She sounded as though she might cry, but she held her head high and glared at Kate. "I don't want to be friends with you anymore, Kate Milton. I only want Patriots for friends." Sarah stormed out the door.

Kate turned to Colin. "I wish I could tell her," she whispered. "Maybe she wouldn't be so mad at me if she knew I was helping the Patriot cause."

Colin shook his head. "You know you can't tell anyone. The redcoats have to believe you're a Loyalist just like your parents. Then they'll never suspect you."

Kate frowned. "Sarah isn't right, is she? It's not the Loyalists' fault."

"No, it's not their fault. She's just hurting and doesn't know what to do about it."

Kate blinked away tears. "Well, hurting me won't help."

"No." Colin put his hand on her shoulder, then went back to his work.

Kate looked around the room. In all the jars of herbs, was there anything that would heal the wounds she and Sarah were feeling in their hearts? Was there any medicine for a broken friendship?

November moved into December. Days went along like usual until one evening during the second week of December, when Colin was again staying late at the apothecary shop while the officers played cards, smoked their long pipes, and visited.

Kate and Colin were trying to read a new medical book by candlelight, but Kate's eyes kept closing. Mama was already sleeping, and Father had sent word that he was delivering a baby and likely wouldn't be home until morning. Kate wished the redcoats would leave so Colin could go home to bed. Then she wouldn't feel guilty going to bed herself.

Suddenly, she heard words that wakened her like a clap of thunder: "Fort Harrison and Mary."

She nudged Colin. "Did you hear that?"

He nodded. On tiptoe, they moved to the closed library door and leaned their ears against it. Kate held her breath so she could hear better. What she heard set her mind whirling. British troops were being sent from Boston to Fort Harrison and Mary in New Hampshire!

"Harrison and the Observers need this news right away!" Colin whispered. He took one step toward the front door, but Kate grabbed his arm.

"You can't leave yet!" she hissed. "The officers might suspect something."

Chairs scraping against the library floor sent them dashing back to their chairs. Kate dropped her head and arms on the table and closed her eyes. After a moment, Colin pretended to be asleep, too.

Officers filed into the room, joking with each other. Kate's heart raced. Beside her, Colin was breathing as hard as if he'd just raced back from the Neck. She nudged him and made herself breathe slowly and deeply, as if she were sleeping.

Boots stopped beside the table. "Time to wake up, lad."

Colin blinked, sat up, and looked at the officers. He stretched his arms over his head. "Leaving?"

"Yes, lad," Captain Ingles answered. "Ye'd best see to banking the fireplace."

Colin pretended to yawn. "See you tomorrow night."

He and Kate stumbled toward the library while the officers left. He made quick work of banking the fireplace, while Kate snuffed the candles. Even with such an important message to deliver, they didn't dare leave the fire and candles burning.

"I'm going," Colin said, throwing his wool jacket around his shoulders.

Kate grabbed her cloak, as well. "I'm coming, too!"

Colin frowned at her and shook his head, but Kate knew he didn't want to take the time to argue.

Snow and ice made it hard to hurry along the dark, narrow streets. Only the moon and stars lit their way. A lantern might have been seen by soldiers or others. They didn't want anyone to remember seeing them on the street so late at night. Not when they were carrying an important Patriot secret!

Colin's house was dark and quiet when they reached it. The family was already in bed. Colin lit the candle on the hall table and carried it with them so he wouldn't fall and make noise. They didn't want to wake Lieutenant Andrews or Lieutenant Rand!

Kate's mind kept saying, *Hurry! Hurry!* but she walked slowly. She tried to remember which steps and which floorboards squeaked.

Creak! She and Colin froze. Kate's heart slammed against her chest. She wasn't as familiar with the creaks and squeaks in Colin's house as she was with her own. Had anyone heard her?

No one stirred. Colin slowly opened Harry's door.

While Colin shook Harry's shoulder, Kate held the candle high so Harry could see who it was. She put her finger to her lips.

Colin whispered in Harry's ear that he had news he must tell him right away.

"Kitchen," Harry whispered back.

Together they went downstairs, stepping over the squeaky places. This time, Kate was as silent as Colin. When they reached the kitchen, Harry opened the barrel of apple cider beside the back door. Taking the tin ladle hanging on the wall, he dipped the cool cider into three pewter mugs.

He handed mugs to Kate and Colin. "If anyone walks in, we'll say I woke up thirsty. I came down for a drink and met you two coming in." He cocked an eyebrow at Kate. "I take it you're spending the night with Susanna?"

"That's right." Kate felt guilty now that she had insisted on coming with Colin. If they were discovered, her presence might look odd to the officers. And if Mama woke up and found her gone, she would worry.

"I know you said we aren't to tell Patriot news in the house," Colin whispered, "but this is too important to wait until morning."

They stood close together beside the fireplace, where they could still feel a little heat from the banked ashes. Kate shivered at the eerie sound their whispers made in the large, dark room.

"What's your news?" Harrison asked.

Colin told how they'd overheard the officers. "General Gage is sending redcoats from Boston to Fort Harrison and Mary at Portsmouth, New Hampshire. They'll go by sea."

"Why?"

"There's only a few redcoats at the fort. General Gage wants more soldiers there in case the minutemen try to take the fort's gunpowder."

In the light of the candle Colin had set on the mantel, Kate could see excitement dancing in Harry's eyes. "The minutemen must get the gunpowder before the soldiers from Boston arrive."

"To do that, they'd have to go into the fort and take the powder from under the redcoats' noses," Colin said.

"Yes."

"But if the soldiers catch them, they might be shot."

"Yes," Harry agreed.

"I mean," Colin looked as though he were trying to put his worst fears into words, "if the redcoats and minutemen shoot at each other, war could start."

"Yes. Mark my words, if General Gage keeps taking Americans' guns and ammunition to use against us, war will surely start. If not at Fort Harrison and Mary, then somewhere else."

Hopelessness filled Kate's heart. She didn't want war. She wanted peace with the king and his troops. She knew that most Patriots only wanted the king to listen to their complaints so that things would go back to being the way they had once been. That was all she wanted, too.

"If this news gets to the minutemen," Colin said slowly, "then Kate and I could start the war because it's our secret."

Harry's fingers squeezed Colin's shoulder tightly through the wool jacket. "This might be the most important news the Sons of Liberty have discovered. The Patriots must hear it."

"I thought the Continental Congress said the Patriots' army wasn't to shoot at the redcoats unless the redcoats shot first."

"That's right. But if the redcoats take all our ammunition, we won't be able to fight. We'll have to do whatever the king says, no matter how wrong it is."

Colin nodded slowly. Kate hadn't thought of that.

Harry rubbed a fist across his stubbly chin. "We need to tell Paul Revere. Portsmouth is sixty miles north, and the roads are covered with snow and ice. Paul's the only man we can count on to get through in time."

Kate saw Colin swallow hard. "Do. . .do you want me to tell him?"

Kate shivered. Would they have to sneak into Mr. Revere's house tonight?

Harry shook his head, his brown hair brushing his shoulders. "No, it's too dangerous. Even though you're only children, if you were caught entering Paul's house, the British might become suspicious. Mark my words, when they find the Portsmouth minutemen know the redcoats are being sent from Boston, General Gage will try to find how the news got out. We don't want anyone to remember you two from both Uncle Firth's house and Paul's the same night."

Colin yawned and picked up the wool blanket that was folded neatly at one end of the tall-backed settle. Kate yawned, too. Now that they'd passed the news and worry on to Harry, she was tired again. "I'm going to bed," Colin said, and Kate decided she would climb into bed with Susanna. She would be sure to wake up early in the morning so Mama would never know she was gone.

But Harry grabbed Colin's arm as he started to lay down on the settle. "Oh, no, you don't. You need to go back to Uncle Firth's and sleep in the library. That way the officers will find you there in the morning. No one must know you came home tonight. We don't want anyone to think you had a chance to tell

Father and me what the officers said."

Colin sighed. Kate didn't want to go out in the cold and snow again any more than Colin did, but she knew Harry was right. They slipped quietly out the back door while Harry went to dress.

CHAPTER 14

The Raid

Harry got the message safely to Mr. Revere. Kate wondered what excuse Mr. Revere used to get out of town. General Gage didn't let people into or out of Boston without a pass anymore. To get a pass, you had to have a good reason to leave. Kate smiled at the thought of Paul Revere saying, "I'm off to warn the minutemen that you're sending soldiers to Fort Harrison and Mary." No, Mr. Revere would have come up with another reason.

Three days later, Colin told her Paul Revere was back. Kate was surprised he'd made the dangerous ride so quickly. Every day he was gone, Kate had prayed that Mr. Revere would be safe, the message would get through, and war wouldn't start.

Mr. Revere told Harry what happened at Fort Harrison and Mary. Harry and Uncle Jack printed the news in the *Boston Observer*.

Paul Revere had reached the minutemen before the soldiers from Boston arrived at the fort. In the middle of the night, the minutemen went to the fort in Portsmouth Harbor in boats.

The British captain in charge of the fort fired three times at the minutemen, but he hit no one. The captain knew he didn't have enough soldiers at the fort to win a battle, so he surrendered.

Patriots, Loyalists, and redcoats in Boston were all shocked when they heard the news. Minutemen had taken a British fort without anyone on either side being wounded or killed!

Harry grinned when he told Colin and Kate the news. "The minutemen carried away ninety-seven kegs of gunpowder and about one hundred guns and hid them. The minutemen need those guns and ammunition. They wouldn't have them without you two."

Kate couldn't help but be proud as she heard the town talk about the minutemen's raid. Lieutenant Rand and Lieutenant Andrews told the family that General Gage was mad that news of his plans had leaked out.

Mr. Revere made Colin and Kate gifts: small silver whistles shaped like spy glasses with the words "Boston Observer" carved on their sides. Kate carried hers with her everywhere. She would stick her hand in her apron pocket, feel the satiny smooth silver, and smile at the memory of Mr. Revere's and Harry's praises.

Kate's parents didn't like the news about Fort Harrison and Mary one bit. Mama was at the apothecary when Colin told them what had happened at the fort—without telling his and Kate's part in it, of course. Mama set the blue bottle she was dusting back on the shelf with a thud. "The minutemen must have known General Gage was sending soldiers to the fort." Her lips were pressed tight with disapproval.

"I suppose so," Father agreed.

Kate was checking the wooden medicine box Father kept in the trunk on the back of his carriage. It was her chore to keep the box stocked with twine, splints, bandages, sponges, medicines, and things to make pills and powders. She kept her eyes on her work, afraid to look up at her parents' faces.

The feathers in Mama's duster fluttered over a row of large jars with curving blue letters. "A spy must have told them."

Kate's heart lurched against her chest. She opened her mouth, but she couldn't say anything.

"Maybe one of his own soldiers," Mama continued. "I think it's awful, a British soldier betraying his country."

"Maybe it wasn't a soldier," Father said. "Maybe it was a Patriot who overheard the plans."

Kate glanced up quickly at her father, but he seemed absorbed with the medicine he was measuring.

Mama picked up a small metal scale in one hand, dusted the cupboard beneath it, and slammed it back down with a crash. "Citizens shouldn't betray their country, either," she snapped. "I'm just so tired of this terrible—" Her voice caught, and she broke off without finishing the sentence.

"Surely whoever told thought it was the right thing to do." Father's voice was grave.

"People like Jack and all the other Patriots always think they're doing the right things. But look what a mess they've made of Boston and of our lives!"

Colin shifted his shoulders uncomfortably. "They haven't done anything but ask the king to put things between England and the colonies back the way they were years ago, before the Stamp Act and the Tea Act, and—"

"They haven't done anything?" his aunt interrupted him, her voice shrill. "They've done everything! It's because of them the harbor is closed. I'm tired of making do with whatever food we can get. I want sugar and molasses instead of dried pumpkin for baking. I want new clothes for my family." She snatched up Kate's quilted skirt between her thumb and forefinger. "Look at this old thing! I've mended a dozen holes in it this winter, and it's too short for her. I'd be able to buy Kate a new dress if the port opened."

"But dear—" Father tried to hush his wife, but for once Mama wouldn't listen to him.

"I'm tired of sharing my house with strangers, too. I'm tired of our families arguing. Remember the good times our families used to have together? Now you and your brother-in-law don't even talk to each other!"

Father's lips curled just a little. "That's not the Patriots' fault, dear."

"Everything is the Patriots' fault!" She stamped her small slippered foot on the wooden floor. Kate had never seen her mother so upset.

"But, Mama," Kate said, "even Father says the king is punishing Boston more than is fair."

"I don't care. If I knew who the spy was that told General Gage's plans for Fort Harrison and Mary, I'd turn him in myself."

The marble pestle Colin had been holding hit the countertop and rolled onto the floor.

Father looked down thoughtfully at the pestle that had landed by his feet. Then he turned back to his wife. "You don't mean that. The spy could be someone you know, maybe even someone you care about."

Mama picked up the pestle and slammed it down on the counter. Her blue eyes were almost black with anger. "Spies make things worse. I want life to go back to the way it used to be."

"Turning against our neighbors isn't the answer."

Mama tugged at her lace-trimmed mobcap. "You call yourself a Patriot," she said to Colin, "but I know you also believe in doing what's right. Wouldn't you turn in a spy?"

"Maybe not, if he was someone I knew."

Mama threw up her hands in exasperation. "You're just as stubborn as your father, Colin Lang! You may not have joined the rebels who threw the tea in the harbor, but you're a Patriot just the same. Can't you see that all of you Patriots are hurting Boston?"

"I don't believe that," Colin said softly. Kate knew her mother's sharp words had upset him. Still, his voice sounded calm and reasonable.

But Kate knew her mother had refused to listen to reason.

Feelings grew worse between the redcoats and Patriots during the winter. The redcoats were afraid the Charles River would freeze over and that the minutemen would cross the ice to attack the troops.

But the river didn't freeze over. It was a mild winter, which was good for everyone in Boston. Fuel was scarce. A colder winter would have meant the poor people would have suffered more. The Patriots were sure God made the winter mild to help them.

Hopes for peace grew dimmer. The Patriots were preparing

more and more for war. Patriot gunmakers were busy in all the colonies, making muskets for the minutemen. Paul Revere and other silversmiths made bullet molds. Colin's mother, Harry's wife, and other Patriot women gave their silver and pewter dishes and candlesticks to be melted down and made into bullets. Kate wondered if Lieutenant Andrews and Lieutenant Rand noticed the dishes and candlesticks missing from the house.

Larry came to town often, bringing things to market. He always stopped by to visit Colin and Kate. He told them how he and his father spent their evenings in front of the family fireplace carving wooden bowls and spoons the minutemen would need if war came.

Kate was glad there had been no fighting between the redcoats and minutemen. So far, the only people killed had been British deserters who had been caught and shot at the common. Each time it happened, Kate thought of Mr. Lambert. Where was he? Was he safe?

In February, General Gage's men tried to take the ammunition stored at Salem. Harry told Colin and Kate that Mr. Lambert, the deserter they'd helped escape, was living near Salem. He was helping train the minutemen.

The Observers hadn't been able to get a message to Salem. General Gage had locked Paul Revere, Harry, and some of their friends in jail at the fort on Castle Island to keep them from telling Salem. So now the Observers knew that the general had his own spy in the Observers.

Even without the Observers, Gage's men weren't able to take Salem's ammunition.

March fifth was the fifth anniversary of the Boston Massacre.

People gathered at Old South Church to remember those who'd lost their lives at the hands of British soldiers. The building was packed. People were crushed together in the pews. The aisles were filled. Men even stood on the two-foot-deep windowsills. Kate knew the streets were crowded, too. Thousands had turned out.

Kate went with Colin and his family, but when she glanced up at the balcony, she saw that her parents were there, too. They sat where young Josiah Quincy had been the night of the tea party. Kate could still remember his chilling words that night:

"I see the clouds which now rise thick and fast upon our horizon... to that God who rides the whirlwind and directs the storm I commit my country."

Kate wondered, *How close is the storm of war now?*

Colin nudged her elbow and pointed toward the front of the church. Kate almost laughed out loud when she saw Dr. Warren, the Patriot leader, climb into the church through the window above the high pulpit! He hadn't been able to make it through the crowd.

Dr. Warren was the one who had written the Suffolk Resolves that Colin and Harry had printed and Paul Revere had carried to the Continental Congress at Philadelphia last summer. Dr. Warren had come to the print shop to thank Colin's father for doing such a quick, good print job.

Wealthy John Hancock, who had been the leader of the Continental Congress, and Sam Adams, one of the smartest Patriot leaders, were beside Dr. Warren.

Forty British officers took the best pews at the front of the church and sat on the steps that led to the high pulpit. Colin and Kate exchanged worried glances. There was a rumor that General Gage was going to arrest the Patriot leaders today. The Loyalists had even made up a song about hanging them.

The redcoats couldn't frighten the Patriot leaders from speaking. Dr. Warren told the story of the Boston Massacre. He reminded the people of all the reasons they were proud to be English citizens.

"It isn't our aim to become a separate country from Great Britain," he said. "Our wish is that Britain and the colonies grow stronger together. But if our peaceful attempts aren't successful and the only way to safety lies through war, I know you will not turn your faces from the enemy."

The soldiers jeered. The crowd cheered. But no one was arrested at the meeting after all. Was it because the soldiers were afraid the crowd would turn on the redcoats if they arrested the popular leaders? Kate thought the leaders must have been frightened, even though they weren't arrested.

Out in the street after the meeting, Kate hurried to join her parents. The crowd about them parted to let Sam Adams and John Hancock through. Kate saw her mother's icy blue glare as the men walked past. Kate knew Mama hadn't changed her mind about Patriots.

In the days that followed, the Patriot leaders quietly slipped out of town, one by one, until only Dr. Warren was left.

The thunder of war sounded louder than ever.

CHAPTER 15

Danger

Kate smiled as she entered the printing shop. Spring had come at last, and the air outside was filled with the chatter of birds and the smell of cherry blossoms. The shop still smelled like ink. Uncle Jack always said ink was his favorite smell because ink printed words, and words were man's most powerful tools, next to faith in God.

Harry, Colin, and Uncle Jack looked up from their work and said hello. Colin handed her a freshly printed newspaper. "Read what Patrick Henry said."

Kate read it aloud.

" 'We have done everything that could be done to stop the storm from coming. There is no longer any room for hope of peace. If we want to keep those rights for which we've been struggling for ten long years, we must fight!

We shall not fight our battles alone. There is a just God, who rules nations. He will raise up friends to fight our battles for us.

Is life so dear or peace so sweet as to be bought at the price of slavery? Forbid it, Almighty God. I know not what course others may take, but as for me, give me liberty or give me death!'"

Prickles ran up and down Kate's spine. The words filled her with a tingly sense of awe. She would always remember these words, she promised herself, and one day she would repeat them to her children. Still, she wondered how Patrick Henry could be so certain. Was it really so bad to live under Britain's rule? She was fairly sure she would never choose to die, no matter how unfair Britain's taxes might be.

"Do you think he's right?" she asked her uncle. "Do you think we'll have to fight?"

Uncle Jack looked very serious. "I think he's right."

Harrison nodded as well.

Kate and Colin walked outside. The sun still shone, warming the cobblestones. Redcoats, tradesmen, and housewives coming from market still filled the street. Idle craftsmen still sat on barrels and benches, visiting. Birds still chattered and cherry blossoms still perfumed the air.

But nothing was the same.

The next day, Kate saw people all over town reading the *Boston Observer* and heard them repeating Patrick Henry's words. In the afternoon, when Father said they could go, she and Colin hurried to Uncle Jack's shop with Liberty at their heels. They'd just arrived when a clattering in the street drew everyone to the door. Kate couldn't believe what she saw.

Lieutenant Rand and three other officers were riding their horses through the street. A large group of soldiers followed on foot, calling insults at the Patriots and laughing. Rand carried a large straw man. There was a grin on the lieutenant's face that made Kate's skin crawl.

People in the street hurried to get out of the horses' paths. Then they stopped and watched to see where the soldiers were going. Everyone knew what the straw man was for.

So did Kate. She'd seen others like it often enough.

As the officers pulled their horses to a stop in front of the shop, Rand leaped off his horse. He grinned at Colin and his father, then he and one of the other officers stopped a foot in front of them. Liberty growled deep in his throat, peeking at Rand from behind Kate's skirts. People in the street drew nearer, but Kate knew they couldn't stop the redcoats.

The other officer carried a rope with a noose at one end. He tossed the other end over the shop sign's metal pole, then hooked the noose over the straw man. Kate's stomach tightened when they pulled the straw man up, letting it swing in the breeze. She knew what they were doing. It was called hanging someone in effigy. They were pretending to hang Uncle Jack.

A copy of the *Boston Observer* was pinned to one straw hand. Rand grabbed a pipe from a nearby shopkeeper. He held it beneath the paper until it started on fire. Liberty yelped and scuttled away.

Colin darted into the shop. He grabbed the bucket of water that always stood beside the press. Kate knew the straw would go up like kindling and could start the building on fire. Water sloshed over the floor and Colin's shoes as he raced out the door with the bucket. The straw man was already one huge flame. The officers and his father had backed away.

Colin tossed the entire bucket on the burning form. Most of the fire went out in a hiss of smoke. The rope continued to burn, scorching the wooden shop sign.

Uncle Jack grabbed his composing stick, stuck it through the noose, and yanked the rope down. He stamped the flames out until only a smoking black circle remained.

Lieutenant Rand sat astride his bay horse and watched. Finally, he leaned over the horse's neck. "Patrick Henry may not be afraid of war, but you should be, Mr. Lang. If war breaks out, the treasonous printers will be among the first prisoners of war." He yanked at the reins, turned his horse, and galloped up the street, hooves clattering against the cobbles.

Colin's fists curled into balls. "I hate that man!"

His father's arm slid around his shoulders. "We're to love our enemies, Son. He needs our prayers, not our hate."

"Aren't we supposed to love everyone not just our enemies?" Colin asked.

"Yes, but it's hardest to be nice to our enemies."

"If that's true, why are you nicer to Lieutenant Rand than to Uncle Firth?" Colin stormed into the street, his wet shoes slapping against the cobblestones. Kate looked after him unhappily. She knew he wanted to be alone.

Kate was glad the next morning when her father asked her to work in the medical garden. It felt good to be outside in the sunlight with the birds singing and the smell of fresh earth. Her fear and anger over Lieutenant Rand's straw man lightened a little as she worked, pulling the tiny weeds that were growing around the young herbs.

The medical garden was more important than ever since the harbor had closed. Now when Father ran out of medicines and herbs, it was difficult and expensive to replace them unless he could get them from the garden. Kate sat back on her heels for a moment, enjoying the sunshine on her face, but she knew Mama would scold her if she came in with her face all red from the sun. She tightened the blue ribbons beneath her chin, pulling the sides of her huge round straw hat down over her cheeks.

Colin joined her in the garden and began turning the soft soil with a wooden rake. As they worked, the sound of fifes and drums playing a British march grew steadily louder, until it drowned out the songs of birds in the nearby trees. Colin and Kate moved to the white picket fence surrounding the garden to watch a regiment of redcoats parade past. Brass buttons and musket barrels flashed in the sun. Six young Patriot boys followed along singing "Yankee Doodle" at the top of their lungs.

"When the British troops first came to Boston, I thought everything would get better," Kate said. "Instead, everything got worse." She leaned against the fence. "Now, Sarah blames everything on the Loyalists—but I know that people like Mama and Father aren't to blame for everything that's wrong."

"Are you and Sarah friends again?"

She shook her head. "No. Sarah says she hates Loyalists and won't be friends with me anymore."

"I'm sorry, Kate."

"I always thought everything would work out between Britain and the colonies. But if Sarah can hate me because my parents are Loyalists and our fathers can stop talking to each other, maybe Britain and the colonies will stay angry, too. Maybe all this tension will never go away."

"Maybe."

Kate wrapped her fingers around the top of a picket in the fence and watched the troops disappearing down the street. "Everyone in Boston seems angry these days. People keep talking about war. Sometimes, Colin, I'm so scared."

He put a hand on her shoulder. The warmth of his hand comforted her, but she knew the thought of war scared him, too.

The next evening, Dr. Milton sent Colin to his father with a message to meet him after dark at the print shop. Colin exchanged looks with Kate, his brows raised in a silent question, but then he ran off to do what he was told.

Kate wanted to ask her father why he wanted to meet with Uncle Jack. Her curiosity made her feel both nervous and hopeful, all at the same time. His face was so grave, though, that she didn't dare ask him any questions.

The next morning, Father looked the same as ever as he went about opening the apothecary shop. Kate could hardly wait until Colin came. She was certain he would tell her what had happened.

Later, as they again worked in the garden, the children talked in excited whispers.

Colin, his father, and Harry had pretended to go to bed early the night before, Colin told Kate. They said good night to the family and officers. Then they sneaked out an upstairs window.

When they reached the print shop, Kate's father stepped out of a shadow and joined them. Uncle Jack made sure the wooden shutters were closed over the windows. Inside, Harry lit a single candle from a warm coal in the banked fireplace. In the wavering light of the candle, the three Langs faced Dr. Milton.

Colin's father crossed his arms over his chest. "You haven't spoken to me for six months, Firth. Now you order me and my sons to the print shop in the dark of night. Why?"

"General Gage is planning to take your press and arrest you for treason."

"No!" Colin yelled. He couldn't bear it to be true! His father and brother couldn't be arrested!

His father put his hand on Colin's shoulder. "Quiet, son. How do you know this, Firth?"

Dr. Milton hesitated a moment. "An officer I trust told me. He knows my sister is your wife."

"Why arrest us now?" Harrison asked.

"A ship arrived this week from England with a letter from the king to General Gage. The king told him to be tougher on the Patriots," Dr. Milton said. "You and your father need to leave town."

"Gage won't give us a pass out of town when he wants to arrest us," Uncle Jack said. "Maybe Harry or I could sneak out of town, but how could we sneak both our families out?"

Sweat trickled down Kate's spine as she listened to Colin's story. She remembered the deserter she and Colin had seen captured at the gate. Would that happen to Harry and Uncle Jack?

"Then your father said, 'I've been thinking about this for hours.'" Colin continued with his story.

"General Gage won't hurt your families," Kate's father had said. "It's you and Harry he wants. I promise to watch out for your families until you can return or they can join you. Because I'm a Loyalist doctor, I have a pass that lets me enter and leave Boston freely. The guards at the Neck see me so often that they don't even search me. I can sneak you out in my carriage."

Harry grinned. "That's a great idea!"

Relief poured through Kate as she listened. It was the perfect plan! She felt so proud of her father. No matter what he believed, he would always stand by the people he loved.

Colin shook his head when he saw Kate's excited face. "My father said, 'No.'"

Uncle Jack had shaken his head and crossed his arms over his large chest. "I won't let you put yourself in danger. The officers at our house would quickly find we'd left town. When they found you'd left town the same night, you'd be arrested."

Dr. Milton's arms had swung wide. "What else can you do?"

"We can find a way out of Boston ourselves." Uncle Jack raised his eyebrows and looked at Harry. "Can't we?"

Colin knew he was asking Harry whether he could get them out the same way Harry had helped other deserters out of Boston.

Harry nodded. "We'll find a way."

"If you can't find another way out," Dr. Milton said, "promise you'll let me help you."

"I promise. I'll never forget this, Firth, not the warning or the offer to put yourself in danger to help us."

Colin had thought the candlelight reflected off unshed tears in his father's eyes. A moment later he'd decided he must have been wrong. He'd never seen his father cry.

Uncle Jack cleared his throat. "Colin said something to me yesterday that's been bothering me ever since."

Colin had looked at him in surprise. What had he said?

"He said he didn't understand why we were nicer to our enemies than to you, Firth." Colin's father held out his huge, ink-stained hand. "Our families have worked together down through the years. I'd like us to be friends, in spite of our differences. I'm asking you to forgive me."

Slowly, Kate's father took his brother-in-law's hand. "And I as well."

"You told me often that God says we're to pray for our leaders," Uncle Jack said. "Maybe that's a good place to start over."

"For King George?" Kate's father asked.

"Yes—and the Patriot leaders."

"Oh, all right." Dr. Milton had grinned. "I guess they can all use the Lord's help. I only hope it's not too late for peace."

"If war comes," Harry said, "the leaders of both sides will need the Lord's help more than ever."

The four joined hands in the middle of the dark room. They prayed for wisdom for King George and the Patriot leaders and for peace in America.

After Kate's father left, Uncle Jack had put a hand on each of his sons' shoulders. "We've printed only what we believed was right. We have to trust that God will make a way of escape for us."

Harry had left to talk to friends in the Sons of Liberty who could help them find that way of escape. Colin and his father began taking apart the press. "We make our living by it," Uncle Jack said. "We can't let it be destroyed." He knew friends who would hide the press in their cellar.

Kate blinked tears from her eyes as Colin finished his story. "What will your family do now?"

Colin shrugged. "Father told me to come to work here just as though everything was normal. We're waiting for Harry to tell us what to do next."

Only an hour later, Harry stopped by the apothecary shop. The Langs' escape was arranged. "Tomorrow is Easter Sunday," Harry reminded them. "The soldiers won't dare arrest us until after church. That will give Father and me time to say good-bye to our families."

Kate looked at Harry. "You have to leave?" She already knew the answer. Would baby Paul remember his father when he grew up? Kate could not hold back the tears that filled her eyes.

After church the next day, Harry told the other family members and Lieutenant Andrews, who always joined them for services, that he and his father wanted to check something at the shop before Sunday dinner.

"See you at dinner," Uncle Jack said. He smiled at Kate's parents. "You and Kate will join us, won't you?"

The Miltons nodded and smiled. "We'll see you later," Father said, his voice calm and sure.

Kate watched as Colin and his mother and sisters walked home. They were chatting and laughing as they walked, as though inside their hearts weren't breaking with fear and sadness. They didn't want Lieutenant Andrews or anyone else to see how frightened they were.

Would Harrison and Uncle Jack escape? When would their family be together again?

Kate prayed all the way home.

∞ CHAPTER 16 ∞

♪ Mission of Mercy

B y Tuesday evening, Colin and his family still hadn't heard whether his father and Harry were safe. "They must be," Colin told Kate. "If they'd been caught, the soldiers would have told us."

Kate was certain Lieutenant Rand would have loved to have given the bad news. The officer had been furious when he'd found the two Lang men had left town. *He must have known General Gage was planning to arrest them,* Kate thought.

A few days later, when Kate and Colin stepped through the front door of his home, they heard a man's voice they didn't recognize coming through the closed sitting room door. The next voice they did know: Lieutenant Rand's. They silently exchanged looks, then leaned their ears against the door to listen.

The voice they didn't know was speaking now. "You and Lieutenant Andrews are to report to the common as soon as possible, prepared for an expedition."

"Lieutenant Andrews isn't here," Lieutenant Rand said, "but

I'll get the message to him."

Kate and Colin stepped quickly from the doorway. Opening the front door, Colin pretended they were just entering the house as Lieutenant Rand and a soldier came out of the sitting room.

The soldier nodded at the children and left. Lieutenant Rand frowned at Colin. "Do you know where Lieutenant Andrews is?"

"I haven't seen him, sir."

Rand grabbed his hat from the hallway table. "I'm going looking for him. If he gets back before I do, tell him to wait for me here."

Kate watched Rand hurry down the street in his red coat and black hat. The officers were to be "prepared for an expedition," the soldier had said. That meant General Gage was sending his soldiers out of Boston, likely to take another town's gunpowder. *We should tell Paul Revere,* Kate thought, *but how many men is Gage sending and where?*

Kate and Colin worried about it for fifteen minutes, pacing back and forth in front of the fireplace, talking in whispers. They could hear women's voices in the kitchen, and Kate knew Colin's mother and sisters must be making supper. "Should we ask your mother?" she whispered.

Colin shook his head. "I have to figure out what to do." All of a sudden, he sounded more like a man than a boy.

When Lieutenant Andrews walked in, Susanna was with him. Her hand was tucked into the crook of his elbow.

"Lieutenant Rand is looking for you, sir," Colin said.

Kate almost blurted out that he was to go to the common,

but she remembered just in time that she wasn't supposed to know that!

Lieutenant Andrews didn't answer. Instead, he looked at Susanna. Their faces were filled with worry. The officer removed his hat and turned to Colin. "While we were walking by the common, an officer stopped us. I'm to report there right away."

So he'd already heard the message.

Susanna said, "Boats are waiting by the common to take soldiers across the river." She glanced at Lieutenant Andrews and back to Colin. "It's not a secret. Anyone from town who goes to the common can see what's happening."

"Is it a secret where the troops are going?" Colin asked.

"Yes." Lieutenant Andrews played with his hat and bit the corner of his bottom lip as if he couldn't decide whether to say more.

"They're going to try to take more of our ammunition, I suppose," Colin said.

Lieutenant Andrews took Susanna's hand. "When I came to America, I expected only to follow my orders and serve the king. I didn't expect to meet Susanna or find I agree with the Patriots' beliefs. I didn't think I would ever betray my king and fellow soldiers, but to do otherwise would be to betray my conscience."

Kate waited for what he would say next, her heart beating faster and faster.

The officer took a deep breath. "It's rumored we're going to Concord, on the other side of Lexington. Maybe we are to take the Americans' arms there in obedience to King George's recent orders. You must warn the Sons of Liberty, Colin."

Colin ran out of the house with Kate right on his heels.

They headed for Paul Revere's house. When they reached the house in North Square, Colin banged on the door.

Kate looked over her shoulder nervously. The streets were filled with redcoats dressed for battle. "Try not to look so upset," she hissed. She tried to laugh as she said the words so that the officers would think nothing of two children out paying a call. She knew many marines were quartered in nearby houses, including Major Pitcairn, one of the best-liked British officers—even by the Patriots.

Mr. Revere greeted them with the smile he always wore. "Young Lang. Mistress Milton. You must be here about the delivery. I heard only an hour ago that it arrived safely."

"Delivery?" Colin stared at him blankly. "Oh, the delivery!" Kate knew Mr. Revere must be speaking about Uncle Jack and Harry. They were safe! Joy and relief flooded her in spite of the hard news they carried.

"Thank you, sir, but that isn't why I'm here." Colin whispered Lieutenant Andrews's message.

Mr. Revere nodded. "I've heard the same from two other sources."

Kate was disappointed that Mr. Revere already knew their news.

"To hear it from more than one Observer only makes it more likely the news is true. It was brave of you to come. Tell no one else," Mr. Revere warned.

Would Mr. Revere ride again tonight for the Sons of Liberty? Kate wondered. If he did, he'd have to sneak past the soldiers at the Neck or the warships in the harbor.

If there was war, would Harry and the other minutemen face

the officers who had been living in their homes? Lieutenant Andrews had shared his army's secret, but he hadn't said he would desert and become a Patriot. Could Andrews shoot at Harry or Harry at him?

Kate's stomach felt sick.

As the children headed back to Kate's house, they saw Dr. Milton's carriage leaving. To Kate's surprise, Larry was on a horse beside the carriage. "Uncle Firth!" Colin sprinted down the street after the carriage, and Kate struggled to keep up on her shorter legs.

Her father drew on the reins and looked down at the children. "Larry's father is ill," he said. "We're on our way out to their farm. I may need to operate. I could use your help, Colin."

"May I come, too?" Kate asked.

Her father hesitated. "Your mother may not want you to go."

"May I go ask?" she pleaded.

Her father nodded, and she dashed for the house. Her mother met her at the door.

Mama smiled as Kate fought to get the words out between her gasps for air. "Save your breath," she said. "I know what you're going to ask. And I've also come to realize how important healing is to you. So long as you stay with your father, you may go."

Kate gave her mother a grateful hug, then ran back to the carriage where Father, Colin, and Larry were waiting.

The wheels clattered over the cobblestones. Kate looked back. Her mother was still standing in front of the house, staring after them. Her face was lined with worry, and Kate suddenly realized how much courage it must take to be a parent and let your children grow up. Especially in dangerous times like these. Kate waved her hand at her mother, hoping Mama would know how much she loved her. Her mother's face lightened as she returned the wave, then turned to go back inside.

They stopped at Colin's house to let his mother know where they were going, and then they were on their way. "It would save us a lot of time if we could take the Charlestown ferry from the north end of Boston," Father grumbled. "Instead we have to go south across the Neck, then north. It will take us twice as long to get there. I hope the extra time won't cost Larry's father his life."

There was a moment at the Neck when Kate didn't think they'd be allowed to leave Boston. The guards had told Father that he and Kate could leave but not Colin or Larry. Dr. Milton convinced them that Larry's father was truly ill, that Larry was needed to show him the way to the farm, and that he needed Colin to assist him.

They'd been driving a long time when Kate looked across the river toward Boston. She could see campfires on the common and candlelit windows, but darkness pressed all around them. A lantern swung from each side of the carriage roof, helping light the way for the horses. The night sounds of owls, insects, and toads kept them company.

Colin pointed out two lights, higher than any others, to Dr. Milton and Kate. "Someone must have hung lanterns in the tower of Christ Church," he said. "Isn't that strange?"

CHAPTER 17

War!

When they arrived at the farmhouse, Dr. Milton grabbed his black bag. "Colin, help Larry with the horses. See that you're quick about it. Bring the medicine chest."

Kate had been worrying about something all the way from Boston. Mr. Revere had told them not to tell anyone else Lieutenant Andrews's secret, but the silversmith hadn't known she and Colin would be leaving town that night, traveling the very road the British would likely travel to reach Concord. He hadn't known Kate and Colin would be at a farmhouse just outside Lexington, the town the Redcoats would have to pass through on their way.

Larry was helping Colin unhitch Dr. Milton's horses from the carriage. Kate took the opportunity to whisper into Colin's ear. Colin nodded, then took a deep breath, and turned to Larry. "Larry, can you get a message to the minutemen around here?"

Larry's hands froze on the reins. "Tonight?"

Colin nodded, darting a look over his shoulder at the farmhouse. Kate's father had already gone inside. Colin told

Larry Lieutenant Andrews's secret while they took the horses to the barn to be fed, watered, and brushed down.

"Guess I'm not too surprised," Larry said. "This afternoon the minutemen were called to Lexington Green when British officers were spotted on the roads. When none of our lookouts saw troops coming, the men were sent home."

He grinned at Kate and Colin across the horse's back. "If the redcoats are figurin' to find any guns at Concord, they're goin' to be mightily disappointed."

"Why?"

"Paul Revere warned the Concord Patriots on Sunday that the redcoats were beginnin' to act a might suspicious, pullin' men off duty to train. Concord seemed the likely place for the redcoats to head. The Massachusetts Congress was meetin' there. Would've been easy for Gage's men to arrest all the most powerful Patriot leaders in Massachusetts. Then, too, it's the nearest place to Boston with a good supply of ammunition and guns."

"How do you find out so much, Larry?"

"Livin' in the country isn't like livin' in Boston. We don't have redcoats tellin' us what we can and can't do and livin' in our houses. We don't have to worry 'bout the redcoats overhearin' us if we talk 'bout Patriot doin's. Sunday I visited cousins in Concord. We had a grand time hidin' things."

"Hiding what things?"

"Ammunition and guns, of course." He snorted. "The redcoats will never find them. We dropped bags of bullets in the swamps, and we buried the cannons in a farmer's field."

Kate and Colin burst out laughing at the thought of a farmer plowing over cannons.

When the horses were cared for, Larry saddled his father's only other horse. Then he raced toward the house to check on his father. Soon he was back carrying an old squirrel gun.

"We'll stop those redcoats," he told the children. He swung himself up onto his horse's back. "Thanks for the warnin', friends."

He was off. Would he warn the minutemen in time to truly stop the redcoats?

Father frowned at the children when they finally went inside. "I thought I told you to hurry." He didn't waste time with more scolding. Instead, he quickly told Colin what was wrong with Larry's father. He was going to operate, and Colin would need to help. "You can make yourself useful, as well, Kate, by handing me things as I need them."

Father took instruments from his black bag and laid them on the kitchen table, where he'd be operating. Kate pulled off her cloak and wrapped one of her father's black aprons over her dress to protect the blue homespun from getting spattered with blood.

The fireplace's heat warmed away the chill from their night ride. Like all kitchen fireplaces, it was as wide as she was tall and almost as high. Kate could smell cornmeal mush cooking slowly in the large black kettle hanging from a crane over the low flames. The smell reminded Kate that she hadn't eaten since noon, and her stomach growled. There was no time to think of food now, though.

Hours later, about two in the morning, when a horse's hooves were heard slamming against the dirt farm lane, Colin and Dr. Milton didn't even look up from their patient. Kate, however, was weary from holding the lantern high so that her father could see. Larry's mother took it from her hand to let her rest, and Kate stepped out onto the front porch to breathe the night air. A moment later, the hoofbeats drew nearer. With a thrill, Kate heard a man call, "The redcoats are coming! Patriots turn out!" Then the sound of hooves headed back down the lane.

When she stepped back inside, her father had paused in his work. In the light of the lantern, he looked across the wooden table at Colin. Kate saw Colin look back at him without saying a word. Then they both went back to work. The redcoats and minutemen might be planning to meet, but Kate knew they both agreed that their duty now was to save the man in front of them.

Kate's head was starting to nod when a sharp noise startled her awake. Colin's head jerked up as well.

"Gunfire!" Father exclaimed. "The locals must be waking the countryside, letting them know the redcoats are coming."

Soon they heard a bell ringing. Larry's mother said it was the bell from a church at Lexington, another way to wake the people. Before long other church bells from nearby villages joined in. The gong of bells kept up all night.

Kate's father drew the last stitch at about four in the morning, closing the operation. Larry's father was still alive. Kate knew he was still in danger, though. Many people died from surgery because of infections.

Larry's mother gave them cornmeal mush for breakfast. To pay for the operation, she gave Dr. Milton a large smoked ham. Colin put it in the trunk the doctor kept on the back of his carriage, while Larry's mother wrapped in rags three stones she'd heated in the fireplace. Kate, Colin, and Father placed them at their feet in the carriage to ward off the cold morning air.

They were on the road before four-thirty. Dogs barked and howled. Church bells still sounded through the darkness. Candles lit farmhouse windows, and they weren't the only ones on the road. Men on foot and horseback were hurrying toward Lexington.

"Fools," Father muttered, slapping the reins against the horses' flanks. "Don't they know better than to anger the king's troops?"

Neither Kate nor Colin answered. Kate gripped the edge of the carriage seat, swaying as the horses moved along the rutted road only a little faster than a walk. They had sixteen miles back to Boston. Kate knew her father didn't want to tire the horses too soon.

When they neared Lexington Green, where Kate and Colin had watched the minutemen practice months before, the gray sky of dawn revealed the shadows of men in front of the meetinghouse. The road ran alongside the green, and beyond the meetinghouse, Kate saw a dark column moving closer, growing larger and larger. "Redcoats!" she whispered.

Father urged his horses to the side of the road, beneath a large tree beside a rock wall. They would have to wait until the redcoats passed to continue.

A drum began its *rat-a-tat-tat*. They heard the captain order the minutemen to fall in. The men formed two lines in front of the meetinghouse. There were only about seventy of them, Kate guessed—farmers and craftsmen from the way they were dressed. About forty townspeople looked on from doorways and windows and behind stone walls.

Was Larry with the minutemen? Kate wondered, leaning forward on the seat to see better in the dim light. The lanterns still swung from the carriage top, but they were no help any longer. Colin lifted the glass sides and blew out the candles.

Two men hurried behind the minutemen carrying a trunk. Kate recognized one of them: Paul Revere. So he'd made it out of Boston to warn the countryside after all. Maybe Larry's warning hadn't been needed.

"Let the redcoats pass. Don't fire unless you're fired upon!" the captain called to his men.

A moment later, the redcoats marched past the meetinghouse and onto the green. "There are a lot more redcoats than minutemen!" Colin said.

Father nodded grimly. "Even the most hotheaded rebel wouldn't be foolish enough to fight against such odds."

Colin nudged Kate and pointed out Major Pitcairn, who was quartered with Paul Revere's neighbors. He was one of the redcoats' leaders.

The redcoats stopped about 150 feet from the Patriots. Major Pitcairn rode up to the minutemen, his sword drawn. "Ye rebels, disperse! Lay down your arms! Why don't ye lay down your arms?"

There was a flash of gunpowder, the roar of a musket. Then another and another!

Colin leaped to his feet, setting the carriage rocking, but Kate cringed against her father's shoulder. She couldn't tell who had fired first. Now both sides were firing! Gunpowder smoke filled the air.

Some minutemen scurried away, dodging redcoats' musket balls and bayonets. Some hid behind trees and walls or headed toward nearby buildings. Others stayed where they were. The redcoats hurried after the minutemen. Bodies were falling from the musket fire! A minuteman not much older than Colin was hit in the chest with a musket ball. He crawled away, bleeding heavily. Kate knew she was going to be sick. Her father put his arm around her while she leaned out the carriage window.

Major Pitcairn whirled his horse around. His sword flashed as he brought it down in a motion Colin knew meant to stop firing. But the redcoats didn't stop firing! Minutemen shot from the green, from behind a stone wall, and from nearby buildings.

Horrified, Kate watched a redcoat jam the bayonet on the end of his musket into a fallen Patriot. Her stomach lurched again.

Major Pitcairn fell with his horse. Had the friendly officer been hit? Kate breathed a sigh of relief when the major stood. His horse had been hit, though.

A musket ball whizzed over the carriage, and Father yanked the children out of the carriage. "Get behind the stone wall!" he ordered. He followed them, keeping hold of the horses' reins, which wasn't easy. The bays tried to bolt, frightened by the muskets.

Minutemen raced to get away from the redcoats. Some fled down a road. Most crossed a swamp to reach safe land.

Only minutes had passed when the fighting ended. Kate's anger boiled over as the redcoats cheered. How could they cheer killing and hurting people? Their officers struggled to get the troops in order again. Only one or two redcoats had been wounded and none killed. Soon the cheerful troops set off down the road toward Concord.

Father grabbed his black leather bag. "We'd best see if we can help any of these foolish rebels."

The children followed him. Already some of the wounded were being carried to nearby homes and Buckman's Tavern. The man Kate had seen bayoneted was dead. So was the young man she'd seen crawling away. In all, eight men were dead. Kate was glad to see Larry wasn't among them. Nor was Larry one of the ten wounded.

Kate clung to her father's sleeve, trying her best not to be sick again. If she truly wanted to be a healer, she knew she could not let such sights frighten her. She had often helped her father treat patients with illnesses and broken bones. She'd seen her share of blood and dying. But she had never seen violence like this.

It's the wounded who are important, not me, she told herself again and again. She made herself watch carefully as her father used a steel probe to find musket balls, then used a bullet extractor—shaped much like scissors—to remove them. Someday, she told herself, she might have the opportunity to do this herself. After the musket balls were removed, Dr. Milton let Colin put plasters from the medicine box on the wounds. Then Kate bound them up with strips of material she ripped from her petticoats.

They were there for hours, first helping the wounded, then eating lunch at Buckman's Tavern. While at lunch, they were surprised when Colin's father and Harrison joined them, guns in their hands. They found out that Uncle Jack and Harry had been staying at a farm near Lexington since leaving Boston. The Langs had fought on Lexington Green!

Harry looked pale. "The man next to me was killed by the redcoats. He never fired a shot. One minute he was alive and the next he was dead. You were right, Colin, when you said it's easier to kill a man than to keep him alive."

Suddenly a man rushed in. "Redcoats are headed back this way! Concord's men are chasin' them! Patriots turn out!"

Harry and Uncle Jack grabbed their guns and jumped up. "We have to go," Uncle Jack said. "Tell your mother we're safe, Colin. We'll be in touch."

Kate's heart sank as they ran into the tavern hallway and out the front door. If they kept fighting, would they ever see them alive again?

Father pushed his chair back from the table. "We had best make ourselves useful, Colin." He looked at his daughter. "I want you to stay here, Kate. We'll bring the wounded back here, and you can help us then—but your mother would never forgive me if I didn't do my best to keep you out of harm's way."

Kate could tell from his face that there was no point arguing. Her heart racing, she watched from the tavern window as they rode away. Before long, they were back with the carriage full of wounded men. After that, Kate was too busy to be afraid.

"Hello, Kate."

Kate looked up in surprise from the wound she was bandaging. The wounded man she knelt beside was Lieutenant Andrews! A musket ball had hit him in the thigh.

Lieutenant Andrews told them a bit of what happened at

Concord. The town militia had treated them politely, escorting them into town with drums and fifes. But when Major Pitcairn ordered his men to destroy a bridge, fighting started.

When the redcoats headed back to Lexington along the tree-lined road, the minutemen and other colonials had kept up a constant fire. The redcoats had been sitting ducks in the middle of the road while the minutemen shot from behind trees, bushes, fences, and sometimes from houses.

"We didn't stand a chance," Lieutenant Andrews said, gritting his teeth against the pain as Dr. Milton removed the musket ball. "Many of our soldiers have been killed or wounded."

So the redcoats have "won" the battle on Lexington Green, Kate thought, *but the Patriots are "winning" the rest of the battle. The Patriot who had shot Lieutenant Andrews will never know that the officer had tried to help the Patriots by telling Colin and her the redcoats' plans,* Kate thought as Colin and her father moved on to another wounded man. The sound of musket fire and shouting continued while they worked.

"There will be no turning back now," Father said grimly late that afternoon as they were finally riding home.

Questions ran through Kate's mind. What would happen next? How many minutemen and redcoats would die or be maimed? What would happen between friends and families who were on opposite sides of the conflict? How would the redcoats treat Patriots in Boston? Would the Patriots be safe?

The time Kate had dreaded for so long had come. She gripped the edge of the seat until her fingers hurt.

"It's a war now," Colin said softly. "Will I have to fight?"

Dr. Milton sighed. "Not yet. You're still a boy. But if the

war lasts another year or two, it's very likely you'll be called on to fight. You'll be a man, after all."

Another year or two of fighting? Kate gasped at the words. Surely, it couldn't last that long!

"I'm not sure I'm ready."

Kate's father smiled a little. "To be a man or to fight? You've no choice in one and little in the other."

Colin lifted his chin. "If I have to fight, I'll have to carry a gun, but I want to carry a doctor's tools, too. Maybe I can be a doctor's helper for the army. Will you teach me all you can?"

"Me, too, Father?" Kate looked up into her father's face. "I can be useful." She had learned something today: Battlefields were places of killing, but they were places of saving lives, too. "Plenty of women are healers. You'll need all the help you can get."

Her father looked down at her. Then he sighed. "I'm afraid you're right, Kate. But I can make no promises now. I'm too weary. We need to get you home to your mother."

Kate leaned her head on her father's shoulder. The months ahead would be frightening ones, she knew. But everything she had seen today convinced her even more that she wanted to play her part.

I know I'm only a little girl, she thought sleepily, *but God, please make me useful.*

As her eyes sank shut, she was certain that one way or another, God would answer her prayer.

Betsy's River Adventure

Veda Boyd Jones

A Note to Readers

While the Lankford and Miller families are fictitious, their journey from Boston to Cincinnati mirrors the experiences of hundreds of families during the early 1800s. When the British, who were fighting against Napoleon in Europe, began kidnapping American sailors and illegally forcing them to work on British warships, President Jefferson ordered all American ports on the East Coast closed.

As a result of this action, merchants, shipbuilders, and the businesses who provided supplies for them went out of business. Rather than go through years of unemployment, many families moved to Pittsburgh, Cincinnati, and other growing cities in the interior of America to start new lives. While some of the young Americans who had been captured by the British managed to escape and some were eventually released, many others simply disappeared and their families never learned what happened to them.

For Marshall, Morgan, Landon, and Jennifer,
with love

Contents

❧ CHAPTER 1 ❧

The Plan

"Cincinnati!" Betsy Miller wailed to her friend Mary. "It might as well be the moon."

"As if someone could go there," Mary said with a sniff.

The two girls huddled in heavy cloaks on their favorite pier at Boston Harbor and watched the waves. A few boats bobbed on the water a mile or so out.

"Father says a frontier town like Cincinnati could use a doctor, but I don't think that's the reason we're going. I think it's because Uncle Paul wants to go, and he's talked Father into it. With the embargo, there isn't much shipbuilding going on, and he needs work."

Betsy glanced down the wharf. The shipyard where Paul Lankford had worked was unnaturally silent. The cold sea wind whipped her hair into her eyes, and she pushed back the brown curly locks. She wrinkled her nose at the fishy smell on the brisk breeze.

"But why Cincinnati?" Mary asked. "I thought Pittsburgh was where riverboats were built."

"I don't know why. All they said was we were going as soon as arrangements were final. They've been planning this for months, but they just told me. And, of course, George is going." Of all her relatives, George Lankford was her least favorite. He was only eleven, two years her junior, but he was a good foot shorter than she was, and he never let her forget that she was extremely tall for a girl.

"How's the weather up there?" he'd ask every time she saw him, which was frequently since their parents were close friends as well as family.

The teasing was one thing, but he was also her exact opposite. While she was shy, he was outgoing and impatient with her reluctance to speak or act upon a situation until she had studied it. Answering the teacher's questions in school dismayed her, but George would wave his hand to get the teacher's attention.

It had taken her two years to become good friends with Mary, and now she was being jerked out of a comfortable situation and thrown into a new place where she'd know no one. She'd have to make new friends. George told her it would be a great adventure. Betsy thought of it as torture.

"Do you think you'll see wild Indians?" Mary asked.

"I fear we will. We'll probably be scalped before we reach Ohio," Betsy said with a shudder. "I don't want to go. I don't want to be constantly badgered by George. He delights in embarrassing me."

Betsy shook her head, remembering the time George had taken her lunch pail and put it on the shelf at the front of the schoolroom. He'd had to move a chair over and climb up, but she had easily reached it from her standing height. The other students had watched her face turn as red as a burning hot coal. They'd laughed, and she'd grabbed her pail and run back to her desk. She'd sat staring down at her desk while school went on around her.

"What you ought to do is get him back. Embarrass him," Mary suggested. "Let's go over to my house. It's getting colder."

Betsy nodded and got to her feet, but she still looked out at the water. It was probably useless—this vigil she kept of going to the pier every day to look out toward the sea. Her cousin Richard was an American sailor who had been kidnapped and forced into naval service by the British over a year ago. It was unlikely that he would be released while the Napoleonic War still raged, because the British needed good sailors like Richard. Hundreds of American young men had been impressed, as they called it. Their families had no idea where they were or if they still lived.

Betsy felt powerless to help Richard, but going to the harbor made her feel closer to the older cousin who had always been kind to her and who had taught her to play the violin. Her gaze swept the harbor one final time; then she turned away from the water.

The girls trudged to Mary's one-story frame house and sat by the fireplace with their hands and feet stretched out toward the warming flames. Betsy had suggested they meet at the pier since it was where the girls had spent many hours talking in the summer, confiding in each other and watching the ships. It seemed fitting that she break the news of the move there where they could be alone.

Now she heard the clatter of dishes as Mrs. Stover worked

in the kitchen. In one corner of the big room, Mary's younger brothers argued over some wooden blocks. The baby cooed in a cradle near the fire. Mary rocked the cradle with her foot as they talked. "What did you mean about getting even with George?" Betsy asked.

"I don't know. Do things to him like he's doing to you."

"It's not possible to embarrass George Lankford. Besides, he's not short for his age; I'm just tall for mine." At five-foot-nine, she towered over everyone in the school. Only one eighth-grade boy came close, and he was a half inch shorter. Her mother told her that she was having her growth spurt early and the others would catch up, but that wasn't much solace now.

"You wouldn't tease him about his height. You'd have to pick something that bothers him."

Something that bothers him. That will take some thinking.

"You could play all kinds of tricks on him on the trip," Mary said. "But you have to promise to write and tell me all about them."

"Promise," Betsy said, looking down at her hands. This had possibilities, but something kept niggling at her mind, resisting the plan. "This wouldn't be the Christian thing to do, would it, Mary? Pastor would say it was wrong."

"Isn't what George is doing to you wrong?" Mary argued. "If he does unto others as he wants them to do unto him, then he wants to be teased."

"I suppose you're right, although that seems a little backward. Still, I ought to teach him a lesson so he'll stop this. Mother says if you do something over and over, it gets to be the normal thing for you to do, even if it's something bad. If I don't stop George from teasing, he'll be doing it to everybody."

"Exactly."

But what could she do to him? Betsy pondered while she walked home in the shivering cold. A cloud blanketed the sun, and the late Saturday afternoon seemed dismal, matching her mood.

She opened her front door to be met by none other than the object of her thoughts.

"Hey, Betsy," George called with his head tilted back and his hands cupped around his mouth. "How's the weather up there?"

She ignored him. After all, what reply could she give that wouldn't call even more attention to herself? As it was, the grown-ups in the parlor were all staring at her. Her parents, George's folks, and Richard's mother and father had stopped talking.

"Betsy, I'm glad you're back," her mother said. "We're discussing the move." Betsy had always wondered how her petite mother had married such a tall man. Betsy's father, Dr. Thomas Miller, measured in at six feet three inches, and she figured she must have taken after him. He was an awesome figure of a man—one who commanded respect.

He now spoke in a deep baritone voice. "We've booked passage on the schooner *Columbia* from Boston Harbor and up the Delaware River to Philadelphia. We'll depart Wednesday, March 4. At Philadelphia we'll ship our belongings on freight wagons to Pittsburgh. Then we'll take the stagecoach."

George's father continued their itinerary. "We'll work together to build a large flatboat at Pittsburgh. I've heard there are many swindlers who sell boats that use inferior wood or who don't caulk the joints correctly. We'll be using that wood to build our houses, and we want the best." His recitation sounded as if it were his side of a discussion that had been held earlier.

"We may be in Pittsburgh several weeks while we build the boat," Father continued. "Then we'll float down the Ohio River to Cincinnati. That shouldn't take but a couple of weeks, since it's all downstream. By the time we get there, school will not be in session, but Mother will help you with lessons, and you can start again in the fall in a new school."

He looked kindly at Betsy as if he knew how important school and books were to her. There had been times when she had thought of them as her only friends. Of course she had a copy of the Bible, which she had read cover to cover. She also had copies of four Shakespeare plays and a slim volume of poetry.

"I understand there's a library in Cincinnati," Mother added.

That surprised Betsy. She had thought there would be Indians. A library was a civilizing touch to a frontier area she considered beyond the outskirts of the United States. Oh, she knew Ohio was a state in the new country, but that didn't mean it was a place she wanted to go.

"I'm sure it will be fine," she said. It wasn't as if her opinion really mattered. The adults must have made all the plans months ago, but she'd only been told about it the night before. She noticed the papers Father held. He'd probably gotten the tickets. March 4. In a week and a half, they'd be on their way to Cincinnati.

Uncle Charles and Aunt Martha, her cousin Richard's parents, were staying in Boston. They would keep vigil until their son was released from the illegal British impressment or they found out what had happened to him. And they would be in Boston to welcome him home should he return from the war. Betsy tried to push that worry from her mind.

"It'll be great," George said. "Jefferson and I are going to fight Indians."

"The Indians are friendly," Father assured the boy.

"Jefferson is moving, too?" Betsy asked in alarm. She couldn't stand George's dog. George had wanted to name the dog Thomas, but Betsy's father didn't like the idea of sharing his first name with a pup. So George had settled for Jefferson.

"You can't think I'd leave Jefferson behind," George said as he jumped, trying to touch the top of the door frame that led into the kitchen.

Betsy sighed in disgust. Now she'd have to put up with that dog as well as with George. She didn't know which was worse. The dog always sniffed around her heels, calling attention to her. But then George delighted in making her the center of attention, too. Those two belonged together. And she was going to get them both.

Mary's suggestion that Betsy get even with George was sounding better and better. In the next ten days before her family left Boston for good, she and Mary would have to map out the plan.

The next few days flew by. Betsy continued to go to school, but in the evenings she helped her mother pack.

"We can't take everything with us," Mother said. "We're going to let Pastor have this bed. His family's growing by leaps and bounds."

"This is my bed," Betsy said. "What will I sleep on?"

"We'll get something else in Cincinnati. We'll take the big bed because my grandfather brought it from England. It was my mother's, and she gave it to me."

They sold some of their belongings, gave other things away, and the rest they packed in wooden crates and trunks.

The day before departure arrived, Betsy and Mary, arm in arm, walked home from school.

"Have you come up with any ways to get George?" Betsy asked.

Mary grinned mischievously. "We have to stop by my house; then I'll walk you home." When they reached her home, she ran inside and reappeared a minute later with a cloth-wrapped package. She held it out to Betsy.

"What's this?"

"Smell it," Mary said.

Betsy unwrapped the bundle. Her nose wrinkled before she could rewrap it. "Whoo! What is this?"

"Limburger cheese. I got it from a peddler on Beacon Street. If you unwrap it and put it with George's clothes, they'll all smell terrible." She laughed.

"How will that embarrass him?"

"Nobody will want to be around him. He always wants to be the center of attention, and that will take care of that."

Betsy nodded and stuck it in her empty lunch pail. She could still smell the stuff. That would get George. "Thanks. Got any other ideas?"

"You'll have to come up with them as you go. Who knows what will happen on your trip? I wish I were going with you."

"Me, too." They had reached Betsy's house, and they stood in the cold wind. Betsy didn't know how to say good-bye to her friend.

"I have a secret," Mary said. "Promise you won't tell."

"Who could I tell? I'm leaving."

"The embargo President Jefferson declared makes Father angry. I heard him tell Mother that the store will go out of business if he doesn't get some goods from England to sell, and that's not going to happen as long as the ports stay closed. He said there were opportunities on the frontier. He mentioned Ohio."

"Do you think you'll move west?" Betsy whispered in awe. Could it really happen? Would her best friend move to Cincinnati, too?

"I don't know. But don't be surprised if someday I knock on your door and say, 'Remember me?' Wouldn't that be something?"

"Mary, that would be the greatest thing. Once we get settled, I'll go to the river every day and look at the boats and pray that you're on one of them." In a way it would take the place of going to the harbor to look for Richard.

The two girls hugged, and then Betsy hurried inside the empty house. Their belongings had been taken to the schooner earlier that day, and all that was left was bedding.

After a sleepless night spent on the floor, Betsy and her parents arose at dawn and made last-minute preparations for the trip. Betsy carried blankets, Richard's violin, and her lunch pail, which secreted the awful-smelling cheese.

"I have a surprise," Father said. As they walked toward the dock, he paused at the livery stable. "I've decided to take Silverstreak with us. If George can have Jefferson on board, surely we can take our mare.

Betsy hugged him. "Oh, Father. I hadn't even hoped that we could take Silverstreak. I couldn't bring myself to tell her good-bye." Together they went inside the stable and bridled the horse. Mary, books, the violin, and Silverstreak were all Betsy's dearest friends. She was taking three of them with her, and maybe Mary would show up someday, too.

Betsy shifted her load of blankets to the mare's back, and they walked on toward the *Columbia*. The *clomp* of Silverstreak's hooves on the planks of the dock was a reassuring sound to Betsy. She led the horse onto the ship and to the special roped-off section one of the crew showed her. She was tying the mare to a pole when she heard George's voice behind her.

"We won't have to send a sailor up the mast. We'll just ask you when you sight land again," he said.

She ignored him.

"You bringing that horse?" he asked.

She glanced at him. "Of course. Father will need her when he makes calls on patients."

Jefferson ran up to Betsy and sniffed her feet. The small brown dog came upon the pail she had set down and shied away from it, backing right into Silverstreak's makeshift stall. The horse reared; the dog yelped and ran to George.

"Keep your horse away from my dog," George said.

"Keep your dog away from my horse," Betsy said.

A tight smile crossed Betsy's face, and she glanced at the lunch pail that held the stinky cheese. This trip just might be fun.

⌒⌒ CHAPTER 2 ⌒⌒

The Journey Begins

Betsy stood at the rail and watched the sailors on the wharf make last-minute preparations to cast off. Lines were tossed to sailors in longboats who strained as they rowed, pulling the ship out to sea. Betsy and George had been warned to stay out of the way of the crew, who were scurrying between the two masts and readying the sails. Betsy had counted twenty-three other passengers, but none of them were children.

Betsy's mother came up behind them. "Did you put the blankets in the stateroom?"

"Yes, Mother." Betsy had already been below deck to her family's small stateroom. Although the schooner line that ran the regular route between Boston and Philadelphia advertised the accommodations as elegant, Betsy would have argued with that description. It was a stark room that smelled bad, but they wouldn't be on the boat for long. She wished they were already in Philadelphia, and she wished they weren't going at all.

"It will be a better life," her mother said, as if to herself.

"Mother?" Betsy glanced down and saw tears in her mother's eyes. Didn't she want to go, either?

Mother took a deep breath and lifted a hand in farewell to Uncle Charles and Aunt Martha, who stood on the dock. As the ship shifted beneath them, Mother said, "We are leaving your brothers here."

"Oh, Mother." Betsy's three stillborn brothers had been buried in the churchyard. Many times she had wondered what her life would be like if her brothers had lived. The house wouldn't have been as quiet, of that she was sure. It would have been more like Mary's house with constant activity and noise. Betsy hugged her mother's petite frame.

"I know their spirits are with God," Mother whispered. "But this is hard."

Betsy swallowed back tears, but a few found their way down her cheeks. She'd tried to be strong about this move, but now that her mother had let her emotions show, Betsy couldn't hold her tears at bay.

"Is it raining up there? On our big day?"

Betsy stared hard at George, who looked as if he was uncomfortable with all the crying. She almost felt sorry for him. Even though he had referred to her height again, he sounded as if he were trying to cajole her out of her sadness. Maybe she should reconsider her plan of getting back at him.

"George is right. Today is no day for tears. We're starting a new adventure, Betsy. And we should start it with glad hearts." Mother kissed her and moved down the rail to stand by Father.

Betsy gazed back at the wharf and at Richard's folks, who were growing smaller by the minute as the schooner moved away from shore. They had always been kind to her, just like their son. When Richard had first gone to sea, he'd entrusted his prized violin to Betsy's keeping, telling her to keep practicing while he was gone. She'd offered it back to his parents when she found out about her move to Cincinnati, but they'd both said Richard had wanted her to keep playing.

"When Richard returns, he can travel to Cincinnati to get it back," Aunt Martha had said. "Maybe we'll come with him."

She'd said "when" Richard returned, not "if" he returned. Betsy wanted to have the same faith that Richard would return from this war that shouldn't even involve their country.

Jefferson tugged on the hem of her skirt, and she looked away from the receding shore and toward the pesky dog. "Keep that dog away from me."

George jerked at the line that held the dog, and Jefferson yelped. Curious sailors glanced their way as they adjusted the sails that had caught the wind. They spared a quick look at George but seemed to study Betsy. She just knew they were staring at her because she was so tall.

"I'm going below," she told George and stepped carefully across the deck toward the steep stairs that led to the staterooms. Once in the safety of her room, she picked up the violin case and drew out the lovely instrument and the bow. She finished one slow, melancholy song that fit how she was feeling then forced herself to strike up a bright tune to lift her mood.

Mother was right. She should look on this move as an adventure. Once she had hit the last quick note, she put away her violin with a new resolve and made her way to the top deck to check on Silverstreak. She'd heard that some animals didn't take to the motion of the boat, and she hoped the mare wasn't suffering any pangs. Certainly motion sickness hadn't affected Jefferson.

Cold wind whipped at her hair and pushed her long skirt against her legs as she crossed from the stairwell opening toward the makeshift stall. Now that they had left the bay, wind that had been blocked by land filled the sails, and the ship cut a sharp line through the water.

"Betsy!"

She turned and sidestepped just in time to avoid being hit by George as he swung on a rope that dangled from a crosspiece on the mast. He swayed back and forth like a pendulum and let out a loud whoop.

"You rapscallion!" a sailor yelled. "Let go of that line!"

"George, what are you doing?" Betsy grabbed the rope to stop the motion while George held tightly to the end. "You'll cause a shipwreck!"

George dropped to the deck with a thud. "I was just seeing if I could swing. I didn't hurt anything."

"Don't touch these lines," the sailor ordered. Betsy grabbed George by the arm and dragged him along with her toward Silverstreak's stall. Her face burned from the confrontation, even though she wasn't the one who'd done something wrong. "We're going to be on this ship for four days. You'd better stay out of trouble."

George edged around the stall and took a defensive stance, feet shoulder width apart, head cocked back. "I was just looking around. I'm not hurting anything. Swinging on that rope wasn't going to cause a wreck. The worst it could do was move the sail, and it didn't. I tugged on the rope before I put my weight on it."

"Just be sure you don't cause any more alarm for those sailors. They already have their eyes on us. Father said to stay out of their way."

Betsy turned her attention to Silverstreak and stroked the horse's mane. The animal seemed to be taking the swaying motion of the ship without a problem. When Betsy looked back over her shoulder for George, he was gone. She shouldn't have to worry about him. Where were his parents anyway? She ducked around barrels and poles until she located her folks and George's. They were standing by the rail looking toward home. Betsy looked past them at the shoreline, which was barely a brown spot on the horizon.

If her second brother had lived, he would have been George's age. For the second time that day she wondered what her life would have been like if he had lived. Surely he wouldn't have been the rambunctious type like George, whose curiosity and eagerness were always making him the center of attention.

Seagulls cawed overhead. Betsy glanced up and watched them circle and occasionally dive in the water in search of fish. She pulled her cloak more tightly around her shoulders and found an unoccupied spot in the sun where she could sit with her back braced against a wooden box that also blocked the brisk wind. The sun felt warm as she watched the seascape. Waves broke against the ship and sprayed a fine mist on the edge of the deck but didn't reach her. Time passed slowly, and she felt herself slipping back into that melancholy mood again.

Betsy must have dozed off, for the next thing she knew, she was in the shade and the chill of March had settled inside her. The sun was higher in the sky than before, but they had changed directions. Father had told her they would tack many times, or they would go too far out to sea. She couldn't see any shoreline now but knew it couldn't be too many miles away. In her secluded spot, she could watch the activity of the sailors and study the passengers who were huddled in small groups here and there. The cold sent her down below, and she found her mother tidying their room.

"I was about to search for you, although it wouldn't take long to find you on a ship this size. Are you feeling better now?"

"Yes, Mother. And you?"

"I'm fine. Sometimes we have to let our feelings out so that we can move forward in life. I'm anxious to get settled in Cincinnati. Your father says it will hold many opportunities for us."

"Yes, Mother," Betsy said, although she had no idea what those opportunities would be.

"Did you pack something in your lunch pail for us? Our passage includes our meals, but I'm wondering how good the cook is." Her mother held the pail that secreted the stinky cheese, and Betsy quickly shook her head.

"No, I'll take that. Shall we join the others?" she asked in an effort to change the subject. They walked into the main cabin, which was dominated by a long table. Quiet conversations buzzed as the passengers ate the meal of stew and hard bread. George sat on the floor with some strangers at the far end of the room, which Betsy guessed was some thirty feet long. She ate quickly then returned to the stateroom with her mother.

"I had this trunk brought in here instead of stored with the others below," her mother said. "We might have use for it."

Betsy recognized the trunk and quickly unbuckled the straps. Inside, wrapped in clothes for safekeeping, she found her beloved books. *Macbeth* was on top, so she pulled it out, deciding she'd have lots of time for reading while they traveled to Philadelphia. The afternoon passed with her curled up in a dim corner, poring over the volume.

The next day passed while Betsy alternated between reading and sitting in the sun on the deck, watching the sky and the seagulls and the waves. Occasionally she'd catch a glimpse of land before the ship tacked and headed back to the open sea. Her father assured her the zigzag course was the straightest way the ship could travel south. George stayed out of her sight, and she decided to give up her plan of making him miserable. If he continued to avoid her, they'd get along just fine.

On the third day the sun failed to peek out from behind heavy clouds, and the wind howled around the sails. By midmorning snow fell heavily, disappearing into the water but piling up on deck. Betsy helped Father cover Silverstreak's stall with canvas to protect the horse. After that, the snow made the deck treacherous to walk on, so she merely stuck her head out from below deck to check on the horse.

Even with fewer sails up in an effort to control the ship's motion, many of the passengers got sick from the constant tossing of the ship. Betsy's mother and George's parents suffered seasickness, and Betsy stayed in the tiny stateroom to care for them. The ship sailed out of the storm by late afternoon, but that night few passengers sat at the long table.

Betsy coaxed weak tea down her patients' throats, and her father decided they would all sleep in the one room for warmth and so he could also help with the sick. Before bedtime, Betsy, her father, and George prayed for the recovery of the patients and for a safe journey's end. Betsy changed into her nightdress behind a curtain, laid down beside her mother, and pulled heavy quilts over them. George curled up in the corner with his dog.

After a restful night, Betsy awoke and reached for her traveling dress. It wasn't lying on the trunk where she had left it. A quick glance around revealed Jefferson curled up in it. "Give me my dress," she whispered, careful not to wake up the others. She and her mother had sewn the dress especially for the trip, and now that dog had shed hair all over it. She jerked on it and Jefferson gave it up with a sharp bark. Betsy stared at it in horror. The hem of her brand-new dress was in tatters where the dog had chewed on it in the night. She couldn't contain a squeal of anger.

"What is it, dear?" her mother asked in a voice that showed she was recovering.

"Jefferson has ruined my dress," Betsy said in a low tone.

"It wasn't his fault," George said. "He got cold in the night, so I covered him with it."

"Then it's your fault," Betsy said, turning on him.

"Let me see it," Mother said. She studied the torn places. "You can turn up the hem and conceal the holes. My sewing kit is in that trunk." Betsy rummaged in the trunk for the necessary items, while George and Father helped the patients into the main cabin for morning tea. Betsy turned up her hem three inches and stitched it, all the while plotting revenge on George and his dog.

She put on the dress and wished she had a looking glass, although she had a good idea what she looked like. In a few hours they would dock in the biggest city in the United States, and she would look like a tall gangly girl in a dress that she'd outgrown.

Once again George had managed to embarrass her. But it would be the last time. Somehow she had to get even. She'd teach him a lesson he needed to learn. She'd even the score.

CHAPTER 3

Betsy's First Chance

As the ship made its way up the Delaware River, Betsy marveled at the city around her. Almost fifty thousand people lived in Philadelphia, and it looked as if half of them were on the docks. Other ships were loading and unloading. They had already passed three ships that were headed out to sea or maybe up to Boston, she thought longingly for a moment, before thoughts of this huge city pushed her old home out of her mind.

Other passengers crowded the deck as they watched the city landscape pass by. Even Mother was topside. Although the afternoon wind was still freezing cold, the sea had calmed down, and Mother said the brisk air made her feel better.

"Betsy, as soon as we dock, take Silverstreak off and to the end of the wharf out of harm's way," Father said. "Keep George with you. Your uncle Paul and aunt Eleanor are still under the weather, and it'll take all their strength to make sure their belongings are unloaded and kept together without having to keep an eye on George as well."

Betsy nodded. She didn't want to leave the deck, but she slipped downstairs and got her violin and her lunch pail then returned to watch the sailors skillfully maneuver the ship into port.

"George, stay with me," she ordered.

George's eyes shone with excitement—or maybe it was mischief she saw in his bright eyes, Betsy decided. As soon as the gangplank was in place, she untethered Silverstreak and led her off the ship. George held onto a rope he had tied around Jefferson's neck. The dog ran ahead as far as the eight-foot rope allowed.

They clomped across the wooden planks and onto the cobblestone street at the end of the wharf.

"Wait here," Betsy said.

"Look, black people," George said and pointed at a group gathered around a barrel.

"Pepper pot, smoking hot!" They hawked their wares.

"Here, hold Jefferson a minute. I want to see what they're selling."

George flung the rope into Betsy's hand before she had time to object, not that he would have listened. He rushed off toward the black people.

Betsy had seen a black person once in Boston but not up close. Through lowered lashes, she watched the encounter between George and the street sellers. They were talking to him, asking him questions. . .or was it the other way around?

She tied Silverstreak to a hitching post and was in the process of tying Jefferson to the same post when a wagon drawn by a pair of horses clopped by. One moment she held the dog's rope in her hand, and the next moment he was gone, barking and chasing the wagon. Riding at the back of the wagon was another dog.

"George!" Betsy yelled as she ran after the wagon. Who would have thought a wagon could travel so fast over the uneven cobblestones? Betsy splashed through a puddle where some of the stones had sunk. She glanced back to see that George was running behind her.

The wagon stopped farther along the wharf next to a pile of empty crates, and the driver hopped down and loaded a couple chests. Jefferson barked and climbed the pile of crates so that he was level with the other dog. One crate toppled as Jefferson climbed to another. His bark turned to a whine.

"Come down, Jefferson," George called a second before he climbed on a low crate. He reached for another one, but it teetered a moment and then fell.

"George, don't go up there," Betsy cried. "You'll fall. They can't hold you."

"How am I going to get Jefferson?" George retorted and edged toward another crate.

Jefferson was standing on a high crate, not moving. He seemed frozen in fear. The driver of the wagon had returned to his high seat and yelled, "Giddyup." The horses responded, and the wagon lurched away, with the dog barking a farewell at Jefferson.

Jefferson didn't bark back. He looked at George and put a paw out to move toward him, which dislodged another empty crate. It crashed to the ground, barely missing George, who still clung to his spot in the pile.

It serves them both right, Betsy thought. George shouldn't have run off, leaving Jefferson with her, and Jefferson was turning out to be as impetuous as his owner. She stepped back and assessed the situation. Was this her chance at getting back at the dog for chewing her dress? And at George for embarrassing her all those times?

No, this was a matter of the two of them getting hurt. It wasn't the same thing. Besides, Father had told her to watch after George, and she'd better fulfill that responsibility. She pushed a fallen crate over beside George.

"Step here, George, and climb down. If we build a couple steps, you should be able to get your dog."

George shot her a grateful look and followed her order. Once he was safely on the ground, he helped Betsy push a crate right below the area where Jefferson hovered, and she held it stable while George climbed on it.

It wasn't enough. Betsy found another crate that could be moved without bringing the whole pile down.

"I'll sit on the bottom crate and hold this one in place," she said. George climbed on the lower one, then carefully crawled onto the second crate. He stood and stretched for the dog, but he was still a good six inches short.

"Come here, Jefferson," he called, but the dog didn't move.

Betsy watched him cajole and plead with Jefferson, but it did no good. She looked around for another crate, but the two they had stacked were fairly unstable even with her holding on. She didn't want to do it. She couldn't do it, but did she have a choice?

"Come down," she ordered her younger cousin, sighing

impatiently. "I'll try to get him."

George quickly hopped down and took his place on the bottom crate.

"Hold this one tight," Betsy said as she crawled onto the second crate. She gingerly pulled herself to her full standing height.

"Tell him to face this way," she said.

George commanded his dog, but Jefferson didn't budge. Betsy reached for him and pulled his back end off the crate so that he had to shift his weight or fall. In an instant she had him in her arms.

"Jefferson!" George shouted as he jumped up to take the dog. The crate he'd been steadying tipped, and Betsy grabbed the one above it to avoid taking a tumble. She felt Jefferson slide in her grasp, and she held him as tightly as she could with one arm.

"Sit down!" she shouted.

George plopped back down and steadied the second crate until Betsy had climbed down, then he popped back up and took the frightened dog in his arms.

"Jefferson." He stroked his dog on the forehead. "Don't run away like that again. You should have stayed with Betsy."

"Richard's violin!" Betsy cried. In her haste to chase Jefferson, she'd left it next to Silverstreak's hitching post. She dashed back down the street toward the horse and sighed with relief when she spotted the violin case and her lunch pail exactly where she'd left them.

George, with Jefferson's lead rope wrapped around his hand, loped up behind her. "You run fast for a girl," he said.

She nodded. Since she'd hemmed her skirt up to hide the

holes Jefferson had created, she didn't have to hike up her skirt to run or even to walk. Not that she would forgive the dog for that.

"Father!" George yelled as their parents made their way toward the hitching post. "Betsy saved Jefferson's life," he declared in a loud voice that stopped other pedestrians, who turned to hear the story.

All eyes focused on Betsy, and she blushed crimson as George explained about the crates and the other dog. George had a flair for the dramatic, and once again he had made her the center of attention even when she'd done him a good turn.

"You should see her run," George said. "She's so tall she has a long stride."

If possible, Betsy turned even redder.

"That's wonderful, Betsy," Mother said. "Let's gather our things and start for the inn."

Betsy gave her mother a grateful glance as the small group of travelers picked up their possessions and walked on.

"What about Silverstreak?" Betsy asked Father.

"I'll get her to a stable as soon as we get your mother settled."

Mother's skin was still pale, and her step was slow as they walked the block to the inn where they'd be spending two nights.

As soon as Mother and Betsy were in their room, Father left them to attend to traveling matters. He promised Betsy he'd show her around the city later that day.

It was after the evening meal before Betsy and Father knocked on the door to the Lankfords' room at the inn. Father had decided to take George along on their tour of Philadelphia, despite Betsy's protest. The last thing she wanted was to share her father with George! But Father had insisted George's parents would appreciate the silence George's absence would allow.

"Are all the details taken care of?" George asked, when Father had answered all of Uncle Paul's questions and the threesome was on the street outside the inn. Before Father could answer, George yelled, "A lamplighter! Do you think he'd let me light one?"

He didn't wait for an answer but flew down the street to the side of the man climbing the ladder beside the lamppost.

"What do you use for fuel?"

Betsy could easily hear George's excited question, but she had to strain to hear the lamplighter answer, "Whale oil."

"It sure smells. Could I light one?"

George followed the lamplighter to three posts before the lamplighter let him light one. The poor lamplighter must have figured that was the only way to get rid of the boy.

"Father, why don't you order George to stay with us?" Betsy asked. She normally wouldn't question Father's judgment, but George was back to his old tricks, being the center of attention.

"Oh, he's a boy and just naturally curious. If I thought he was annoying the lamplighter, I'd stop him. He learns a lot by asking questions. He's a smart boy."

Betsy stopped and looked at her father. Was he disappointed that his only child was a daughter? Did he want her to be more forthright and less shy? She couldn't help her personality, could she? She would never speak to a stranger the way George had just done.

"Did you see me?" George asked when he returned to Betsy's side.

"Yes," was her only reply.

Father showed them the statehouse where the Constitution had been signed. He pointed out the University of Pennsylvania, too.

"The medical school here is excellent. I visited the Pennsylvania Hospital briefly today and talked to several doctors about new procedures. Have you thought about becoming a doctor, George?"

So Father did want a son! He wanted someone to follow his lead and become a doctor. Betsy's posture slumped, and she looked down at the street as they walked along.

"I want to make things," George said. "Maybe ships like my father makes. Or maybe new things that haven't even been invented yet."

"There's a whole new world out there," Father said, "and we're going to be a part of it."

Betsy wanted to be part of it, too, but she felt that Father was talking only to George, a boy—a curious boy. She listened inattentively during the rest of their walk and was glad when they returned to the inn for the night.

At sunrise the next morning, the Millers and the Lankfords stood under the willows near the navy yard with hundreds of other worshipers for the Reverend William Staughton's service. The pastor was fiery in his delivery of the sermon. He shouted about human failings. He thundered about God's love.

When he read a verse from Isaiah about God's treatment of Israel, he caught Betsy's attention. "When thou passest through the waters, I will be with thee; and through the rivers, they shall not overflow thee." Betsy knew he wasn't talking about their journey, but she took heart that God would be with them as they traveled. She dwelled on that while the pastor yelled about confessing. He roared about salvation. And he tore the air with his loud hallelujahs.

"He knows how to rile up a body," George said. He and Betsy followed behind their parents as they walked back to the inn.

"Yes, he's a powerful speaker," Betsy said. She much preferred the preacher at home who spoke more softly, but she had to agree that Pastor Staughton had reached a lot of people with his booming voice.

That was the biggest church service she had ever attended. No wonder it had been outside. A building couldn't hold that many people. And everyone had been quiet, so the preacher could be heard. Only the noise of the river had disturbed his words.

Betsy looked toward the Delaware River. Maybe Mother would let her go to the wharf this afternoon for a last look at the water that flowed to the sea—one of God's greatest creations. She shuddered at the thought that she might never see the ocean again.

CHAPTER 4

The Stinky Cheese

At daybreak the Millers and the Lankfords stood at the stagecoach office, loading their belongings onto the top of the stage. Betsy didn't trust the driver to safely anchor Richard's precious violin, so she stood in the doorway of the cab and leaned over the top.

"Move, George," she said. He had climbed all over the stage to inspect it and now sat on top in her way. He shifted a little, and Betsy secured the violin between bags.

"Take your valise," Paul Lankford instructed his son. "Here's another bag. Can you push it over there?"

Betsy ducked inside the cab. The interior of the stage allowed room only for passengers, and this time the six of them would be traveling alone. Even though George was small, there wasn't room for another person.

Betsy was appalled that Jefferson was allowed inside the coach with them. She sat beside the door and hoped George and his dog would be against the other door on the other side. That would be as far away from him as she could get in the cramped interior.

Within a few minutes everything was loaded. The driver came out of the stagecoach office with a satchel. "U.S. Mail" was printed on its side.

"He's putting it in the front boot, under the driver's box," George informed her. He had his foot on the passenger step, and of course he sat down on the bench seat directly opposite Betsy.

"Heyah," the driver yelled at the two teams of horses, and they were off.

George kept up a constant stream of chatter, pointing out landmarks they'd already seen as they rode across the uneven streets. Betsy figured he'd give a tree-by-tree description as they traveled the three hundred miles to Pittsburgh, but she watched the landscape move by, too.

Soon they approached the bridge over the Schuylkill River and awaited their turn to cross. The clomping of the horses' hooves echoed as they crossed the first long wooden expanse. Betsy had never been on a bridge this tall before, and she strained to see over the edge into the water below. George was hanging out the window.

"Look how high we are," he said. "How would you make a bridge like this?"

"In sections," his father answered. He poked his head out the other side of the stage. "Each arch is supported by stone piers. It's like a wharf, but it goes across the river instead of into the bay. It has to be tall enough to allow sailing vessels to pass underneath."

They were headed downhill now as they had crested the first arch, and Betsy braced herself against the window. Their descent was quick, but going up the steep second arch was a long process. By the time they had descended the final arch, Betsy was ready for level ground. As they rounded a curve and she could look back at the three arches, she saw another stagecoach on the bridge. Its passengers were walking across the bridge so the horses would have an easier pull.

Traveling was tiring, Betsy discovered. They jolted along at a fairly good clip on the turnpike, and every ten miles they stopped and paid a toll. Every time they stopped, George jumped out and let Jefferson run around. Betsy checked on Silverstreak, who was tied to the back of the stagecoach.

By dusk, Betsy was ready to scream. Jefferson had climbed all over her and everyone else. Good thing he was a little dog, but that didn't change her opinion of him licking her shoes and barking when they passed any wildlife or livestock. She tried to take a nap, but every time she'd nod off, they'd hit a bump and her head would hit the back of the cab.

She ached all over when they stopped for the night at an inn beside a toll booth. There weren't enough beds, since other travelers had stopped before them, so she claimed the floor with the quilts she'd used for cover in the cold coach. Next to her was Richard's violin and her lunch pail. Even with the lid on, the pail leaked whiffs of the putrid cheese. She was tired of carrying the pail, and she was ready to get on with the plan of keeping George from being the center of attention. Certainly today he had monopolized the conversation.

"We're going fast," he'd said after their third stop to pay the toll. "It won't take us long to get there."

"Eight days," Father had told him.

"It won't take us eight days at this speed," George had said.

"This is the easy part," Father said. "We're on level ground.

We have to cross the mountains."

"It may take us awhile going up, but coming down should be real fast," George had reasoned. "We could make it in seven days."

"You're using good logic," Father had said. "It does take longer to go up than come down, but the mountains will take longer than if we were on level ground, like now."

How could Father talk to George like that without yelling, "It'll take eight days! Now be quiet."

As she lay on the pallet on the floor of the inn, Betsy thought of how she could use the cheese. She doubted she could get it into George's valise without someone seeing her. However, she might be able to smear the cheese on the handles. When they loaded their belongings that morning, Uncle Paul had picked up the valise by the bottom and held it up so that his son could grab the handles. If they followed that pattern tomorrow, George would get smelly cheese all over his hands. Knowing George, he'd rub his hands on his clothes and make them smelly, too. Then he'd have to ride up with the driver in the cold wind. And he not only wouldn't be the center of attention, the silence in the cab without his chatter would give the others a welcome rest.

Betsy set the lunch pail near the fire so the cheese would soften in the night and fell asleep thinking that Mary would be pleased with her. When they got to Pittsburgh, Betsy would write to her friend and tell her how well the cheese worked.

Early the next morning, as soon as they had breakfasted, Betsy slipped outside with her gear. The temperature was nicer, more like spring, but the air still held a bit of winter's chill. She stowed the violin in the rear boot and set her lunch pail on the side of the stage that couldn't be seen from the inn. She stuffed the quilts and her cloak in the cab. She'd smear the cheese before she put on the bulky cloak, so it wouldn't get in her way, and she wouldn't soil it. The driver was hitching the horses, but he paid no attention to her. Where were the others? She stepped back into the inn.

"George, are you ready?" She couldn't see him in the dining room.

"He's out back getting Jefferson," her mother answered. "Could you carry this please? Your father is fetching Silverstreak, and I think we'd better hurry before our driver gets impatient."

Betsy picked up the bag. "I can carry another one. Is George's valise ready?"

"Why thank you, dear," Aunt Eleanor said. "It's right here." She pointed to it and then gathered her own belongings.

Betsy fairly skipped outside. This was better than the plan, but she didn't have much time. She heaved her mother's bag onto the luggage rack then disappeared behind the stage to do her duty on George's valise.

The smell of the cheese nearly gagged her. It had gotten stronger in the tightly closed pail. She quickly opened the package, careful to keep her hands on the packaging and not touch the moldy cheese. She smeared the handles with the soft cheese, and for good measure spread some on the top, too. Then she quickly ran to the bushes on the far side of the road and tossed the cheese. Mother and Aunt Eleanor were on the small porch, and Father, Uncle Paul, and George were coming around the side of the inn.

"Load them up," the driver called. Betsy giggled. She'd actually done it without being seen. She sauntered toward the group and petted Silverstreak while Father tied the horse to the back of the coach. Another stagecoach was loading behind them, and the driver yelled, "Load them up," again.

Betsy stood on the passenger step and started to climb into the cab, but Father stopped her. He'd come around to the side where George's valise sat on the ground.

"Find a place for this, Betsy," he said.

"But that's George's bag," she said. "Where's George?" She glanced inside the cab and saw George already in his normal seat, holding Jefferson.

"Hurry," Father said. He was holding the bag on the bottom and handing it up to her. He wrinkled his nose and glanced around as if looking for the source of the odor. What could she do? She froze.

"Betsy?"

She reached for the handle, trying to lift the bag with two fingers, but it was too heavy, and she had to take it from her father with a firm grip. She could feel the slimy cheese residue on her hand but held her breath and shoved the bag on top of the coach. The valise teetered, so she wedged her foot against the wheel rim and hoisted herself up to stuff the bag in place. At that moment the impatient horses shifted, causing the wheel to turn slightly. Betsy lost her foothold and pitched headlong onto George's bag.

She gagged and pushed herself off the luggage rack. The stuff was in her hair, on her face, on her hands. She screamed, and Father reached for her.

"Don't touch me," she shrieked and jumped off the stage. She whirled around and saw the others staring at her from inside the cab. She'd made herself the center of attention. *Stop,* she told herself. *Calm down.* She had to get the cheese off.

Father leaned toward her then backed away. "Betsy, what's that smell?"

"Limburger cheese," she mumbled and darted to the well at the side of the inn. She lowered the bucket and pulled it up, spilling cold water on her dress.

"Betsy, what have you done?" Mother had climbed out of the stage and stood beside her. "What is this in your hair?"

"Limburger cheese," Betsy said again, this time more plainly. She plunged her hands into the water and splashed some on her face, scrubbing at the cheese.

"You can't wash your hair now and travel all day with wet hair. You'd catch your death of cold," Mother said. "Where did you get this cheese?"

"On George's bag," Betsy said.

"George Lankford," Mother called toward the stage. "Get out here this minute."

"No, Mother. He didn't put it there. I did," Betsy said in a small voice.

"Load them up," the stage driver yelled.

"We've got to go," Mother said. "We'll straighten this out on the way."

They walked back to the stage, and Mother climbed inside. Jefferson barked and jumped out of George's arms and onto the narrow floor when Betsy sat down by the window.

"You stink," George said.

She ignored him.

Jefferson growled; then he howled, and he backed away from Betsy.

The stage lurched and pulled away from the inn, and the chaos inside the coach grew louder.

"Make Jefferson stop," Betsy commanded.

"He can't help it. You smell bad," George said.

Betsy glanced at the others. George's parents looked bemused. Father's nose was wrinkled, and his eyes were sharp on her. She couldn't bring herself to look at Mother. They were disappointed in her behavior, and they had a right to be.

"It was a harmless prank," Mother said in a loud voice to be heard over Jefferson's whining. "Where did you get the cheese?"

"I brought it from Boston." Betsy could have placed the blame on Mary, but that wasn't honest. Mary may have given her the cheese, but she hadn't forced her to use it. Betsy was already in big trouble. To lie would have made it worse. That was one of God's commandments, and Mother said to break one was a sin.

"You put it on George's valise?" Aunt Eleanor asked.

"Yes."

"Why?" Father asked.

What could she say? That George teased her too much, and she couldn't stand it anymore? That she wanted to make him pay? That Father really wanted a son and he was stuck with her? A too-tall gangly girl.

Jefferson let loose with a long howl and some short yaps, saving Betsy from answering.

"This can't continue," Mother said. "Thomas, would you ask the driver to stop? Betsy had better sit outside until she airs out."

"But, Mother," Betsy began then stopped. She deserved this. She deserved to be punished. And she couldn't stand the yelping of Jefferson anymore. At least sitting outside she'd be away from George and his dog.

Father hailed the driver who pulled up on the reins. The gruff fellow didn't look any too happy to have a smelly passenger sitting beside him on the driver's box, but he scooted over to make room for Betsy.

The March wind whipped against her, and she shivered into the quilt that she wrapped tightly around her, keeping her hands deep in the folds. She wished she could put on her hat, but with the cheese smell still in her hair, the hat would be ruined.

When they stopped to pay the first toll, George jumped out of the stage with Jefferson.

"How's the weather up there?" he called, but Betsy ignored him. She wallowed in her misery, and although her conscience argued with her, she vowed to find another way to teach George a lesson.

CHAPTER 5

The Embarrassing Horse Ride

At the end of the second day of travel, under the watchful eye of her mother, Betsy scrubbed the cheese off George's valise and apologized for playing what the family was calling her "harmless prank." She took a bath, washed her hair, washed her too-short traveling dress, and hung it in front of the inn's fireplace to dry.

The point of her whole ordeal with George was to make him as miserable as he'd made her by embarrassing her. And that plan was to get him isolated, to not let him be the center of attention that he seemed to thrive on. All she'd managed to do so far was embarrass herself. She sat in front of the fire and finger-combed her hair until the curly brown locks were dry.

"I'm sorry," she'd heard her mother say to Aunt Eleanor. "That action was so out of character for our shy Betsy. I don't know what got into her, but I'll talk to her."

And her mother did talk to her. It wasn't a discussion; it was a lecture about how unladylike her conduct had been. About how it wasn't the Christian thing to do to play pranks on George.

About how we must all get along on this trip. About right and wrong.

She knew all that. And she knew she had been wrong. The next time she planned how to get George, it would not involve other people.

How did George so effortlessly hurt her feelings? Did he plan those things out? Or was it a natural part of his personality to embarrass her? She would teach him to think more about other people's feelings. How exactly to do that escaped her for the moment, but she gave it a lot of thought as the journey continued.

The days of riding in the stage fell into a pattern. Part of the time they were walking, letting the horses pull the stage up the steep mountains without the added weight of passengers.

"We may as well have walked all the way to Pittsburgh," George complained.

"At least we're not carrying our bags," Betsy had pointed out to him, one of the few times she directed a sentence his way. Mostly she stayed to herself—out of George's way.

She missed Boston. She missed Mary. What would she be doing now? Did she go down to the harbor to look for Richard?

On Sunday, the group didn't observe a day of rest.

"I believe the Lord will understand that we must travel," Mother told Betsy. "Although He also must know how weary we are from the trip."

Father led an early worship service before they climbed back into the stage, and Betsy played a hymn on the violin. She found solace in her music, and she prayed that she would find a happy life in Cincinnati. She desperately needed a new friend.

"Today's the eighth day," George announced on Monday. "We'll get to Pittsburgh today, won't we?"

"We should," Father answered. He was still as patient as ever with George, to Betsy's dismay. "I suspect it will be early evening when we arrive."

George talked a blue streak the entire day. He asked about Pittsburgh, about building the flatboat, about where they would stay, and about when they would leave for Cincinnati.

But it was Betsy who spotted Pittsburgh first. The telltale sign was the haze of smoke that hung over the horizon.

"They have factories," Father said. "Lots of them—and they burn coal. That's what makes all that haze."

They were still a few hours from settling in for the night. They had to wait for their turn on the ferry that would take them into Pittsburgh where they'd stay in yet another inn.

All along the riverbank were little wooden huts. Children scampered around, shouting as they played tag. Their voices carried to the ferry dock and combined with the sound of hammering from across the river. It was quite a noisy din. Betsy's senses were reeling from the smoke and the noise. Pittsburgh wasn't the country town she had thought it would be. It reminded her of the manufacturing part of Boston. Would Cincinnati be like this, too?

Once they were settled at an inn for the night, Betsy fell into a deep sleep and awakened again to the clattering of hammers.

"What are they building?" she asked Mother at breakfast. Both families were grouped around the large table at the inn.

"Boats, of course, but there are a lot of foundries for ironwork, too. We'll explore today while your father and Uncle Paul make inquiries about the boat."

"Can I go to the stable and see Silverstreak?" This time Betsy turned to her father.

"That would be very helpful," he said and told her the name of the stable and gave her directions. "She could use a good grooming and some exercise, but that will have to wait. Your uncle Paul and I want to see if there are some adequately built flatboats before we make lumber purchases to build our own."

"Can I go with you?" George asked.

"It would be best if you stayed with the women today," his father replied. "Once we start building, you'll be part of the crew."

"If we build," Father said, "it will take awhile, and we won't be able to make the trip with the others when the thaw comes. The innkeeper said at the first sign of the spring floods, the river is crowded with boats."

"But we aren't going as far as the Louisville Falls. We're stopping at Cincinnati, so we don't need the high water," Uncle Paul said.

The two men left, still discussing whether to buy a boat or build it.

"Can we go down by the river?" George asked.

"Perhaps you and Betsy can after we walk around this area," his mother said. "I don't want you down there alone."

Wonderful, Betsy thought. She had to watch out for George again.

Betsy coughed when they walked outside the inn. The haze was the same as yesterday. Women on the street wore black with a little white lace peeking out of their bonnets and collars.

She imagined they had to change the white lace quite often. Everything seemed various shades of gray.

The foursome walked the area around the inn, George in the lead with a long rope tied around Jefferson's neck and Betsy and the women following behind. They paused to glance inside the brick mercantile stores that lined the streets.

"We should make a list of supplies we'll need," Mother said to Aunt Eleanor. "There are plenty of mercantiles here with everything we'll need in Cincinnati."

"I wish we knew what could be purchased there and what we must take with us," Aunt Eleanor said. "Perhaps the men will know more when they return."

They walked down one side of the street for several blocks and up the other side of the street, then returned to the inn.

"You may go to the stable now, Betsy. Do you remember the way?" Mother asked. Betsy nodded, for she had noted the stable's location on their walk.

George piped up, "Can I go with her and then to the river?"

"That will be fine, but be back before noon," Aunt Eleanor said. No one had asked Betsy if it was all right for George and Jefferson to tag along. She sighed. Was there no escaping this boy and his dog?

He dashed ahead of her, staying in sight, so she didn't have to walk with him. When he reached the corner where they were to turn to get to the stable, he waited.

"Hurry up, Betsy."

On purpose she slowed her step. It was a small victory, but this was her errand, and she wouldn't be bullied about by George. Once she made the corner, George again ran along ahead of her, stopping now and then to look at stores or businesses.

She didn't know what his hurry was. When he reached the Blackburn stable, he didn't go inside in search of the horse but stayed outside.

"Coming in?" Betsy asked as she swept regally by him.

"No, Jefferson and I'll wait, but don't take long. I want to go down by the river."

Betsy ducked inside the dimness of the stable and found the mare with no difficulty, even though she was in the last stall on the left. A stableboy was brushing a horse in a stall she passed, but she walked like she knew what she was doing, and he didn't bother her. She gave Silverstreak a good grooming, knowing that would please Father, and leaned her head against her only friend. She wished she could take the mare out for a ride. And why not? Silverstreak needed the exercise, and Father would be grateful that she'd done it.

She'd have to talk to the stableboy, and that wasn't something she wanted to do. Maybe she could get George to do it. She strode purposely back outside.

"What kept you so long?" George asked.

"We're going to take Silverstreak out for a ride. Tell the stableboy what we're doing," she ordered.

"I'm not riding that horse," George said. "Come on. Let's go down to the river."

"We can ride Silverstreak and get there a lot faster."

"I'm not riding that horse," George repeated.

"Are you afraid of her?" Betsy asked. Surely not. But now that she thought about it, he'd given the horse a wide berth the entire trip on the boat and in the mornings and evenings when she and Father had tied Silverstreak behind the stage.

"I'm not afraid of anything," George said. "I want to walk, so we can look in the storefronts and see everything. Besides, Jefferson can't ride."

"Oh," Betsy said. "Well, come talk to the stableboy."

"No, you want to ride, you talk to him."

Betsy took a deep breath. She couldn't talk to a complete stranger, could she? She heard Silverstreak's neigh from inside the stable, and her desire to exercise the horse and make Father think she was useful was stronger than her fear.

Please, God, give me courage, she silently prayed as she pivoted and marched back into the stable. She explained to the boy, who was probably only a year or so older than she.

"I can see the horse knows you," he said and helped her saddle the horse with a saddle that rested over a rail. It wasn't a sidesaddle like she was used to, but that was okay. She'd ridden on Father's saddle once and had found it gave her better control of the horse.

The next time she exited the stable, it was atop the mare.

"Ready, George?" She didn't mind being high above him this time. From her perch on the mare she could see him scurrying ahead, pulling Jefferson behind him.

He darted down Market Street for a block and then turned immediately onto Water Street. There was the Monongahela River.

Children played among the wooden shacks. Clotheslines sagging with laundry were strung between the shanties. Someone yelled, "Tomorrow's the day. It's thawing." Men scurried about carrying crates to the flatboats that lined the banks. Boys threw rocks at the thin ice that hugged the shoreline.

All this activity caused Silverstreak to neigh and rear. Betsy held on and reined her in, but the boys and girls stopped their play and ran over to see the horse.

"Is it yours?" a bold boy asked.

Betsy didn't answer. George had sidestepped away from the horse, but now he drew a bit closer.

"It's her father's horse, but she gets to ride it sometimes," he said.

"Can I ride it?" the boy asked.

"Sure," George said. "Can't he, Betsy?"

The cold of the March day didn't bother Betsy anymore. She felt her cheeks flush. "George," she hissed in a low voice. "You know I can't let anyone else ride her without Father's permission."

He shrugged his shoulders as if saying that was her problem, not his. Like always he was trying to be the good guy, be liked by everyone, be the center of attention.

"I have to get her back to the stable," she said. "George, come on."

"I'll stay here," he said and squinted at the sun that struggled to burn a hole through the hazy air. "It's not noon yet."

"Let us ride the horse," the boy spoke up again.

Betsy didn't answer.

"Ah, she's the only one with legs long enough to reach the stirrups," George said. "Let's do something else."

Betsy glanced down to see that a length of leg was showing below her dress on both sides of the man's saddle.

Mortified, she pulled the reins to the left and turned Silverstreak. She dug her heels into the horse's sides, and the mare cantered away from the group of children.

CHAPTER 6

A Muddy Mess

Betsy stood at the edge of the group of crude dwellings and watched George in action. She'd groomed Silverstreak after she'd returned the mare to the stable then trudged to the river. She wished Aunt Eleanor hadn't asked her to keep an eye on George. If Aunt Eleanor hadn't actually said the words, Betsy would have left him and returned alone to the inn.

George fit right in with the other boys. He didn't tower over them like she did. He had their attention, too, like always.

"Toss it in here, Johnny," he directed one of the boys. So he already knew them by name.

Johnny dropped a wooden contraption, which Betsy guessed was supposed to be a miniature flatboat, into the river. The boys ran along the side, tracking its progress.

"Look at it go now," George shouted. "The current's got it."

"It's gone," Johnny called. "Long gone."

A bulky-looking man strode quickly to the boys. "Did you use my good lumber for that toy? And my nails?"

"We thought we could catch it," Johnny explained. "George thought it up."

"Get back to the hut," the man ordered. "You boys find something else to do."

The boys dispersed in different directions. George glanced around then headed for Betsy.

"Hey, it's the girl who wouldn't let us ride the horse," a boy said in a loud voice.

"We'd better get back," George said, as if he hadn't done anything wrong.

Betsy stared at him then walked away from the river without saying a word.

As soon as they'd eaten the noon meal, Betsy asked her mother for paper and a quill pen.

"I thought you'd be wanting to write," Mother said as she rummaged in the trunk for the items. "I'll post a letter to your uncle Charles and aunt Martha and tell them of our progress. Perhaps they've heard from Richard by now." Betsy sat at the small table in their room and wrote:

> *Dear Mary,*
> *How I miss you. Have you gone to the wharf to look for Richard? I miss him, too. And I miss the ocean.*
> *George is worse than ever. He talks to every stranger we see, desperate to get attention, even from those he doesn't know. The Limburger cheese got all over me instead of George. It was awful. I had to ride with the driver of the stage instead of out of the wind inside the cab.*
> *Today George made fun of me in front of some strange children by the river here in Pittsburgh. I was on*

Silverstreak and my legs were showing below my dress. That is the worst thing he's done.

I have to think of ways to get him back. I'm out of room on this sheet, but I'll write again when we get to Cincinnati.

All my love,
Betsy

"I'm finished, Mother," Betsy said.

Her mother took the page and folded it once and once again then wet a wafer and glued the edge. "Write Mary's name and Boston on here. As soon as I write my letter, we'll find the post office. I want to send these postpaid. We don't want to force a hardship on Mary when she picks up the mail."

Betsy nodded. If the embargo had affected Mary's family as she'd hinted, she might not have an extra twenty-five cents to pay for the letter. She wrote the address and then let her mother have the table as a writing surface. Betsy sat on the bed and read from her book of poetry until her mother was finished. Mother asked the innkeeper about the post office, then the two set out the few blocks to post their letters.

"Betsy, is something wrong?" Mother asked as they walked along. "You're even quieter than ever. Is it George? You didn't say a word to him over our meal."

"George delights in embarrassing me. He made fun of me when we were at the river." Betsy told her mother about the incident.

"I don't think George intends you any harm. He's high-spirited, and he doesn't think before he says things."

"He's mean, and I want to embarrass him."

"Hmm. So that's why you put the Limburger cheese on his valise. Betsy, do you think God wants you to get even with George?"

Betsy hesitated, then said slowly, "I think He wants George to learn to respect other people."

"Yes, I believe that's true. But do you think it's up to you to teach George? Wouldn't that be his parents' job?"

"I don't see them doing anything about it. George doesn't say bad things when they're around except, 'How's the weather up there?'"

Mother smiled. "I'm sure that can get irritating. We have opposite problems. When I was your age, I was the shortest person in my class in school. The other girls and boys used me as a measuring stick. Each time someone passed my height, he bragged about it to the others. It wasn't long until the only ones who were shorter than me were those several years younger."

They had arrived at the post office, and Mother talked with the postmaster and paid for the letters to be sent to Boston. On their walk back to the inn, Betsy returned the conversation to her mother's problem.

"Did you ever want to get even with those children who made fun of you?"

"At first I did. But through the years I learned to accept myself as I was. And my mother talked to me about our Lord wanting us to turn the other cheek. He wants us to forgive those who trespass against us rather than get even with them."

"But, Mother, that's easy for you because you're so beautiful. Others want to be like you. Nobody wants to be like me." Betsy blinked back tears.

"That's not true, dear. You're so pretty with those blue eyes. When you're excited about something, they sparkle so. And your hair—all those curls and that rich brown color. Aunt Eleanor's commented on how lucky you are to have such curly hair. Your height should be an asset. You should stand tall and regally. You're growing into a real beauty, Betsy."

"You're my mother. Of course, you would think so," Betsy said, but she felt better.

"Just wait. In a few years you'll have lines of suitors waiting to have you notice them. And you must be kind to each of them, just like you must be kind to George now. He's impetuous and doesn't always think before he blurts out something. Forgive him and forget it."

Betsy mulled over her mother's words that afternoon as she walked to the shops again with the women. At least George had convinced his mother to let him go to the river on his own. Later that evening the Lankfords joined the Millers in their room to discuss the next phase of the journey.

"Then we're going to build?" George asked.

"Yes," George's father said with a grin. "We've ordered lumber delivered to a site where we can work on it. The flatboats we saw aren't sturdy enough, and the lumber isn't the quality we want in our houses."

Betsy thought that was an established fact from the way Father and Uncle Paul had talked that morning. Father always wanted to check every option, but Uncle Paul had pushed for building the flatboat since before they had left Boston.

"I saw lots of flatboats at the river today," George said. "They said the wind shifted, and the thaw is here. Can I help build our boat?"

"Of course," Uncle Paul said. "We're going to need all the help we can get, so we can build it quickly. We can use your help, too, Betsy."

Everyone turned to look at her, and she tried to shrink further into the bed where she was sitting. She didn't know what she could do to help, and she sure didn't want to be around George day after day. Even though she was going to try to forgive and forget like Mother had suggested, staying away from George would be the easiest way to do that. On the other hand, this might be her chance to show Father that she was as good as a boy. He'd seemed pleased about her exercising Silverstreak and had said that working with her horse could be her daily chore.

"Eleanor and I have started a list of supplies we'd like to take with us," Mother said. "We'll start shopping tomorrow. When will our movings arrive, Thomas?"

"Not for another couple weeks," Father said. "Freight travels slowly. Even though the teams of oxen are strong, pulling loads up those mountains will take some time. If we're going to get an early start on the flatboat tomorrow, we'd better turn in."

George's family left for their own room, and after everyone got ready for bed and Father said the nightly prayer, he blew out the lantern. Betsy lay on her pallet on the floor and stared through the darkness toward the ceiling. What was she doing in Pittsburgh, Pennsylvania? What sort of life waited for her in Cincinnati? Would the air be foul like here? Would there be a lot of children like the ones who lived in the shacks by the river? Those were travelers waiting for the thaw, so they would be moving on. But would there be a lot of children in her new town? Would there be someone like Mary? And someday would there be lines of suitors wanting to meet her like Mother said?

The next morning at breakfast, the inn vibrated with activity. Travelers, who had lived at the inn instead of in the huts by the river, bustled about preparing to leave.

"The thaw's here. We're shoving off," one man said. "The river rose ten feet last night."

"Can I go watch?" George asked. "Can I?"

"I suppose," his mother answered, "if Betsy will go with you. There's too much activity for you to go alone today."

"She'll go. Won't you, Betsy?" George said. Betsy glanced at her mother, who had raised her eyebrows as if to tell her this was her chance to forgive and forget.

"All right," she said and nodded.

"Stay out of the way of the travelers," Mother said.

George raced outside to get Jefferson, and Betsy followed more slowly. She had changed from her too-short traveling dress. She wanted to present as respectable a picture of herself as possible.

"Come on," George shouted. "We'll miss them leaving."

Highly unlikely, Betsy thought and was stunned when they arrived at the river to find half the flatboats already gone. Unlike the waiting attitude of yesterday, today the air was filled with excitement. People on board the boats called good-byes to those still on shore, and polemen called orders from one side of the boats to the other. Betsy lifted her long skirt and stepped gingerly to avoid soft ground and mud holes created by earlier melting snows.

"Stay back here," she told George as she watched men trying

to coax livestock on board. Horses neighed and cows mooed as men led them onto flatboats. Jefferson barked. Some boys were chasing chickens and putting them in a coop when they caught them.

"Hold Jefferson," George said and thrust the dog's rope into Betsy's hand. George jumped in the fray and chased the chickens toward the boys, although he didn't make any move to catch any of the hens.

"Fresh eggs for the journey," a girl said who opened and shut the coop's door as the boys stuffed the fowl inside.

"Maybe fried chicken would be better," George said.

Jefferson yelped and ran around and around Betsy, twisting the lead rope.

"Stop that," she ordered and took a few steps forward trying to get the dog under control. He was headed straight for a muddy area. Too late. The dog circled her again and the rope bound her legs together. She tottered, unable to catch her balance, and plopped backward on the muddy ground.

Jefferson barked and jumped on her with his muddy paws, and Betsy stuck her hands in the soft ground to lever herself up. It was no use. She'd only succeeded in getting her hands covered with muck. She pushed the dog away, but he barked and howled and jumped back on her, trying to free himself from the tangled rope that still bound Betsy.

"What are you doing?" she heard George shout.

She glanced up and saw George and the other boys running toward her.

"It's all right, Jefferson. I'll free you," George cooed to his dog.

"Jefferson! What about me?" Betsy exclaimed. The boys were laughing now, and she felt that familiar heated flush creep up her cheeks. *Forgive and forget.* That's what her mother had said. But her mother didn't spend time around George and his smelly dog. Her mother wasn't the one who now sat in a mud hole with her dress wet and filthy and at least seven boys laughing at her.

"Johnny, come load," a voice called, and the boys dispersed, leaving George wrestling with the rope.

"Lift your feet," he said, and Betsy struggled to get the rope untangled.

Finally it was unwound from her legs, and George held the lead rope in his hands. Jefferson no longer danced around and yelped. He sat quietly beside his master.

Betsy pushed herself to her feet.

"We are going back," she said. "Come, now."

"But I'm helping them load and everything," George said.

"I said now and I mean it." With all the aplomb she had, a muddy Betsy walked tall and regally toward the street that lined the river. George and his dog followed.

~ CHAPTER 7 ~

Building the Flatboat

By late afternoon, Betsy returned to the river's edge with Mother and Aunt Eleanor and George. Betsy wasn't about to take George down there by herself, and Mother had agreed with her after she'd helped Betsy clean up and wash out her dress. So they all set out for a walk. Jefferson was tied to a post behind the inn.

The riverfront village was deserted. Flatboats that had lined the river had cast off from the landings and were already on their way to points west. Although the din of hammering and sawing from factories still reached Betsy's ears, they were sounds she was becoming used to. Now the silence of the riverfront was eerie. No children's shouts and laughter split the air. The bustle of the morning could have been in her imagination.

"We missed it," George said, as if it were Betsy's fault.

"There will be more travelers through here," Mother said. "I heard talk at the inn about this being a late start for the first leaving. It's usually in February, but this year winter stayed longer. We'll still have high water when we can start our journey again, with no chance of ice chunks to harm our boat."

"Who told you that?" George asked. "Maybe I can talk to him."

"For what reason?" Aunt Eleanor asked her son.

"To find out more about the travelers. Maybe more boys will live here for a while. Somebody to play with," he said with a sideways glance at Betsy.

He'd better look for someone else to play with, Betsy thought, because it sure wasn't going to be her.

"There won't be much time for play," Aunt Eleanor said to her son. "If the men get their lumber delivered today, they'll be ready to begin on the flatboat tomorrow. Your father drew up plans for it before we left Boston. He's anxious to get started, and he's counting on you for help."

"Oh, I want to help," George said. "I like building things."

The foursome walked six streets from the river to the public square, the Diamond.

"A lot of the wagons are gone," Aunt Eleanor said. "I guess we should have walked farther around the square this morning."

"We got a lot of things on our list, and Saturday's another market day," Mother said. "I wonder how long we will be in Pittsburgh."

She repeated the question that evening after dinner when the two families once again visited in the Millers' room.

"That depends," Father said, "on how many men we can find to help us build the boat. We've put the word out today that we'll be hiring and hope for men to come by the site tomorrow. The lumber is there, and Paul has approved it."

"Not a knot in it," Uncle Paul said with pride. "You can't use knotted wood for a boat. Water pressure can push the knots out and sink the boat."

Early the next morning Betsy, George, Father, and Uncle Paul walked out to the building site. Betsy and George sat on lumber to weigh it down while the men sawed it to length.

"It'll be fourteen by fifty feet," Uncle Paul said. "Narrow enough to get through tight places and long enough to hold our movings."

"George, over here," Father called.

And that was the way most of the morning passed. Betsy held boards for Uncle Paul, and George held boards for Father. Betsy glanced over at Father, who was in a discussion with George. Of course George could talk to a wall, so that was no surprise. But it rankled, just the same. Was Father thinking of George as the son he didn't have?

Betsy did exactly what Uncle Paul asked her to do, determined that she could do a boy's job as well as a boy and certainly better than George.

By late morning a few men had drifted to the site, asking about the job. And before noon, Father had hired three men and sent Betsy back to the inn. George was allowed to stay.

Betsy walked slowly back to their lodgings, wondering why Father preferred George to her. What had she done wrong?

She found Mother and Aunt Eleanor packing food from the inn to take to the men.

"They'll be too dirty to come in for the noon meal," Mother said. "So the innkeeper has allowed us to take food to them. We can use your help carrying."

"I can't go back," Betsy said. "Father doesn't want me there."

Mother set a pot of beans down on the table with a *thump*. "What did he say? What did you do? Why did he send you back here?"

"I don't know," Betsy said and held back a sob. She knew all right. He wanted George. He wanted a son.

"I'll talk to Thomas," Mother said thoughtfully. "This is unlike him."

Betsy carried a basket and followed the women the few blocks near the river where the men were laying out the framework of the boat.

"There are extra men here," Mother said in a low voice.

"Yes. Father hired them this morning."

"I see." The women left the food, and Mother said they'd come back for the pots and dishes a little later. She spoke a moment with Father then walked back to join Betsy and Aunt Eleanor.

"A couple of the men are a little rough," Mother explained as they walked back to the inn. "Their language isn't something that Father wants you to hear."

"But he lets George hear it," Betsy said.

"I suppose since he's a boy, the men feel it won't offend him. Sometimes, Betsy, it's a mixed-up world. No one should speak in a manner that would offend another person. But that's not always the way it is. Your father wants to protect you from this."

So she would not be allowed on the building site except to deliver food. George and her father would become even closer, and there was nothing she could do about it.

For the next week, Betsy shopped with the women and tightly packed their purchases in crates for the trip. She exercised

Silverstreak each morning and afternoon and learned the city of Pittsburgh. She explored the ruins of old Fort Pitt and visited Grant's Hill on the eastern edge of the settlement. At the foot of the hill was Hogg's Pond—home to wild ducks and half-wild hogs. After the pigs caused Silverstreak to shy and almost unseat Betsy, she cut the pond from her exercise route.

And she secretly worked on a surprise for Father.

At noon she carried food to George and the men. George strutted around and practically crowed that he was allowed to participate in such an adult project as building a boat.

Most of the time Mother and Aunt Eleanor accompanied Betsy, but on Wednesday of the second week, they had returned to the farmer's market, and Betsy made the trip to the site by herself on horseback. Baskets of food were strapped across the horse, and after Betsy delivered the food, she waited for the men to eat so she could load the utensils and return them to the inn.

George had taken Jefferson out to the site and had him tied to a post, but Betsy took no chances with the food. Once she had loaded the plates with fried chicken and bread, she put the pan of fried chicken high on top of a pile of lumber—out of Jefferson's reach.

She retrieved it when the men asked for more chicken and served them.

"I want another piece," George said not one minute after she'd asked if he wanted more. She pretended not to hear him and asked Uncle Paul a question about the boat building. Out of the corner of her eye, she watched George get up and walk to the chicken. Good. He had to serve himself. He tried to reach the chicken, but it was over his head, so he jumped and grabbed for the handle of the pan. He succeeded in bringing the pan right down on his head. Since he was looking up, the handle hit him in the eye.

To Betsy, the accident seemed to take place in slow motion. She screamed and jumped up when she saw the heavy pot fall, but she couldn't reach George in time to prevent the injury.

Father examined the bump on George's head and the gash under his eye. Blood trickled from the wound. "Betsy, take George back to the inn. Wash his wound and put the white ointment on it that's in my bag. George, you get to take the rest of the day off to play. Your wound isn't serious, but you may develop a headache from that bump. Betsy will stay with you."

"I'll load up the pots and dishes, and we can walk beside Silverstreak," Betsy said.

Once she got him in the Millers' room at the inn, she obeyed her father's instructions. George winced but didn't cry when she bathed the wound with well water.

"You're going to have a black eye," Betsy said. "It's already starting to turn."

"A shiner? I'm going to have a shiner?" George seemed elated with the information that would have mortified Betsy. How could he enjoy the prospect of having people stare at him and wonder what had happened to his eye?

"Probably take it a week to disappear," Betsy said, drawing on her knowledge of her father's experience. Sometimes in Boston she'd accompanied him on calls, so she could watch the patient's children, her father had said, but mostly she watched what he did for the sick.

When the women returned laden with more purchases, they made a fuss over George. But he seemed restless once the women went to the Lankfords' room to pack the household goods in crates.

"Let's go down to the river to see if any other travelers have come," he suggested.

"No. Father wanted you to rest, so you should remain quiet."

"But what's there to do here?" His hand motion took in the tiny room. "What do you do all day?"

Betsy didn't want to tell her younger cousin, but she felt responsible for his accident and wanted to make up for it. "I've been studying the *Navigator*." She held up a copy of the traveler's guide to the western rivers. "It tells how to get down the Ohio."

"Father has a copy of that, but reading isn't really doing anything."

"I'll be right back," Betsy said and left her room to fetch Uncle Paul's copy of the *Navigator*. When she returned, she opened it and handed it to George.

"Look at this page on shoving off at Pittsburgh," she said. "There's a large flat bar at the mouth of the Allegheny, nearly meeting the foot of the Monongahela." She read aloud, " 'There is, however, a good passage between these two bars, in a direction a little above the Point or junction of the two rivers, towards O'Hara's glassworks. Before you get quite opposite the Point, incline to the left, and you will get into the chute, keeping the foot of the Monongahela bar on the left hand, and the head of that of the Allegheny on your right.' "

"Sounds hard," George said.

"But it's not. Look," she said and drew a folded copy of

the Pittsburgh newspaper, the *Gazette*, from the trunk. "I'm drawing pictures of the river on this paper. Try to block out the words and focus on my lines. See, here's the river and the two sandbars. This X is the glassworks. You've seen it across the river. This arrow shows the route we need to take to avoid the sandbars."

George examined her drawing. "This is good," he said, and Betsy let out a breath she was unaware she'd been holding.

What was she doing? She certainly didn't need George's approval of the way she was passing time waiting for the boat to be finished.

George flipped to the next drawing. "How far have you gone down the river?"

"Not too far. I have about eight maps drawn. How much longer will it take to build the boat?"

"It's going fast with so many workers," George said with pride in his voice. "We should caulk with oakum and pitch on Monday, but Father says he wants that to cure good before we turn the boat. While it's curing, we're going to start the walls of the cabin."

"But how long?" Betsy asked again. George was like Uncle Paul. He had details in his mind and couldn't answer a simple question with a simple answer.

"Hard to say. It depends some on the weather. But I imagine in another two weeks of work we'll be ready to go."

Two weeks to work on her drawings. She could probably have them done by then.

CHAPTER 8

Danger on the River

The boat turning took place two weeks after work had commenced on the flatboat. The large, awkward structure needed to be turned over so that the bottom could rest in the water. Extra hands were needed to wield the monstrous frame into the river. The men had rolled it to the water's edge on logs and then piled huge rocks on one side to weigh it down.

Betsy and George and the women helped some of the men hold ropes to steady the boat as others lifted it with poles, setting and resetting them as the edge of the flatboat opposite the water lifted higher and higher. The weighted-down side was underwater, and within minutes of the pushing of the poles and pulling of ropes, the boat flipped over and settled on the Ohio River.

Cheers rang out from the workers, and Betsy joined in. Another phase of the building began as the workmen prepared to build up the sides and put a roof over the living quarters for the families.

"The hard part's done," George told Betsy as if he knew

what was involved in building a flatboat.

"At least my part is done," Betsy said and dropped her rope. She and the women returned to the inn and the packing. Their movings had arrived by freight wagon and were being stored in one of the huts on the riverfront. Some of those crates needed to be repacked since they'd been damaged in the move.

"Good thing we got rid of so many things in Boston," Mother said. "How will we ever fit all of these crates on the boat?"

"We'll pile them high," Betsy said.

"Your father wants to buy glass here for our windows, but I don't know where we can put it. Perhaps he should purchase it and have it sent on the merchant ships. We can't take all the supplies it will take to build a house in Cincinnati."

The night after the boat turning, Father brought a man to the inn for dinner and introduced him as Marley.

"He's a bargeman who'll help us get down the Ohio," Father said. "Marley's made twenty trips down the Ohio. He knows every crooked turn of that river."

"And there are many," Marley said. He was a short, stocky man but appeared to be all muscle, not fat.

"Betsy and I've made maps of the river," George said, and Betsy gasped. She'd let him work on the maps that one day when he'd gotten his black eye. It had healed now, but she felt like giving him another one. He was claiming responsibility for her work.

"Have you now?" Marley asked. "Can I see them?"

"Sure," George said. "Where are they, Betsy?" Almost as an aside he added, "Betsy did most of them."

With all eyes on her, Betsy excused herself and went to

her room to get the maps. When she returned, George was explaining about the *Navigator* to Marley.

"I know the fellow who writes that guide, and he's thinking of putting maps in it someday. But it will take some time for him to draw them up and get them printed." Marley reached out and took the maps Betsy had drawn on the newsprint. The others crowded around his chair to look them over.

"Now this is some fine studying of the guide," Marley said. "You sure you haven't been on this river before?" He laughed a loud, friendly laugh.

"This is fine work," Father said and looked directly at Betsy. "We'll rely on you and Marley to get us to Cincinnati without mishap."

"Oh, there'll be mishaps," Marley said. "Most folks think they're going on holiday when they set out. They think they can just sit and gab on the boat, but they learn soon enough that it's not that way. There's lots of work to be done to keep the boat in the current and not caught in an eddy or stranded on a sandbar."

Betsy had read enough to know exactly what he was talking about, but George looked a little puzzled. He probably thought he'd fish the whole time.

The men talked of the boat construction and when departure day would come. A new man had been hired to lay up the fireplace so they could cook on the trip. The brick would be used again for their house.

Although it was enlightening to hear these things, Betsy let her mind drift to the actual journey down the river. Now that she had studied the bends and curves and sandbars, she was anxious to begin the trip.

From under lowered lashes, she studied Marley. She had seen him in church the two times they had attended local services. He'd sung hymns in a deep bass voice—a loud voice, much like his laughter. She supposed he was loud because of yelling orders on flatboats. His eyes twinkled when he caught her watching him, and she quickly looked down at her hands.

After Marley left, Father said that he had been searching for a Christian man to pilot them down the Ohio and was pleased that Marley had agreed.

"Be kind to him," he said to Betsy. "He's known some tragedy in his life." He didn't elaborate, and Betsy was left wondering what that tragedy was.

Another week passed. Betsy finished reading the *Navigator* as far as the Cincinnati port. Her mother had taken her to one of the two bookstores in Pittsburgh and let her pick out several books to add to her limited collection, calling them part of her education. They had intended to continue sums and writing and reading study, but her mapmaking study combined all three in a way that satisfied Mother. And that was fine with Betsy. She figured her schooling would be ahead of whatever type of school was held in Cincinnati.

Betsy accompanied Father to a chemist and mineralogist who was trying to establish a manufacture of acids. The doctor had already found many native materials for making drugs, and Father purchased several medicines to take to Cincinnati and arranged for further orders.

The day before leaving arrived, and the women helped the men load the boat. They evenly stacked crates and trunks in certain positions to guarantee a balanced boat.

"Can't have one corner in the water," Marley said. "Put that one down here, young George."

"Hold this blanket," Mother instructed Betsy. They strung it on rope as a room divider under the roofed area, separating the sleeping areas from the cooking and living area.

By nightfall the boat was loaded and only lacked perishables and Silverstreak. Early the next morning the travelers loaded the horse and George's dog and climbed on board, and the next phase of the journey began.

"Cast off that line," Marley ordered, and Uncle Paul unlooped the cable on the dock and jumped on board.

Betsy sat on a crate near the front of the flatboat with her maps in hand. Father held a great long oar on one side of the boat, and Uncle Paul did the same on the other. Marley steered from atop the roof with a long sweep that acted as a rudder.

Although she didn't say a word, Betsy watched with great interest as Marley maneuvered the boat between the sandbars of the Allegheny and the Monongahela that she had read about and mapped out. They shot by Hamilton's Island in a chute that was narrow and rapid, and then they were truly in the Ohio River.

Within minutes they had left the smoky haze and the noise of manufacturing behind them. Betsy sighed. Marley may have said it wasn't a holiday, but it seemed like one to her. The April sunshine warmed her all over, and George and his dog were at the stern behind the enclosed space and as far from her as possible. They floated past farmland and brushy undergrowth so thick she couldn't see through it.

"Push off toward the left," Marley called to Uncle Paul. Betsy admired the way her father and Uncle Paul worked in tandem, as if they could predict the other's move with his sweep.

As they rounded a bend, they met with head winds. Betsy pulled her cloak around her against the chill. For the next hour they made slow progress against the wind. Once around another curve, the wind switched again, and they picked up speed.

"How far will we get today?" she asked Marley, who had traded places with Uncle Paul and was now manning one of the long poles.

"Depends. Could make twenty or twenty-five miles. Where do you have us on the map, little lady?"

He always called her that. At first Betsy thought he was making fun of her, since she was taller than he, but she soon discovered that "little lady" was his title of respect.

"I have us past Hog Island and headed for Dead Man's Island."

"Right on target. See those willow branches in the middle of the river?" He pointed. "Look to the left."

"Oh, yes, I see them."

"That's all you'll be seeing of Dead Man's Island. The water's still too high to show the land. But we know it's there, so the good Lord willing, we won't be caught unawares." He turned toward Father. "Get ready to move her to the right." He shouted orders to Uncle Paul, who stood atop the roof with a tight grip on the sweep.

George came back around the little house with Jefferson on his heels.

"Did you say Dead Man's Island? How many men have been killed there?"

Trust George to want gory details, Betsy thought.

"Too many to count," Marley said. "In flood times there's not even a leaf to warn travelers about the trees underneath the water. Many a flatboat has been stove in and sunk in a minute's time. Now, bear hard to the right," he shouted to Uncle Paul.

Within a few minutes they had successfully passed the ripples above Dead Man's Island and swept to the right of it.

"I like the fast water," George said. He fashioned a chair out of a crate and stuck his fishing line in the river.

"Do you have any bait?" Betsy asked.

"No. But I'm going to dig for worms when we land for the night. Then we'll have fish for supper tomorrow."

Betsy doubted it. She hadn't known George to be much of a fisherman, even in Boston. He was too impatient to sit still for long.

At noon the women served a lunch of beans that had cooked all morning over the fire in the little house. The fire kept the shelter warm, and from time to time Betsy disappeared inside to stand by the fireplace. She checked on Silverstreak, who was tied at the stern and who seemed to be taking the riverboat ride in stride.

The afternoon passed pleasantly enough with the same atmosphere of peace and tranquility. The silence was only broken by the low murmuring of voices on the boat, birds chirping, and an occasional fish near the bank, jumping and splashing. They met three keelboats working their way up the river and called to each one. Betsy never tired of watching the landscape pass by. There were hills, long forest slopes, and meadows. Trees had budded green, and occasionally a redbud and white dogwood brightened the underforest.

"We're going to be looking for a place to tie up for the night," Marley told Betsy late that afternoon. "We'll be wanting daylight to get our cable secured to shore and not be landing on any sandbars in the process."

Was he asking for her opinion? Surely not, but he looked at her with raised eyebrows.

"See any place on your map that looks good?"

Betsy consulted her well-thumbed copy of the *Navigator*.

"The book says that if we land, we'll have considerable loss of time and some hazard," she said.

"But we'll all be needing sleep, and if we keep going, we'll have to keep a good lookout to stay in the current. Your father's plan is to tie up at night and move on at first light."

Betsy bent over her maps. "After we clear the next bend, there's a little cove."

"I was thinking the same thing," Marley said. In a louder voice he announced to the others that they were planning to land.

Around the next curve, there appeared to be a fork in the river, but Betsy knew it was deceptive. A peninsula stuck out far enough that travelers couldn't see around it as they could see around most islands. The *Navigator* warned that it had fooled many travelers who thought it was a shortcut to straighten out the river.

"We can't go too far in the cove, or it'll be hard to get out tomorrow," Marley said. "But we want our cable to reach both shores. If my memory serves me right, there's a tie-up tree on the left. Look there."

So Marley knew all along that this is where we would stay the night, Betsy mused. But he had been nice enough to ask her advice, because she had worked hard on her maps.

Uncle Paul rowed in the skiff to the shore and secured one cable from the left side of the flatboat. Then he rowed to the shore of the peninsula and secured a cable from the right side of the flatboat.

"Can I go on the land?" George asked, once the boat was secured for the night. "I need to dig for some worms."

"I'll take George and Betsy ashore," Marley said. "There's a creek where we can fill the water buckets with cleaner water than we can pull out of the Ohio."

Although she wasn't keen on being in the skiff with George, Betsy longed to stretch her legs and explore a bit.

Marley rowed them the short distance to shore and pulled the skiff up on the bank so Betsy could get out without getting wet.

"Creek's right down that way, little lady."

While Marley showed George where grubs would be hiding under some downed limbs, Betsy carried one water bucket and wandered through the underbrush toward the creek that emptied into the Ohio. She gingerly watched her step on the uneven forest floor.

She wasn't fifty feet away from the creek when from the corner of her eye she caught a movement. She lifted her gaze to stare straight into the eyes of an Indian!

CHAPTER 9

The Graves

Betsy froze. The Indian, a boy about her age, stood beside his horse, which was drinking from the creek. He said something that she couldn't understand.

He said it again.

Betsy finally found her voice and screamed, "Marley!"

"Marley?" the Indian repeated.

Betsy twirled when she heard running footsteps behind her.

Marley burst through the undergrowth with George on his heels. Marley looked at Betsy, then at the Indian. He said something in a different language to the boy, and the boy responded and grinned.

"It's okay, Betsy. This is Running Fox. We're friends."

"You know this Indian?" George asked.

Marley took on a haunted look. His eyes narrowed and a frown line crossed his brow. He breathed out a sigh. "He's from a settlement not far from here. I know it well."

"Then he's friendly?" Betsy asked.

"Very friendly," Marley said. Again he spoke to the boy in his native language. The boy answered and motioned behind him.

"He's been looking for a stray," Marley said.

Betsy heard a distant mooing that seemed to come from upstream.

The Indian boy cocked his head as if he'd heard it, too, and immediately mounted his horse. He called something to Marley, and Marley held up a hand in farewell.

"How do you know him?" George asked as they filled their buckets with creek water.

Marley hesitated, then said, "At one time I lived with the Indians. Let's get back to the boat. We need to settle in before dark."

Whatever Marley knew about the Indian boy and the settlement, he didn't want to talk about, Betsy quickly decided, as they made their way back through the undergrowth toward the boat.

George stopped to pick up a small bag, which Betsy figured held his worms and grubs for fishing. She moved to his other side as far from the bag as she could get.

They climbed back into the skiff, and Marley rowed them to the flatboat. The evening settled around them. Father offered a prayer of thanks for the safe start on their journey, and they ate with the light from the lantern making soft shadows on the boat.

After dinner Betsy played a few tunes on the violin until Jefferson howled in competition with her music. Then she put the instrument away and sat near the edge of the boat, listening to the night sounds of the river.

George plopped down beside her.

"Why do you think Marley lived with the Indians?" he asked.

Betsy had been wondering about the same question. "I don't know. Did your father tell you anything about him?"

She couldn't see his face in the darkness, but Betsy could see by the way he tilted his head that he was trying to remember.

"He said they'd looked a long time to find someone like Marley to take us down the river. Most of the bargemen are rough, noisy men. They brag and fight each other a lot." George sounded like that was something he'd have liked to have seen.

Betsy nodded. "I heard Father tell Mother that Marley was a good Christian man who would fit in with us. He told me that Marley had known tragedy, and I should be nice to him."

"You think his tragedy had something to do with the Indians?"

Betsy shrugged. "Maybe."

"How are we going to find out?" George asked.

"I suppose we have to wait for him to tell us. And we aren't going to pester him, George. We may never know."

"I wonder if my father knows."

Again Betsy had been thinking along those same lines, and she wasn't pleased that she and George had the same thoughts. Still, she would look for an opportunity to talk to Father tomorrow.

The April night was chilly, and Betsy settled near the fireplace in the enclosed area to sleep. The others crowded in, and she didn't have room to roll over.

The next morning at dawn, the men untied the cables and shoved off with their long sweeping oars. They pushed off the river bottom for as long as their oars would reach, then rowed into the main channel of the wide Ohio.

George immediately tossed out his fishing line. Betsy edged over to her father's side of the boat.

"We need to take Silverstreak off the boat tonight if possible and give her some exercise," Father said.

"How can we do that?" Betsy asked. "She can't get in the skiff."

Father laughed. "You're right. Only if there is a landing can we take her off. We'll have to watch for a ferry landing or a wharf. It may be a day or two. Would you check the *Navigator*?"

"Yes, Father. Oh, I've been wondering about Marley," she said as if it were an afterthought. "He's a very nice man. What tragic thing happened to him? Did it have to do with the Indians?"

"Turn port side," Marley called from his position high atop the roof. "Sandbar."

Father turned his attention to his long sweep and pushed hard against the bottom of the river. The boat moved toward the left and glided into the stronger current.

Betsy thought she would have to repeat her question, but Father turned back to her just then.

"Marley confided in me, and I cannot break his confidence. If you get to know him well, he may tell you of his past tragedy. He's known sorrow, but he's overcome it with God's help. It's his story to tell, not mine."

How could she get to know Marley? It wasn't in her nature to jabber on like George did at times. It had taken her courage to ask Father about him, and she wasn't really shy around Father.

She knew he loved her, even though she still felt he wished she were a boy, and knowing that he loved her gave her courage to talk to him when she couldn't talk to others.

In Pittsburgh Father had told her to be kind to Marley. She could do that. He had charged forward to rescue her from the Indian, even though it turned out she didn't need saving. He had been open to her few questions about their trip, and he had asked her about her maps. They were developing a solid friendship. She would treat him as she wanted to be treated, just as the Golden Rule said.

With that decided, Betsy spent the rest of an uneventful day enjoying the spring sunshine and studying the maps to find a place to exercise Silverstreak.

"Can we get to Steubenville by dark?" she asked Marley when he took a shift on the starboard side where she sat studying the guidebook.

"We've been doing well today. We might make it. Need to go shopping?" he teased.

Betsy laughed. "No. I need to take Silverstreak for a ride."

"Hey, Jefferson needs to run, too," George piped up. Betsy was unaware he had moved over to her side of the boat.

"Just keep him away from Silverstreak," Betsy said.

"There's plenty of room for you two to keep a distance," Marley said, and Betsy studied him. Did he know about her feud with George? They'd been getting along better, but she hadn't forgotten how he'd embarrassed her when the Pittsburgh settlement travelers were pushing off.

"There's a new courthouse at Steubenville," Marley said. "And a new jail, if we need to lock one of you up."

"Are there a lot of criminals there?" George asked.

"No more than anywhere else, I reckon," Marley said.

"Are they Indians?" George asked, and from Marley's expression, Betsy figured George had asked one too many questions.

"No," Marley said. "You have something against Indians?"

"No. Just wondering," George said, and he went back to where he had left his fishing line dangling in the water.

They traveled longer that day, and by dusk they arrived at Steubenville and tied up for the night. Father and Betsy unloaded the mare, but it was Father who rode her through the streets and out into the country.

"You'd better stay with the women," Father had said, "since it's near dark."

Although Betsy was allowed to walk the length of the main street with the others, she'd hoped for the freedom of a ride on the horse. The cramped quarters of the boat bothered her. She'd been used to the limitless feel of gazing at the ocean. The river, although wide, was bordered by forests and fields and hills. It was a closed-in feeling. How did people inland adapt to this? The sea called to her, and she wanted to answer.

The sea reminded her of Richard, and she wondered where he was on this April evening when the first star could now be seen. Was he fighting on a British ship or was he back in Boston? Maybe once they were settled in Cincinnati they would hear from his folks.

"Let's get back on board," Mother said. "We need to fry up those fish, and Father will be back soon."

Betsy couldn't believe George had caught enough fish for

supper, but he had, and he wasn't letting her forget it, either.

After the meal, Betsy laid down early for the night. Two days on the river, and the time ahead stretched out in front of her endlessly. What waited for them at journey's end?

At daybreak, the men pushed off again, and by midafternoon they tied up at Wheeling.

"Betsy, it's your turn to exercise Silverstreak," Father said. "We will only stop for an hour at most, so take care to be back here soon."

Betsy glanced at the sun's position, then rode the horse down Wheeling's one street. Once they passed the last building, she let Silverstreak have her head and run wild. The wind whipped Betsy's hair, and she celebrated her freedom by laughing aloud. All too soon she gauged the sun had drifted a half hour toward the western horizon, so she turned the horse back toward town.

"Fried chicken tonight," Mother announced once they were back on the river. "What luck that we landed here on market day."

Betsy groomed Silverstreak, then took up her usual position, sitting on a crate and studying her maps.

"Where are we tying up for the night?" she asked Marley.

"Near Little Grave Creek."

"The mounds," Betsy said with awe. The *Navigator* had given a detailed account of the ancient big mound and the smaller ones near it. "Can we explore?"

"I reckon if your folks say you can," Marley answered.

"What mounds?" George asked from the other side of the boat.

That boy had hearing that would put a dog to shame.

"Nothing really," Betsy said. "Just some big hill." There was no reason George needed to come along.

"An ancient Indian burial ground," Marley explained. "We'll have to land quick so we have some daylight left."

Betsy sought Mother and asked permission to explore the big mound. Then she stood at the helm and waited for it to come into sight.

"Look," George said from right beside her. "It's steep."

"'It's an eighty-degree angle,'" Betsy read from the *Navigator*. "'It's seventy-five feet tall and one hundred eighty yards around the base.'"

"Can we climb it?"

Should they climb a grave? Betsy had always been careful not to step on graves in the cemetery next to the churchyard back in Boston. It might be disrespectful to the Indians, and that might upset Marley. She didn't want to risk that.

As soon as the flatboat was secured for the night, Betsy, George, and Marley departed in the skiff and quickly reached ground.

"I'm going to the top," George shouted and took off.

Betsy glanced at Marley.

"Can't stop him," Marley said. "That's one curious boy. You can go look it over, if you want."

The mound was covered in trees. Betsy hiked up her dress and began the long climb, holding onto low branches for balance. George was halfway up. Marley stayed at the foot of the mound.

"It sounds hollow," George called down from his lofty perch.

He was beating on the slanted ground with a downed branch.

The *Navigator* had said it sounded hollow, too, but Betsy couldn't detect that from the sound she heard. She rested against a very tall oak and began the steep climb again. "It's caved in on top," George yelled back.

By the time Betsy reached the peak, George was down in the sinkhole, which was about four feet deep. Only his head peeked out of the deep basin. "I'm looking for some Indian stuff," he said, "but there's nothing here but more brush."

Betsy walked around the perimeter of the sinkhole. He was right—nothing there but brush. She looked off in the distance, searching the plain below for the ghost town that was mentioned in the guidebook. There it was, an old town that never took root once Wheeling was established. Only some old tumbled-down buildings remained. Odd. White man had tried to put a town here and failed where the Indians had declared the land a cemetery. The old white oak near the basin was a good four feet in diameter. How old did that make this mound? A hundred years? Two hundred years?

"Help me out, Betsy," George ordered.

Betsy's thoughts were pulled to her cousin who was trying unsuccessfully to climb out of the sinkhole.

"Now why would you climb in there if you didn't have a way out?" she asked. Here was a golden opportunity to embarrass him, and there was no one around to notice it.

"There aren't any footholds. Come on, give me a hand."

"Say 'please,' " she said.

"Betsy. Are you going to help me out or not?"

She had to help him out, or Marley would climb that hill

and get him out. "Say 'please,' " she said again.

"Please," George said finally.

Betsy knelt on the ground and reached for him with one arm while circling a tree as a brace with the other arm. George grabbed her hand and walked up the sinkhole wall.

"Thanks," he said grudgingly.

"You're welcome," she said with a tilt of her head. "Are you ready to go down? Marley's waiting."

The descent was as difficult as the climb because of the steep slope. Betsy inched her way, but George scampered down. When she was on level ground, Betsy discovered Marley had spent his waiting time gathering rocks and was placing them in the form of a cross at the foot of the mound.

Betsy began picking up some stones and put them in the formation. George helped. "Marley," Betsy said, "do you think the Indians buried here went to heaven? I mean, if they didn't know about the Lord, how could they be saved?"

That question had first crossed her mind when she read about the mounds.

"Well, missy, I don't rightly have an answer. I just don't know. That's one of the mysteries of God. I guess we'll find out soon enough."

"I guess we will," Betsy said.

They finished the cross in silence.

CHAPTER 10

The Deserted House

On the fourth morning of the river journey, Betsy faced the stern of the flatboat and watched the Indian mound disappear from view. When she could no longer see it, she turned around and settled onto her usual crate seat. She consulted the maps to guess how far they would get that day.

The river curved past Big Grave Creek and churned in a narrows. The men hugged the right shore and got the flatboat through the ripples.

"I like the faster water," George said.

It was more adventurous, and Betsy was surprised to find that she also liked the ripples. "We're headed for Captina Island," she said. "Big curves coming up."

The river switched back on itself before it turned again to the southwest.

"Hey, look. Other travelers," George said.

Not only was there another flatboat ahead, it appeared to be stuck.

Betsy consulted the guide. "There's a sandbar at the lower

end of the island and then two narrow channels with swift water. They must have snagged."

"Ahoy," Marley called to the stranded travelers.

Betsy could see two men and two women working on a portion of their boat. A couple of children sat on the roof.

"We've got a hole," one man called. "Hit a log."

"Have you got oakum?" Marley asked.

"No, we've used it all."

Marley looked at Father as if asking a question.

"Where can we tie up?" Father asked.

After some maneuvering, the men managed to get the boat in a position so it wouldn't float down the river or hang up on the close sandbar. The three men loaded mending supplies in the skiff and rowed upstream about fifty yards to the stranded flatboat.

Betsy watched them caulk the joints. George wandered into the covered area, then returned to where Betsy was sitting, carrying his family's shelf clock.

"What are you doing?" Betsy asked as he placed it on a high crate so the weights hung in the air.

"This wasn't keeping good time before we left Boston. I'm going to fix it."

"What do you know about clocks?"

"I can learn," he said. He took the back off the clock and pulled on the weight, then pushed the pendulum so it would start. "This gear makes this gear turn, which makes this one turn the hands," he mumbled as if to himself. "If I turn this one, then this—"

"George, what are you doing with that clock?" his mother

asked. She stood outside the flatboat house, looking as if this wasn't the first time she had caught George operating on something.

"I'm fixing it," he said. "It's been losing time."

"Do you know how?"

"I'm figuring it out," George said.

"Perhaps you'd better wait until your father can help you with it," Aunt Eleanor said. *She has the patience of Job*, Betsy decided. *If George were my child*. . . Well, that wouldn't bear thinking about.

George reluctantly carried the clock back into the covered area and returned with a lost look on his face.

"I wish we could go ashore again," he said.

"Well, we can't."

"I wish we could do something exciting."

"We are. We're floating down the Ohio River. Some people back home would think that was pretty exciting," Betsy said.

"Maybe. But being stuck on a boat all day and all night is downright confining."

It was a thought she'd had before. It was scary how she and George thought so much alike at times.

"I wish I could help those people. I could fix that boat. I helped put oakum on this boat."

"Quit wishing and do something," Betsy said.

"There's nothing to do."

"Then invent something," she said.

George mumbled something and wandered away from what Betsy considered her area.

Betsy read her maps and saw no place of great interest

coming up that day. There were several places they could stop and exercise Silverstreak, but Father might not want another delay.

With that in mind, Betsy walked along the narrow passage beside the covered area to the stern and untied Silverstreak.

"You only get to walk a few feet then turn around," she said, "but it's better than nothing." Betsy quickly tired of the routine but counted fifty turns before she tethered the horse.

Traveling down the river gave her different landscapes to view, but being tied up in one spot during the day was downright boring.

Betsy walked along the narrow passageway toward the front of the boat and glanced toward the stalled travelers. They were still working on the hole, but it looked like they were making progress.

Her foot stumbled on something, and she tried to regain her balance.

"No!" she screamed, and the next thing she knew, she was in the frigid water. She came up sputtering and grabbed for the boat but missed before her heavy skirts took her down again. She bobbed back to the surface.

"Man overboard!" George called.

The children on the roof of the flatboat house were screaming. Everyone on both boats was yelling at her, Marley louder than anyone.

"Splash with your hands. Kick your feet," he shouted. Betsy did her best, but back under the water she went.

She coughed when she resurfaced and beat the water with her hands, but down she went again. Each time she submerged, she seemed to go deeper and take longer to come up to the top.

"Betsy, give me your hand," Mother cried when Betsy came up yet again and gasped for air.

She quit splashing the water and reached for Mother, who was lying on the boat with her hand outstretched. But Betsy couldn't reach her.

"Grab this," George called and threw a rope that hit her in the head. Down she went once more, and this time she thought she would never breathe air again.

But she resurfaced, and this time she grabbed the rope—her lifeline. Mother and Aunt Eleanor and George pulled her toward the boat. With shaking hands Betsy gripped the wood, then climbed onto the boat, with her mother pulling on her arms.

"Build up the fire," Mother ordered Aunt Eleanor. "Let's get these wet things off you, Betsy. Are you okay now? How did this happen? Did you lose your footing?"

Through chattering teeth Betsy muttered, "I tripped on something." She pointed at the narrow passageway beside the covered house and saw string stretched across the walkway. She glared at George.

"You said invent something, so I invented a way I could catch three fish at once. See, I put hooks on three—"

"I don't want to hear it," Betsy interrupted as she lumbered in her soaking wet dress toward the covered area. She left a trail of water behind her.

Mother helped her peel her wet things off, and Betsy wrapped up in a blanket in front of the fire to get warm before donning dry clothes. She could hear Aunt Eleanor lecturing George on making sure his inventions didn't involve other people.

Betsy sat in front of the fire, finger-combing her hair, when the men rowed back to the boat.

"Are you all right, Betsy?" Father asked and hugged her tight.

"I'm cold," she said. "But it happened so fast. I'm okay now."

"That's my girl." He kissed her forehead. "Losing your brothers was bad enough, but I couldn't have stood to lose you," he said as if to himself.

"But you still wish I were a boy," Betsy said.

"Betsy, that's not true. Why would you think that?" Father tilted her chin up so she was looking at him.

"You're always talking to George, saying he's a curious boy."

"He is, and I like to encourage his questions, because I want him to learn; but that doesn't mean I want you to be a boy. You're a wonderful girl, and you're going to be a magnificent woman. Did you hit your head when you fell into the water?" he asked with a smile. He kissed her forehead again. "You're precious to me. Never forget that."

Betsy felt a lurch as the boat was untied and the journey was underway again.

"I'd better take my position with the sweep. We fixed those folks up and got them off the sandbar. They're going to wait for the oakum to cure a bit, then they'll move along. Want to go sit in the sun?"

"Not yet," Betsy said. "I'll stay here by the fire a little longer." Physically, she felt chilled to the bone and couldn't bring herself to leave the heat of the fire. But her heart felt warmer and lighter.

Before noon Betsy took up her normal post with the guidebook. George stayed out of her way once he had mumbled sorry and something about making sure he didn't endanger anyone again.

Betsy just nodded and didn't look up from her book. She tried to search for landmarks the book mentioned, but she couldn't concentrate on the words or the shoreline. She trembled as she stared into the Ohio River that churned along beside her. That last time she had gone under, the river had swallowed her. She'd opened her eyes and seen nothing but water, still muddied from the spring flood. Panic set in.

"How are you doing?" Marley stepped toward her from his post with the long oar. He still watched ahead but withdrew his sweep from the water.

"I'm all right," Betsy said.

"A bit scared?" he asked and nodded, answering his own question. "And rightly so."

"It was dark under the water," she said. "And I was so helpless."

"I know. I was in there once," he said. His eyes looked misty, and he moved back to his post.

Betsy closed her eyes. "Dear God," she whispered. "Thank You for getting me out of the river. Please help me not be scared anymore. Amen." A tear trickled down her cheek, and she wiped it off and took a deep breath.

The rest of the day Betsy sat on her crate. When they docked she felt much better, but she didn't leave the boat with George and Marley when they took the skiff to shore.

There wasn't much to see anyway. That night she dreamed she was under the water again and woke up, gasping for air.

Two more days of travel brought them to Marietta, where they tied up at a wharf.

"Tonight we sleep in real beds," Father said. "Tomorrow is Sunday, and we're taking a day of rest."

The tired travelers unloaded a few bags and found rooms at an inn. Silverstreak was boarded at a stable. On Sunday morning after a breakfast where they sat at a real table, they attended church. Father and Mother visited easily with the townspeople. Betsy smiled at a couple of girls and said hello when they greeted her as they walked by. Odd. In the past she would have been too shy to speak to strangers.

In the afternoon they walked around the town and were glad to get the exercise. Betsy rode Silverstreak, and George threw sticks on the town square for Jefferson to fetch.

"There's a shipbuilding yard here," Uncle Paul said at dinner.

Betsy looked up from her plate of ham and potatoes. Did that mean Uncle Paul might want to stay in Marietta? She liked the town and wouldn't mind it if they stayed here.

"I noticed that, too," Father said. "But there are several shipyards in Cincinnati."

"Yes, and someday a yard will have my name on it," Uncle Paul said.

"We'll shove off tomorrow morning after the women have time to visit the market and lay in some fresh supplies," Father said.

It was midmorning before they boarded the flatboat again. Betsy felt better after spending time ashore. She could face the Ohio again without the trepidation that had haunted her.

She took up her old post with her maps and the *Navigator*

and read the pages about the next few miles.

"Marley," she said excitedly, "will we get to the Blennerhassett mansion before nightfall?"

"Yes, missy. With our late start this morning, I suspect that's where we'll spend the night. There's a stone boat landing where we can tie up real easy."

"Oh, can we go ashore? Can we see the house?"

"It was once a grand place," Marley said. "But last spring a crest of floodwater drowned the gardens and filled the house."

"Have you seen it since?"

"Yes. It's but a ghost of its former self."

"Ghost?" George had edged over by Marley. "What ghost?"

Betsy ignored him. "Where are the owners?" she asked Marley.

"I don't know. All I know are rumors. Aaron Burr was involved with Mr. Blennerhassett in some movement to take New Orleans by force and form a new government there. Both were arrested, and I don't know the outcome of it. Meanwhile the house has been ransacked and left deserted."

"Vice President Aaron Burr?" Betsy asked.

"He was the vice president. Now we have a different one."

"I know. Clinton," Betsy said, remembering that Thomas Jefferson had changed vice presidents for his second term.

"Where is this place?" George asked.

Betsy looked at her map. "About eight more miles. We'll get there before dark."

"I'll ask if we can explore it," George said and disappeared inside the covered area.

"Do you know anything else about the place?" Betsy asked Marley.

"Blennerhassett was quite a curious fellow," the man said. "I never met him, but I heard that he played the cello and did all sorts of experiments trying to invent things."

"Like George," Betsy said.

"Much like George," Marley agreed. "But I think the lad means well."

"What about Mrs. Blennerhassett?"

"I understand she was quite pretty. They had a couple sons."

"Did she play a musical instrument?" Betsy asked, thinking that perhaps the woman had played the violin.

"I never heard anything like that," Marley said. "Although I heard they had some big parties. Half of what's said about them is probably untrue. When people are so wealthy and fall on hard times, there's usually a lot of tales spread about them."

"How much farther?" George asked. "We can go ashore, but we have to be careful, and Marley has to go, too."

"I'd like to see the place again," Marley said.

It was nearing sundown when the travelers approached the east end of the biggest island in the Ohio.

"The other end is owned by someone else," Betsy explained to George. "We must be careful to stay on the deserted side."

Tying up at the stone wharf was as easy as Marley had said, and the threesome jumped off the boat onto the dock.

They walked up a path that was still silt covered from the flood and ambled toward the two-story house. From the back Betsy could see honeysuckle vines on a trellis next to the house. At least the vines had survived the dunking by the Ohio River.

One-story curving wings flanked both sides of the two-story

main part of the house. Even in its deserted state, the mansion remained graceful.

"I'm going to walk down where the orchards were and see if any of the trees have greened up," Marley said. "I'll be back in a moment."

Betsy and George stared at the house. In the fading sunlight, it took on a ghostly air, and that thought gave Betsy an idea.

"I wonder if the old place is haunted. I've heard there are lots of rumors about it. Are you afraid to go in there?" Betsy asked.

"Of course not," George scoffed.

"Go on in. I dare you to climb upstairs and wave from the window."

George glanced around. "Where did Marley go?"

"Down the path. He'll be right back. Afraid?"

George didn't answer but strode toward the front door that stood ajar. When he reached the verandah, his pace slowed. He glanced over his shoulder at Betsy then stepped on the porch. He glanced back one more time before he disappeared.

Marley's Secret

Her plan was simply to scare George as much as her fall into the Ohio River had scared her because of his fishing invention. *He needs to know how his actions affect other people,* she decided.

With lightning speed, she raced to the house and tiptoed up the steps to the verandah. Cautiously, she peered inside the doorway. There was no sign of George. Maybe he was already on the staircase.

She sneaked into the house. Once her eyes were accustomed to the dimness within, she could make out heaps of broken furniture in the large room to her left. Above her the chandelier in the entry hung without one glass globe left intact. A lone candle sat in its holder.

The floor was covered with silt and sand. As she stepped carefully into the next room, she noticed many footprints, as if other travelers had stopped to see the former splendor of the mansion. So this was where Mr. Blennerhassett had played the cello. She could imagine herself standing over by the ornate mantel of the fireplace, playing Richard's violin. Dozens of friends would dance to the sweet music in the large room. What a party they would have, and what an odd thought. She didn't play the violin in front of others. Until this trip she'd only played for Richard and for Mother and Father. Now George's family and Marley had heard her, too.

Above her, she heard George's halting footsteps. She had to act fast. What could she do to make an eerie sound? To her left were broken parts of a rocking chair. She picked up two wooden pieces that must have formed rungs and struck one with the other, making a knocking sound. The footsteps upstairs stopped, and Betsy smiled. She tapped on the wall three times, then repeated the code three more times.

"Betsy," George called from upstairs.

She didn't answer.

"Betsy, is that you?" His voice was quavering now.

She said nothing but instead pounded on the wall with her fist. That movement jarred jagged pieces of a large broken mirror that clung to a frame, and they fell to the floor. Betsy jumped, and the tinkling of breaking glass echoed through the house. A scream came from upstairs.

"Good," she whispered. She silently glided to the staircase and climbed, step by step. She didn't try to mask the noise of the creaky stairs, and for good measure, she moaned as she climbed up and up.

Running footsteps made for the back of the house. With her long legs, Betsy took two steps at a time and quickly reached the second floor. She could hear George scurrying toward the back of the house, and she ran to the first door across from the stairs. The room was empty except for trashed furniture. What had possessed someone to tear up such a grand bed? She started for the second door and knew this was where George was. She could hear whimpering sounds.

She jumped into the second room and yelled, "Boo!"

George was on the window ledge, ready to jump. Betsy watched him grab the trellis beside the window and swing out. She dashed to the window and peered out at the same time that she heard the sound of splintering wood. The trellis was pulling away from the house.

"George!" she screamed.

Her cousin yelled in terror.

Betsy stretched out the window and grabbed the trellis, bringing George back toward the house. "Can you climb back in?"

"No, there's something in there!"

"What's going on?" Marley ran around the corner of the house and reached the base of the trellis.

"Can you help George down?" Betsy called. Her arms ached from holding the trellis in place. She didn't know how much longer she could retain her grip. With Marley's guidance, George inched his way down the trellis, his weight pulling the trellis from the house as Betsy struggled to keep it close. Finally he was on the ground, and she let go.

"Look out!" she cried as the wooden structure crashed to the ground.

"Get out, Betsy," George shouted. "There's something up there." He whirled toward Marley. "We have to get her out before it gets her."

Betsy didn't wait to hear anymore. She ran for the stairs. If

George had been hurt, it would have been her fault. And here he was wanting to come back in to save her. She bounded down the stairs and out the front door in time to see George and Marley come around the left wing of the house. She ran toward them.

"Did you see anything?" George asked. "Did you hear anything?"

"I heard a mirror break," she said, trying to catch her breath. She didn't admit that she'd accidentally broken it when she pounded on the wall.

"I heard it, too. Let's get back to the boat." When she didn't move, George added insistently, "Now! That house is haunted."

"There's no such thing as a ghost," Marley said. "There's a logical explanation for whatever you heard." He looked hard at Betsy. She looked away.

"In any event," Marley added, "we do need to get back to the boat. It'll be dark in a few minutes."

"It moaned, too," George said, "and it made a knocking sound in a rhythm, as if it was trying to say something."

"It was probably the wind," Marley said, "making a branch tap against the wall of the house." Again he looked at Betsy.

"What about the orchard?" she asked.

"It's gone. The trees were too young to survive. The power of nature—the floodwaters were too much for them." His voice trembled, and now it was Betsy's turn to look searchingly at him.

Once they were back on the boat, George recounted the excitement in the house.

"There are no such things as ghosts," Uncle Paul told his son.

Father agreed with him. "It was your imagination playing tricks on you."

"But Betsy heard the mirror break, too," George protested.

"A mirror?" Marley said in a low voice that only Betsy could hear. "Not just a piece of glass?"

Betsy turned away and stared at the water.

After dinner while the others were inside the shelter, out of the cool wind that had sprung up, Betsy made her way to the back of the boat to check on Silverstreak.

"Why?"

Betsy jumped at the sound of Marley's voice.

"I didn't hear you come out here," she said in a husky voice.

"Why did you scare George?" Marley asked.

Betsy bit her lip then sighed. "I wanted to scare him as much as I was scared when I fell in the river."

"He didn't mean to harm you, and you meant to scare him."

"I know. And if he'd been hurt it would have been my fault." She felt tears slip down her cheeks. She should confess what she'd done, apologize to George. She knew that, but wasn't it too late?

"You were very scared in the water," Marley said. "I know the power of the river. I know your fear."

"How could you know my fear?" Betsy lashed out. "It was so dark."

He didn't answer for a long while.

"My wife, my baby daughter, and I were caught in floodwaters."

Betsy stood up straighter. Some instinct told her what was coming next.

"Our boat was stove in by trees hidden under the water. She went down in seconds."

"And your wife and daughter?"

"Drowned, I guess—" His voice broke off. He sniffed then continued. "I never found them. I searched for months. Their bodies never washed ashore."

"Oh, Marley, I'm so sorry," Betsy choked out. She laid her head against the horse's neck and cried.

"I wanted revenge," Marley said. "I wanted God to tell me why I was alive and they were dead. I was thrown into a submerged treetop, and it held me above the water. I cursed the rain and the floodwaters. Why did God take my family from me?"

"Do you know why?" Betsy asked on a sob.

"No. They went to heaven, of that I'm sure."

Betsy cried quietly into the mare's mane until she regained control. "So that's the tragedy in your life," she said.

"Yes. Moon Silver and little Sarah are now memories to me, and I think of them every day."

"Moon Silver? She was an Indian?"

"Yes. I lived in her settlement for two years. We were headed west when the boat sank. I returned to tell her family. And I started taking others down the river. I had to tame the river. Prove to myself that I could take families safely down. But I always wait until the spring flood has passed. I warn other families of the dangers of the floodwaters, but few listen to me."

"So that's why you hadn't already gone down the river when we needed a guide."

"Yes. Now I've told you my story. I understand how afraid

you were of the water. But was scaring George the way to handle your fear?"

Betsy looked out at the black night. The flickering light from the lantern inside the enclosure left deep shadows. She couldn't see the water, but she could hear it rush by.

"If I'd looked at my feet, I would have seen the string and not tripped. George shouldn't have put it in the way, but it wasn't exactly his fault. I should apologize?" She asked the question, but she knew the answer. They made their way back to the group inside the shelter. Betsy sat down beside George.

"I made the sounds in the mansion. I'm sorry," she said without preamble.

"You were the ghost?" George said in a loud voice. The others stopped talking.

"Betsy?" Mother said.

"I—I wanted to get George back for making me fall in the river. I wanted to scare him, but I know that was wrong. I'm sorry." She tried to hold back the tears, but the last few moments had been too emotional for her.

"I forgive you," George said. "I shouldn't have put the string in the walkway."

Betsy waited for Mother to chastise her, but no one else spoke for a moment.

"Now that that's taken care of, I think I'll turn in," Marley said. His statement ended the evening, and Betsy cast him a grateful look.

In the morning nothing more was said of the mansion or of Betsy's trick, and she sighed with relief as she took up her post with the *Navigator*.

The last few days had been unseasonably warm. For several days Betsy had sat on her crate seat without her cloak around her, but this day was different. By noon the wind came up, and the sky darkened with huge black clouds.

"We'd best be finding a place to hole up," Marley said. "The sooner the better."

Betsy consulted her maps and found several places that might work, but the first three were already taken by other flatboaters. They waved as they floated by, searching for the next place.

They hadn't seen much river traffic going downriver since they all seemed to be floating at the same rate. But now they discovered just how many other travelers shared the river with them.

George and Betsy made a lean-to out of canvas to cover Silverstreak, and George insisted that Jefferson be allowed inside their little house.

Rain was already pelting down by the time they found a cove where they could tie up for the night. The women fed the fire in the covered area while the men secured the boat. Rain fell hard and steadily throughout the night. By morning it hadn't slackened any.

"We're staying put," Father said. They sat inside the shelter, peering out when an adventurous flatboater would float past. Betsy read in the dim light from the fire and kept pushing Jefferson away. That smelly dog wanted to be close to the fire, too.

Once Marley and Father rowed ashore and found more wood to keep the fire going. By nightfall the rain showed no sign of abating, but by morning it was a gentle rain, and Father and Uncle Paul and Marley rowed the flatboat out of its safe berth and into the current of the Ohio again.

"We must keep a sharp eye," Marley said. "The sand shifts after a heavy rain." Although the men watched, and Betsy read aloud from the *Navigator* about where the sandbars were located, by late morning the flatboat caught on a newly formed sandbar.

"Push off! Push off!" Marley yelled. The men strained against their sweeps. Betsy held her breath as they pushed to no avail.

"Move these crates starboard," Marley said. "The weight on that side should raise this side, and we can push it off again."

Betsy and the others hurried to do his bidding, and although the right side of the flatboat tipped dangerously close to water level, with lots of grunts and muscle power, the men were able to free the boat from the sand's hold.

George and Betsy and the women scurried to move the crates back to even out the load on the boat, and it once again found the river's current and floated downstream.

Everyone was wet, and once the rain stopped for good, the travelers changed into dry clothes.

"We'll make clotheslines out of these ropes," George said, and Betsy helped him string rope across the boat.

"We look like a Monday washing day back home," Mother said once they hung all the clothes out for the sun to dry.

Back home. It had been days since Betsy had wondered about Mary and the ships in Boston Harbor and if Richard had returned from the sea. A wave of intense homesickness washed over her. It was as dark as the waters of the Ohio River.

CHAPTER 12

The Holdup

The next few days fell into a pattern. Good weather returned, and with it, traffic on the river increased.

"Why didn't we see other boats before?" Betsy asked. "It seems everyday we see more and more."

"At first we must have been traveling at about the same speed," Marley answered. "So the only travelers we saw were the ones who were stranded or keelboats that were going upriver. Some of these boats are merchant boats. They stop fairly often so we can overtake them."

Not only did they overtake them, Mother bought goods from one merchant. He sold a bit of everything, and Mother even found a book to add to Betsy's collection.

They also started stopping at wharves when it wasn't time to stop for the night. Father said Silverstreak would lose muscle tone if she wasn't exercised each day, so they took the opportunity to unload the horse at least once a day.

On the evenings when they tied up at a settlement's wharf, there would be other boats tied there. Occasionally in the coves where they'd stay for the night there would be others, too. Once they all went ashore and shared dinner with another family. They sat around a campfire, and when Father suggested that Betsy get her violin, she complied.

These were friendly folks, and she doubted that she would ever see them again, so she struck up a tune, and they sang along.

Some days Betsy and George guessed how many boats they would see along the way. Keelboats counted, too.

"At least we've never been passed by a flatboat," George said. "We've got a pretty fast boat."

"Yes," Marley said, "and a sturdy one. The extra time your father took working on this boat has made it hold up when a lesser boat would have sprung a leak."

"My father's going to own his own boatyard soon," George said proudly.

"Yes, and it will be a quality outfit," Marley replied.

Jefferson barked, which usually meant he heard wildlife along the shore or more river traffic.

Betsy heard the noise before they rounded the bend in the river and came upon two boats fastened together near the middle of the channel. The noise almost drowned out her words.

"What is it?"

"A sawmill," Marley said. "That paddlewheel between the boats powers the saw." He called directions to Father and Uncle Paul, and they steered the boat to the left of the floating sawmill.

Late that afternoon they tied the boat at the rickety dock near the mouth of Salt Creek. The three men were busy applying oakum to the stern. Uncle Paul had noticed a place that might be a potential trouble spot.

"Best to take care of it before we spring a leak," he said.

"What about Silverstreak?" Betsy asked her mother. "Can I take her for a ride without Marley? There are some fields on the other side of the trees, and there's even a salt lick not far from here." She had just read about it in the guide. "That must be why this dock is here."

Mother scanned the shoreline. "It looks all right, I guess. But take George and Jefferson, too."

Betsy hadn't exactly avoided George since the episode at the Blennerhassett mansion, but she hadn't sought him out, either. Now she called to him and asked if he wanted to go ashore. She knew what his response would be. Within a few minutes Betsy and George were ashore. They followed a narrow path, with George and Jefferson staying way behind Silverstreak.

"I'm going to look for the salt lick," George said when they came to a point where the wooded path forked. He tugged on the rope that was tied to Jefferson, and they headed west while Betsy turned Silverstreak in the opposite direction.

"I'll be back in a little while," she said. "Stay out of trouble. We'll go back to the boat together." A little way past the woods that fronted the river, a wide field opened up. Betsy let Silverstreak canter. The mare threw her head up and raced through the new green grass. If she didn't know better, Betsy would have said the horse grinned at having freedom of movement again.

They'd been on the river for fifteen days. They were all tired, but Marley said they should reach Cincinnati in another four days on the outside—three if everything went well. She didn't know what lay in store for them in Cincinnati, but she was ready for a real home with a real address. Then she could write to Mary again and hope for a letter in return.

April wildflowers dotted the pasture to her right, and she rode among the blues and the yellows and sweet scents of the early flowers. Perhaps she and Mother could put out flowers at their new home. She could transplant wildflowers, and there would be many more to choose from in May.

To her left was a dogwood in full bloom. She rode under the tree, ducking so she wouldn't get hit by the low branches, then she stopped Silverstreak and sat up straight. It was as if she were a part of the tree. To her left, to her right, below her, and above her were the fragrant white blossoms.

She breathed in deeply and sat still a few moments until Silverstreak neighed. When the mare reared her head, she hit a branch, so Betsy carefully guided her out from under the tree.

The sun was getting low, and she knew she should find George and return to the confinement of the boat. With a sigh she turned away from the lovely tree and headed back in the direction she had come.

George was nowhere to be seen. She whistled, thinking Jefferson might respond with a bark, but heard nothing. Once she reached the fork in the wooded path, she rode west over a mile, toward where she suspected the salt lick was located, but she didn't see George. He probably couldn't have covered that much ground on foot in the time she'd been riding Silverstreak. Where could that boy and his dog have gotten to?

Leave it to George to get lost the one time they were trusted enough to go ashore alone. She turned Silverstreak toward the river and slowly headed back through the woods toward the flatboat. Glancing left and right, she searched for George and Jefferson. She found him hiding behind a big tree about two hundred yards from the river.

Before she could say a word, he held his finger to his lips for silence. The alarmed expression on his face made her bite back the words that rose to her lips. She turned Silverstreak around and rode her back up the path, then tied her to a tree. Gingerly Betsy walked toward George, who was still staring at her with huge eyes.

She tiptoed to his hiding place.

"What are you doing?" she whispered.

"There's a strange man on the boat," George whispered back.

"Probably just another traveler."

"I don't think so. Look!"

Betsy peeked around the side of the tree at the boat. It was a good two hundred yards down to the water's edge, and she couldn't see details clearly, but the stance of the men signaled danger. Father, Uncle Paul, and Marley faced the man. Mother and Aunt Eleanor hovered near the opening to the covered area.

"What are they doing?" George asked.

"I don't know." She saw the setting sun reflect off something in the stranger's hand. Betsy gasped. "I think he's got a gun."

"Is he robbing them?"

"We've got to do something. He might hurt them."

"What can we do?" George asked.

"Let me think. Did you find the salt lick? Did you see any men there?"

"No, I didn't get that far. Jefferson chased a squirrel, and I had to chase him."

"So there's no help there. If we run down to the boat, he'll see us and that won't do any good."

"We need to catch him by surprise and tie him up," George whispered. Betsy nodded. She looked around for another boat or a little skiff, but their flatboat was the only one on the river.

"How do you suppose he got here? By foot?" Betsy asked in a hushed whisper.

"Must have. He'll have to come up the path, won't he?"

"He should. Where's Jefferson?"

"I tied him to a tree back there," he motioned through the woods but off the path. "Once I saw that man, I didn't want Jefferson barking. Look!"

Father was handing the man something, probably money they had saved to start over in Cincinnati. The man stuffed it in a bag and waved the gun around. Betsy could hear him speak, but she couldn't make out the words. From his arm motions, she guessed he was telling them to stay on the boat.

"Can you get Jefferson's rope without making him bark?" she asked. "Maybe we can trip him. One of us on each side of the path, and we'll jerk it up when he passes."

Without saying a word, George sneaked back into the woods. A couple minutes later he was back with the rope.

"I told Jefferson to stay."

"The man's leaving," Betsy whispered. "Give me that end." She silently crawled across the path and hid behind a large oak. Leaning back into the trail, she covered the rope with some leaves, cringing when they made a rustling sound. George buried the rope on his side of the path.

"When he gets to this spot, pull on it," Betsy said.

She peeked around the tree and saw the man jump off the dock and bolt toward them. He wasn't fifty feet away when Jefferson barked. That dog again! The robber paused a second and cocked his head as if listening. Jefferson barked again, and this time the sound was farther away. He was probably chasing another squirrel. The man seemed satisfied that nothing was coming his way and scurried forward.

Betsy held her breath as she listened to the man's running steps crackle the leaves that littered the path. He came closer, closer. When he was almost upon them, she glanced across the path at George. He was staring at her, his huge eyes the only thing she noticed on his face.

"Now!" Betsy yelled, and they both jerked on the rope.

The man let out a curse as he fell. Before he could struggle to his feet, George jumped on his back, and Betsy wound the rope around his legs. The man shook George off, but when he finally managed to stand, the rope made him stumble again, and down he went.

"Get him!" Betsy shouted and jumped on his back along with George.

"Betsy! George!" Father called. The three men came running up the sloping path.

Marley reached them first and pounced on the man. Father tied the man's hands behind his back with one end of the rope, leaving the other end wound around his legs.

Then Father grabbed Betsy and held her close. "We were so frightened that he would find you out here," he said.

"We got him good," George bragged.

"You sure did," Uncle Paul assured his son as he hugged him.

Marley picked up the bag the robber had carried. "I believe we'll be taking this back." He reached inside the man's coat and pulled out the gun. "I don't believe you'll be needing this where you're going." He turned to the other two men. "We can turn him over to the law in Adamsville."

"I'll get Silverstreak," Betsy said and explained where he was tied up. "I'll be just a minute."

The men hustled the prisoner back down the path to the boat.

"Jefferson!" George called. He whistled, but there was no sound from the woods. "Jefferson!"

"Which way do you think he went?" Betsy asked.

"Back toward the salt lick, I think," George said and started up the path.

"Hop on, and we'll find him," Betsy said.

"I'll walk," George said.

"Suit yourself." Betsy moved ahead on Silverstreak and called for Jefferson. Who would have thought she'd have to be looking for that dog? But George had captured the robber by getting Jefferson's rope and setting the dog free. It was the least she could do.

At the fork in the path, Betsy turned toward the west. "Jefferson," she called. As soon as the woods gave way to clear fields, Betsy urged Silverstreak into a canter. If George and Jefferson had come here before, it seemed logical that the dog would return, unless something else or some other animal claimed his attention.

Soon she could no longer hear George yelling and whistling

back in the woods. The sun was nearly down. Riding in the dark on unknown ground was dangerous. A mile later she turned the horse around and retraced her steps, although she still hadn't found the dog.

She saw George walking along the edge of the woods, still whistling and calling for his dog.

"We have to get back to the boat," Betsy told him.

"But Jefferson's out here somewhere."

"We'll find him tomorrow, first thing. Hurry, it's getting darker by the minute. Jefferson's a smart dog. He'll be all right."

George yelled for his dog all the way back to the boat, but there was no telltale barking in response. He lumbered onto the boat. The eyes that had been saucer sized an hour earlier were now small with pain. Betsy knew how she'd feel if it had been Silverstreak out there alone, and she patted George on the back.

"We'll find him tomorrow," she said and explained to the others that they hadn't found the dog.

"He'll get hungry and come looking for us," Aunt Eleanor told her son.

Betsy groomed Silverstreak, then joined the family for prayer before another meal of beans.

"Thank you, God, for delivering us from evil," Father ended grace. "And please help us find Jefferson, so that we may reward him for giving us his rope."

The prisoner was tied to a post on the side opposite the dock. Father untied his hands so he could eat then retied them.

"Jefferson!" George called toward shore every few minutes.

In desperation to get him to stop yelling, Betsy pulled out her violin. Jefferson had always howled when he heard her play.

She'd thought of him as a bad critic, one more strike against him, but Father had explained that dogs seemed to hear high pitches better than people, and that he probably liked the high notes she reached.

She played songs with high clear notes and was about to put away the violin for the night when she heard a bark from the woods.

"Jefferson!" she said.

George must have heard him, too. He was already on his feet and reaching for the lantern. Uncle Paul followed his son.

"Jefferson!" George called. He whistled for his dog as he jumped off the boat onto the dock. "Here, boy."

Betsy could hear the dog rustling leaves as he bounded down the path, barking and yelping. She struck up another tune, and Jefferson started his howling.

A few moments later a triumphant George returned to the boat carrying the little dog. Uncle Paul followed right behind him with the lantern.

"Don't you ever run away from me again," George lectured his dog. "We were all worried about you."

Not all of us, Betsy thought out of habit, then hastily amended that thought. She had been worried about the dog because he meant so much to George.

"Thank you, God, for returning him safely," she whispered.

CHAPTER 13

Stuck!

Early the next morning the travelers floated down to Adams-ville, where the men rowed the prisoner to shore. Father had assured Betsy that all their cash was safe now, and that the money hadn't been as important as the lives of his family.

"I was terrified that robber would find you and George in the woods," Mother said. "But I guess I didn't have to worry about you two. You worked together. I'm proud of that, Betsy."

Betsy nodded. She really hadn't thought about working with George. It had just happened.

Once the men returned to the boat, they cast off again, and Betsy took up her usual post with her maps.

"If we travel late this evening, we can make it to Limestone Creek, can't we?" Betsy asked Marley. The sun was staying up a little later each day, and she wanted to claim those few minutes as travel time.

"We might be tying up in the dark," he said, "but that's a big landing. There are bound to be lanterns out."

By dark they were still on the river, determined to make it

around the bend to Maysville on the Limestone. An hour later they tied up at the landing, one of several boats secured there. Father exercised Silverstreak on the main street, and the next morning they shoved off at sunrise.

"How far can we get today?" George asked after they had breakfasted on the river.

"If we can get to Bullskin Creek tonight," Betsy said, consulting her maps, "we might be able to make it to Cincinnati by tomorrow night."

"Two more days!" George exclaimed. His excitement matched Betsy's as they pushed on down the river. Even the adults caught the contagious fever of journey's end. They made good time, and by early afternoon they were nearing Bracken Creek.

"Stay port side," Marley called from the roof where he was steering the boat with his wide sweep. Father left his position on the left side and crossed to push off with Paul.

"Push! I can see the sandbar," Marley called. "It's farther out."

But they couldn't move in time, and the boat snagged on the bar, stopping so suddenly, Betsy slid off her perch on the crate. Marley had squatted on the roof, but Father and Uncle Paul both fell on the deck. Inside the shelter, Mother and Aunt Eleanor screamed as crates came crashing to the floor. Jefferson howled, and Silverstreak whinnied.

"Wow," George said. He was sprawled on the deck near Betsy's feet.

"Are you all right, Maggie?" Father quickly gained his stance and ran inside the enclosure. He appeared a moment later at the doorway. "We have a few displaced items but nothing major. Anyone hurt?"

Betsy rubbed her arm that had scraped along the crate but didn't say anything. She made her way down the narrow aisle beside the enclosure and settled Silverstreak.

"Let's get her off the bar," Marley called. "Any leaks?"

"None here," Uncle Paul called from aft. He examined the boat and declared it seaworthy. Then the work began.

The travelers stacked their heavy belongings on the freed side of the boat, so the side that was buried in the sandbar could be shoved loose.

They pushed, pulled, and tugged but the flatboat remained still. Another flatboat passed by them, careful to stay on the far left, away from the grabbing sandbar.

"Can we help?" a bargeman from a keelboat called a few minutes later. This boat was making its way up the Ohio and was positioned below them.

Marley quickly conferred with the men on the keelboat, and they threw a rope to the flatboat.

"They'll try to pull us out. If they stay in the channel, the current will help. Get ready to push."

All three men pushed off the sandbar with their long sweeps. On the keelboat, some bargemen pulled on the rope and others pushed on their long poles. The flatboat rocked and at last was freed from the sandbar.

Betsy and the others quickly redistributed the weight of the crates, Marley untied the rope, and the bargeman pulled it aboard the keelboat.

"Many thanks," Father called to them.

"Think nothing of it," the bargeman called.

"That was nice of them to help us," George said as they got underway again. "But why didn't that other boat stop?"

"It wasn't the Christian thing to do," Betsy said, "going by us like that."

"There could have been many reasons," Mother said. "It's not for us to judge what's in the hearts of others."

"Does this mean we won't get to Cincinnati tomorrow?" George asked.

Betsy glanced at the sun, but Marley answered before she could estimate the distance and the hours of sunlight left.

"This delay has cost us dearly in time. We'll spend two more days on the river," he said, "but that will let us get to Cincinnati in the daylight instead of at night. That will make it easier."

Perhaps, Betsy thought, but she had hoped that this would be her last night of sleeping on the boat.

By the next evening, excitement aboard the boat was a tangible thing. George skipped along the deck, Betsy's violin had never had a happier voice, and Jefferson barked at every bird along the shore. They anchored near Little Indian Creek, and Betsy had a hard time falling asleep.

At daybreak the travelers cast off for the last time. By afternoon George was dancing across the boat, and Betsy was calling off each landmark they passed.

"That's Little Miami River," Betsy said. "It's not far now." She stood on her crate, as if that bit of additional height could make her see farther.

George stood at the bow. "Look!" he shouted a few minutes later. "Cincinnati!"

Mother and Aunt Eleanor stood beside Betsy and stared at the shoreline. Dwelling after dwelling came into sight. It wasn't the size of Boston, but it was the biggest town they had seen since they left Pittsburgh.

"We're home," Mother said, "at last."

"Home?" Betsy echoed. Not home. Boston was home. They were in Cincinnati.

"Yes, home," Mother said in a voice that brooked no argument. "This is our new home." Betsy didn't reply, but her excitement at finally arriving dimmed.

They docked and unloaded Silverstreak. Father tied her to a hitching post while they walked to a public house on the main street. As soon as they had washed up and drank a refreshing cup of tea, Father turned to Betsy.

"Take Silverstreak to the stable and arrange for her board." He handed her several coins.

"You want me to go alone?" she asked.

"Yes, please. The innkeeper said Potter's stable is a few blocks farther down this street but on a corner, so it faces north."

"But, Father, you want me to talk to the man at the stable?"

"Yes, Betsy. I need to arrange for storage for our movings and get them off the boat this afternoon. Take George with you."

"But I can help you," George protested.

"Yes, you can. After you help Betsy with Silverstreak," Father said.

Betsy and Marley walked side by side toward the boat, while George raced with Jefferson to the river.

"You have a problem with the horse?" Marley asked.

"No," Betsy replied. "I have a problem talking to strangers."

"Now I never noticed that," Marley said. "You took right up with me."

"You're different," Betsy said.

"No. I'm the same as everyone else. Give people a chance, Betsy. They're just like you and me."

She nodded but didn't reply. She'd taken up with Marley because Father had said he had overcome tragedy and she should be nice to him. He didn't seem like a threat to her. Surely everyone hadn't overcome tragedy. But could there be something in their lives that they struggled with, too?

They arrived at the post where Silverstreak was hitched, and Betsy untied her.

"Come on, George," she called.

"I'm coming," he said but stayed a good ten feet behind her with Jefferson yapping at his feet as they made their way back down the main street.

Once they passed the inn, Betsy scrutinized each corner, looking for the stable. Four streets later she found it.

"You want to talk to the man?" she called back to George, who still lagged behind.

"You do it, but hurry up so we can get back to the boat. They've probably already found a place to store our movings and are unloading."

Betsy stood outside the stable and looked into the dim interior. Stalls lined both sides of the barnlike structure. She could make out a figure near the back.

"Come hold Silverstreak," she ordered George, as she mustered her courage to go inside. She had done this in

Pittsburgh, but Silverstreak's keep had already been arranged, and it was a boy she'd talked with. She'd known that they'd be leaving town shortly, so it didn't matter what the stable boy thought of her.

"No. Tie her up," George said from the street.

A couple of boys about George's age walked around the corner. "Why are you afraid of Silverstreak? Are you afraid of all horses?" she asked in exasperation. The two boys snickered as they walked by, and George turned a brilliant shade of red.

Betsy stared at him. He was embarrassed. She'd tried so many ways to embarrass him that hadn't worked, and then out of the blue, she'd done it. It didn't feel as good as she had thought it would. An eye for an eye—that was her purpose: to humiliate him the way he'd humiliated her. But this vengeance didn't sit well with her. Turning the other cheek was much more her philosophy. Why hadn't she seen that before?

She turned and walked purposefully into the stable, leading the mare.

"I have a horse to board," she said to the man, who was walking toward her. "Dr. Thomas Miller is the owner, and her name is Silverstreak. I'll be exercising her most days. What's the charge?"

He named an amount, and she paid him a week's board.

She led Silverstreak into the stall the man pointed out and promised the horse she'd return later that day to ride her.

"When you come back, I'll tell you the best roads to take," the man offered.

"Thank you," she said. He had been quite nice. Maybe Marley was right, and she needed to give others a chance instead of being too shy to speak.

By the time Betsy and George arrived at the river, Father, Uncle Paul, and Marley were unloading the boat and putting the crates on a flatbed wagon.

"We're headed to the river warehouse," Father said and motioned to a nearby building. "Not far to move our things, and from the looks of the clouds, we'd better hurry."

Betsy glanced up and watched dark clouds soar across the sky. There was strong wind up high, but on the ground the wind wasn't nearly as fierce.

The rain held off until nightfall, and by that time all the Millers' and Lankfords' belongings were safe and dry in the warehouse. Father, Uncle Paul, and Marley had found a place to anchor the flatboat so that it could be torn apart for the lumber to start on the houses.

"First we'll build ours," Father said when the two families gathered around the dinner table at the inn. "Then we'll all live there until we can get Paul's up. We'll find a suitable place tomorrow."

"And I'll be finding a keelboat that wants another hand," Marley said.

Betsy gasped, surprised that he was leaving. Yet she'd known that he was hired to take them downstream. Now his job was over, and he'd want to get back to his home base. But he'd become part of her family.

"When will you be going?" she asked.

"Not for a few days anyway," he said. "I need to get some land legs, and I'll help take the boat apart."

CHAPTER 14

Rising Waters

In steady rain the next morning, the men walked the streets of Cincinnati to find a good location for the Millers' house, then they checked at the land office.

"We've found the right place," Father reported at noon. "We'll be living on Sycamore Street. There's a vacant area right on the corner. We can have the entry to our house on one street and the entry to my surgery on the other."

"What about our house?" George asked.

"We'll get to that after we build the first one," Uncle Paul said.

The rain continued in the afternoon. Betsy's hat and cloak didn't keep her dry as she hurried up the street toward Potter's stable. She wasn't going to ride Silverstreak in this downpour, but she could groom the mare and let her know that she hadn't been deserted. For once George hadn't tagged along. He'd stayed to play with Jefferson on the covered back porch on the inn.

Betsy darted under the porch roofs of the mercantiles as she made her way down the street. The rain pounded down and seemed to gain in intensity. When would it stop?

She didn't stay long at the stable but talked with Mr. Potter and learned more about the town. She asked about the library, and he told her where it was located. He didn't know the times it was open, but she vowed to find out. She had allowed her books to be stored in the warehouse in the trunk, so there would be one less thing to step around in their small room at the inn, and anyway she'd be able to read other books at the library soon. She'd only retrieved her Bible and writing materials out of the trunk before it was taken to the warehouse.

The rain seemed to have let up when Betsy left the stable and ran from covered porch to covered porch through the shower back to the inn, but soon another storm moved through, dropping buckets of water on the soggy town.

By the next day, Betsy was sick of rain. Was this typical of Cincinnati's weather? Would her new home mean living in constant rain? She sat downstairs in the parlor of the inn and stared out the window. For the moment the rain had turned to drizzle, and ten minutes later she saw sunshine for the first time in days. The street was one continuous mud puddle. The only solid ground—and it was mushy—was in the yards beside the houses where spring grass grew. Even with the rain over, it would take some time for the ground to dry out.

Just then Marley clomped up the side steps to the inn and barged inside. "River's rising," he announced. "We're watching it, but it could come out of its banks before evening."

"But it stopped raining," Betsy said. "Surely it won't go any higher."

"It's still raining upstream," Marley said, "and that water will flow this way. According to the rain barrel next to the warehouse, we've had over fifteen inches of rain. That's a lot of water. Where's your father?"

"Upstairs. I'll fetch him."

Betsy returned with her father and Uncle Paul and listened to the men talk.

"That warehouse is too close to the river. It could go under. Anything in there that needs moving?" Marley asked.

"My books," Betsy said. "Oh, Father, I left my books in the trunk."

"We'd better move things to higher ground," Father said, "just in case. Let's check around."

Father, Uncle Paul, and Marley left the inn, and Betsy watched until they disappeared from sight. They didn't walk down the muddy street but stepped gingerly from yard to yard.

An hour later by the grandfather clock in the parlor, they returned and stood on the front porch.

"Betsy, we're going to need everyone's help to get our movings out of the warehouse. Mr. Potter says we can store things in the stable for the time being. He has a couple of empty stalls. But we can't get a wagon down this muddy street. Get the others." He motioned to his mud-covered feet. "I shouldn't go inside. And tell your mother to wear my old pair of boots."

Betsy quickly climbed the stairs and called to the women. George and Jefferson ran to the front porch from the back porch of the inn. Soon they all traipsed to the river warehouse, single file, finding the most solid footing they could.

"Oh, my," Mother exclaimed as they looked at the Ohio River.

"It's coming up a foot an hour," Marley said, after conferring with some bargemen who had tied up at the public landing.

Jefferson barked, and George trudged into the muddy street to pick up his dog. Jefferson had sunk to his stomach in the mire.

George placed the dog on the flatbed wagon that was stored beside the river warehouse.

"Stay," he said. "I'll get you on the next trip."

It was eight long blocks that sloped upward to Potter's stable, and Betsy made sure she and Mother carried the trunk that held her books. In some places they couldn't avoid the mud. Her shoes were caked with it, making each step harder. For once she was glad she was wearing her too-short traveling dress that Jefferson had chewed on. It kept the hem from getting so muddy and weighing her down.

They formed an odd parade walking to the stable. Father and Uncle Paul carried two crates between them, balancing one on top of the other. Aunt Eleanor and George carried a trunk, and Marley carried one by himself.

Mr. Potter directed Betsy and Mother to the stall where they deposited the trunk with the books.

"Let's hope the next trunk isn't as heavy," Mother said.

"Silverstreak can help," Betsy said. "That way I can carry the smaller crates on horseback." She saddled the mare and guided her the long, but less muddy, way to the warehouse. Still the horse's hooves were plastered with mud.

Marley handed Betsy two valises. She hooked one over the saddle horn and propped the other in front of her. From his perch on the flatbed wagon, Jefferson barked at the horse as

Betsy maneuvered her toward more solid ground.

"Stay." Betsy repeated the order George had given earlier and was amazed that the dog obeyed. Getting stuck in the mud must have made a great impression on him. She glanced at the river. It had taken much less than an hour to get the first load to the stable, yet the water was more than a foot higher than the last time she'd she seen it.

Betsy took her load to the stable and returned again.

Other men were at the river warehouse now, carrying stored goods to higher ground. They worked quickly and with little talk.

This time Father helped Betsy load a heavier crate. She secured it with a rope around the saddle horn and balanced it in front of her.

"Just take it as far as the porch at the inn, then return," Father said, an urgency in his voice.

Betsy urged Silverstreak forward. She passed Mother and Aunt Eleanor carrying the headboard of Grandmother's bed between them. George struggled up the porch steps with a large basket, and then he headed back while Betsy deposited her load.

By her fifth load to the porch, the river roared only inches below its banks. As George helped Betsy stack her crate on the porch, someone on the street cried, "She's out of her banks!"

That was impossible. How could it rise so fast?

George dropped his end of the crate and yelled, "Jefferson!" He turned and ran toward the river, his shoes throwing mud behind him.

Betsy climbed on the mare and followed him. She pulled up

Silverstreak when she saw the river. How had this happened so fast?

Water gushed around the wheels of the flatbed wagon where Jefferson sat howling. George dashed into the waist-high water, which knocked him off his feet and carried him downstream a good ten yards before he regained his footing and waded out of the floodwater. Looking like a drowned rat, he ran to Betsy.

"Help me get Jefferson!" he pleaded. "You're tall, so the water won't be so high on you."

Betsy glanced around. Where were her parents? Too far down the street to help now. She urged Silverstreak through the water, but the mare shied and reared. Quickly she dismounted and tied one end of the rope that she'd used to secure the crates around her waist and the other to the saddle horn.

"You're going to have to mount Silverstreak," she told George.

"I can't," he said.

"You have to. Jefferson's depending on you."

George took a deep breath, put his foot high in the stirrup, and swung into the saddle.

"Now pull on the reins if I need you to back her up and pull me out of the water," Betsy ordered. She stepped into the raging floodwaters and felt the rush of the water against her legs. With great determination she took one step after another until she reached the wagon.

She climbed up on the wheel and reached for Jefferson. The dog backed away from her.

"Tell your dog to come here," she called to George.

"Betsy!" Father yelled from a block away.

"Jefferson, go to Betsy," George shouted.

The dog inched toward her. When he was in reach, she grabbed for the muddy creature and cradled him in her arms. Now to get down from her precarious perch on the wagon wheel. She felt the wagon lurch under her feet, and with a quick prayer for courage, she plunged into the water.

This time she went under, and in the brief moment that she was submerged, she relived her earlier nightmare of being in the murky Ohio. She fought her way to a standing position and made sure Jefferson's head was out of the water. A glance at the edge of the floodwater assured her that George still sat in the saddle. Father stood behind Silverstreak. Mother and Aunt Eleanor stood at a distance, their eyes opened in horror.

"Hurry, Betsy," Mother called. Betsy stepped staunchly away from the wagon and into the torrent. She immediately lost her footing and went under again. The rope pulled at her waist, and quickly she was back on top of the churning water. She moved toward the edge of the water, half swimming, half walking.

Step by step Silverstreak moved back, keeping the rope taut between them. Jefferson didn't move in her arms. She glanced down and saw his eyes frozen in fear. They probably matched her own. Six more steps, five, four. Each step became easier as the water became shallower. Three, two, one. She stepped out of the water and into mud.

She shivered as George climbed down from Silverstreak and grabbed Jefferson. Father hugged Betsy and led her away from the rushing water that was now encroaching on the area where they stood. The dog barked and licked George's face.

Silverstreak whinnied, and Betsy leaned on her as they moved farther up the street, out of the water's reach.

"Let's get you to the inn," Mother said. "Whatever possessed you to go out into that torrent?"

"I had to. Jefferson was trapped," Betsy said through chattering teeth.

"Look!" George cried. She turned and watched as the floodwaters washed over the wagon and carried it downstream. She shook, not from the wet and cold, but from fear.

Father supported her on one side and Mother on the other as they made their way to the inn.

"Silverstreak?" Betsy asked.

"Your uncle Paul's taking her to the stable," Father said. "Our movings?" she asked.

"All safely out of the warehouse," Mother said. Aunt Eleanor hustled George and Jefferson along the street beside them.

Two hours later Betsy was warm and dry again. She sat with George and Jefferson on the front porch of the inn. Their parents and Marley had moved the rest of their belongings from the porch to Potter's stable. The sun was still shining, the rain was over, but floodwaters continued to rise. The adults were helping other townspeople move their belongings to higher ground.

"Marley said the river should crest sometime in the night," George told her. "But it won't get up here."

"That's good."

"Betsy, thanks for saving Jefferson. I don't know what I'd do without my dog. It's a good thing you're so tall, so you could go in after him."

Betsy stared at the house across the street for a full minute then turned to George. "If you think it's a good thing I'm tall, why do you always tease me about my height? 'How's the weather up there?'" she mimicked.

"No reason. Something to say, I guess. Get a rise out of you."

"Don't do it anymore."

"All right, if it bothers you," he said.

"That's it? You won't do it anymore?"

"No. You're so quiet, Betsy. You should have told me before that it bothered you. It bothered me that you asked if I was afraid of horses in front of those boys at the stable."

"I didn't mean to embarrass you, and I felt terrible afterward. I think we should treat each other the way we want to be treated."

"You mean like the Golden Rule says?" George asked.

"Exactly. George, why are you afraid of horses?"

"They're so big." He looked at the floor of the porch instead of at her. "I rode Jacob Baker's horse back in Boston, and it threw me off. I've never been back on one until today."

"Silverstreak's big, but she didn't throw you," Betsy said. "Sometimes you have to face your fears. If you want, I'll teach you to ride. Then you won't be afraid anymore."

"Thanks, Betsy. I'd like that," George said.

"I'm going inside," Betsy said. She left Jefferson and George and climbed the stairs to the Millers' room. With quill pen in hand, she sat at a small table and reflected on her conversation with George. Then she began her letter to her friend in Boston:

Dear Mary,
    We are home. Our eventful journey has left its mark on me. I'm not as shy as I was. And George and I have declared a truce. We may even be friends.

Grace and the Bully

Norma Jean Lutz

A Note to Readers

While the Ramsey and Morgan families are fictional, the troubles faced by people living in Cincinnati during 1819 are all too true. Now known as a Midwestern city, Cincinnati in the early nineteenth century was part of America's western frontier. During the time of this story, Cincinnati's lifeblood, the Ohio River, was so low that boats couldn't travel on it. Many people lost their jobs, and many families went hungry.

At that time, states printed their own money. The value of the money varied from day to day, and when there were financial problems, the money often became worthless. This confusing situation caused many problems that took more than a hundred years to straighten out.

Because there weren't radios or televisions, musical instruments were very important forms of entertainment for families in the 1800s. Having a piano or parlor organ in the home became common, and by the end of the century, most girls were expected to know how to play the piano at least a little.

To Gene and Barbara Yeager
The two of you are the epitome of the fruit of the Spirit gentleness.
I cherish your friendship.

CONTENTS

CHAPTER 1

Trouble at School

Excitement tumbled and bubbled deep inside ten-year-old Grace Morgan's stomach, making it difficult for her to pay attention. Her chin rested on her hand as she stared out the schoolhouse window.

The crowded classroom on the first floor of the brick building was not only noisy, but stuffy, too. The classroom upstairs, where the older students attended, was just as crowded. Thankfully, Grace's seat was by an open window, where she could feel the soft spring breeze blowing in. She didn't mind that she had to share a seat with Amy Coppock. Amy had been her friend for almost two years.

April meant that her fifth-grade school term was nearly over. That in itself was enough to make Grace want to turn handsprings. But today was much more exciting than the close of school. Tonight she and Mama would pen the order for her brand-new piano!

She'd dreamed of having a piano for months. Finally, Papa said that with the contracts for two new steamboats, there would be enough money for a piano. Grace sighed as she thought of the pictures in the catalog she and Mama pored over night after night. But now the decision was made. Papa said the steamboat *Velocipede* would be leaving in the morning, and the order would go onboard with the outgoing mail!

Shifting in the small, hard seat, Grace brought her attention to the front of the room, where Mr. Inman tried his utmost to work on recitation with a group of first- and second-grade students. Mr. Inman's stand-up white collar, which that morning had looked starched and spiffy, now looked rather wilted. His black bow tie drooped, as well.

Grace had decided months ago that Silas Inman was too kind and gentle to be a teacher, especially in this crowded room. The older boys talked out of turn and kept a ruckus rumbling most of the time. Last year's teacher, grouchy old Mr. Travers, seemed harsh and mean, but at least the boys had behaved.

Out of the corner of her eye, Grace saw Raggy Langler shoot a spitwad right at the back of her cousin Drew's head. Drew Ramsey sat two rows over with the sixth graders. Grace watched as he reached up to remove the wet mass from his hair and turned around to scowl at Raggy. Even from two rows over, she could sense Drew's disgust. Drew had told her there were never boys like Raggy in his school in Boston.

Poor Drew. Ever since he'd arrived from Boston two months ago, several of the boys had made fun of his dapper clothes and Boston accent, but Raggy was the worst. As Mr. Inman turned his back, Grace stuck her tongue out at Raggy, making Amy giggle. Raggy shook his fist at her and mouthed the threat, "I'll get you."

Grace just turned up her nose and ignored him. Amy nudged Grace, then pinched her own nose, indicating that Raggy smelled bad. Grace nodded in agreement. Raggy's dark hair was matted, his clothes were worn and frayed, and his neck was the color of dirty dishwater. His nose seemed too long for his angular face. The boy was continually scratching, and Grace was certain he must have lice.

On their shared slate, Amy and Grace were supposed to be working their multiplication tables, but instead, Grace had drawn a stick-figure girl sitting at a piano. Amy knew all about the new piano that would soon be coming to the Morgan household, and she was happy for Grace.

"I wouldn't even want a piano," Amy had said that day at recess time. "Then Mama would make me practice every day. I'd hate that." She screwed up her pretty face at the very thought.

But Grace didn't see it that way. It was as though her fingers hungered to move over the smooth ivory keys and coax out melodies to accompany her singing.

Last year, the church her family attended had purchased a piano. But only Widow Robbins was allowed to go near the fine instrument. No one was even supposed to touch the dark mahogany lid to take a peek at the shiny row of black-and-white keys. Grace told Mama that was unfair. Mama just said, "Rules are rules, Gracie. You know that."

Now that Grace had celebrated her tenth birthday, she hated being called *Gracie*, but still Mama, Papa, and even her older brother, Luke, insisted on calling her that.

Just then, Mr. Inman finished with the younger children and called the class to order. His efforts were rewarded only slightly as the older boys continued to whisper and laugh. Raggy had a handful of followers who mimicked his every action, especially Wesley Smith and Karl Thompson.

"As we approach the closing of the school term—" Mr. Inman began. He was interrupted with cheers from Raggy and those around him.

"Yea, hooray!" they cried in chorus. "No more school!"

Mr. Inman's soft brown eyes were troubled as he surveyed the culprits. Tugging at his dark chin whiskers, he began again. "The superintendent of schools has asked that all classrooms have a presentation prepared for the closing-day ceremony. Be thinking of how our classroom can contribute to the program, either individually or as a group."

Amy's hand shot up, and when the teacher called on her, she said, "Grace Morgan can sing, Mr. Inman. She has the most beautiful voice in the world. Nicer than a nightingale."

Grace felt herself blushing. She had no idea Amy was going to blurt out such a thing. Often she sang for family gatherings. A few times she'd even sung at church. But singing in front of the entire community would be quite different.

"Thank you, Amy." To Grace, he said, "Would you please have a song prepared for the program, Grace?"

"Yes, sir," she answered, feeling giddiness building inside her. Now she had one more exciting thing to look forward to.

From the back of the room, Raggy said in a loud whisper, "Dapper-Dandy Drew could show us how to talk Yankee talk."

Drew's hair—the color of corn silk—didn't quite cover his ears, and Grace saw them turn red right up to the tips. How she wished she could do something to cheer up Drew. She tried to imagine what it would be like if she were to lose both her parents to such a wretched disease as yellow fever. That's what had happened to Drew just last winter.

Grace turned to give Raggy her worst scowl. He was such a beast.

Mr. Inman gave Raggy, whose name in class was *Russell*, a warning to keep silent, but the warnings carried little weight.

Raggy mostly did whatever he wanted. And that seldom meant schoolwork.

In the past, Raggy had showed up for school only about half the time, but recently his attendance had become almost perfect. Grace believed that Raggy came to school only to take part in tormenting poor, defenseless Drew.

At last, Mr. Inman completed all the instructions regarding the school-closing ceremonies, which, he said, would include a parade down Main Street. Amy and Grace nudged one another at the prospect of a parade. What fun that would be!

Class was then dismissed, and Grace went to the cloakroom to fetch her tin pail from the shelf. Drew was right there beside her. Out in the schoolyard, Amy called out a good-bye as she and her older brother, Jason, headed west down Fourth Street toward their home. Grace often wished Amy lived nearer to Deer Creek so they could walk home together.

Before going out of the fenced schoolyard, Grace said to Drew, "Wait a minute." Sitting down in the dirt, she proceeded to unbutton her hightop shoes and pull off her long, itchy woolen stockings. The shoes, which had been purchased at the shoemaker's last autumn, were now much too tight.

"Grace, what are you doing?" Drew protested. "You can't walk barefoot in these filthy streets."

"Of course I can. Just watch me." She jumped up and wiggled her toes in the dirt, making little dust puffs. "*Ahh*. Now my feet are finally free."

Drew shook his head in disbelief. "No girl in Boston would walk home from school barefoot in the dirt." He paused a moment as he studied Fourth Street. It was nearly three inches deep in dirt. "But then, in Boston there are no dirt streets."

"Oh, come on, Drew," she said, hurrying on ahead of him

and turning off Fourth Street to Walnut. "Forget about Boston for a while. Let's go down near the landing and look at the *Velocipede* before going home." Grace wanted so much to help Drew forget about past things and for him to be as happy about Cincinnati as she was.

"I thought you weren't supposed to go near the landing by yourself," Drew countered, hurrying to catch up with her.

Grace gave a little giggle. "I'm not by myself, silly. You're with me. And besides, we won't go all the way to the landing. We'll just look down from Second Street."

She knew Drew wanted to hurry home. Among other things, Drew was frightened of the many pigs that ran wild on the streets. The helpful pigs ate the garbage that was thrown into the streets every day by the town's residents.

"I know you're wary of the pigs, Drew," she told him as patiently as she could. "But we'll find two big old sticks, and if any pigs come along, we'll just whack them on the snout."

Grace had never had a pesky pig attack her, but she knew other children had been attacked and seriously hurt. The gruesome stories had scared Drew.

Grace pointed to a yard where several large shade trees grew. "There should be a couple of sticks under those trees." But before they could head that direction, out from between two buildings came Raggy along with Wesley and Karl. They whooped and hollered.

"Dapper Drew! Dresses up in pretty clothes! Looks like a dandy!" Raggy called out in a singsong voice.

Quickly the other two took up the chant: "Dapper Drew! Looks like a dandy!"

Grace caught the look of fear in Drew's eyes. These boys were more frightening to him than a whole herd of pigs.

CHAPTER 2

The Fight

Grace stopped stock-still and turned about to glare at the trio. "You boys hush your mouths!" she demanded. "Leave us alone!"

Drew seemed confused, but Grace knew if he shot off running, they'd be after him for sure. "Pay 'em no mind at all, Drew Ramsey," she said in a loud voice. "At least your name is better than *Raggy*." She spit out the word with all the disdain she could muster.

But Raggy's attention was not on Grace. Coming closer, the tall boy reached down to grab a handful of the dirt from Walnut Street and flung it at Drew. "Now the dandy's a *dirty* little dandy," he said and roared with laughter.

"Stop that!" Drew protested. In vain he tried to brush off his nice navy coat and matching trousers. As Drew looked down at the mess, Raggy gave him a sudden shove, dumping him into the dirt.

Grace could stand it no more. She began twirling around, swinging her tin pail as she went. Coming up right behind Raggy, she whammed him in the back of the legs with the pail. Raggy yowled with pain. The blow knocked him off balance, causing him to stumble. As he did, he grabbed one of Grace's shoes that she'd dropped.

"Got your shoe!" he hollered as he ran off, but Grace was in hot pursuit.

"Stop that thief! He's a thief! Stop him!"

Not looking where he was going, Raggy ran smack into a well-dressed gentleman with a top hat and pearl-handled cane. "Here, here, you ragamuffin!" protested the man. "Watch where you're going!"

"Stop him!" Grace kept yelling. But Raggy threw the shoe as hard as he could and raced on down the street. His friends had long since disappeared.

With the help of the kind stranger, Grace retrieved her shoe from within the high wrought-iron fence of a fine home, then retraced her steps to where Drew stood waiting.

"You know, Drew," she said as she tried to catch her breath, "if we stick together, we can whip that terrible Raggy Langler."

But even as she said it, she could tell Drew had no desire to whip anyone—even someone who'd pushed him into the dirt. It was as though there were no life in her cousin at all.

"Why do they allow ruffians like him to attend our school?" Drew wanted to know. "He should stay in Sausage Row where he belongs."

Drew was referring to the run-down district near the landing where the poorer people of the city lived.

"Papa says the city voted to pay the way for a few indigent children to attend as well as those of us who *can* pay the subscription to go to school." Grace felt proud to know these facts, but it was only because she sometimes sat on the stair landing and listened to the grown-ups talk. She was always sent to bed before serious talk began.

"But why someone like Raggy?" Drew asked. "He doesn't even want to learn."

"It's because of the washerwoman he lives with. Emaline Stanley is her name. She took Raggy in when she found him roaming around Sausage Row all alone. I hear tell she's plumb set on him getting educated." Grace chuckled. "They say she barged right into a meeting of the board of trustees to have her say."

Drew shook his head. "Doesn't she realize the boy's not worth it?"

"I guess not. You know, Drew, the Reverend Danforth says we're supposed to love everybody, but I don't see how anyone could love that dirty, mean-mouthed Raggy."

As they talked, they approached the brink of the hill. Walnut Street, like most of the north–south streets in town, led down toward the public landing at the bank of the grand Ohio River.

Grace loved the sight of the landing as it spread out before them. The wide cobblestone landing was flanked on the north by a row of stately buildings, housing factories, mills, and warehouses that thrived on the river business. At one end of the landing was the brick factory, at the other end was the glassworks.

Situated on the far side of the glassworks was the boatbuilding business in which Papa and Luke were involved. Papa had told her many times, "Grace, someday you'll see dozens, and perhaps even scores, of steamboats plying these waters. And mark my words, the queen city of Cincinnati will be smack dab in the middle of it all!"

The awe and thrill in Papa's voice never failed to stir something inside of Grace. How she wished Drew could be as impressed by this growing frontier city as she was.

"There it is!" she cried out as they approached Front Street. "There's the *Velocipede!*" The queenly steamboat sat high and proud near the landing, among lesser keelboats, barges, and a few meager flatboats, which carried individual families and all their earthly belongings.

"You see steamboats most every day," Drew commented dryly. "Nothing to get worked up about."

"But this steamboat will carry the order for my new piano!" she said, bouncing up and down on her bare toes.

Drew stopped beside her to study the river. "Why is the stern-wheeler out so far?" he asked.

Now Grace stopped to look, as well. "The water's low. Papa says it's because there was so little snow last winter and so little rain this spring."

"What happens if the water goes lower?"

Papa and Luke had told Grace about a summer many years ago when the river was dry for a number of months. But that was before they depended on steamboats to bring so many supplies from New York and New Orleans.

"It won't go any lower," she assured him—and assured herself, as well. "The spring rains will come soon. Just wait and see. Then, instead of complaining about the dust in the streets, you'll complain about all the mud." Grace didn't even want to think about the prospect of a business slowdown on Cincinnati's public landing, especially if it meant a slowdown on the arrival of her piano.

The walk to Front Street had taken them a few blocks out of the way in their journey home. Before turning to walk back up the hill to Third, Grace sat down to put on her shoes and stockings so Mama would never know she'd been running barefoot all over the city.

Looking up at Drew, she asked, "Are you going to do something special for the school program, Drew?" She hopped up as they resumed their walk toward home.

Drew gave a shrug.

"You told me you learned Greek and Latin in Boston. Why don't you recite a piece in Greek?" She laughed as she thought of it. "That'd show that old Raggy a thing or two." But she could see her great idea sparked little response in Drew. If she could speak another language, she'd teach it to Amy. Then they could talk about Raggy, and he'd never know what they were saying.

They were almost to the two-story brick home where Grace lived on Symmes Street. She stopped a moment at their front gate, where her mama had planted masses of rambling roses and honeysuckle bushes.

"In the morning, Papa and I will take the order for my piano down to the steamboat," Grace said. "If you want to go with us, come by earlier than usual."

Drew nodded in agreement. "Bye," he said giving her a listless wave.

Grace watched as he walked slowly toward the plank-covered log cabin situated in a clearing near Deer Creek. There, Drew lived with his older brother, Carter; Carter's wife, Deanna; and their two little ones, Adah and Matthew. Even though Carter had built a loft for Drew, Grace knew that, with two toddlers underfoot, it was a crowded place.

Opening the gate, she gave a sigh. It just didn't seem right that she should be so happy and Drew so sad. Although Drew's bedroom in the loft was nice, it was no doubt shabby in comparison to the fine room and fancy furnishings he'd enjoyed in Boston.

As she approached the front door, she could smell the wonderful aroma of her mama's beef stew. She burst into the roomy kitchen, where Mama was bent over the butcher-block table, stirring batter in a crockery bowl.

"Mama," she called out, "I'm home!"

Mama looked up and brushed a strand of chestnut-colored hair from her forehead with the back of her hand. "Gracie, what happened to you? Your bonnet's down and your hair's a fright!"

From the pantry, Grace heard snickers from Regina Watson, their hired girl. Grace ignored the snickers since it seemed Regina was always laughing at her. Quite honestly, Grace had forgotten that her bonnet had fallen back during her wild encounter with Raggy.

"Too much running at recess, I guess," she said quickly. She decided not to tell Mama about the chase, especially not while Regina was listening.

Just then, Regina emerged from the pantry carrying two pies. She was a thin girl with stringy hair and a mousy face. "Gracie is forever running," she said. "A few chores would settle her down, I'd say."

Regina accused Grace of being petted because she was the youngest. If Grace weren't so polite, she'd tell Regina that Luke had called the hired servant "an addlepated girl with half the sense God gave a goose." Instead, she simply ignored Regina. Hugging her mother, she breathed deeply the aromas of yeasty dumpling batter.

"Go wash your hands and brush your hair, then come and tell me about your day," said Mama.

Grace pinched off a tiny bit of dough and popped it into her mouth. Her news couldn't wait until after a washing. "Mama," she said, "you'll never guess what—I'm going to sing at the school-commencement exercises!"

Mama stopped stirring batter now and raised her eyebrows. "Why, fancy that, our little Gracie singing in front of all those people!"

Regina came to take the bowl from Mama's hands and began dropping spoonfuls of the batter into the boiling stew.

"Mama, please," Grace protested. "I'm not 'Little Gracie' anymore. I'm ten years old." She leaned against the heavy butcher-block table and went back to her story. "It was because of Amy that I was asked. She told Mr. Inman that I have a beautiful voice."

"And you certainly do." Mama waved her flour-covered hand. "Now go do as I said, please."

Backing away toward the kitchen door, Grace added, "Will you and Papa help me choose the perfect song to sing?"

Mama nodded as she turned to dip her floured hands in a basin of water and wipe them on a linen towel. "We'll talk at supper," she said. "Go on now."

"And after supper we'll write out the piano order?"

Mama looked up and smiled her warm, kind smile. "That's exactly what we're going to do."

Grace almost slipped and said she'd looked at the *Velocipede*, but she caught herself in the nick of time. She wasn't supposed to come home by way of Front Street.

Strolling out of the kitchen, Grace gazed down the hallway at the brand-new parlor Papa had built just last year. When it was finished, Mama had purchased flowered wallpaper at the mercantile store and had it hung, along with heavy dark green drapes. Between the whatnot shelves and the fireplace was the very spot where Grace's piano would sit. By using her imagination just a bit, she could actually see it sitting there and see herself running her fingers over the keys. She could even see pages and pages of music on the stand.

Halfway up the stairs, she hung out over the balustrade to gaze again at the empty space on the carpet where the piano would be placed. In just a few months it would be there. She could hardly wait!

CHAPTER 3

The Piano Order

The oil lamp made a warm golden glow in the center of the dining table as Mama laid out the quill, ink, sand, and paper. There, too, was the flickering candle to use for sealing wax.

"We'll work at the table," Mama said, "so we can sit together. There's room for only one person at the secretary."

All the fixings from dinner had been cleared away. Regina had gone home, taking a few of the leftovers with her in her wicker basket. Grace was quite thankful that Regina did not live with them.

Mama spread out the catalog to the page they'd marked. "Now, you're sure this is the one?" she asked.

Grace nodded, so excited she could barely speak. "I'm sure."

The handsome-looking piano was mahogany and looked every bit as nice as the one at church. *Just let cranky Widow Robbins have her old piano,* Grace thought. But she would never say such a thing out loud.

Mama picked up the quill to dip in the ink.

"May I, Mama? May I write the order?"

Mama looked surprised. "Why, I suppose you can." She handed the quill to Grace. "I'll read out the words and numbers."

Writing the order made Grace feel just like a grown woman. Why couldn't Mama and Papa remember how grown-up she was becoming?

When they were finished, Mama said, "Thad, would you come here a minute? We're ready for the banknote."

Grace's broad-shouldered papa seemed to fill the room when he entered. He pulled out the other cane-bottomed chair and sat down.

"Let's see here now," he said, picking up the order. "My, my. Would you look at Gracie's beautiful penmanship?"

Grace wanted to protest again about being called *Gracie*, but it seemed easier to say so to Mama than Papa. Papa always looked at her with a merry twinkle in his eye. "Thank you, Papa," she said instead.

"By the time the leaves turn and the pawpaws are ripe, we'll have a house filled with music."

"We already have a house filled with music, Papa," Grace countered. "Your fiddle does that."

Papa reached out to gently pat her arm. "Now, I'm trusting that you'll be making music much more grand than my screechy old fiddle."

Grace laughed at his joke, but she thought his fiddle music was wonderful.

She watched as Papa's strong hand took the quill to write out the banknote for a partial payment. Because of Papa's successful boatbuilding business, he had a great deal of money now in the Branch Bank at Fourth and Vine.

"Lavina," she'd heard him say to Mama just last week, "when the two steamboats that Luke and I are building now are finished, we'll be just about as wealthy as Chesman Billings."

The very thought made Grace gasp. Mrs. Chesman Billings

had come to Mama's sewing circle one time. Grace had never seen such an elegant and stylish dress as this lady of wealth had worn. Mr. Billings's landholdings in the city of Cincinnati were extensive. Amy's father also owned several prime lots along Fourth Street. Perhaps one day Grace and Papa and Mama would live in a fine house farther up on the hill.

"Here you go, Gracie," Papa said, handing her the note. Carefully she folded it inside the order and Mama helped her secure it with sealing wax. On the outside of the paper, she penned the address of the piano factory in New York, carefully wiping the quill when she was finished.

"This occasion calls for a celebration," Papa said. "How about a song before going to bed?"

Moving to the parlor, Papa took his fiddle down from the special shelf he'd made. After tuning the strings, he struck up a merry tune that he'd learned from a keelboatman. Grace sang all the verses, with Mama and Papa joining in harmony on the chorus:

The boatman is a lucky man,
No one can do as the boatman can,
The boatmen dance and the boatmen sing,
The boatman is up to everything.
Hi-O, away we go,
Floating down the river on the O–hi–o.

Grace rolled up the carpet and danced a jig as she'd seen the swarthy boatmen do. From her favorite spot on the bluff high above where Deer Creek emptied into the Ohio, she often watched the keelboats and the larger heavy barges moving up and down the river. Traveling upstream meant teams of muscular rowers must work the long oars. On top of the low, boxy cabin sat the fiddler, sometimes wearing a slouch hat upon his head and a bright bandanna at his neck. The boatmen rowed to the rhythm of the fiddler's music. But when the way was easy traveling downstream, the boatmen passed the time dancing jigs. The happy tunes and fancy steps stayed inside Grace's head.

Mama laughed when they finished the last verse and the final rousing chorus. "When your piano is here, Grace, perhaps our music will consist of something other than boatmen ditties."

Grace nodded. "I'll learn church hymns, Mama," she agreed. "But I'll always love the happy boatmen songs."

Later, as Papa opened the big family Bible and read the scriptures, Grace's thoughts turned to Drew's problem that day with Raggy Langler. When they prayed, she asked Papa to say a special prayer for Drew to be happy.

Drew sat at the small table in the center of the cabin. Bent over his Latin textbook, he read the words by the flicker of the lamp. Matthew and Adah were at last quietly sleeping on the trundle bed. When the little ones were awake, Drew found concentration impossible.

He tried to read several pages of Latin every evening. Sometimes, if he had the time and the extra paper, he meticulously worked on translations. One time Deanna asked him why he worked so hard on his Latin studies, but Drew found he just couldn't explain. "I like Latin," was all he said.

It was as though he owed it to his father and mother. His parents had made sure he had the finest education that Boston could offer; now it was upon him to maintain what he'd received. And it certainly wasn't going to happen at the crowded school he currently attended.

Once, he'd called it a "charity school" in front of Grace, and she'd become upset. "It is not a charity school," she protested. "It's a public school. Papa pays a subscription just like everyone else."

Drew hadn't meant to hurt his cousin's feelings, because he liked Grace. But he knew the amount of subscription was a paltry sum. After all, the concept of the school was to cater to all—even creatures such as Raggy Langler.

Drew's older brother, Carter, sat across from him, polishing and cleaning his musket and filling the room with the aroma of flaxseed oil. The small cabin seemed to shrink when Carter was there. His very presence loomed over Drew like a shadow. Because Carter had been away from Boston for so many years, Drew barely knew him. They were worlds apart. It was strange, but Drew felt lonelier when his brother was home than he did when he was away.

"Drew," Deanna said softly, "it's time you were in bed."

"Yes, ma'am," Drew answered politely. Closing his book, he went to the basin near the cabin door, poured a little water from the pitcher, and washed his face and hands. There was lye soap nearby, but he hesitated to use it unless he was really dirty. He felt guilty using the family's supplies. His older brother had come to Cincinnati with nothing and had worked hard to eke out a living. Even now they had little to spare. Drew felt he was just another mouth to feed.

As Drew moved to the ladder that led to his loft, Deanna came to put her arm about his shoulder. "Sleep well, Drew."

"Thank you."

Her touch, which felt so like his mother's, made hot tears burn in his eyes. He turned away and blinked them back.

Carter said, "Good night, Drew." But he never looked up

from his prized gun.

Back home in Boston, when his parents were still alive, they closed each evening with scripture reading and prayers—but Carter seemed to have forgotten all about God—except to accompany his family to church each Sunday. Pulling off his waist shirt and breeches and pulling on his nightshirt, Drew wondered himself if God were still around.

Lying on his small cot, he stared through the semidarkness at the slanted roof just a few feet above his head. Drew sighed. From beneath his pillow, he brought out the smooth piece of wood that he was carving with his sharp penknife. Father had told Drew many times that he had just the right touch to make a piece of wood come alive.

Now that the days were longer and light came in the small window, he often carved and whittled after going to bed. But tonight he was too tired. Holding up the wood in the shadows of the loft, he smiled. The shape was that of a sleek cod-fishing schooner such as those docked in Boston Harbor. Carving the ship helped him to remember Boston.

Just then, he remembered he was to leave for school earlier the next morning. Climbing out of the bed and moving to the ladder, he called down softly, "Deanna?"

"Yes, Drew?"

"Will you wake me earlier in the morning? I'm to go to the landing with Grace and her father before school."

"I'll rouse you," Carter answered, "when I go out to cut the wood."

"Thank you," Drew said and returned to bed. Carter's words were like a slap. When Drew first arrived in Cincinnati, Carter had asked him to split kindling, but Drew had never swung an ax in his life. Although Drew was more than willing to learn,

Carter had no patience to teach him.

"You might get your clothes dirty," Carter had said.

The comment cut deeply. Drew had no other clothes to wear. While he'd seen many well-dressed men, especially around the business district of Fourth Street, he was dressed differently than most of the other boys.

In the low bureau at the foot of his cot were the portraits of Mother and Father. Father had commissioned them to be painted only a few months before they died. Sometimes Drew allowed himself to take them out and look. But very rarely. . . and only when he was alone. He never wanted his brave older brother to see him cry.

He had very nearly cried that afternoon when Raggy attacked him. In the darkness, Drew smiled as he remembered the sight of Grace swinging her tin pail with all her might.

While Drew hated having a girl stand up for him, he appreciated Grace's friendship. He knew she was on his side. She didn't have to invite him to come to the steamboat with her in the morning. He would have to remember to thank her for her kindness.

Drew was happy that Grace invited him, but he knew being near a steamboat might remind him of the sad journey down the Ohio a few months ago. He'd have to be careful not to cry. Again.

✎ CHAPTER 4 ✎

News from the Landing

A light patter of rain was falling when Grace heard Drew's knock at the kitchen door the next morning. He was early. She and Mama and Papa hadn't finished breakfast yet.

Grace left her place at the table to answer his knock. "Come in," she said. Drew's solemn face lit up as he smelled the aroma of Mama's flapjacks.

"Good morning, Drew!" Mama called out. Without asking, Mama fetched another plate from the cupboard. "You might as well have a few flapjacks and a slice of ham while you wait."

Drew sat down at the table without being asked twice. By the time Grace had gone upstairs to fetch her cloak with the hood, Drew had polished off the plate of food. Grace wondered if he'd had much breakfast at Carter's house.

She'd heard Luke and Papa talking about Carter. When Carter had first arrived in Cincinnati, he'd worked at the boatworks for a short time but then decided to go out on his own as a tanner. What he didn't take into account was that there were already more than a dozen tanyards and no need for a new one. He hadn't done as well as he'd hoped, so Papa had offered to let him come back to the boatworks. Carter had turned down the offer. Papa had told Luke, "Carter is too proud."

Maybe Carter doesn't have enough money to feed Drew properly. That thought worried Grace. Carter worked some days at the tanyard. Other days he chopped wood and went hunting in the nearby forests.

She learned these things while sitting on the stair landing, listening to the grown-ups talk.

"Thank you for the breakfast, Aunt Lavina!" Drew called to Mama, as he followed Papa and Grace out the door.

Grace figured there wasn't a more polite boy than Drew in the whole state of Ohio.

The landing was a busy place. Horses whinnied as they pulled wagons full of boxes, bags, and barrels close to the boat for unloading. Black stevedores shouted to one another and tossed about heavy bags of flour as though they were feather pillows. Several fine carriages, harnessed with smart-stepping horses, were hitched nearby as passengers said good-bye to friends and family in preparation to embark.

Papa was a friend of the captain of the *Velocipede*, so he strode up the broad gangplank as though he had a ticket to ride all the way to Pittsburg, Pennsylvania. Captain Micah Wharton was down on deck, greeting passengers and overseeing the loading so all was done in an orderly manner.

"Top o' the morning to you, Thad Morgan!" Captain Wharton called out when he saw Papa. Grace liked the captain's cheery voice, his ruddy red cheeks, and his broad, thick mustache. "And here's Gracie, too. To what do I owe this special visit?"

After introducing Drew to the tall captain, Papa explained, "Grace has a letter to go in the mailbag, Captain Wharton."

The captain raised his bushy eyebrows. "It must be terribly important to be hand-delivered to the captain."

Grace was bursting to tell. She held up the folded and sealed letter. "It's my order for a new piano! It's coming from a factory in New York."

"Is that a fact?" The captain reached out his large, big-boned hand. "I'll see to it that it's delivered safely." He slipped the order into the pocket of his greatcoat with its shiny brass buttons. Looking wistfully out at the river, he added, "If we don't get a little rain, we may not see you again until this time next year."

Hearing those frightful words, Grace stopped still. But then came Papa's reassuring voice. "See those clouds?" Papa waved to indicate the overcast skies. "The Lord willing, the spring rains will come. And probably too much, as usual. That's the way it seems to happen around here."

Captain Wharton shook his head. "I want to think you're right, Mr. Morgan, but. . ." Just then, the captain's attention was diverted. "Hey there!" he yelled out to a carriage that had just pulled up and blocked the loading area. "Excuse me, folks. I must go see about this." And he was gone.

Grace turned around to see Drew standing by the deck railing, running his fingers gently over the carved and polished wood. There was that sad look on his face again. Adjusting her tin pail on her arm beneath her long cloak, she went over to stand beside him.

"Do you like steamboats?" she asked.

"I suppose so. That is, I like the way they're made. Especially the fancy woodwork."

Papa walked up behind them. "Time for you two to scoot off to school."

Grace looked up at Papa. "But I wanted to say good morning to Luke since we're so close. May I, please, Papa?"

Grace's older brother, Luke, was one of her favorite people in the whole world. When Luke took pretty Camille for his bride, Grace wept. She was jealous of Camille for taking Luke away from her. But now the hurt was almost gone. Sometimes she was allowed to go to Luke and Camille's new home and stay overnight. That was fun.

Papa was looking at her with a twinkle in his eye. "Only if you promise to stay just a moment, then run on to school. You don't want to be responsible for making Drew late."

Following Papa's long strides down the wide cobblestone landing, Grace looked through the raindrops at the row of tall three- and four-story buildings that lined the landing. Each one was home to a thriving business. She wanted to comment on them to Drew, but she saw he wasn't noticing them at all. Drew was glancing wistfully back at the steamboat.

At the boatworks, the skeletal frames of the two new steamboats were taking shape. Nearby stood a large building where Luke oversaw the work on the steam engines. Luke was standing outside, talking to the men who were working on the boat frames.

When they called out to him, he turned. Running to lift her up and swing her around, he said, "Gracie! What are you doing at the landing? This is a school morning."

Once he'd set her down, Grace explained about the order for her brand-new piano.

"Ah, so you're finally getting your piano? Papa's little pet," he teased. "I suppose if you wanted the scepter from the king of Prussia, he'd get that for you, too."

"Oh, Luke, that's not true. When I learn to play, the piano will be for all the family. You can come and listen."

Luke screwed up his face and stuck his fingers in his ears.

"And listen to you play sour notes? Not on your life."

She started to smack him but couldn't get her arm out of her cloak before he jumped, laughing, out of her reach.

Papa had been talking to his workers, but now he turned to tell Grace and Drew to get on their way. "You'll have to hurry now."

"Yes, Papa." Grace turned to see Drew picking up scrap pieces of wood and slipping them into his pocket. Drew was handy with his penknife. She'd seen the whistles and tops he'd carved for Matthew and Adah.

"Come on, Drew!" she hollered to him. "I'll race you up the hill!"

If Drew really tried, Grace was sure he could easily win the race. But he gave the race only a halfhearted try. By the time they reached the schoolhouse, huffing and puffing, the gray clouds had broken apart and the warm sun was out.

Later that morning at recess, Grace told Amy about the incident the day before with Raggy.

"How I wish you walked home the same direction as Jason and me," Amy said. "With Jason around, Raggy would never bother you or Drew."

Grace knew that was true. Even though Raggy Langler was big for his age, Jason was bigger. How nice it would be to have a guardian nearby like Jason Coppock.

Amy leaned toward Grace and confided, "Mama says that when Raggy was younger, he helped deliver wash for Emaline Stanley. Now all he does is run loose all over town and cause mischief."

Emaline was the washerwoman for Amy's family, so Amy would know. Grace shook her head at the thought of dirty, lazy Raggy. "And helping Emaline with the deliveries is the least he could do for being allowed to live in the lean-to behind her shack."

Tired of talking about Raggy Langler, they turned their conversation to the school program and the pretty new dresses they would wear.

"If I had to stand before the entire city to sing, I'd be petrified," Amy said.

"I'm excited and a little nervous," Grace said, "but I'm not afraid." It was difficult to explain just how much she loved singing in front of people.

Suddenly, loud shouts sounded from a far corner of the playground. Looking that direction, Grace felt her heart sink. Raggy, Wesley, and Karl had Drew cornered near the fence and were taunting him. Other boys stood around laughing. Grace hated the onlookers for not helping Drew.

"Come on, Amy," she said. "Drew needs our help."

"You go," Amy said. "I have an idea."

Without a look back, Grace ran quickly toward Drew, yelling at the boys to get away and leave him alone.

Raggy stopped and glared at her. "Fellows, this little wildcat-gal's the one that smacked me on the legs."

"Yes, and I'd do it again as quick as you can draw a breath, Raggy Langler," Grace told him.

With attention shifted away from him, Drew tried to make a break, but Karl and Wesley blocked his escape. "Oh, no you don't, dapper-boy," Karl mocked.

Raggy gave a raspy laugh and spit a stream of " 'baccy juice," as he called it. "Our fancy boy here needs a little gal to come rescue him. *Tsk, tsk,*" he said through his teeth. "Ain't that a sight?"

Just as Grace despaired that nothing but the recess bell could save Drew, a shout sounded behind her. "Get on out of here, you no-good scalawags!"

Jason Coppock was striding forcefully toward Raggy, and following him was Amy, sporting a wide grin!

CHAPTER 5

Yost's Mercantile

At the sight of the taller, stronger boy coming toward them, Wesley and Karl fled. Raggy stood his ground for a moment, calling after his pals not to run, but it was no use. They were gone.

"Go on," Jason said to Raggy. "Slither out of here like your two snaky friends. And in the future, pick on someone your own size."

"Just you wait." Raggy shook his fist at Drew, whose face was as white as a bedsheet. "I'll get you when you ain't got no little gal to hide behind." With that, he ran off to another part of the schoolyard.

"Well, what're you looking at?" Jason said sternly to the other boys standing about. Suddenly the crowd melted away.

Once Drew could find his voice, he thanked Jason.

"Think nothing of it," Jason said smiling.

"I don't know why those boys dislike me so," Drew said, his voice still shaky. "I've done nothing to harm them."

Jason laughed. "That has nothing to do with it, my friend. Ruffians like that are always looking for fresh prey. You just happen to be it."

Drew shook his head as though he couldn't believe it.

"You're from Boston, as I remember it." Jason had his arm about Drew's shoulder and was leading him to a shade tree where they sat down on the grass. "Surely you had Raggy's kind in Boston."

"Not where I lived," Drew said quietly.

"Well, let me tell you about boys like Raggy. All you have to do is stand your ground, and they'll hightail it. Every time."

While Drew politely thanked Jason for the advice, Grace could see he wasn't truly convinced. It was just like when she told him that a smart smack on a pig's snout would send it running. He simply didn't believe her.

The clanging of the bell broke into the conversation, and soon they were standing in their straight lines, ready to march to their classrooms. Grace gave Amy a wink and a grin as they saw Raggy trailing at the end of the line. With a friend like Jason Coppock, Grace reasoned, perhaps Drew would learn to laugh and have some fun.

Saturday was Grace's favorite day of the week. No school meant she could go to the market with Mama. The busy marketplace was filled with wagonloads of meat and produce from the outlying farms. Grace loved the sights and sounds and the hustle and bustle. Often she'd asked for permission to do the market shopping alone. "I can do it, Mama," she'd say. "I've watched you, and I know how to find the firmest heads of cabbage and the plumpest plucked hens."

But Mama always said no. "You're too little to shop alone. Some of the merchants in the market can't be trusted."

But earlier this week, Grace had tried a new approach. She had asked that Drew go along and that Mama allow the two of them to do the shopping. "Perhaps Drew can make purchases for Deanna," Grace had suggested. Once Grace saw she had Mama's full attention, she added, "Deanna would surely welcome such help."

When at last Mama gave in and reluctantly gave permission, Grace realized she'd not even asked Drew. When she did ask him, he seemed willing enough. At least Grace was right about Deanna.

"What a relief it will be not to have to make my way through the crowds with two little ones in tow," she said.

So it was settled. Before dawn on Saturday morning, Drew was at the Morgans' back door with Deanna's list in his hand and a basket on his arm. Mama instructed Grace several times about how to dicker for the best prices.

"When you've finished at the market," she added, "please stop at Yost's Mercantile for a paper of pins and a yard of sprigged muslin."

To the store, as well! Grace could hardly believe her good fortune. This made her feel more grown-up than ever.

The sky behind the hills to the west of the city showed barely a smudge of pink as Drew and Grace walked toward the lower market. A broad roof covered most of the area between Main and Sycamore and was supported by triple rows of brick pillars. But the sides were all open.

Since Drew had never before seen an open-air market, Grace showed him around and introduced him to the merchants she knew. Many of the farmers drove their wagons through the dark of night to vie for prime positions at the market. Feeling quite important, Grace taught Drew how to squeeze the cabbages to be sure they were not rotten in the center.

"Wait until summer, when the grapes come in," she told him

as she chose a fat hen hanging from the racks. "There will be great baskets full of them, and you eat until you cannot eat any more." Talking about the juicy grapes made her mouth water.

"I'm not sure Deanna's budget could purchase that many grapes," Drew commented.

Grace wanted to say that Carter could earn fine wages at the boatworks, but she held her tongue. After all, Drew wasn't responsible for Carter's actions.

At Mr. Koenig's wagon, she found the firmest cabbages, and at Mr. Frey's wagon, she purchased the eggs. In her basket was a linen towel in which she was to wrap the eggs. Just as they were walking back through the rows of jammed-in wagons, Grace whispered, "Look there, Drew. It's Raggy Langler."

Raggy was slinking about the edges of the market area. As they watched, he slipped up to the back end of a wagon, reached in to grab a large white turnip, and then fled.

Grace gave a loud *whoop* and pushed through the crowd in that direction. "Stop that boy! He's a thief!" But no one was quick enough, and Raggy was long gone.

Leaving the market, they walked up Main toward Fourth Street and Yost's Mercantile. Muttering under his breath, Drew said, "It must be awful to have to steal for food."

Grace looked over at Drew in surprise. He sounded almost as though he felt sorry for Raggy. She knew she'd never steal, no matter how little she had. Wanting to change the subject, she said, "Mama gave me enough extra for each of us to have a stick of peppermint. You like peppermint, don't you?"

"Who wouldn't like peppermint?" he answered dully.

Grace was convinced nothing could ever excite Drew.

The heavy door of the mercantile was propped open, but the fresh spring air couldn't soften the strong mixtures of aromas inside the store. Here one could find everything from ax heads and kegs of nails to buggy whips and bolts of cloth. The store was fairly bristling with business.

Once inside, Grace was surprised to see Jason Coppock with a broom in his hands, sweeping the wooden floor. When he greeted them with a smile and a wave, Grace noticed that Drew brightened some.

"Amy never told me you worked for the Yosts," Grace said.

"I just started today." Jason waved his hand at all the merchandise and added, "Until I learn where everything is, I'm doing odd jobs. But soon I'll be a clerk." There was a note of pride in his voice. "Hey, Mr. Yost," he called over to a scar-faced man behind the counter. "We have a couple of customers here."

"Hi, Grace, Drew," Zachariah Yost greeted them cheerily. "What can I do for you today?" In spite of his terribly scarred face, Mr. Yost was a kind man and a good friend of Grace's brother, Luke.

Grace pulled out her list. "Mama needs a paper of pins and a yard of sprigged muslin."

"Pins and muslin, coming right up," he said. Pulling down the bolt of cloth and laying it on the counter, Mr. Yost asked, "How's your brother Luke doing these days? I don't see him much anymore."

"He and Papa are working hard to finish the two steamboats as soon as possible. Mama says they barely take time to breathe," Grace answered.

Mr. Yost chuckled at her comment. Carefully he measured and cut the muslin, folding the piece and returning the bolt to the shelf. "Now just tell me what those big old boats are gonna float on?" he asked. "From the looks of things, the river'll be down to a trickle in a few more weeks."

Grace didn't want to hear those words. True, there still hadn't been any hard spring rains, but they would come. She was sure of it. "Papa says the spring rains are just late," she told him.

"Late, huh? Well, I guess the snows were late, too. Don't forget, Gracie, there was very little snow all winter. Maybe the snows will come in June to raise the river level," he joked.

Grace quickly changed the subject. "Drew and I would each like a peppermint stick, as well, please."

"Two peppermint sticks." He added the items to the list, then took the wide-mouth jar from a shelf and brought it down to the counter where they could choose their own.

After Grace paid Mr. Yost, Drew suggested they put the cloth and pins in his basket since it wasn't as full as hers.

"Good idea," Grace agreed. "Now let's get on home and show Mama what a good job we've done."

As they moved toward the door, Jason called out, "Has Raggy Langler bothered you anymore?"

Grace answered by telling him they'd seen Raggy swiping vegetables at the market earlier.

Jason nodded. "I'd suspect no less of the ruffian." Giving the broom a couple more swipes, he added, "Remember now, Drew, what I told you about the likes of Raggy."

Drew nodded. "Yes, Jason. Thank you."

Grace was anxious to get home to see the pleased look on Mama's face. Regina could not have done as well. Perhaps now Mama would no longer call her *Gracie*.

As they walked down the hill, Grace asked Drew what he thought of the market, but his comments were vague. Sometimes Grace wished she could do things and go places with fun-loving Amy rather than glum Drew. Amy and she would have giggled and laughed throughout the entire morning.

Just as they were ready to turn the corner at Fourth and

Main, she heard Drew give a groan. "Oh no," he said. "Not again."

Raggy Langler was coming toward them with a menacing scowl on his face.

"I heard you calling me a thief at the market awhile ago," Raggy said.

"I called you a thief because you are a thief," Grace returned.

"Don't make him any madder," Drew muttered, stopping in his tracks.

"So the Boston dandy goes to market with his little basket on his arm," Raggy taunted as he drew nearer. "Let's see what dapper-boy buys at the market." Bumping into Grace, Raggy grabbed at Drew's basket, yanking out the piece of muslin.

Unbalanced, Grace nearly fell, but righted herself just in time. She could only hope no eggs were broken. Raggy whipped out the cloth and draped it over his dirty hair. In a singsong voice, he said, "Oh look, I'm dressed like the dandy from Boston."

"Give that back," Grace demanded. "That's my mama's cloth. I'll call the watchman on you."

Raggy was dancing about, raising a cloud of dust beneath his feet and having a great time with his own jesting. "Now there's no big boy to save you," he taunted, waving the cloth in the air.

Grace knew the watchman who held this area was a tall, friendly man named Mr. Gedney. If only. . .

Suddenly, at the top of her voice, she began to scream as though she were dying. "Help, help, Mr. Gedney! We're being robbed!"

"Quit that caterwauling," Raggy demanded.

But Grace wouldn't stop. She screamed and hollered and yelled and stamped her feet. "Give me back that muslin!" she yelled. "You terrible, no-good thief!" Curtains rustled at windows as people peered out. Mr. Gedney came running up the hill toward them with his large rattle stick in his hand. As soon as Raggy spied him, he threw the sprigged muslin in the dirt and ran down a side street as fast as he could go.

"I'm sorry, Grace," Drew said as he picked up the cloth and shook out the dust.

"What's going on here?" Mr. Gedney demanded. He was panting heavily from his uphill sprint. "Oh, it's you, Grace Morgan. How are you, young lady?"

"Not very well, Mr. Gedney. That mean old boy tried to take our things we bought at the market."

"Come on," Drew said to Grace. "There's nothing he can do now."

"Who?" Mr. Gedney wanted to know. "What boy?"

"Raggy Langler is his name," Grace told him.

Mr. Gedney nodded. "I know him. He's the boy who lives with Mrs. Stanley."

"That's the one," Grace said. Drew was beginning to walk on down the hill. "Drew, wait for me!" she called out.

"All the watchmen from here down to the public landing have chased that boy at one time or another," Mr. Gedney told her. "But I'll keep my eye out."

"Well, he didn't really take anything, Mr. Gedney. I mean"— she tried to explain as she started walking after Drew—"he did take something, but he gave it back again."

Mr. Gedney nodded. "I'll keep an eye out just the same."

"Thank you, Mr. Gedney!" Grace called back as she ran to catch up with Drew. When she was beside him again, she asked, "Why'd you say you were sorry awhile ago? You didn't do anything."

"I know," Drew said, his eyes sad. "That's why I apologized. I didn't do anything."

Last Day of School

Drew said good-bye to Grace at the front gate and politely thanked her for inviting him to go along. "I really did enjoy the market," he told her, "and the peppermint stick."

"You're welcome, Drew. See you tomorrow at church."

He nodded and went on his way.

When Grace presented to Mama the basket containing one cracked egg and a yard of dirty sprigged muslin, Regina said to Mama, "I knew you should never have let her go to the market alone. She's just too little."

Grace glared at the hired girl. "I am not too little. There's a boy named Raggy Langler who torments Drew terribly. He tried to take Drew's basket, and he pushed me. We saw him stealing turnips in the market."

"The boy would never have bothered you if I'd been with you," Regina put in. "Or your mama."

Sometimes Grace wished Regina didn't work for them. She could help Mama with some of the work, if only Mama would let her.

"How was it you were able to get the cloth back?" Mother asked in a kind voice. It was good to know she wasn't angry at Grace.

"Mr. Gedney, the watchman, heard me yelling and came running."

"Why didn't this bad boy named Raggy just run off with the cloth? Why did he throw it down?"

Mama's question surprised Grace. She shook her head. "Because if he kept it, Mr. Gedney would have run after him and he would have been a thief."

"But you say he stole turnips?" Mama took the items from the basket and began putting them away.

Grace didn't understand what Mama was getting at, nor did she want to know. Raggy Langler was a mean, horrible boy, and that's all there was to it. "He stole the cloth, then threw it in the dirt," she said trying to make the story worse. "He pushed me so hard that, if I'd fallen, your cabbages and turnips would have been full of dirt and the eggs all broken."

"I believe at prayers tonight, we shall pray for Raggy Langler," Mama said. "Now go to your room and freshen up. We'll have cabbage wedges with our salt pork for lunch."

Not only did Mama pray for Raggy that night, she also instructed Grace to pray for him at church the next morning. Now that was going to take some doing!

On Sundays they walked to church with Carter, Deanna, and little Matthew and Adah. Grace's bonnet was new. The ruffles and ribbons fascinated two-year-old Adah.

"Pitty ribbon," she said, wanting to touch the bonnet. Grace adored cute little Adah with her mop of copper-colored curls.

Four-year-old Matthew held tightly to Drew's hand, and Grace noted how the little boy dogged the steps of his young uncle. Carter, as usual, had little to say. Grace couldn't imagine being as quiet as Carter Ramsey. What a chore that would be! Mama and Deanna, on the other hand, always chatted nonstop.

As they entered the sanctuary, Widow Robbins was seated at the piano, playing a grand hymn. Before the piano had arrived, Grace had hated her family's second-row pew, but now she was thankful. Grace watched every move Widow Robbins made as her fingers scooted over the glossy keys, amazed at the combination of sounds that came out. Someday she would know how to create lovely music on her very own piano.

The Reverend Danforth's message lasted for several hours. Sometimes there would be a break, during which they sang hymns from the hymnbooks. If Grace had her way, they'd sing for hours and take a break to listen to a short sermon!

Although Grace only listened halfheartedly, at one point she heard the reverend say that it was God's will that all should come to repentance—that God willed no one to perish or be lost. Grace wondered, *Does that include people like Raggy and the riffraff that live in Sausage Row?* Then the Reverend Danforth added, "By our love and our example, we draw others into the kingdom."

After church, Grace thought about what those words meant. No matter how she twisted and turned them around in her head, she just couldn't see any way she could love Raggy Langler or set an example for him. She wanted to strike him and make him leave Drew alone forever.

The day of the school-commencement exercises broke sunny and bright. Grace wanted more than anything to enjoy every moment of the day, but the conversation she'd overheard the night before between Papa and Luke kept echoing in her mind. There still hadn't been a drop of rain, and the low river level meant no barges, no keelboats, and no steamboats. Grace had never seen the beautiful Ohio River so low. That in itself was scary enough.

But sitting quietly on the stair landing, she'd heard Papa and Luke talking about yet another problem—the Cincinnati banks.

"They've extended too much credit," Papa said.

"But all banks out West have operated on credit," Luke protested. "There's no other way to make it go."

"Yes," Papa answered in a low voice, "but all cities aren't suffering from lack of river traffic. It would be a double blow for us if the banks folded."

For the first time ever, Grace stopped listening and crept back into bed. What did it mean to have the banks fold? Did that mean the banknote Papa wrote for the piano would not be any good?

Grace and Amy were currently standing in front of the schoolhouse. They were in their proper position, along with hundreds of other students, waiting for the parade to begin. All of Fourth Street was decked out in bunting and banners. Grace reckoned most of the city had turned out for the occasion. It felt nice, and a little strange, to feel the warm sun on her head and face. But none of the girls wore their bonnets, and the boys had left their caps off. All the children were to be bareheaded, wear light-colored clothing, and wave streamers as they proceeded down the broad street, singing as they went.

With a pounding of the bass drum and clash of cymbals, the band struck up a lively tune and the parade was underway. Grace marched and sang and waved her streamer with all the others. At the corner of Fourth and Broadway, she saw Papa and Mama standing at the curbing with Luke and Camille. She smiled to them and waved her streamer with more enthusiasm. It was good to see Papa smiling. There had been worry lines on his brow for many weeks.

The parade led to the town square, where the children were seated on the grass. On the bandstand stood Hugh Sutton, superintendent of the city schools, who called the crowd to attention. Acting as master of ceremonies, Mr. Sutton announced the special presentations from each classroom.

When it was Grace's turn, she stood and walked proudly to the platform. The leader of the band put his pitch pipe to his lips to give her the correct key. Looking out over the thousands of faces, she searched for Mama and Papa. When at last she spied them standing beneath a sprawling oak tree, she sang to Papa the clear sweet melody of "A Mighty Fortress Is Our God." A hush fell over the crowd as the words of comfort touched fearful hearts. Coming to the second verse, she sang:

Did we in our own strength confide,
Our striving would be losing
Were not the right Man on our side,
The Man of God's own choosing.
Dost ask who that may be?
Christ Jesus, it is He;
Lord Sabaoth, His name,
From age to age the same,
And He must win the battle.

Even as she sang, Grace wondered if Jesus would help them win their battle against the awful problems of a dry river and banking systems that were falling apart. Could she be as certain as the hymn stated?

After the presentations, speeches, and prayers were completed, there were games and picnics beneath the cool shade of the trees in the square. Mama had brought Grace's school bonnet along, but no one else was wearing one, so she convinced Mama to let her run bareheaded throughout the afternoon.

She introduced Amy and Jason to her family. Jason politely invited Drew to join in the races and games with him and his friend. Grace was surprised and pleased when Drew agreed.

Amy's little sister, Leah, was a toddler near Adah's age. Amy and Grace had great fun walking among the crowds with Leah in tow. Thankfully, Raggy had not appeared that day. Nor had she seen Wesley or Karl.

As they sat in the grass near the bandstand, listening to the rousing band music, Grace mentioned the boys' absence to Amy.

Pulling Leah into her lap, Amy said, "But they're the indigent students, remember?"

"What do you mean?"

"Grace, think about it. Can you imagine their dirty clothes in the parade along with all the pretty linen dresses and the other boys' white shirts and nice bow ties? Why, they don't even have shoes!"

Grace felt silly that she'd not thought of that before. It was true. When snow was on the ground, Raggy wore a pair of boots that looked as though they'd been cast off by someone much larger than he. As soon as the frost was off, he was barefoot again. What shoes would he have worn in the parade?

Suddenly, Grace felt a little ache deep in the pit of her stomach. An ache she couldn't explain, and one that didn't want to go away.

CHAPTER 7

Drew's Challenge

Whippoorwills echoed their lonely calls in the trees above Drew's head. The dense grove of buckeye, sycamore, and honey-locust trees blocked out the dimming June sky. Only through a few patches in the leafy boughs could he see the stars beginning to come out. Beside Drew, Grace sat quietly as she stared down the bluff at the wide muddy bog that was once a rushing river. The ferries that used to carry folks back and forth from the Kentucky side to the Ohio side were landlocked and useless.

It wasn't like Grace to be still or even to sit still. Drew knew she was worried about her family. And he was worried, as well. The saddest thing to Drew was that Grace never mentioned her piano anymore. Had she lost hope?

If Drew hadn't liked Cincinnati when he first arrived, he liked it even less now. The entire city seemed to be falling apart. Land prices had caved in and factories were closing their doors. He understood some of what was happening, but most he did not.

"It's not just the lack of river traffic, is it?" he said to Grace, breaking the silence.

Grace turned to him. Her bonnet hung down her back by its ribbons. "You mean why the businesses are failing? No, Drew, it's not just the river."

Drew brushed leaves off his homespun trousers. After school let out, Deanna had found some old clothes of Carter's and cut them down for Drew. The feel of linsey-woolsey took some getting used to, but at least he would no longer be called a dandy. "I've asked Carter about things, but he won't talk."

"Same with Papa," Grace agreed. "He says I'm too young to understand. But I've heard plenty of talk between him and Luke and with Mama, too." She pulled at the tuft on a purple thistle weed. It broke apart in her hands. "I heard Papa call it a *depression*. He says now that Americans are trading with the British rather than fighting with them, British products are cheaper than our products. That puts American factories out of business."

Drew thought about that for a minute. "But the banks. . ."

"I don't understand, either. All I know is that the banknotes that *used* to be worth something aren't worth anything now."

"Carter said he was glad he didn't have any money in a worthless old bank."

"This is one time your brother may be right."

Drew looked away for fear he might see Grace cry. When she spoke again, Grace said, "Papa and Luke both trusted the bank, and now they have nothing. And the money they expected to receive from the sale of the boats won't be coming. The buyers can't come downriver to fetch them." Pulling her hankie from her apron pocket, Grace blew her nose. "Papa doesn't even know if the owners still have the money to buy the boats."

After a moment, Drew tried to change the subject. "Carter wants me to go hunting with him."

Grace brightened a bit, tucking her hankie back in her pocket. "That's good, Drew. At least you'll be helping. I wish I could do more to help."

"I'm sort of afraid of the musket."

Grace nodded. "You can get over being afraid."

"Do you think so?" Drew sometimes envied Grace's fearlessness.

"Carter may not talk much, but I imagine he'll be a good teacher."

Drew thought about that. "He's not very patient. I mean, he's not very patient with me. He's pretty patient with Matt and Adah."

"That's because they're his own. That's different. He probably expects more of you because you're older."

"When he's gone from the house, I've been practicing splitting kindling."

"Have you?" Grace's look of surprise pleased Drew. "I'm proud of you. How're you doing?"

"Not too well, but I'm not giving up. Deanna's been helping me keep the secret."

"I've been lending a hand around the house more, too, since Mama had to let Regina go." She gave a little laugh. "I used to wish Regina didn't work for us. Now I'm sorry I had those thoughts. Regina needed the work, and Mama needed her help."

"You couldn't have known how things were going to change."

"I know, but I'm still going to be more careful about my thoughts." Methodically, she pulled the ribbons of her bonnet through her fingers. "I wish we could do more, Drew. I wish we could help somehow."

Drew knew what she meant. Now that circumstances in the city had seen a downturn, Drew felt even more guilty for eating at Carter's table. Many nights he ate only half of his portion and made sure Matthew and Adah took the rest. Then he went to bed dreaming of the heavy-laden table at his old home back in Boston. There were delicacies there, such as rhubarb pies, which he doubted he'd ever taste again. After his parents had died, it was discovered that the embargo and the war had destroyed their business. There was no money left, and strangers now lived in his Boston home.

"Come on," he said, jumping to his feet. "We're certainly not doing much good up here."

"You're right," Grace agreed as she stood and brushed dirt and leaves from her skirt, "but it's good to get away for a few moments. Even if the view does look down on a dried-up river."

They walked quietly down from the bluff together, crossing the small bridge over Deer Creek. Drew walked Grace back to her house before returning to Carter's small cabin at the edge of the woods. He filled the water bucket at the well and, heaving with all his might, carried the sloshing bucket into the kitchen for Deanna. Soon his muscles would be as strong as Carter's.

Deanna smiled and thanked him, and little Matthew came running to greet him.

"Uncle Drew," he said, "look." He held up a whistle that Drew had carved for him, which was now in two pieces. "Adah broke it," he declared. "She's a bad girl."

Adah clung to her mother's skirts, sucking two fingers of her free hand. When she heard her brother's accusations, she ducked her head.

Drew took the pieces of the whistle. "She didn't mean to break it," he said. "And I can easily make another."

Matthew began to bounce around. "Would you, Uncle

Drew? Please, would you?"

"We'll look for a just-right willow branch tomorrow."

Just then, Carter appeared at the door. "Tomorrow you may be busy, little brother," he said. "Come out to the well. I want to teach you to dress out the game. Bring that sharp knife of yours."

Drew gave a little shudder as he thought of the blood and innards he was about to see. But he straightened himself, pulled his knife from his trouser pocket, and followed Carter out into the dooryard. A flickering lantern sat on the edge of the well, spreading light on the ground where Carter had placed two dead rabbits.

"Just do as I do," Carter said, lifting one of the rabbits by its hind legs. Taking his knife, he carefully made a clean slit down the midsection of the rabbit.

Drew took a quick breath and held it. Giving himself no time to think, he did the same. Within minutes, two rabbits were skinned and gutted. Drew was pretty proud of himself, and once it was over and the entrails were lying on the ground, it didn't seem half bad. Like Grace said, he could get over being afraid.

Without the fur, the rabbits looked pretty skinny. As though reading Drew's thoughts, Carter said, "They've about run all their winter fat off." Taking water from the dipper hanging on the well post, he rinsed both carcasses. "But wild game may be all that will grace our table until things change."

Drew wanted to ask questions, but he held his tongue.

Heading toward the house, Carter volunteered one more comment, "And the game is staying further and further away from all this so-called civilization."

That night's supper was salt pork and Indian corn pone,

but Deanna seemed delighted that she now had two rabbits to stew.

The next morning, Carter woke Drew early. Drew quickly dressed and ate, then helped Deanna pack their lunch of dried beef, biscuits, and water. Drew followed closely behind Carter as they made their way across Deer Creek and headed in a northeasterly direction until they were far from the noisy city.

Drew had never been in such dense wilderness, but he rather liked the solitude. Silently, Carter pointed out tracks and signs of game.

Before the day was out, Carter placed his prized musket in Drew's hands and showed him how to pour in the correct amount of powder and tamp it in. Then he demonstrated wrapping the lead ball with the cloth and tamping it down.

"This is the safety cock," Carter said, placing the percussion cap in place. "When you're ready to fire, you pull it back to full cock, then let her fly."

Drew nodded, wondering if he would falter when it came time to fire.

"Someday," Carter said softly, "I'm gonna have me a good rifle."

A few moments later, Carter pointed out a fat grouse sitting crouched beneath a bramble bush. As Drew aimed at the bird, his hands began to quiver and shake. He forced them to be still. Slowly he let the hammer fly, and the explosion slammed his shoulder. The grouse flew away unharmed.

He waited for Carter to berate him, but his brother only remarked, "Being hungry can help make you a crack shot."

It was true. When they stopped at a stream for a drink and to eat their lunch, all Drew could think of was rabbit stew! After that, he pictured food on the table every time he aimed.

Late in the afternoon, he had a bead on a squirrel sitting high in a beech tree. Slowly, slowly he let the hammer fly, and the squirrel fell to the ground with a *thud*.

Drew wanted to laugh and shout, but instead he handed the musket to Carter and ran to pick up his kill. When he came back, Carter patted his shoulder and said, "Good shot. You must be real hungry!" As they laughed together, Drew wondered why he and his brother couldn't have more moments like this.

A few days later, Drew and Grace were sent to the market to see what they could purchase. In just a few weeks the open markets in Cincinnati had totally changed. The grapes, melons, and tomatoes that Grace had promised would not be coming. No milk, cheese, or fat hens. The drought had affected the crops. Most of what little the farmers had produced, they were using themselves. And what was brought in to market often went by begging because so few people had money to make purchases.

In spite of the early hour, the air was still and hot. Under the roof of the vast market, there was only a smattering of wagons. And the produce looked pitiful. Drew was almost embarrassed to approach the farmers. Grace did a little dickering and purchased a bag of snap beans, two small heads of cabbage, and a few eggs. Before they turned for home, Drew suggested they go to Yost's.

"But we've no money for candy," she protested.

"I know, but I'd like to say hello to Jason."

Grace looked at him. "Do you think he still has a job there?"

Drew shrugged. "Let's find out."

"Let's do. If he's there, I can find out how Amy is, as well."

They hurried in the direction of Fourth Street. Inside the store, there was only one other customer. Mr. Yost hailed them as they entered. "Say there, Grace, Drew," he said with a cheery smile. "Did you come to buy me out?"

Grace chuckled at his silly remark. "I don't think we're in a position to buy you out today, Mr. Yost. We're looking for Jason. Does he still work for you?"

"Well," Mr. Yost said slowly, "he doesn't exactly work *for* me. I guess you could say he works *with* me now."

"What do you mean?" Drew asked.

Mr. Yost leaned against the counter and gave a little sigh. "When the crash hit, I had to let my workers go."

"I know how that is," Grace put in. "Papa and Luke had to do the same at the boatworks."

Mr. Yost rubbed at a scar on his face and nodded. "It's the same everywhere. In Pittsburgh and Lexington, too, I hear. Well, anyway, that Jason just wouldn't go." He chuckled as he thought about it. "Jason said, 'You can't pay me, but you can teach me. Let me stay and do what I can, and you teach me all about the mercantile business.'"

Drew nodded. He knew he liked Jason Coppock. That boy was smart.

"So," Mr. Yost went on, "he comes every day. We wait on a few customers, and then I teach him how to make orders, how to stock, and how to keep the books." He laughed again. "'Course, there're no orders to make, so we pretend a great deal."

"So where's Jason now?" Grace asked. Drew was just ready to ask the same thing.

The light in Mr. Yost's eyes faded just a bit. "Today Jason is at home helping his family move."

"Move?" Grace asked. "Are they moving away from Cincinnati?"

"Oh, no, Gracie, they're just moving to another part of town. You see, they've lost their house."

Drew felt his stomach lurch, and he heard Grace gasp. "Oh no!" she said. "Poor Amy. Poor Mr. and Mrs. Coppock." Drew knew that Grace had been frightened her own family might lose their house after she learned that Mr. and Mrs. Chesman Billings, the richest people in Cincinnati, had lost all their holdings.

"Lots of people are losing houses and land right along with their businesses," Mr. Yost told them. "That's what happens when people live on credit. Me, I've tried to pay for everything as I go. My ma and pa taught me that long before they died." He shook his head. "But even still, we may not make it through this."

"Where'd the Coppocks move to?" Drew wanted to know.

"They found a small cabin over by Mill Creek."

"That's clear out of town!" Grace was incredulous.

"Yep," Mr. Yost answered, "and they were plenty lucky to get it."

Before Grace and Drew left, Mr. Yost held out the candy jar. "Here," he said, "each of you take one. They're getting more stale by the day." He smiled. "I promise I won't tell if you won't."

Drew hated to take something without paying, and he could see Grace felt the same way. But the shopkeeper insisted.

Soon they were carrying their basket between them, walking down the hill, sucking on their peppermint sticks.

"What are you thinking about, Drew?" Grace asked as she licked the last of the peppermint from her fingers.

They had just passed the corner where Raggy had accosted them so long ago. Drew hadn't seen Raggy for weeks. "I was just thinking," Drew answered, "that if things keep going as they are, Raggy Langler may become the best-dressed fellow in Cincinnati."

CHAPTER 8

Surprise in the Country

The Fourth of July, usually a rollicking celebration in Cincinnati, was quiet and subdued that summer. The city council voted to dispense with the great parade and instead encouraged citizens to become involved in the soup kitchens that had been set up in each part of the city. There were a few firework displays that evening, but they didn't amount to much.

Grace was disappointed. She'd looked forward to the holiday as a diversion from the gloom about her. Still, she knew the city leaders were right. How could they celebrate when people were starving?

However, a nice surprise did come a few days later. In the mail came a letter from Samantha and Owen Tate. The Tates were relatives of theirs who lived on a farm several miles north of the city. Grace wanted to open the letter right away, but Mama said they must wait until Papa came home.

It was later than usual when Papa arrived home that night. Grace wanted to show him the letter immediately, but again Mama said to wait. "Let Papa eat supper and rest his weary bones," she said. Even though Mama was tired from all the daily household chores, she still took extra care to protect Papa and make him comfortable each evening.

Finally, after their meager supper was finished, Grace brought the letter to the table. "Look, Papa. A letter from Samantha and Owen. May I open it?"

Papa smiled. "Of course you can, Gracie. Let's hope it's full of good news. I could use some."

Carefully Grace peeled open the seal and spread out the paper. She read: " 'Dear Thad, Lavina, and Gracie. . .' " Grace looked up. "When is everyone going to stop calling me that?" she asked.

"Go on," Mama insisted. "What does Samantha say?"

Grace read on:

We've heard about the hard times in the city. The drought here has been bad, as well, but we do have plenty to eat. Owen has dug the foundation for the new room on the house. We could use help in framing and finishing it.

Why don't you come for a visit and lend a hand? Have Luke and Camille come, too. It would be good to see you again. Tell Grace I have a surprise for her to see.

Love,
Samantha

Grace looked up to see Mama smiling. "A trip to the farm," Mama said softly. "That would be nice."

"And listen to this part!" Grace said. "At the bottom it says, 'Our baby is to arrive around Thanksgiving time.' "

"Oh, Thad, do you hear that? Samantha is to have her first baby! What wonderful news!"

"May we go, Papa? They need our help. You heard what she said. May we?" *A surprise!* Samantha had said there was a surprise. Grace wondered what it could be.

"She did say they need help," Papa agreed. He leaned back in his chair. "I guess nothing here will spoil while we're gone."

Grace could hardly contain her excitement. How good it would be to have something to look forward to once again. "Papa," she said, "may we take Drew along?"

When her father paused before answering, she added, "He can work hard. Why, he's even learned to swing an ax."

"Doesn't Deanna need him there, Grace?" Mama asked.

"As Drew himself said, he's just another mouth to feed," Grace answered. "They barely have enough to eat now."

Mama and Papa looked at one another. Finally, Papa said, "Let's ask Carter. If he agrees, it's all right with me."

Grace jumped up from where she was sitting. "Please, Papa, may we take the lantern and go to Carter's house tonight?"

"Grace," Mama protested, "your papa is weary. Let him rest."

"It's all right, Lavina. Carter's gone out hunting nearly every day. I'd just as well go while he's at home." He stood up from the table. "Leave the dishes and grab your bonnet and come with us," he said to Mama.

She nodded. "It would be good to spend a little time with Deanna," she said. "Thad, would you go to the cellar and bring salt pork from our barrel? We shouldn't go empty-handed."

Grace was already running upstairs to grab her bonnet from off the hook in her room. She and Drew were going to go to the farm! Carter just had to say yes.

And Carter did say yes. His only condition was for Drew to cut extra wood for Deanna's cookstove before he left.

Carter had carried a couple of cane chairs out to the back stoop, and he and Papa sat in the warm night air, talking softly. Inside Mama played with little Adah while she chatted with

Deanna. Grace and Drew ran about the clearing, helping Matt catch fireflies.

Stretched on boards at the edge of the clearing were the skins that Carter was tanning.

"This is the one I shot," Drew said, pointing to the golden brown squirrel hide. "Carter says he'll teach me to make a pair of moccasins with it. And in the fall, if I shoot a deer, he'll teach me to make leggings."

Grace noted the pride in his voice. Perhaps Drew was finally adjusting to his new home.

The next day, Papa began making arrangements for their trip. To rent a wagon for the trip, he had to write a promise to the liveryman that he would bring back produce from the farm in payment.

The morning they were to leave, Drew was at their house before daybreak. Mama made sure he ate another biscuit before they left. Mama had also packed a lunch to eat on the way, which now sat by the front door in a basket.

Luke and Papa had walked to the livery to fetch the wagon, and Grace sat on the front steps waiting. Her insides were a jumble of fluttering butterflies. It had been months since her family had been out to visit the Tate farm.

She kept wondering about the word *surprise*. Samantha had written in the letter that a baby was on the way, so that wasn't it. With a slam of the door, Drew came out carrying a buttered biscuit.

"Thank you for asking me to go along, Grace," he said.

Grace wondered if she remembered to say thank you half as many times as Drew did. "I wanted you to go see the farm. It's ever so much fun."

"What's it like?"

"Fields of grain that seem to stretch out forever," she explained. "And a barn full of hay with cows, horses, and pigs. Oh, and there are geese, too."

"Are the geese mean?"

Grace laughed. "They're just like the pigs on the street, Drew. You take a big stick to them."

Just then, around the corner came Papa and Luke with the wagon. Harnesses jingled, and the team of sorrel horses whinnied and snuffled and bobbed their heads as Papa pulled them to a stop. "Whoa there!" he called out.

"Mercy to goodness," Mama said as she came out carrying the basket. "That's enough commotion to wake all the neighbors."

Mama was probably right. Grace was quite sure no one else in the neighborhood was up this early. The buckboard had two sets of seats up front with a long bed in back and high sideboards. Luke hopped down to help Camille up into the back seat. Grace and Drew clamored into the wagon bed. Once Mama and Papa were on board, they were off.

They took Hamilton Road north out of the city. In no time at all, they were traveling along the curving road that cut through dense stands of trees. Occasionally they came upon open farmland where acres of wheat, oats, barley, and corn had been planted. Cozy little houses snuggled into hillsides flanked by smaller smokehouses, outhouses, sheds, and at least one towering barn.

Grace had heard many times what fertile farmland their state enjoyed. And it was true. But Papa commented on the scrawny crops: "They should be a full foot taller by this time of year."

Mama replied that they should all be praying for rain.

Grace breathed in the clean fresh air and grinned at Drew. She didn't want to think about droughts, bank failures, or financial disasters. This was a holiday, and she was determined to enjoy it to the fullest.

"I hope there are baby kittens in the barn," she said.

"I like kittens," Drew said. "I had a kitten of my own in Boston."

"Your very own?"

Drew nodded. "She even stayed with me in my room."

Grace thought that would be nice. A cuddly little kitten lying on her bed. "Say," she said, "maybe that's the surprise."

"What surprise?" Drew asked.

"In Samantha's letter she said there was a surprise for me to see. Maybe it's a kitten."

Over her shoulder, Mama said, "Grace, if the surprise is a kitten, you cannot bring it home."

Grace thought for a moment. "And since I've seen kittens before, the surprise must not be a kitten."

When the warm sun was straight up in the sky, Papa stopped at a stream and allowed the horses to drink. Grace and Drew hopped down and helped spread the quilts in the grass. They opened the basket and enjoyed a picnic lunch of salt pork, slices of bread with cheese, and boiled eggs. No one commented that it wasn't a very elegant picnic lunch. It was too lovely a spot and too nice a day to complain.

Papa brought a dipper of water for the ladies, but Grace and Drew knelt down at the edge of the gurgling stream and scooped up handfuls of clear, cool water. "It's a far sight cleaner than Deer Creek," Grace said.

Just then, Drew flicked cold water on her.

"Why, you. . . !" She scooped water in her cupped palm and

flung it at him, splashing him square in the face.

Drew burst out laughing and ran from her reach as she chased him through the trees. She very nearly caught him, but since he'd been spending time in the woods with Carter, he was much more agile than when she'd first met him. For the life of her, she couldn't keep up with him.

Papa's call put a stop to their game, and they came laughing and panting to the wagon. Later, Grace realized that it was the first time she'd ever heard Drew laugh—really laugh!

As dusk began to gather, the rocking of the wagon lulled Grace into a deep slumber. The next thing she knew, a loud voice called out, "Hello, hello! Welcome! We thought you'd never get here! Come on down. Owen can take care of the team. I know you're tired."

Even in her half sleep, Grace recognized Samantha's friendly voice. Rubbing her eyes, she sat up. Drew was still fast asleep on his pile of quilts. She reached over and gave him a shake. "Sleepyhead, wake up! We're here!"

Lanterns were swinging over the back of the wagon. "Well, well. If it's not our little Gracie."

That was Owen's voice. "And who is this?" he wanted to know.

Drew was sitting up and stretching.

"This is Drew," Grace said. "Carter's younger brother."

"Of course, of course. Come on, now," he said, giving them each a hand. "Samantha has a supper all laid out."

Following the soft yellow lantern light, the two went up the path to the back door. Tantalizing food aromas met them before they entered. Grace was sure nothing had ever smelled so good. There on the table were platters of frizzled ham, bowls of seasoned potatoes, and wedges of cooked cabbage. But on the sideboard was the best of all—squash pies. Grace hadn't seen a pie for ever so long.

Grace and Drew ate without talking. Grace wasn't sure if it was because she was too tired to talk or too hungry. But as she cut into her thick slice of golden squash pie, she remembered about the surprise.

"Samantha," she blurted out, "you said there was a surprise for me to see."

"And there is. There surely is," Samantha said.

"May I see it?"

"It's in the barn," Samantha explained.

"May we take the lantern out to the barn to see?"

"No surprises tonight, Gracie," Mama said firmly. "To bed with you as soon as you finish eating."

Once Grace and Drew were bedded down on quilts in corners of the kitchen, she was glad Mama had said no. Her full stomach had made her very sleepy. As she dozed off, Grace knew it wouldn't matter if there were no surprise at all. Just being at the farm was a good enough treat!

CHAPTER 9

Drew's Gifts

Early the next morning, Grace was awakened by the sounds of Samantha filling the cookstove with wood. When she looked over to wake Drew, he was gone. How could he be up before her?

"Samantha!" she said, jumping to her feet. "Where's Drew?"

"He volunteered to chop kindling for the stove." Willowy Samantha leaned down to grab another chunk of wood, shoved it in the stove, and slammed the iron door shut. Corn mush bubbled in a pot, and tall, round biscuits sat on a tin ready to go into the oven. Outside a noisy old rooster hailed the morning with his loud crowing. How could Grace have slept through all this noise?

As she hurriedly folded quilts, she asked, "He hasn't been to the barn, has he?"

Samantha laughed. "Do you think I'd let someone else see the secret first?"

Grace felt a stab of guilt. That's exactly what she'd thought. Just then Mama came in from the living room. Grace ran to give her mother a hug. Mama's face seemed free of worry lines for the first time in many days. "Mama, may I run to the barn before breakfast?"

Mama shook her head. "Breakfast first, Gracie."

Grace wanted to complain, but seeing Mama so relaxed made her keep still. She wanted nothing to ruin this perfect day.

The men were outside studying the foundation for the new room and planning the day's work. Quickly Mama, Camille, and Grace helped Samantha put breakfast on, and then they called everyone inside. Grace saw Drew's eyes brighten at the grand array of food on the table. Since there weren't enough chairs, Drew and Grace filled their plates and ate on the back stoop.

Chickens scratched about the yard. Several tall white geese strutted proudly, giving an occasional honk. The smell of the clean country air invigorated Grace and made her want to run and shout.

"I don't know which is best," Grace told Drew, "the sweet clean air or the scrumptious food."

Around a mouthful of biscuit, Drew mumbled, "Both."

Grace laughed as the boy with impeccable manners sopped gravy with his biscuit and swiped a drip off his chin with his sleeve. When his plate was clean, Drew said, "Samantha told me this morning that she's been carrying water from the well to her garden each day."

"Looks like it needs it."

"We could do that."

Grace stopped with a spoonful of mush in the air. "That's a nice thought. Between us, we can carry twice as much water as Samantha in her condition." Cleaning up the last of her bowl of mush, she jumped to her feet. "Come on, there's so much to do. And we have a surprise to see!"

"Don't tell me to come on," Drew teased. "You're the one who slept all morning."

"Slept all morning? Why, Drew Ramsey, you. . ."

She smacked at him with her spoon, but he ducked quickly into the kitchen.

When breakfast dishes were cleared, Samantha finally announced that it was time to go to the barn. Drew and Grace ran circles around Samantha, laughing and giggling as they followed the dusty path from the house to the barn. Chickens squawked and scattered from in front of the trio. Rhythmic sounds of hammering and sawing filled the air as the men framed in the new room.

Samantha chatted about how pleased she was that they'd come and how excited she was about the new bedroom. When they reached the barn, Drew helped her pull open the heavy door. Grace squinted at the dimness and inhaled the smells of leather, fresh hay, and animals. Owen's prize horses were stabled in the barn, but most of the cows and pigs were outside in the pasture.

After a moment, Grace heard faint *baa*-ing. "Sheep?" she asked, making a guess.

"Over here," Samantha said, leading to a far corner. There, in a small enclosure, were two nanny goats and three of the most darling white kid goats Grace had ever seen.

"Goats!" she exclaimed. "You have goats! Oh, Samantha, this is a wonderful surprise. Where did they come from? May we pet them?" She wanted to touch their silky fur.

Samantha reached up to get a bucket from a hook and then fetched a small stool. "An old peddler came by awhile back with these nanny goats, and it just took Owen and me one look. . . . We couldn't resist. We just had to have them. And a few weeks later, both gave birth—to these three." She gestured to the kids.

As Samantha opened the gate to the enclosure, the nearest

nanny goat moved cautiously away. "Come now, Josie," Samantha cooed to the nanny. To Grace and Drew, she said, "They're not sure they trust me just yet. So you two just watch until I finish milking."

"Milking? You're going to milk them?" Grace was fascinated. Such small animals giving milk! She watched carefully as Samantha fastened the nanny's head in a stanchion to keep her still. Streams of milk echoed with a *ping-ping-ping* as they hit the tin bucket. Soon the white foam rose to the rim where Grace could see it.

"These little critters give a lot of milk," Samantha told them. She handed the full bucket to Drew. "Set that over by the door so it won't get spilled, and I'll let her loose."

Samantha unfastened the stanchion and then repeated the process with Annabelle, the other nanny. Once she was done, she opened the gate to let Drew and Grace into the enclosure. "Walk slowly now, so as not to startle them."

Grace knelt down in the hay to pet one of the kids. The coat was warm and silky to her touch. She rubbed its head and the kid pushed back. "Look, Samantha! Look how she's trying to butt."

"You're right, that is a she. A little nanny," Samantha said. "You should see them butting one another. Like three little children romping together. Cutest thing you ever saw."

"Are these ones nannies, too?" Drew asked, his arm about the necks of the other two kids.

"On your right is a billy goat, a male," Samantha replied. "The other one is a nanny."

"Will they run and play with us?" Grace wanted to know.

Samantha nodded. "They'll give you a merry chase. You'll have to keep a close eye on them."

"Let's work for a while," Drew suggested to Grace. "Then we'll come back and play with them later this afternoon."

"That's a perfect idea."

"Work? And what work will you be doing?" Samantha led the way out and closed the small gate to the enclosure.

Drew looked at Grace as though waiting for her to speak. But she said, "You tell her. It was your idea."

His face flushed pink as he said, "We'd like to carry water to your garden while we're here."

"Why, Drew, thank you." Samantha leaned over to put her arm around him and kissed him squarely on the cheek. Now his face grew even redder. "What a relief it'll be to have a rest."

Time passed quickly as Drew and Grace carried heavy buckets of water to the rows of vegetables. The hot sun bore down on their heads. Grace found wearing her bonnet was much more comfortable than having it hanging down her back. Owen gave Drew a felt slouch hat to wear to shade his face.

They hoed weeds in the corn patch, then picked a basket of snap beans. Mama and Camille picked cucumbers and cooked up vinegar syrup to make pickles. There were carrots, turnips, and cabbages ready to be picked. Along the fence grew vines of ripening melons and pumpkins. Grace wished she lived on a farm with all this food growing everywhere. The open-air market didn't seem half so much fun. Before supper, Drew and Grace released the goats and played tirelessly about the farmyard.

The next day, Drew found several pieces of scrap lumber lying about where the men were working. Taking them to Samantha, he said, "I noticed you have no whatnot shelf in the house. I can make one from these pieces. Would you like that?"

"Drew, you'll never know how much I'd like that. Owen is

able to put up a barn and drive a nail straight, but fancy work is not his cup of tea."

Drew had his trusty knife, and in the evenings, while Grace ran about playing with baby goats, Drew carved a delicately detailed whatnot shelf.

The days were passing too swiftly for Grace. She wanted this holiday to last forever. But within a week, the room was framed and finished, and there were even two glass windows hung. In the living room, Samantha's new whatnot shelf was mounted in the corner by the fireplace. Even Owen commented on what a craftsman Drew was.

The women packed foodstuffs to take home. Some would pay the liveryman, but there was still plenty to share with Carter and Deanna. There were green pickles, blackberry preserves, blocks of cheese, and baskets of goose and chicken eggs. One bag of wheat and another of corn lay in the wagon bed.

On the last afternoon, Grace and Drew sat under a leafy buckeye tree with the nannies and their kids munching grass nearby.

"Samantha says goats grow up and come fresh much quicker than a cow," Grace said.

"Come fresh?"

"Give milk."

Drew nodded. "Oh."

"And she says they eat very little, and that they'll eat most anything. They don't need a big pasture like a cow."

"I heard Samantha say that." Drew was lying on his back staring up at the cloudless sky.

"Drew, you know how we're always wishing we could do more to help out our families?"

"We do what we can. Now that I can shoot the musket and

skin my own game, I feel I'm pulling my share of the load."

"What if we could do more?"

"More? How?" Drew sat up and looked at Grace. "I can tell you're thinking about something. What are you cooking up?"

"What if we could sell goat's milk?"

"It'd spoil before we got it back to Cincinnati," Drew said.

"What if we took the milk-giver with us?"

Drew smiled. "You want to take one of the nannies?"

"Yes, I want to take Annabelle." Grace smiled. "Her kid is weaned from her."

"Your mama would never allow a goat in your yard."

"A few months ago she might not. But now that there's little food and no money, she might not be so hard to convince."

Drew thought about it. "It'd be fun to have Annabelle with us," he said.

"I agree. Shall we go ask?"

"Let's go!"

First they went to find Samantha, who was out in the garden. Grace asked if she'd part with Annabelle. "I was hoping you'd ask," Samantha answered.

Mama and Camille were in the kitchen cutting up a roasting hen for supper.

As Grace expected, her mother protested. "Gracie," she said, "you don't know a thing about taking care of a goat. You're too young for that much responsibility."

"I'm not too young," Grace protested. "I can learn. We'll have milk to drink and some left over to sell."

"But you don't know how to milk a goat."

"Samantha's already taught me. There's nothing to it."

Just then, Drew spoke up. "I can build a pen and a stanchion, Aunt Lavina."

Now Mama hesitated. It was a good sign.

Then Drew added, "And I'll even help Grace take care of Annabelle."

Grace could see her mother weakening. "I suppose we could see what your papa thinks."

Papa thought it was the smartest idea he'd heard in a long time. "Fresh milk every day! Why, Lavina, who could argue with that?"

So it was settled. Owen wove a tether rope for them with a handy slipknot so Annabelle wouldn't get away from them. The next morning when they packed the wagon, the men tied Annabelle to the back.

Grace had thought she would be sad about returning to the city, but now that she had Annabelle, she was excited. Loud good-byes and thank-yous were exchanged as the wagon pulled out of the Tate farmyard. The return trip would be slower since the wagon was weighted down with supplies.

Annabelle wasn't sure she liked leaving the farm. She bleated most of the way. Mama put her hands over her ears. "Such a racket! She sounds worse than a colicky baby."

Papa answered, "You won't care about the noise when she gives buckets of milk."

Grace didn't mind the noise at all. What fun she was going to have with her new pet.

CHAPTER 10

Annabelle's Accident

The next morning, Grace and Drew were ready to launch into their milk-selling business. But while they had plenty of milk to sell, they'd forgotten one small detail. Few people had the money with which to make a purchase.

Drew had a small wagon in which to carry their crocks of milk. They walked from house to house, pulling the wagon and asking if anyone wanted to buy some milk. People sadly shook their heads and closed their doors. Grace and Drew went home discouraged.

It was Drew who came up with the idea of bartering. "No one has any money," he said, "but people have things they might want to trade."

"That's a wonderful idea," Grace agreed.

"Let's begin with Yost's Mercantile," Drew suggested. "We'll ask Deanna and Aunt Lavina what they need from the store, and then we'll ask Mr. Yost if he'll trade the items for goat's milk."

And that's just what they did. Zachariah Yost was delighted with the plan because he and his wife had two small children. At last, Grace felt she was truly being a help to her family.

When Papa learned of their plan, he commended them. To Mama he said, "Gracie and Drew make a fine business team."

Grace basked in his praise, but she still wished he'd stop calling her *Gracie*.

Annabelle's tether rope was seldom used. Grace could go nowhere but what the bleating nanny wasn't right on her heels. Grace used the rope only when she took Annabelle into town.

"That silly goat would sleep with you if she could," Mama said in exasperation.

And Grace wished Annabelle could sleep with her. The enclosure Drew built was situated in a corner of the small area behind the house, but Annabelle spent little time there. Not because the pen wasn't sufficient, but because the goat cried when no one was around. Grace had never before had a pet, and Annabelle's antics made her laugh with glee.

And laughter was sorely needed, for as the hot, dry summer wore on, conditions in the city worsened. Food supplies dwindled, and people went hungry. There weren't as many hogs roaming the streets these days. Papa heard that people were catching them and eating them. Grace knew butchering a large animal in the heat of summer meant meat that rotted quickly. People became very ill eating spoiled meat. Knowing this made her even more thankful for the small store of food they now had in the cellar.

Papa and Luke talked about another trip to the country. They planned to help other farmers with building projects in trade for food. Grace thought it was a good plan and was pleased that her papa thought of it.

For the most part, Grace had shoved the thought of her new piano far into the back of her mind. It seemed selfish to want a luxury such as a piano when people were hungry.

However, one day as she and Drew were on an errand for Mama, with Annabelle on her tether rope, Grace was again thinking about her longing for a piano.

They were coming back from Yost's Mercantile when Grace had a bright idea. "No one's in the church on a Tuesday," she said to Drew. "Let's stop in for a minute."

"Grace, you don't like the long hours at church on Sunday. Why do you want to go on a Tuesday?"

Grace studied Drew. His unruly mop of hair stuck out every which way beneath his cap. The cut-down trousers were already too short for him. Deanna had once said that Drew grew at least an inch a day. Where he used to be pale and wan, he was now ruddy and sunburned. Drew looked nothing like the dapper boy who came to them from Boston.

"I do so like church. . .at least part of church," she retorted.

"Only the music."

"Nothing wrong with that. Music holds a sermon in itself." Tugging on Annabelle's rope, she called out, "Are you coming with me or not?" The nanny, who was attempting to nibble tufts of dried grass growing at the edge of the street, bleated and gave a little leap as she scurried to follow along.

"Grace, what're you going to do?"

"The way things look, I may never have a piano of my own."

"You're not going inside the church?"

"People go into the church all the time to pray. Why can't I?"

As Drew caught up beside Grace, Annabelle gave him a playful butt on the leg. He reached down to scratch her head. "That's not exactly true," he said to Grace. "You're not going to pray, are you?"

She smiled. "I can pray while I'm looking at the piano, can't I?"

"Grace!"

"I just want to lift the cover and touch the keys. There's no reason why I can't touch it. It's not fair for Widow Robbins to be the only one allowed to play it."

"You'll have your piano someday, Grace, I just know it. Deanna always says to me, 'Let patience have her perfect work.'"

"I know. Mama quotes the same Bible verse to me all the time. And I am being patient. Very patient. But while I'm being patient, I can still look at the church piano."

They came down Walnut Street to where the stone church with its towering bell steeple loomed on a corner lot.

"What will you do with Annabelle?" Drew asked.

"You hold her and stand outside to keep watch. We'll go to the side door. There's a little grass under the tree there. Annabelle will like that."

The shade cast by the church felt good to Grace's hot feet. Here the blazing summer sun had not totally scorched the scrubby grass. "Stay on the steps," she instructed Drew. "If you see someone coming, rap hard on the door." She handed Annabelle's rope to him.

Reaching out to take it, Drew said, "I shouldn't help you get in trouble, you know."

"There'll be no trouble, Drew." She stepped up on the cool stone step. Glancing about, she saw no one. The brass knob turned easily in her hand. "I'll leave the door ajar. Remember, rap hard."

Drew nodded, then sat down on the step and let Annabelle's rope out to give her wide range of the available grass.

Inside the church, the air was cool, with a kind of musty aroma. Grace made her way past the rows of pews to where the lovely piano sat. Soft light from the window fell across the shiny wood, making it gleam. With trembling fingers, she reached for the little knobs in the front and lifted the cover. It folded back once, then lifted once more to expose all the neatly lined black-and-white keys. Nervously, she glanced over her shoulder. The sanctuary was still empty and quiet.

Her heart was fairly thudding in her throat. She spread her skirt and sat primly on the stool, then allowed herself to actually reach out and touch the keys. They were as cool and as glossy as she knew they would be. Without pressing a key, she trailed her fingers up and down the keyboard. In her mind, she saw how Widow Robbins's fingers pounded out the chords for the hymns every Sunday. She wondered if there was a lighter way to make the melodies come to life.

From the music rack, she pulled down the hymnal and fanned through the pages. If only she knew how to read the notes. Surely it wouldn't hurt to press just one key. She did so, and the sound of the note startled her. She pressed another and then another. Within a few moments, she found sets of notes that sounded pleasing together and others that grated on her ears.

A little noise sounded behind her, making her gasp. Turning around, she said, "Oh, Annabelle, it's only you."

Then she jumped from where she was sitting. From the nanny's mouth hung a partially chewed hymnal. Down on the aisle were three more that also were partially chewed.

"Annabelle! What are you doing in here?"

"And I might ask you the same thing, young lady!" There at the door stood the Widow Robbins.

Grace froze. Where was Drew? Why hadn't he rapped on the door?

Widow Robbins snapped her parasol shut and tucked it

beneath her arm. With a scowl on her thin face, she walked slowly up the aisle. Her long, black silk dress made little swishing noises as she picked up bits and pieces of chewed hymnals along the way.

"Just wait until I talk to your parents about this," she said sternly, her eyes narrowing. "Not only have you broken the rules about not touching my piano, but you have allowed this mangy animal inside the house of God."

Grace stood to her full height. "Annabelle isn't mangy. And she didn't mean any harm. I didn't bring her in, she. . ." Grace stopped. She'd better not say that she'd left Drew to guard the door. Where could he be? She knelt down to take the hymnal from Annabelle and placed it on a pew. The edges were a mess. Annabelle bleated and gave Grace a gentle butt on the arm.

The widow stepped to the piano, took out her lace hankie, carefully wiped down the keys, and then quietly closed the lid. "You are never to touch this piano. Is that clear?"

"Yes, ma'am." Grace twisted the ends of Annabelle's dangling rope.

"Now take that creature and leave the premises. I'll discuss this with the Reverend Danforth, and then we'll pay a visit to your parents and discuss your actions."

"Yes, ma'am," Grace said again. She tugged at the rope and started down the aisle, then stopped. "I'm very sorry about the damage Annabelle caused. But I think more people should be allowed to use the piano," she said boldly. "After all, the church belongs to everyone."

Widow Robbins pressed the hankie to her forehead, then made scooting motions with her hand. "Go. Leave, before my anger takes over."

Out in the hot sunshine, Grace looked up and down the

street for Drew. Nothing. Something had to have happened. But what?

All she knew to do was to head toward home. No sooner had she left Walnut to turn onto Second Street than Drew came running toward her from a side street.

"Hey, Grace! I almost caught him!" he called out.

"Drew Ramsey. How could you? I left you to guard the door, and you deserted your post." She stopped and waited for him to catch up. Perspiration dripped from his beet-red face. His hat was scrunched in his hand, and he was heaving great breaths. Suddenly his words registered. "Almost caught who?" Grace wanted to know.

"Why, Raggy. Who else?"

"You were chasing Raggy Langler?"

Drew beamed a wide smile. "I was."

"Why? What did he do?"

"He tried to come at me and grab Annabelle's rope. So I stood up to him and gave him a hard shove."

Grace could barely believe her ears. "Then what?"

"He tried to fight back, but I tripped him. When he started to run, I tied Annabelle to the doorknob and chased him. Almost caught him, too."

Grace shook her head. This was almost worth getting caught by Widow Robbins. She had touched the piano, and Drew had chased Raggy. Two splendid victories!

When she told Drew about Annabelle getting loose and what happened to the hymnals and about the widow coming in, he was crestfallen. "I'm sorry. Your papa will be angry with you. What do you think will happen?"

"If Raggy tried to steal Annabelle, you did the right thing. Whatever happens will happen."

Mama was embarrassed and quite distraught following the visit from the Reverend Danforth. Papa didn't seem quite as upset as Mama, but Grace was duly scolded by both and sent to bed early that night. Mama and Papa agreed that somehow Grace would have to pay for the hymnals, no matter how long it took.

"Perhaps I can find people who will pay cash for Annabelle's milk," Grace said solemnly. "Then I'll be able to pay the debt." But the thought made Grace feel bad since she'd hoped to use the milk to help Mama and Papa.

Sitting on the edge of her small rope bed, she gazed out the window, wishing she were outside playing because it was cooler. Only a slight breeze ruffled the treetops, and it was stuffy and hot in her bedroom.

The thought of Drew chasing Raggy through the streets amazed Grace. When she had asked him what he would have done if he'd caught Raggy, Drew had said he didn't know. With Raggy's larger size, he could whip Drew. But Drew had saved Annabelle. If Raggy had stolen the nanny, he'd probably be having her for supper right about now.

Grace was sorry the hymnals had been chewed up, because she loved the fine songbooks their church owned. But she'd never be sorry she touched those lovely ivory keys. Closing her eyes, she made herself remember how they felt beneath her fingers. *Let patience have her perfect work.* Waiting was so hard, how could it be a "perfect" work?

CHAPTER 11

The Storm

Because of Annabelle's size, Grace had a hard time leading her around. When Drew wasn't with Grace, Annabelle nearly dragged Grace by the tether. But when left in her enclosure, the goat made such a racket that the neighbors complained. Grace lived on a crowded street where the houses were close together. The offer of goat's milk did nothing to appease the disgruntled neighbors.

"We need our sleep," said Mr. McClarren, who lived directly behind them. Mrs. McClarren had five little ones to take care of, and she heartily agreed.

There was nothing to do but let Drew take Annabelle to his house. In the clearing near the banks of Deer Creek, there were fewer houses nearby. Drew dismantled the enclosure and used the rough planks of lumber to construct a new one behind the Ramsey home.

Even though she knew it was for the best, Grace was sad to have to part with Annabelle. Of course, she'd see the goat often, but it wasn't the same as having her right outside the back door.

Both Matthew and Adah were delighted to have Annabelle at their house and squealed with delight when she licked their hands.

Being nearer the woods turned out to be much better for Annabelle. She could be tethered among the trees far from the house, where she could eat grass and weeds to her heart's content.

It was a muggy, still day in late August when Drew and Grace decided to go for a trek up past the bluff and take Annabelle with them. The city was hot and depressing. Grace had never seen Papa so sad. He'd had some work to do in the country helping farmers with building projects, but not enough to support their family. The drought had ruined the gardens and fields of most farms in the area.

Although Carter continued hunting, he often came home empty-handed. The drought had driven the small game deeper into the dense forests and up into the hills, where spring water sustained them.

When Grace and Drew took Annabelle up into the woods, Grace could forget the awful problems. On this day as they started out, little Matthew put up a terrible squall to go along. Usually Deanna distracted him or talked him out of it. But for once, Deanna seemed unable to cope.

"Perhaps this one time," she said, looking at Grace and Drew with tired, pleading eyes.

Grace knew that short-legged Matthew would slow them down and keeping an eye on him would be a worry. Taking Annabelle was problem enough. But how could they say no?

"All right," Drew said. Grace was glad he was the first to answer. "Come along." He reached out his hand, and Matthew ran to grab it.

Down through the dry creek bed they went, Annabelle bleating with joy at every step. Since following the creek bed was easier than walking through dry, prickly underbrush, they followed it awhile, then made their way up the other side to higher ground.

Usually the woods were much cooler, but today the heat penetrated through the green canopy of tall trees.

Grace sang songs as they walked along. Matthew loved the boatmen songs and asked for them over and over. Usually Grace could sing them all and never get tired, but today the air was so heavy, it was as though she couldn't get her breath. After an hour or so, they came to a clearing, and she suggested they tether Annabelle and sit down.

"Annabelle sure is producing milk," Drew said. "How long do you think it will last?" He pulled out the canteen he'd filled with well water and handed it to Grace.

"I'm not sure. I'll have to ask Samantha." She took a swallow of the warm water and let it trickle down her dry throat. Matthew was fascinated with the way Annabelle cropped the grass. He sat close by the goat, watching her every move.

Drew took back the canteen and offered it to Matt. "Just a few swallows, Matt," he said. "We need it to last till we get back."

Matt nodded and tipped the canteen carefully.

Grace loosened the strings of her bonnet. "I believe this has been the longest summer of my life." Sprawled out on the grass, she was painfully aware of how short her dress was becoming. She'd grown a few inches during the summer just as Drew had. But there'd be no new dresses for school.

Matt looked up from watching Annabelle. "What's that noise?"

Grace sat very still for a moment. "It's rumbling."

"Could it be. . . ?" Drew asked.

"Thunder?" Grace queried, jumping to her feet.

They couldn't see the horizon through the dense trees. The sky above them was still sunny and hazy blue.

"Let's go look!" Grace pulled up the tether stick and pulled on Annabelle, who wasn't ready to leave this lush pasture.

Drew came from behind and gave the goat a shove just as another rumble sounded. "It is, Grace! It's thunder! I bet it's going to rain. And when it rains, the river will be up—"

"Hurry!" Grace interrupted with panic growing in her voice. "We've got to get home!"

"Why? It's just rain. I want to be in the rain."

"I should have known from the heavy, still air," Grace said, pulling on the goat's rope as hard as she could and heading quickly back the way they came. "It gets still like that before a bad storm. Papa's warned me, but I forgot. It hasn't rained for so long."

"I'm scared," Matt said.

"Maybe we could find a cave," Drew suggested, taking hold of the younger boy's hand and hurrying his step. "Carter says there're lots of caves out here."

"If we happen upon a cave, we'll sure crawl inside, but it's foolish to try to hunt for one."

Just then the crashing sound of thunder echoed above their heads and a cool wind swished through the tops of the trees. Annabelle bolted, and Grace nearly tumbled as she tried to follow.

"It's almost on us!" Grace called out.

Matthew began to cry, so Drew stopped to take him up piggyback. This slowed him some, while Annabelle dragged Grace on ahead. They were about halfway back to Deer Creek when they could see greenish-gray clouds boiling up in the west. Grace felt two fat raindrops hit her face. So long they'd prayed for rain, and now it had arrived in a furious storm. It just didn't seem fair.

"See that big tree?" Drew called out. Rain was falling in gray sheets. "Let's get under there and stay!"

"Let's do!" Grace answered. She pulled and tugged on the rope as Annabelle kicked up her heels and bleated out her misery and fright. The sunlight was gone, and even though it was early afternoon, it was dim as dusk.

"I want my mama!" Matthew cried as Drew set him down beneath the tree.

Grace wished Matt were back with his mama, but she didn't say so. After all, her own mama would be worried, as well. Thunder crashed about them like giant cymbals from the marching band. It felt good to have the hard, pelting rain out of their faces. Grace's petticoats clung to her ankles. She put her arms about Annabelle's neck and tried to calm the frightened goat.

"I just remembered, Drew," Grace said. "Papa said never to stay under a tree in a thunderstorm."

"Carter said something like that to me, too," Drew agreed. "But it's so bad right now we have no choice. We need to watch out for Matt."

"Take me home," Matthew whined as he rubbed his eyes with his fists.

Just then a clap of thunder caused Annabelle to leap in the air, and the wet rope slipped from Grace's grasp.

"Oh no!" she cried. "Annabelle, come back! Drew, help!"

Quickly Drew heaved Matthew up on his back. "Follow her, Grace! We're right behind you!"

Sliding on the wet leaves, Grace sped out in the direction Annabelle had taken. Thankfully, it was toward home.

The three had not gone more than a few yards when a blinding flash of light filled the air around them and a crash sounded so loud it made Grace's ears ache. She turned to look and was aghast to see that the fierce lightning had sent the massive tree they had just been sitting under crashing to the ground.

Drew stopped, as well. They were numb with shock.

"Drew," Grace said, "I think Annabelle just saved our lives."

"She did that, all right." He adjusted the weight of the whimpering Matthew. "Hush now, Matt. It's all right. We're headed home." Then he laughed out loud. "Home," he repeated, "where Annabelle will probably be waiting for us as if nothing had happened."

Grace joined in the laughter, but her voice was all quivery. She couldn't wait to hug Annabelle's neck. The rain had lessened some and the wind had calmed. By the time they reached Deer Creek, water was rushing freely down the creek bed. No more walking in the dry bed. They made their way to the rickety old bridge and crossed there.

The sight of flowing water thrilled Grace. Maybe this meant there'd be river traffic soon.

Annabelle was indeed waiting in the dooryard of the Ramseys'. Deanna's look of relief when she met the three drenched children at the door told them how worried she'd been. She stoked up the cookstove and made them stand by it until they stopped shivering. Cups of hot cider helped take the chill off.

"Earlier today, I never thought I'd be cool again," Grace said between chattering teeth. "Now look at me."

Deanna offered to let Grace put on one of her old dresses, but Grace insisted that she go on home so Mama wouldn't worry. But first they told Deanna the story of how Annabelle saved their lives. Even Matt helped add a few vivid details.

"*Boom!*" he said, flinging his hands in the air. "The big old tree went *boom* and fell down."

"If you hadn't chased after the goat. . ." Deanna shook her head and bit her lower lip. "God watches after His own," she said. Her voice trembled as she spoke.

The welcome rains fell off and on for a number of days, until finally one morning Grace heard the most beautiful sound. The melodious tones of a keeler blowing his tin horn echoed through the valley. She was eating breakfast when she first heard it.

She gobbled down her food and told Mama she was going to Drew's to help with Annabelle. By the time she reached Drew's house, Annabelle had been fed and was tethered at the edge of the clearing.

"Drew," Grace said, "did you hear the horn?"

He nodded. "I did. At least the barges and keelboats can get through."

"Let's go see."

"See what?"

"The boats come in, silly."

"From the bluff?"

Grace shook her head. "From the landing."

"But your mama won't like that. We can watch from the bluff."

"From the bluff we can see them come downriver, but only on the landing can we see them unload." She started out as though she expected him to follow. "It's been forever since a boat unloaded, and I don't want to miss it."

She could tell he was thinking about it, but in a moment he

was by her side. "I hope we don't get into trouble," he said.

"We'll watch the boats from the landing just for a little while. Then we'll come back and help Deanna with her chores."

Sure enough, three keelboats were at the landing. One was larger than the rest, with space for eight rowers for traveling upstream. This keelboat had a large, boxy cabin in the center where passengers could get shelter from the weather.

Grace led Drew to an opening between a warehouse and the saddlery where they could see but not be seen. She made sure they stayed on the other side of the landing from the boatworks just in case Papa and Luke might be around. However, since work had come to a complete standstill, the men seldom came to the landing anymore.

From the talk on the landing, Grace and Drew learned that these boats had come up from St. Louis just as soon as the rains began.

Suddenly Grace gave a gasp. Emerging from the cabin of the larger boat was a lovely lady dressed in a fine traveling frock the color of moss in the woods. Her bonnet was lined with ruffles, and the bow was tied smartly beneath her proud chin. Long gloves graced her slender arms up to her elbows. She looked as though she'd stepped out of a fashion catalog from Yost's Mercantile rather than from the cabin of a boat. Grace could only stare, her mouth gaping.

CHAPTER 12

Sadie Rose

Drew, do you see that lady?" Grace asked in a whisper. She looked over at Drew, who was bug-eyed, as well. "I'm not blind," he said. "What do you suppose she's doing coming here? There's nothing in Cincinnati."

They waited a minute to see if a gentleman came to her side. A small crowd was gathering on the landing. The news had traveled that a trickle of river traffic had begun. Perhaps someone would soon come down to meet the well-dressed lady.

"Do you suppose she's traveling alone?" Grace whispered.

Drew shook his head. "Impossible."

But the lady, with her head erect, proceeded to lift the skirt of her empire dress and walk across the running board of the boat to the gangplank.

"Maybe it's not so impossible," Grace said. "She may have a good deal of money and she may need help with her bags." Pulling Drew's sleeve, she said, "Follow me. Hurry."

"Grace, we can't. . . ."

"Then I'm going alone, and I'll have all the coins to myself."

Pushing through the crowd, she sensed Drew was on her heels. Boldly Grace walked right up to the lady. Up close she was even lovelier, with cheeks as smooth and rosy as a fresh peach. Grace could see she wore "paint" on her lips, making them redder than they really were. She'd heard stories about painted ladies. A little shiver ran up her spine.

"Hello, ma'am," Grace said, suddenly wishing her dress were not so small and faded. "Welcome to Cincinnati. My name's Grace Morgan. My father builds boats over at the boatworks down there." She waved toward the far end of the landing. Grace didn't want this fine lady to think she was some waif from Sausage Row.

A smile made the picture-perfect face come alive beneath the delicate bonnet. "Well, good morning to you, Grace. And who might this be?" She motioned to Drew, who stood at Grace's elbow.

"Oh, this is Drew Ramsey, my cousin. He's my friend, too. You can call him Drew."

The lady adjusted her ruffled parasol and held out a dainty gloved hand. "Drew, Grace. My name is Sadie Rose. I'm honored to make your acquaintance."

"Sadie Rose," Grace said softly. "That's a beautiful name. Sadie Rose what?"

"Just Sadie Rose. It's enough, don't you think?"

"Oh, yes, ma'am. It's perfect," Grace replied. Why, Sadie Rose even smelled like roses. "Where are you headed?" Grace asked, suddenly remembering her mission.

"I'm going to stay at Kingsley's boardinghouse."

"Drew and I know right where that is. We can show you the way and carry your bags, as well."

Again came the smile that seemed to light up the entire landing. "That's a kind offer," said Sadie Rose. She gave her reticule a little shake. Grace could hear coins jingling. "Of course, I'd make it worth your while. Wait here while I see about having my trunk carried up later."

Since the streets were still fairly muddy, Grace deemed it best that they take Sadie Rose up Lawrence Street, which was not quite as steep as the others.

The bags were heavy, and before they were halfway to the boardinghouse, Grace and Drew were puffing.

"I hope it's not too much for you," Sadie Rose said.

"Oh no, ma'am, not at all. Drew and I like to work. We work all the time. That is, we would work all the time if there were more work to do."

"I've heard your city has suffered hard times this summer."

"You heard the truth," Drew put in.

"How long are you staying?" Grace asked between breaths.

Sadie Rose paused. "I'm undecided just now," she said.

Grace knew it was rude to ask too many questions, but she couldn't help herself. She wanted to know everything about this lady. "How did you travel all that way by yourself with those ornery boatmen?" she asked.

"I paid for protection."

Grace gave a little chuckle. "That's a smart plan."

Drew wasn't so sure. "I've heard of boatmen who've killed their passengers just to get the money," he said.

Sadie Rose stopped and looked at Drew. "Those passengers were probably snooty dandies from back East who thought they were better than those of us out West. You have to understand the boatmen in order to get along with them."

Grace saw Drew's ears turn pink. He used to think anyone on this side of the Allegheny Mountains was some kind of mindless ruffian. But he was learning differently.

"Mrs. Kingsley's boardinghouse sits at the end of this block, Miss Sadie Rose."

"Good. And you can just call me Sadie Rose. Plain and simple."

"Yes, ma'am, Sadie Rose," Grace answered.

At the front porch of the boardinghouse, Drew and Grace struggled to get the heavy bags up the steps. Once they did, Sadie Rose pulled open the reticule and placed two coins in each upturned palm. Grace hadn't seen a coin for many months. It felt cool and solid in her fist. She looked at Drew and smiled. Now she could pay for the damaged hymnals at the church.

"May we show you anything else in town, Sadie Rose?" Grace wanted to know. "After you've unpacked and settled in?"

"Why, yes. Do you know a man by the name of Eleazar Dunne?"

Grace felt Drew looking at her. "Yes, ma'am, I surely do. And I can take you right to the door of his place." Drew nudged her in the side with his elbow. She ignored him. "We'll be right here on the steps waiting for you, Sadie Rose."

"Thank you, children," replied the melodious voice. "How kind you are to a stranger."

Just then, the portly Mrs. Kingsley appeared at the door, wiping her hands on her apron. "Ain't takin' no boarders, 'less you got real money," she said curtly. "No credit."

"Good morning, Mrs. Kingsley," Grace said, stepping forward.

"Well, morning, Gracie. What are you doing around here?"

Ignoring the question, Grace introduced Sadie Rose and assured the matron that Sadie Rose was good for the rent money.

Mrs. Kingsley squinted at the immaculately dressed lady standing on her porch. "Very well, I'll take your word for it, Grace." She pushed the door open farther and stepped back to let Sadie Rose inside.

When the women were out of earshot, Drew said, "Grace Morgan, have you gone daft? We can't take her to a tavern! Especially a tavern on Front Street! Your mama will tan your hide and hang it up to dry if she ever finds out."

"If she ever finds out. But she won't. And this money can pay for new hymnals at the church. And maybe even a little food, if there's any food left in the city to buy." Grace sat down on the top step of the porch to wait. "These are desperate times, Drew. Desperate times call for desperate measures."

Once she'd said the words, she was pleased at how grown-up it sounded. Maybe when she handed the money to Mama, she could say, "Now, please don't call me *Gracie* again." But how was she going to explain the money without telling the story? She'd have to think of something.

Drew, she could tell, was still stewing about going to a tavern on Front Street, but Grace pretended not to notice. Presently, Sadie Rose came back out the door. Gone was the moss green traveling dress with matching jacket. Now there was a beautiful afternoon dress of the finest raspberry-colored taffeta Grace had ever seen.

Jumping to her feet, Grace said, "Sadie Rose, you're so beautiful!"

Sadie Rose just smiled. "Thank you, Grace. Now, shall we be on our way?"

"I've never heard of a lady traveling alone on a keelboat, and I never heard of a lady going alone to a tavern," Grace said. "What will you do there?"

Sadie Rose's lilting laughter bubbled like a little stream up in the hills. "By my leave, Grace, you're about the most curious girl I've ever met. If you must know, I'm the new singer and piano player for Mr. Dunne."

Grace felt her heart pick up a beat. She glanced over at Drew, whose eyebrows were raised. "You know how to play the piano?" Grace asked.

"Been playing since I was knee high to a mosquito."

"And you sing?"

"Like a bird."

"Grace sings," Drew said, hardly able to keep out of this conversation.

"Does she now?"

"Oh, Drew," Grace said, but inwardly she was glad he'd told Sadie Rose.

"Yes, ma'am," Drew went on. "Last May she was chosen to sing at school commencement."

Last May seemed like such a long time ago to Grace. The long, hot summer had not been fun at all.

"If you're such a good singer," said Sadie Rose, twirling her parasol, "let's hear you sing something."

Grace never had to be asked twice. She burst out in a lively boatmen song. On the chorus, Sadie Rose joined in but moved a couple of notes higher to harmonize perfectly.

When the song was over, Sadie Rose said, "Your cousin was right, Grace. You do sing well."

"Thank you, Sadie Rose. Your voice is like an angel's."

"An angel I am not, but I thank you kindly for the sentiment."

"Right down there is Dunne's Tavern," Grace said, pointing down Front Street.

"I see the sign," said Sadie Rose. "You two can run on now." Again Grace heard the lovely *clink* of coins. This time Sadie Rose handed each cousin a single coin. Now Grace had three. She could hardly believe it.

"But you can't stay in this area alone," Drew insisted. "Don't you want us to walk you back?"

Sadie Rose touched Drew's shoulder lightly with her gloved hand. "Young Drew, what a gentleman you are. Thank you, but I need your help no longer today. Mr. Dunne will see to my safe journey back to the boardinghouse."

Grace knew Sadie Rose would be singing at the tavern until the wee hours of the morning. Even in the worst of times, there still seemed to be business at the taverns, especially those down on Front Street. Papa said when times got hard, men either prayed or drank. Grace was thankful her papa prayed.

As she and Drew trudged back through the muddy streets toward home, Grace could hardly keep still. She wanted to laugh and sing and shout. What a splendid day it had turned out to be!

"I can hardly believe such a fine lady would sing at a tavern," Drew was saying.

"There's nothing wrong with singing at a tavern," Grace said in defense of her new friend. But she wasn't sure she was right. She'd heard stories about men fighting and killing one another after becoming drunk at a tavern. One thing she knew for sure—Sadie Rose was a very nice lady.

As she and Drew passed through the edge of Sausage Row, the smells were awful. Sewage and garbage lined the streets. Houses were little more than shacks, nothing like the fine brick home Grace's papa had built for his family. Vacant buildings with boarded-up windows bore testimony of the hard times in the city.

"I suppose we should have gone up to Second Street," Drew said, wrinkling his nose.

Grace silently agreed. Although there might be garbage in other parts of the city, nothing ever smelled as bad as Sausage

Row. In her apron pocket were her three coins. She held them tightly in her fist and kept her hand in the pocket.

"What are you going to tell your mama about the money?" Drew asked.

He must have been reading her thoughts. She was wondering the same thing. "Why, I'll just tell her the truth. That a boat came in, we went to watch, and then we carried bags for a passenger."

Drew nodded. "I guess that sounds fine, but she doesn't like you going to the landing."

"Perhaps the sight of money will make it all right. What will you tell Carter and Deanna?"

"Carter has never forbidden me to go to the landing. . . ."

Just then, a terrible ruckus in an alleyway behind the vacant buildings broke into their conversation.

"Give that back!" they heard a voice yell. "That's mine. Give it back!"

"Someone's in trouble," Grace said.

"Stay out of it, Grace." Drew tugged on her arm, but she pulled away.

"That voice sounds like Raggy." She stopped to listen. "We've got to do something, Drew. Follow me."

CHAPTER 13

A Visit with Amy

Grace backtracked and made her way carefully around a vacant warehouse, hoping Drew was right behind her. Peeking around the corner, she saw two boys, bigger than Raggy, who were taunting him. She motioned for Drew to come beside her and look.

"You stay here," she said softly. "I'm going around the other way. When I give the signal, dive for their knees."

When she arrived at the opposite corner of the building, she could see the boys had something that Raggy desperately wanted. Strangely enough, it appeared to be a piece of blue flowered cloth.

"Rag–gee, Rag–gee," the boys taunted. "Carries his rag with him wherever he goes." The taller boy waved the cloth in front of Raggy like a flag. Just as Raggy leaped to grab it, the boy passed it off to his friend. There were tears in Raggy's eyes.

When Grace saw Drew peek his head around the corner, she waved her hand. The two of them ran, each one toward one of the tormenters, and slammed as hard as they could into the back of the boys' knees with their shoulders. Both boys tumbled to the ground. In a flash, Raggy grabbed the cloth and fled, disappearing around the corner of the building.

"Why, you yellow-bellied little twerps," one boy growled as he struggled to his feet. "I'll grind you to bits and feed you to the crows."

"Come on, Drew," Grace said. "Let's get out of here." But she was quickly and roughly grabbed from behind.

"Not so quick, little girl," the second boy said. "You're gonna pay for buttin' in where you ain't welcome."

"Pay?" Grace said. Reaching into her pocket, she pulled out two of her precious coins. "Look here," she said. "I'll pay."

"Money!" the first boy exclaimed. "She has real money!"

"And it's all yours!" Grace yelled as she flung the coins as far as she could.

Immediately she was released. While the boys scrambled to retrieve the money, she and Drew made their getaway, leaving Sausage Row far behind.

When they were in their own safe neighborhood once again, they slowed their pace. Still heaving to catch his breath, Drew handed Grace two of his three coins and said, "Here, Grace. I want you to have these."

She pushed his hand away and shook her head. "You earned that money fair and square. In fact, I want you to take my last one and keep it, too. There's not enough to pay for the hymnals anyway."

Drew solemnly took the coin. "I'll keep it for you, but it's still yours."

Grace nodded.

They walked along in silence for a time. Then Drew ventured to say, "I thought you didn't like Raggy Langler, but you helped him. That doesn't make much sense to me."

"I guess I just don't like to see bullies win, no matter who the bullies are."

That night at supper, Papa seemed in better spirits than he'd been for many weeks. "With a few keelboats getting through, perhaps trade will begin to pick up," he said. "We'll pray the fall rains come early and are plentiful. Before you know it, the landing could be booming once again."

Mama had cooked up a kettle of the dried beans Papa had brought back from one of the farmers for whom he'd worked. At least it was a change from the steady diet of salt pork and cornbread. Grace noticed that Papa was always careful to say a blessing over their meals, no matter how little they had.

As they were eating, Mama shared her good news, as well. A letter had arrived from Samantha saying she and Owen would be coming for a visit and would bring as many provisions as they could. "Eggs and cheese," Mama said, closing her eyes. "How good that will taste. Maybe watermelon. *Mmm.*"

Later that night, Grace lay tossing about in her bed. The hot August night made sleeping difficult. Not a bit of breeze fluttered through her dormer windows. Grace couldn't seem to get the look of Raggy's sad face from her mind. It was a puzzle. Why would Raggy Langler fight two bigger boys for a little piece of flowered cloth? Although she still didn't trust Raggy, suddenly he didn't seem like such a threat anymore.

A couple of times during the summer, Grace had received permission from Mama to walk to Amy's house, or rather to the cabin where the Coppocks now lived. Since it was situated far on the west side of town, Mama didn't like Grace to go there alone. But when Drew could go along, Mama was more willing.

Even though Grace loved Amy, it made her sad to visit the small cabin and see that the family didn't have many of the nice things they used to have. Mr. Coppock had owned a lot of land, and when prices plummeted, suddenly he lost not only his money in the bank, but the land, as well.

On this day, Grace and Drew were taking a bag of dried beans to the family. The streets were once again thick layers of powdery dust, and the sun bore down hotter than ever. Perhaps Papa's prediction for early fall rain was overly hopeful.

On the way across town, Grace insisted they go by the boardinghouse in hopes of seeing Sadie Rose. Grace desperately wanted to see her new friend once again. She bravely knocked on the front door and asked to see Sadie Rose, but Mrs. Kingsley glared at her sternly.

"There'd be no reason for a girl like you to visit with the likes of Sadie Rose, Gracie. You can't see her anyway because she's asleep. She sleeps most of the day. Every day. Even Sundays!" With that, she closed the door.

Grace was indignant. "The likes of Sadie Rose," she muttered as they walked away. "What a terrible way to talk."

"She didn't mean anything by it," Drew replied. "Remember, Grace, most people don't approve of ladies who spend time in a tavern."

"But Sadie Rose is different."

"From what?"

Grace shrugged. After all, what did she know about ladies in taverns? "I don't know. She's just different, that's all."

Thankfully, Drew didn't argue. He never did.

The Coppocks' cabin sat in a clearing near Mill Creek. Amy was sitting under a shade tree in the front yard, watching her new baby sister and sewing a patch on a pair of Jason's trousers. Her little sister Leah played in the dirt nearby.

A smile lit her face when she saw the pair approaching. Jumping up, she ran to give Grace a hug. "How good to see you again! I miss you awfully." After grabbing up the baby and taking Leah's hand, she led them inside.

Mrs. Coppock greeted Drew and Grace graciously and offered to fix them each a cup of dandelion tea. Though Grace didn't care for dandelion tea, she didn't want to be rude, so she said yes.

Grace wished she and Amy could visit alone like old times at school. If only their families attended the same church, at least she'd see her friend on Sundays. Grace wanted to tell her about Sadie Rose and describe her fashionable frocks and bonnets. She wanted to tell her about seeing Raggy crying over a little piece of flowered cloth.

But a private conversation was impossible. As usual, the visit would be short. Mrs. Coppock was grateful for the beans, but Grace could tell it was an embarrassment to the woman to accept them and to Amy, as well. They had had so much, and now they had virtually nothing. The very thought made Grace's heart ache.

Later that afternoon at Drew's house, he showed Grace the stanchion he'd constructed. "See how it works?" He demonstrated by moving back and forth the slant that would hold Annabelle's head firm as she was milked. They'd been tying Annabelle's head close to a post when they milked her, but the goat moved around more than they'd like.

"Let's try it out," Grace suggested.

Together they went to the edge of the clearing. Drew lifted the tether out of the ground, and they led the goat to the stanchion. It was a perfect fit.

"Get a bucket," Grace instructed.

Drew did so and also brought her the T-shaped stool he'd

made. Grace situated herself beside the goat, just as she'd done for weeks. She firmly grasped the teats and began to pull. "Drew, it works like a charm!"

Streams of milk flowed into the bucket as Annabelle stood still. For once, they weren't losing quarts of milk because of Annabelle's hooves bumping the bucket. Even quiet Drew grew excited.

"Deanna," he called out, "come and see! The stanchion works!"

After Deanna and the children had watched Grace and Drew take turns milking Annabelle, Grace turned to Deanna and asked, "Annabelle is giving so much milk; do you think we could make some goat's cheese?"

"What a fine idea," Deanna said. "I know just where my cheesecloths and wheels are packed away."

"Deanna!" Grace called as the young woman turned toward the house.

"Yes?" Deanna asked.

"Could we keep this a secret from my parents? I'd like to surprise them."

Deanna smiled. "Of course, Grace. Now let's get to work."

Several days later, the cheese-making process was complete. Grace insisted that Deanna keep part of it for her own family. Deanna wrapped the remainder of the cheese in some cloth and placed it in a stone jar for Grace to carry home.

Later, when Mama and Papa tasted the soft cheese spread on some cornbread, Grace studied their faces.

"*Mmm,*" Papa said as he set his cornbread down. "That's about the best cheese I've ever tasted in my life. What do you think, Lavina?"

Grace was surprised to see tears brimming in Mama's eyes.

"I do believe Gracie is growing up, Thad. It's a big job to care for a goat, then milk her and make cheese, as well."

What beautiful words to Grace's ears. She ran to Mama's side and gave her a hearty hug.

A few days later, the Tates' buckboard came rumbling up the street in front of the Morgan home, and Grace ran out the front door to greet them.

Their wagon was laden with bags and barrels. A wicker basket held a fat watermelon, along with a few cucumbers, carrots, and turnips. In a crate were two cackling chickens. Thoughts of tasty chicken and dumplings made Grace's mouth water. Finally, something to eat other than salt pork!

✑ CHAPTER 14 ✑

A Summer Feast

Annabelle's giving lots of milk!" Grace cried out as she ran around to Samantha's side of the wagon. "We've even made cheese."

Owen secured the brake on the wagon. Laughing, he said, "Well, well. Hello to you, Grace. Good to see you."

"Grace Morgan," Mama corrected, "what an improper greeting." To Owen and Samantha she said, "I dare say this child has totally lost all decorum this summer. Everything has been at loose ends."

"Please, Lavina," Samantha said, "don't apologize. We love Grace's exuberance." She patted her large tummy. "I hope our little one is made of the same cloth."

Owen jumped down and came around to assist his wife. While Papa helped Owen unload the wagons, the women went inside to catch up on all the latest news.

Luke and Camille, as well as Carter, Deanna, and the children, were invited for Sunday dinner. It would be a celebration. A summer feast! Grace was ecstatic.

Later that evening, Samantha went along with Grace to Drew's house. When they arrived, Drew had just brought the goat in from her tether. Deanna and the children came out to greet Samantha, and together they all went out back so Samantha could see Annabelle.

Samantha could hardly believe how well the goat looked. "I don't believe Josie is this big," she said, petting Annabelle's head and rubbing her ears. "You've taken such good care of her, Grace. I'm so proud of you."

"Mama didn't think I could do it," Grace said, stretching to stand a little taller.

Samantha nodded. "Sometimes mamas are the last ones to realize their babies are growing up." She smiled. "I'll probably be the same way."

"But I didn't do it all by myself." Grace reached out and grabbed Drew's arm, pulling him forward from where he'd been standing behind them. "Drew helped a lot."

"I'm guessing he built the enclosure and the stanchion."

"You guessed right," Grace said.

Samantha ran her hands over the wooden stanchion. "What splendid workmanship," she said.

Deanna agreed. "Drew's a good worker, and he's a gifted carpenter."

Then they all laughed as Drew blushed and ducked his head.

On Saturday, Owen wanted to see the steamboats, so the men left to go to the boatworks. The women butchered chickens and set them to boiling. Pies were baked and turnips stewed. The kitchen was unbearably hot, but no one seemed to mind.

Seeing and smelling all the scrumptious food made Grace think about Amy in her crowded cabin. How she wished Amy and her family could share in this feast. The more she thought about it, the better she liked the idea. But since this was a family gathering, she wasn't at all sure Mama would agree.

Mama, however, did agree. "Why, Gracie, what a kind heart you have," she said. Mama dumped a basket of dried apples into an iron kettle of boiling water. Later those sweet apples would be the filling for a juicy apple pie. Setting the basket down, Mama said, "We have more than enough food for the Coppocks to join us. You and Drew run over to Amy's and extend the invitation."

"Drew's gone off with Carter, Mama. But I can go by myself."

Mama hesitated. She reached up to take her large stirring spoon down from its hook and stirred the apples thoughtfully.

"If I don't go, how will they ever know they're invited?" Grace reasoned.

"I suppose you're right."

Grace's heart skipped a beat. At last Mama was beginning to trust her. "I'll fetch my bonnet," she said.

"Tell them we'll expect them at three," Mama said.

"I'll tell them." Grabbing her bonnet and tying it beneath her chin, she said, "I'll be back before supper."

"See that you are," Mama answered. "Don't dillydally."

The look on Mrs. Coppock's face when Grace offered the invitation was a sight to behold. Amy, too, fairly fluttered with excitement.

"There's plenty, and we want you to come and be with us," Grace assured them.

"I don't know how to thank you." Mrs. Coppock stood at her doorway with the baby resting on her hip. She'd invited Grace inside, but Grace declined the offer. She had to hurry back home.

"Your family has been more than kind to us," Mrs. Coppock

went on. "Jason and Mr. Coppock are grateful, as well. We'll come along to your home directly from church."

"We'll be expecting you around three." With a wave, Grace turned back down the path. At last she and Amy would have a few minutes alone to talk.

The air was steamy hot, and Grace was grateful for the shade from her bonnet. How she wished she had a fancy dress with a matching parasol to ward off the hot sun.

When she arrived back in town, she made sure her path led past the boardinghouse. There on the front porch sat Sadie Rose! Grace could hardly believe her good fortune. Sadie Rose was dressed in a pink ruffled frock with billowy sleeves and no bonnet. In her hand she held an ivory fan, which she waved slowly back and forth.

Grace nearly ran in Sadie Rose's direction. "Hello!" she called out. "Hello, Sadie Rose!"

Sadie Rose's lovely face broke into a smile that warmed Grace's heart. "Hello to you, Grace. Come set a spell. How have you been?"

Grace bounded up the steps to the porch and sat down in the wicker chair beside Sadie Rose. "I'm quite well, thank you. I stopped by to see you one day, but Mrs. Kingsley said you were sleeping."

Sadie Rose laughed lightly. "Ah yes, sleep. Something I do when others are awake."

"Are you still singing at Mr. Dunne's tavern?"

"That I am. Mr. Dunne, it turns out, is as fair an employer as I've had in quite a spell."

"I'm pleased to hear that."

"He appreciates my singing and my piano music."

"I'm sure you're excellent." Grace had so many questions to

ask. "Sadie Rose, how did you learn to play the piano? Did you take lessons?"

Sadie Rose adjusted her ruffled skirts and gave a little sigh. "It was my dear ma who taught me. Before she died."

"Oh, I'm sorry," Grace said.

"No need to be sorry. It was such a long time ago."

"Sadie Rose, would it be too much to ask. . . ? I mean, well, I was supposed to have a piano. It was ordered, but the bank failures and the dried-up river slowed everything down."

Sadie Rose closed her fan and leaned forward. "Yes, Grace? What is it you want to ask?"

"Could you teach me a little bit about the piano? Just a little? I wouldn't take up much of your time."

Sadie Rose relaxed into her chair. "Why, of course I could teach you. At least a couple of songs anyway. Meet me at the tavern early next Saturday morning. No one will be there then. Can you make it?"

"But I thought you slept late."

"Grace, for you I'd sacrifice my sleep."

For a moment Grace thought her heart would beat right out of her chest. "Thank you, Sadie Rose. I'll be there next Saturday morning."

Grace ran the rest of the way home and barely made it before the family sat down to supper.

Sunday's feast was a magnificent affair. Because Mama's table wasn't nearly big enough, makeshift tables were set up in the dining room by placing long boards over sawhorses. Jason and Drew took their plates out in the dooryard to eat. Matthew, Adah, and Amy's sister Leah, were fed in the kitchen. But Grace and Amy were allowed to eat with the grown-ups.

The men talked of better times and how wise banking practices could prevent such disasters from ever hitting Cincinnati again. At one point during the meal, Grace was surprised to hear Carter say to Papa, "Thad, I want you to know I've changed my mind about working at the boatworks with you and Luke."

Papa's bushy eyebrows went up, but he waited for Carter to have his say.

"I've been doing a good deal of thinking this summer," Carter went on. "It always seemed to me a man could make a go of things by himself. Well, I've tried that, and I've seen my family go without the things they need."

"We've all seen our families go without," came Papa's gentle reply.

"That's true," Carter said. "The difference is, you have something to go back to. I don't. I know the economy will turn around and the river won't be dry forever. I'd have to be blind not to see that steamboats are the coming thing." He paused a moment, and Grace knew that Carter was struggling to say what his heart felt. "If the offer's still good, I'm ready to take you up on it."

It was Luke who answered. "The offer's as good as the day it was given."

Carter nodded. "Thank you, Luke. As soon as you can take me on, let me know, and I'll be there."

After dinner, Papa took down his fiddle, and Grace stood up a few steps on the stairway in the hall and sang for everyone. Soon she had them all clapping their hands and laughing and joining in on the choruses. Hearts that had been heavy with worry and fear were made lighter for having a few hours of fun

Because Grace and Amy were put in charge of all the little

ones while the women cleared the tables and washed dishes, there still was no time for quiet talk. But Grace realized she wasn't quite ready to tell Amy about Sadie Rose. Instead they talked about the opening of school, which was set for the next week.

Amy said she didn't care that she didn't have pretty dresses for the new school term. "I'm just anxious to get back to studying," she said. "Mama and Papa and Jason and I have all agreed that things aren't nearly as important as having one another."

Grace thought about that a moment and realized she agreed. Even though she still longed to have her own piano, she knew a piano could never replace the love of her family.

Owen and Samantha left before dawn the next morning. As the empty wagon rattled noisily down the street, Grace waved and hollered her good-byes, remembering especially to say thank you over and over again. She wondered what her family would have done without the generosity of the Tates.

With the new stock of foodstuffs in the larder, Papa was sure they could make it through until things turned around, which he believed would be very soon.

Mama and Deanna continued to make cheese with the extra milk, and of course there was plenty for everyone to drink. Even Luke and Camille took a share.

All week, Grace stewed about in her mind, trying to think of a way she could meet Sadie Rose at the tavern on Saturday morning. In the end, the problem took care of itself. It was Mama who suggested that Grace take a jar of goat's milk to the dressmaker to see if she could trade for ribbon and lace.

Mama had been rummaging in the chest of clothing in the attic. Out of it she'd pulled two of her own cast-off dresses. "I believe," she said to Grace, "there's enough cloth here to make you a proper school dress. All we need is new ribbon and lace." She gave Grace small snippets of the fabric to match the colors.

Grace could hardly believe her good fortune. If it were not for balancing the full jar of milk, she would have skipped all the way to the dressmaker's shop.

Mrs. Cragle was pleased to be paid with fresh milk. Soon Grace had the silky ribbon and delicate lace tucked away in her pocket, and, bidding Mrs. Cragle good day, she made her way down the hill to Dunne's Tavern. As she did, she kept glancing around, hoping no one watching knew her or Papa.

Before she approached the tavern, she heard the enchanting sound of lilting piano music and the clear, full tones of Sadie Rose's singing. She stopped outside to listen, not wanting to break the spell. It was a hauntingly sad ballad about love being lost. Grace stood entranced, wanting the song to go on forever. When the last note died away, she tapped on the door.

"Is that you, Grace?"

"Yes, ma'am. It's me."

"The door's open. Come in."

Pushing open the door, Grace wrinkled her nose at the heavy odor of beer that hung in the air. She'd often caught the aromas outside a tavern, but inside they were a hundred times worse. She hoped it wouldn't make her sick. Across the darkened room, she could see Sadie Rose sitting at the piano.

A little shiver ran up Grace's spine as she entered the forbidden tavern. She knew if Mama and Papa ever found out, they would never understand.

CHAPTER 15

Piano Lessons

"Come on over here and have a seat," Sadie Rose invited. "It's so good to see you again."

Sadie Rose pulled a chair next to the piano stool. Sitting so close to Sadie Rose, Grace could catch whiffs of the fragrance of roses. Roses smelled much better than beer.

Pointing to a key in the center of the keyboard, Sadie Rose told her it was called *middle C*. Then she explained the octaves and taught her the eight notes in each octave.

"What about the black keys?" Grace wanted to know.

"We call them *sharps* and *flats*," she said. "I'll tell you more about them in your next lesson."

Next lesson! What beautiful words to Grace's ears.

"Do you recognize this melody?" Sadie Rose asked. She placed her right hand on the keys and picked out a simple tune.

"Why, that's 'A Mighty Fortress Is Our God.' My favorite hymn."

"Is it now? It's my favorite, too. It's one of the first songs my ma ever taught me. Look how easy it is. It begins on this C up here and ends on middle C down here." Patiently, Sadie Rose pointed out the notes and then let Grace follow her. Within minutes, Grace had the first few bars down pat.

"I don't play this song very often anymore."

"Why not?" Grace asked. "It's so beautiful."

"It brings back too many painful memories," Sadie Rose said wistfully.

"About your ma?"

Sadie Rose nodded. "When Ma and Pa died, my baby brother and I were given to an orphanage in Philadelphia. It wasn't a very nice place, Grace. I did my best to look out for little Patrick, but I had a difficult time of it."

"Drew's an orphan," Grace offered. "He came here from Boston to live with his older brother. I'm sure glad he didn't have to live in an orphanage."

"Yes, be very thankful," Sadie Rose replied, giving Grace's shoulder a gentle pat. "Before Ma and Pa died, I gave them my word that I would always look after Patrick." Sadie Rose paused and pulled a hankie from out of the sleeve of her blue organdy dress.

"What happened, Sadie Rose? What happened to Patrick?"

"People came," she said in the barest whisper. "Came and adopted him. They—they didn't want me. I said I could take care of him myself, but they laughed at me."

Grace squeezed her eyes tight to blink back hot tears. "That's so terrible," she said. "But you couldn't help what happened!"

"But I promised. I promised Ma and Pa. Now I can't even get their forgiveness."

"No," Grace agreed, "but you can surely get God's forgiveness if you just ask. And that's even better."

As though she hadn't heard, Sadie Rose went on. "The couple who took Patrick away said they were coming out West. I've traveled from town to town, looking for him. That's why I sing in taverns." Sadie Rose dabbed gently at the corners of her eyes. "It earns me enough money to keep on going."

"Why not pray and ask God to help? God knows where your brother is."

"Oh, Grace, you're such a good, sweet girl. But I've forgotten how to pray. It's been so long."

The way Sadie Rose talked to Grace made her feel much older than her ten, almost eleven, years. "Well, I haven't forgotten. Papa reads the Bible every evening, and we pray before going to bed. I can pray for you."

Sadie Rose's face lit up with a bright smile. "Oh, would you truly? I'd like that very much."

"Bow your head," Grace directed. Then she very simply asked God to show Sadie Rose where and how to find her brother, Patrick. Then she added, "And please, Lord, let it happen quickly so Sadie Rose can stop wandering from place to place. In Jesus' name, amen."

Sadie Rose put her arm around Grace's shoulder and gave her a squeeze. "Oh, Grace, you're a good friend. I'm so glad you came to the landing the day I arrived. And I'm pleased to be able to help you learn to play the piano."

They continued working on the melody together until Grace knew it perfectly.

"Next time, I'll show you how to add chords with the left hand," said Sadie Rose.

"I'd better go now. Mama's expecting me." Grace made her way to the back door and gave Sadie Rose a little wave. "Bye now. And thank you very much!"

"Thank *you*, Grace."

With that, Grace slipped out and hurried up the hill. She hugged herself with happiness. She'd actually played a hymn on the piano. And almost as wonderful was the fact that the lovely Sadie Rose had confided in her. She promised herself that she would remember to pray for Sadie Rose every night.

If I were an orphan searching for my younger brother, she thought, *perhaps I would sing in a tavern, as well. Sadie Rose is only doing what she has to do.*

Grace was scolded for arriving home late, but she didn't mind. Being with Sadie Rose was worth all the scoldings in the world.

September's days were no cooler than August's days had been. Sitting in the steamy, crowded classroom at school was sheer torture. Mr. Inman's collar and tie were rumpled my midmorning each day. Periodically he ran his finger around inside the stiff collar as though he wished he could fling it off.

So many things had changed since last spring. Amy was quieter, and she had no new dress to wear. Although Grace's dress wasn't actually new, it was still prettier than almost any other dress in the classroom. How thankful she was that she had a resourceful mama.

Drew now attended school upstairs. Grace missed having him nearby, but she knew he'd be fine. He wasn't a dapper Boston dandy anymore. In fact, at first glance, he looked no different than any other boy at school. His face had lost its pasty color and fairly glowed from a summer of traipsing through the woods.

And, of course, Jason Coppock was in the classroom upstairs, too. He'd keep an eye out for Drew.

Raggy had also graduated to the upstairs classroom, but he seldom attended. Grace thought Raggy looked thinner. If the depression had been hard on her family, she could only imagine what it was like for youngsters like Raggy. And Grace had heard that Wesley and Karl had both left town.

As often as possible, Grace stopped by the boardinghouse in hopes of seeing Sadie Rose. In the afternoons, she might be sitting on the porch catching a late afternoon breeze. Grace would stop and talk with her. Little by little, she was coming to know her friend better. And it was a true friendship. Grace had never had a grown-up for a friend before.

Drew never liked the idea of Grace spending time at the tavern, yet he offered to stay with her each Saturday morning when she went for her lesson. Each time, they took a different route so that, hopefully, no nosy person would see and report them to her papa.

"Mind you," Drew would say, "the more times you go to the tavern, the greater the chance of your being caught."

Grace knew he was concerned for her, but she knew that Drew also liked to be around Sadie Rose. And who could blame him? How could anyone not like such a gracious and lovely lady?

September was drawing to a close when one cool Saturday morning she and Drew were sent to the market. While crops were much smaller than usual, still farmers were bringing in a smattering of fall produce—corn, pumpkins, and squash. Some of the farmers would trade for goat's milk and cheese. Others wouldn't. After selecting three nice squash and several ears of corn, Grace and Drew carried their basket down the hill and stopped at the tavern for a few moments.

By now Grace could play all of "A Mighty Fortress Is Our God" without making a single mistake. Sadie Rose seemed as thrilled as Grace. "I believe you're a natural, Grace. Soon we'll start on another song. Perhaps you'd like to learn a boatman song next."

"I'd like that, Sadie Rose," Grace replied. "Lively boatmen songs make my feet want to dance a jig."

Sadie Rose laughed. "I feel the same way."

"Grace," Drew said to her, "we'd better get home." He was standing by the door with the basket sitting by his feet. "Your mama will have a conniption."

"He's right, you know," Sadie Rose said. "You don't want to worry your ma."

Grace was always reluctant to leave. When she was sitting at the piano with Sadie Rose, she forgot everything else.

Up the street they went with the basket between them. "Step lively," Drew said. "Your mama's expecting us."

Suddenly, from behind them came a loud *whoop*! Grace dropped her hold on the basket and whirled around. There came Raggy, bearing down as fast and hard as he could run. He slammed into Drew, knocking him to the ground and making the basket fly. With one swipe, he grabbed two of the squash and kept on running.

"Come back here with that, you thief!" Grace yelled. "Come on, Drew. I bet we can catch him."

"Let him go." Drew gathered ears of corn and put them back into the basket.

"Let him go?"

"He's hungry, Grace. Let him have the squash." He walked to the side of the street where the third squash had rolled. He brushed it off and placed it in the basket, as well. "Come on. Let's go home."

"What'll we tell Mama?"

"That doesn't seem to be my concern," Drew said almost curtly.

"Are you upset with me?" she asked. She couldn't bear to

have Drew angry with her.

"We shouldn't have been in this neighborhood with our purchases."

"But don't forget, Raggy Langler stole from us one time when we were in our own neighborhood."

Drew was quiet for a moment. Then he said, "He never stole anything, Grace. Remember? He grabbed the cloth, but he didn't keep it."

She knew Drew was right about Raggy and about the area of town they were walking in, but she didn't care. She wanted to be with Sadie Rose, and that was that. "If you don't want to come with me to the tavern anymore, then don't. I don't care."

"But your mama trusts me to be with you, so I don't have much choice, do I?"

Now that the basket was lighter, Grace let Drew carry it alone. She walked on ahead, not wanting to talk.

At the Morgans' front gate, they divided the ears of corn, then she made him take the last squash. Drew did as she asked and went on his way.

When Grace stepped into the kitchen, Mama stood in front of her, an accusing look in her eyes.

Grace wondered how Mama could possibly know about their mishap with Raggy so quickly.

But Mama wasn't concerned about the produce from the market. "Grace Morgan," she said sternly, "I've had a visit from Widow Robbins and two other ladies from the church. They came to tell me you've been spending time at the boardinghouse with a painted lady!" Mama's face looked tired. "Tell me, Grace. Tell me it isn't true."

~ CHAPTER 16 ~

Helping with the Rent

"It's true that I've been visiting with a lady by the name of Sadie Rose," Grace said. "But she's not a bad person."

Why can't old Widow Robbins mind her own business? Grace wondered as she put the ears of corn on the table.

"How on earth did you meet such a woman?" Mama wanted to know.

Grace didn't want to lie. "The day the keelboats came up from St. Louis after the big rain, I asked Drew to go with me to the landing."

Mama sighed deeply and sat down on one of the kitchen chairs.

"The lady needed help, so we carried her bags. She was beholden to us, Mama. We showed her the way to Mrs. Kingsley's boardinghouse. And you know Mrs. Kingsley's is a respectable place."

But Mama was shaking her head. "The landing can be a dangerous place for a little girl."

"I'm not a little girl, Mama. And Drew was with me."

"Then Drew should have reminded you of the dangers."

Grace thought of all the times Drew had followed her into situations that were not of his choosing. He'd been a good friend, and she didn't want to get him into trouble, as well.

"I take all the blame," Grace said. "I shouldn't have been at the landing. But please believe me, Sadie Rose is not a bad lady."

"You keep telling me that you're not a little girl, and yet I find you've been disobedient and that you've been keeping undesirable company behind my back."

Mama smoothed back wisps of her hair, which Grace noticed was growing much grayer. "When I must learn of my daughter's wrong behavior from others in the church. . ." Mama didn't finish the sentence. She stood up and walked over to the corn and began to pull off the shucks.

"I'll talk this over with your papa this evening. I know he will agree with me that you are forbidden to spend time with this woman—this, this Sadie Rose."

When Mama said the name, it sounded like something awful and made Grace feel hurt and angry. But she kept her anger to herself. Somehow she had to make Mama understand about Sadie Rose.

Grace talked to Sadie Rose one more time to tell her what had happened. Sadie Rose gave a kind smile. "I understand, Grace. Your mama's looking out for you in the best way she knows how. You obey her and be thankful to have such a good mama."

Sadie Rose's words made Grace want to cry. How could things be so mixed up?

In late November, the farmers brought their pigs into town to the packinghouses. The air was filled with the frenzied sounds of hundreds of squealing pigs. At least the packinghouses would be busy, which meant the tanners and the chandlers and soap makers would soon have work. Papa said that little rebounds in business were better than no rebounds at all.

After the first snow, Drew bagged his first deer. Grace went to see the carcass, which was hanging in a tree. It was a big buck, and Drew told her he was going to hang the antlers over his bed in the loft right beside the portraits of his mother and father. Grace never remembered seeing Drew so proud or so happy.

Several of his delicately carved boats now lined the mantle over the Ramsey fireplace. Grace heard Deanna repeatedly praise Drew for his skills in woodworking. Drew didn't seem so sad anymore.

Just as Grace's family had shared their provisions with Carter and Deanna, the Ramseys now shared cuts of venison with the Morgans. Thanksgiving dinner consisted mainly of game that had been killed by Carter and Drew.

Although it was difficult, Grace remained obedient and didn't stop to visit with Sadie Rose. However, she often saw her friend about town. When she did, Grace always stopped to say hello. Or she purposely walked by the boardinghouse in hopes of "accidentally" running into Sadie Rose. In her mind, one little greeting broke no rules. By keeping a close watch and timing her walks by Mrs. Kingsley's, Grace continued to see Sadie Rose regularly.

While the citizens of Cincinnati knew that deep snow meant a full river in the spring, still the hard winter only increased the suffering of those who were in need.

Grace celebrated her eleventh birthday during a January snowstorm. Even though there was no party, Mama and Papa tried to make the day as special as they could. Grace thought being eleven would be so much different, but everyone still called her *Gracie*.

It was mid-February when Grace realized she'd not seen Sadie Rose for about two weeks. The heavy snows of January were melting some, and even though it was still cold, at least a person could walk down the streets without wading knee-deep in snowdrifts.

Every day for a week, Grace made Drew walk home from school by the way of the boardinghouse. Still there was no sign of Sadie Rose. Finally Grace could stand it no more.

"I must ask about her," Grace insisted one afternoon after school. "There's no harm in asking, is there?"

"I don't see that there is," Drew answered.

Her cousin now stood nearly half a head taller than Grace. Deanna often said she was going to load bricks on Drew's head to stop him from growing so fast. But he just kept growing. More and more, Grace appreciated Drew's opinions and his quiet wisdom.

"Would you come with me?" she asked.

To her relief, he agreed. Grace tightened her woolen muffler about her neck to better fight the cold wind as they went the few blocks out of their way to the boardinghouse.

Grace went right up and rapped on the door, and Drew stood by her side.

When Mrs. Kingsley opened the door, she said, "I suppose you're looking for Miss Sadie Rose."

"Why yes, we are," Grace answered. "Is she here?"

The matron of the boardinghouse nodded. "She's here, but she's doing poorly. Been down with the fever and chills."

Grace gave a gasp. "I knew something was wrong. May we see her?"

"I can't stop her from having visitors."

Grace waited for Drew to protest, but he was quiet. Together they followed Mrs. Kingsley inside and through a neat parlor area to the curved staircase. Waving to the stairs, she said, "Second door on the right."

As they started up the steps, Grace heard Mrs. Kingsley mutter something about "getting better soon" and "late with the rent." Grace glanced back at Drew and could see he was as concerned as she.

Grace tapped on the door and heard a weak answer.

"Sadie Rose," she said, "It's me, Grace. And Drew's with me."

The weak voice sounded a bit stronger. "Oh, Grace, Drew. Please come in."

Grace opened the door and saw a small chamber that was mostly taken up with a wide chifforobe stuffed full of Sadie Rose's fancy gowns. Lying in the bed with her undone hair flayed across the pillow, Sadie Rose looked small, weak, and vulnerable. There was no paint now, and her cheeks were nearly as pale as the white sheets.

"Grace," she said, "how I was hoping you'd come. How did you learn I was ill?"

Grace rushed to her friend's bedside and knelt down to take her hand. "I just now learned. I hadn't seen you and became alarmed, so Drew and I stopped to see. I'm so glad we did."

"Young Drew," Sadie Rose said softly, looking up at him. "So faithful to your cousin." To Grace, she said, "I know you're not supposed to be here."

Grace ignored the remark. "Sadie Rose, I heard Mrs. Kingsley say something about the rent."

"I wish you hadn't heard." Tears clouded Sadie Rose's eyes.

"Perhaps I chose the wrong time to come to Cincinnati. I didn't know times were as hard as they were." She took a deep breath and coughed. Grace handed her a handkerchief from the nearby table.

"Do you not have enough money for the rent?" Grace asked.

"I kept up, but just barely, until I fell sick. But now I can't work, and I've fallen behind. Mrs. Kingsley tells me she's not running a charity house or a hospital."

"We can bring food," Drew said.

Grace looked up at Drew and felt like hugging him.

"Of course we can bring food," Grace agreed. "And we will." She patted Sadie Rose's fever-hot hand. "You rest now and don't worry about a thing. We'll be back!"

When they came back down the stairs, Mrs. Kingsley was there to meet them. "If her rent's not paid soon," she said, "I'm notifying the officials at the poorhouse."

Grace's hand flew to her mouth to stifle the gasp. Sadie Rose taken to the poorhouse! She felt weak at the knees.

But to her surprise, Drew stepped forward. "No need for that just yet," he said, his voice steady. "Give us a couple of days to see what can be done on Miss Sadie Rose's behalf."

The hefty lady hesitated. "It's not like I want to be cruel," she said, "but I have to eat, too. And I can't afford to keep a room occupied with someone who cannot pay rent."

"Of course," Drew said. "We understand." He guided Grace toward the door. "We'll be back shortly."

"What're we going to do, Drew? Do you have a plan?"

"Part of a plan," he said. "Remember the coins Sadie Rose paid us for carrying her bags the day we met her?"

"Of course," Grace said. "Are you going to pay her rent with her own coins?"

Drew nodded. "It's probably not enough, but it may suffice to calm Mrs. Kingsley and show her we're serious about helping."

"What a wonderful idea."

"You go on home now, Grace. I'll go back to the boardinghouse as soon as I get the food and money. I can take a jar of goat's milk and maybe some cornbread."

"But, Drew, I want to go with you. I want to help Sadie Rose." They'd arrived at Grace's front gate, and she was chilled to the bone. Still, she wanted to go back with Drew to the boardinghouse.

"You can be more help by not worrying your mama." Drew opened the gate. "I promise I'll stop by on my way home and let you know what happened."

There was nothing else she could do, and Grace knew it. If Mama found out, then Grace might spoil her chances of doing anything for Sadie Rose.

Later that evening, Drew stopped by the house under the pretense of delivering a cleaned rabbit for Grace's mama. Before leaving, he slipped Grace a note. When Grace went to her room after evening prayers, she drew out the note. Drew had written these words:

Sadie Rose was thankful for the food. The coins paid a fraction of the rent due. Mrs. K. may take milk for partial trade. We'll talk tomorrow of further plans.

Grace sank down on her bed in discouragement. There had to be a way to help. This was a desperate situation. And desperate situations called for desperate measures!

Grace Takes Action

Grace never undressed for bed that night. She crawled beneath the covers with all her clothes on, waiting for the house to grow quiet. She was determined not to fall asleep. When all was quiet, she got up and pulled on her heavy woolen cloak, first tying her muffler around her neck. Never before had she disobeyed her parents so blatantly. But she simply had to save Sadie Rose from going to the poorhouse.

With barely a sound, she made her way down the stairs and out the back door into the dark, cold night. Gas lamps were lit at every seventh house, and she found herself scurrying from lamp to lamp. It took all her courage to turn down Front Street. While she'd never been frightened there in the daylight, darkness was much different.

Ahead of her loomed the glowing windows of Dunne's Tavern. Pulling the cloak more tightly about her, Grace hurried to the door, where she could hear the shouts and laughter coming from inside. Just as she reached out to open the door, it flew open, and a weaving, staggering man pushed past her, nearly knocking her off her feet.

Taking a breath to muster more courage, she boldly stepped inside the door. Suddenly, the noise subsided and all eyes were on Grace. Remembering Sadie Rose's dilemma, she flung off her hood and stood as tall as she could. "Mr. Dunne?" she said.

A rotund man with bushy hair and beard came toward her. "I'm Mr. Dunne. What're you doing here, little girl?"

"I've come to take the place of Sadie Rose for the evening."

"What?" Mr. Dunne was at first surprised; then he laughed. All around him the other men joined in the laughter and hooted and jeered at her, as well.

"I can play," she said, lifting her voice over the noise, "and I can sing. If you give me a chance, we can all help Sadie Rose." She looked around at the men. "You'd like that, wouldn't you? To help Sadie Rose?"

"Sadie Rose's had a real spell of it. I suppose she does need help." The proprietor of the tavern clawed at his chin whiskers. "Well, I guess it can't hurt." He waved to the piano. "Have a go of it, little girl. Let's hear what your voice sounds like."

Grace removed her cloak and folded it beneath her on the piano stool. It had been several months since she had learned the hymn. Would she remember?

She placed her hands on the keys and began the first few bars of "A Mighty Fortress Is Our God." When the men heard it, one called out, "Say there, this isn't church! Play one of Sadie Rose's songs!" But another said, "Shush your mouth. I wanna hear the hymn."

Grace ignored them all. Once she knew she had the playing down pat, she let loose in her strong, clear voice to sing every word. When she finished the last verse, there were again hoots and hollers, but now their shouts were in appreciation. "More!" they said, clapping. "Sing it again!"

Grace reached inside her sleeve for her handkerchief. Tying the corners to make a little pouch, she held it up. "Here's where you put the money for Sadie Rose." As the little hankie-pouch was being passed around the room, she sang the hymn again. This time she was surprised to see several of the men weeping. Maybe she was helping more than Sadie Rose by her singing.

The next day when she told Drew what she'd done, he was shocked. "Grace, I sometimes think you can never surprise me with your actions, but I'm always wrong. Don't you know you could have been killed down there?"

"I just remembered what Sadie Rose said about the boatmen. If you try to understand people and not act snooty, they respect you." She felt the heavy bag bumping against her leg, where she'd fastened it securely beneath her skirts. "In fact, one of the men walked me to Second Street to make sure I was safe."

Drew just shook his head.

That day after school, they went to the boardinghouse to pay the money to Mrs. Kingsley.

She cast a wary look in their direction when she saw the coins. Although the older woman asked nothing, Grace was sure she was wondering where two children had come up with that much money. With that payment, Sadie Rose's rent was almost current. They hurried up to her room to tell her.

When Sadie Rose heard of Grace's escapade, she laughed right out loud. "Grace Morgan, you are quite a girl." Over and over, she thanked them for helping. Propped up against several pillows, Sadie Rose had a little more pink in her cheeks. "I know I'll be better now. In fact, after drinking the tasty goat's milk, my insides are settling down for the first time in days."

Grace pulled a chair close to the bed. As she did, something fell to the floor. It was a length of blue flowered cloth. Picking it up, Grace felt her breath catch. "Sadie Rose, what's this piece of cloth?"

Sadie Rose reached out to take the cloth from Grace. "That," she said, "is a shawl. Or rather, part of a shawl."

"Part?" Grace scooted her chair closer.

Sadie Rose stroked the cloth tenderly. "It belonged to my ma. I cut it in half when my little brother was taken from me. I kept one half and gave him the other half. Although he was only three, I put it in his tiny fist and said, 'Patrick, don't ever forget me. I'll see you again one day.'"

Grace suddenly pushed the chair back and stood to her feet. "Well now, we'd really better be going. Mama's expecting me."

"Of course," Sadie Rose replied, "and I'm rather tired from all this excitement." Again she gave her thanks as they left.

"Drew Ramsey," Grace said once they were out of the house, "are you thinking what I'm thinking?"

Drew shook his head. "It can't be."

"But we know that Raggy was an orphan and his adoptive parents died."

"That's true, but Raggy's name isn't Patrick."

"Maybe the people who adopted him changed his name."

Drew thought about that. "Possibly. But what can we...?"

"Don't worry. I have a plan."

Drew laughed. "I'm sure you do, Grace. I'm sure you do."

But when Grace arrived home, any plan she'd had was quickly squelched. Once again, she was greeted by a very upset and very disappointed mama. Papa was by her side, and Grace could tell from their expressions that it was not good. Papa asked her to come into the parlor, where they could talk.

"Grace Morgan," Mama began, "I truly thought I'd heard

everything. Now I've learned you slipped out of this house in the dead of night and went down to Front Street to the tavern. One of the most dangerous places in the city. Grace, how could you have disgraced us this way?"

Papa's face mirrored Mama's disappointment. It was enough to break Grace's heart.

"Mama, Papa, I never wanted to disobey you, but I had to go to the tavern. I had to save Sadie Rose's life. They were threatening to take her to the poorhouse."

"Poorhouse? What are you talking about?" Papa said. "You were told not to go see this woman named Sadie Rose."

"I wouldn't have gone to talk to her, but I hadn't seen her in town for two weeks. When we checked on her, we found she was ill with chills and fever." Grace was wringing her hands and trying not to cry. "Don't you see? I'm only doing what you've always taught me, and that's to reach out and help others. Sadie Rose had no one else. The rent was past due. She even said she was hoping I'd come."

"Whoa," Papa said. "I think it's time to hear this story from beginning to end."

Grace sat down by the crackling fire and started at the beginning. She told how Sadie Rose played and sang in taverns so she could earn money to keep searching for her brother. Grace even had to tell how she went to the tavern to learn to play the piano, which made Mama wince.

When Grace finished her story, Papa looked at Mama. "If the church were more generous with their own piano, this might never have happened."

"Thad," Mama said evenly, "we can't blame others for our daughter's disobedience."

"I know I shouldn't have gone," Grace said. "I was trying to let patience have a perfect work. But I wanted so just to learn a song. And now I can play a hymn all the way through. When I played the hymn for the men at the tavern. . ."

"You played a hymn at the tavern?" Papa interrupted.

Grace nodded, and she saw Papa smile.

"When I played the hymn," she continued, "the men were crying. I think men in a tavern need a hymn, don't you, Papa?"

"They surely do," he agreed.

"Thad," Mama said in a warning tone.

"And Sadie Rose needs hymns, too," Grace said, talking faster. "I believe if some of our church ladies would visit her rather than talking about her all the time, she might just come to church." Grace remembered how pleased Sadie Rose had been when Grace had prayed for her. "I think she truly wants to have God's forgiveness."

"Well," Mama said slowly, as though she were thinking it through, "I suppose I could take a couple of ladies with me from the church and call on Miss Sadie Rose tomorrow."

Grace jumped up from her chair. "Oh, would you, Mama? Then I could introduce you to Sadie Rose."

"I'll see if I can arrange that."

"But you, young lady, will still be punished for your disobedience," Papa reminded her. "Not only did you disobey our direct instructions, but I'm also disappointed that you didn't feel you could trust us enough to tell us about the situation and work with us to solve Sadie Rose's problems. You could have been very badly hurt last night. Front Street is not a safe place for a woman, much less a young girl."

"I'm sorry," Grace said. "I should have told you everything from the beginning."

In the end, Mama and Papa set up a list of jobs for Grace to do every evening after school for a week as punishment.

The next day, Grace could barely sit still in the classroom. The large clock mounted in front of the room moved at a snail's pace. At recess she was distracted and barely listened to a word Amy was saying, even though Amy was reporting good news about her father. She said her father had been able to secure a loan from another city and was making plans to start a new business. In spite of the encouraging news, Grace could think only about Sadie Rose and Raggy. Could Raggy actually be Sadie Rose's long-lost brother?

As soon as school let out, Grace hurried outside to meet up with Drew.

"We'll head down to Sausage Row first," Grace said.

"I hope you're right about this, Grace. How will we find Emaline Stanley's place?"

"Easy. We just ask. In Sausage Row, everybody knows everybody."

"But what if Raggy won't listen to us?"

"I don't expect him to."

"You're not making any sense."

"Just follow me and do what I say."

Winter had been especially cruel to the poverty-stricken areas around the landing. The shacks seemed more dilapidated than ever. As Grace had thought, it was easy to find where the washerwoman lived. But would Raggy be there?

As they approached the small house with its little lean-to in the back, Grace saw Raggy. He was taller and more wiry-looking than ever. She'd almost forgotten how long it had been since she'd seen him. Suddenly, she wondered if her plan would work. But it was too late to back out.

"When he comes after us," she whispered to Drew, "you go one way, and I'll go the other. Lead him to the boardinghouse."

"What a crazy plan," Drew said, grinning at her.

"Hey, Raggy!" she called out. "Still carry your rag with you wherever you go?"

Raggy looked around to see where the voice came from. When he spied them, he spouted, "Why, you. . ."

Drew shouted out, "Rag–gee, Rag–gee! Carries his rags with him wherever he goes!"

The plan worked like a charm. Raggy was on their heels like a pup after a rabbit. Grace ran straight up Broadway, while Drew ducked down a side street. As Grace had expected, Raggy went after Drew.

When she hit the front door of the boardinghouse, Grace didn't stop to knock. There in the front parlor sat Mama and Widow Robbins and two other ladies.

"Come on!" she called out, panting and puffing. "Let's go meet Sadie Rose!"

"Grace. . . ," Mama started.

"Your daughter is a little ruffian," Widow Robbins interrupted haughtily.

From behind her, Grace heard Mama say, "She's just a little more energetic than most girls."

When Sadie Rose answered her knock, Grace was pleased to see her up and dressed and sitting by the fire in her Boston rocker.

"Sadie Rose, I've brought company," Grace said, waving the ladies in and then running to the window to see if Drew had arrived.

"Grace," Mama said, "what are you doing?"

"Mama, I'd like you to meet Sadie Rose." Grace motioned

toward her mama but kept looking out the window. Just as she'd introduced all the ladies, Drew came speeding into the alleyway behind the boardinghouse.

"Sadie Rose, quick. Where's the shawl?"

"The what?"

"The shawl. The shawl your mama left to you. Hurry." Grace had no way of knowing how closely Raggy was following Drew.

Sadie Rose stood and walked across the room to her bed. From beneath the pillow she pulled out the cloth. "It's here."

Grace took it from her and flung open the window. Raggy had arrived and was squaring off with Drew, his fists upraised.

"Raggy Langler!" she called out. Raggy looked up at her.

"Langler?" Sadie Rose said. She moved to the window beside Grace. "That's my name—Langler."

"Russell Langler," Grace said this time, using his real name and waving the piece of shawl. "Does this look familiar?"

Raggy stared, unable to move.

Drew, who'd had his fists in the air, backed away, looking more than a little relieved.

Slowly, Raggy reached inside his threadbare shirt, drew out the piece of faded cloth, and held it forth like a flag of surrender.

"Patrick?" Sadie Rose asked softly. "Russell Patrick Langler?"

"Sadie Rose?" came Raggy's small voice. "Is that really you?"

Sadie Rose turned to look at Grace. "Oh, Grace! You were right! We prayed and God heard. He truly heard!" With that, she flew out the door and down the stairs into the snow, not bothering to grab a cloak.

Within moments, the ladies from church witnessed the tearful reunion of the long-separated brother and sister. And there wasn't a dry eye or hankie among them.

～ CHAPTER 18 ～

"Steamboat's A-Comin'!"

In spite of her very grown-up-looking new dress and matching bonnet, Grace could hardly contain her excitement as she stood on the landing waiting for the *Velocipede* to come into view. The winter snows had melted, the spring rains had fallen, and the majestic Ohio flowed full and wide once again.

Grace looked over at Sadie Rose, and they exchanged smiles. The arrival of the new piano meant that Sadie Rose would begin giving paid piano lessons in the front parlor of the Morgan home. That had been Grace's idea. But Mama had had the wonderful idea to hire Emaline Stanley as their servant.

Raggy would continue to live with Emaline until Sadie Rose could save enough money to care for them both and give Emaline something for her years of care. Then Raggy would finally be able to stay with Sadie Rose.

Papa and Luke had completed one of their steamboats, and the buyer was able to make a partial payment. Papa said that was agreeable because as soon as the boat was launched and in business, the owner would be able to pay the balance. Now the second boat was nearing completion.

Drew and Patrick stood off to the side, talking about steamboats. It had been hard to stop saying *Raggy* and to remember to say *Patrick*. But Grace didn't mind taking the extra effort to learn. Now that Patrick was clean, wore nice clothes, and had enough to eat, he didn't look like the same boy. Since Drew understood about being an orphan, he and Patrick had become fast friends. Patrick was even helping with the piano delivery from the steamboat.

Grace and Drew had learned that Patrick was fascinated with Annabelle and wanted more than anything to learn to milk the goat. Grace marveled as she thought about it. That day at the church when he'd tried to take Annabelle, he'd only wanted to pet her.

Grace realized she'd been just as wrong about Raggy as her mama had been about Sadie Rose. They'd all learned a lesson in love.

Suddenly, someone from far up on the landing shouted, "Steam-boat's a-comin'!" The call echoed up and down the public landing and Grace started jumping up and down in spite of herself.

Papa had rented a sturdy wagon, and it was sitting nearby. At last, the proud white boat came into view with its twin black smokestacks pointing skyward.

Presently, the boat was docked, and Captain Wharton strode down the gangplank to greet them. "It's been a long time," he said, laughing and shaking Papa's hand.

"Yes, Captain. A long time," Papa answered. "We've all learned how to be patient." He glanced at Grace and winked.

Then Grace watched as the stevedores guided the crane that lifted the crate containing her piano. Slowly, slowly, it came over to where Papa lined up the wagon. Slowly, slowly, it was let down in the back of the wagon. Grace didn't breathe until it was safely settled. Drew and Patrick climbed into the wagon to hold the crate steady. They seemed almost as excited about the arrival as Grace.

"May I ride home in the wagon with you, Papa?" Grace asked.

"Why, of course, Gracie—excuse me—I mean, why, of course, Miss Grace. May I give you a hand up?" Papa bowed and offered his hand.

As the others boarded the waiting carriage, Grace allowed Papa to assist her into the wagon seat. Papa climbed up beside her, shook the reins, and told the team, "Giddap." Grace straightened her full skirts, adjusted her bonnet, and opened her ruffled parasol to protect her face from the bright spring sunshine.

The wagon clattered over the cobblestones of the landing, taking her new piano home.

American Challenge:
Bonus Educational Materials

Lydia the Patriot:
The Boston Massacre

Vocabulary Words

Bloodyback and **Lobsterback**—disrespectful names that colonists called British soldiers because of the bright red coats of their uniforms
*"Let's see you fire! **Lobsterback**! **Bloodyback**! You won't dare fire!"*

boycott—refusing to have anything to do with something (such as a person, organization, or products) usually to express disapproval or to force acceptance of conditions or terms
*In many ways, life in the colonies was no different than life in England—at least, it hadn't been until people had started to **boycott** British goods.*

colony—a group of people who live in a new territory and are ruled by their mother country
*Since Massachusetts was a British **colony**, Stephen had always accepted that it was logical for British soldiers to be there.*

dillydally—to waste time by hanging around or delaying
*His usual afternoon routine was to wait for Lydia, who liked to **dillydally** after school, and the two of them would walk home together.*

flippant—not having proper respect or seriousness
*"Lydia, don't be **flippant**," warned Aunt Dancy.*

frock—a woman's or girl's dress
*"If I muss up my **frock**, Mama will know something's up."*

goaded—urged and tormented to do something
*"She told me everything—how she **goaded** you into going out."*

haughtily—snobbishly; pridefully
*"I'm not sure even God could love the British," Lydia said **haughtily**.*

Loyalist—a colonist whose loyalty remained with Great Britain
*To be a **Loyalist** meant to support the king and Parliament and accept their right to govern the colonies any way they saw fit.*

massacre—the act of killing a number of people
*"It means that Captain Preston and eight soldiers will stand trial for the **massacre** last week. The prosecuting attorney believes he has enough evidence to convict them of murder."*

merchant—a businessperson such as a storekeeper or shop owner
*The streets had been strangely quiet, even during the hours when **merchants** usually did most of their business.*

midwife—a person (usually a woman) who is trained to help deliver babies
*"The baby is coming tonight, and I'm going to need help. Stephen will have to go for the **midwife**."*

mob—a large, disorderly crowd
***Mobs** broke into houses of British officials or anyone associated with the British government.*

musket—a type of gun loaded from the muzzle (the firing end) and supported on the shoulder for shooting
*Nevertheless, he stood with his feet solidly apart, his **musket** leaning over his shoulder. He was on duty.*

noble—having very high or excellent qualities and character
*Cuyler raised his eyes to the cot across the room and pondered the question. "No matter what any of us thinks, we all have to face that question. If a deadly deed is done in the name of patriotism or loyalty, is it **noble**? If a good deed is done out of fear, does it lack all virtue?"*

oppression—unjust treatment or government
*Still, he committed himself to the one cause he believed in: overthrowing British **oppression**.*

Patriot—colonist who was devoted to defending and supporting the rights of the American colonies and making them an independent country
*On the other hand, to be a **Patriot** meant to detest anything British and do everything possible to throw out the British.*

riot—a violent, public disorder
*He had been at the wrong place at the wrong time when a street **riot** broke out during the Stamp Act.*

threshold—a strip of wood or stone that forms the bottom of a doorway
*Lydia, Stephen thought, would leave the front door wide open and dare British soldiers passing by to cross the **threshold**.*

vigil—staying awake during the time you would normally sleep in order to keep watch and/or pray
*For a long time, Lydia adamantly refused to believe it was over and resisted sleep. She kept her **vigil** at the window and waited for the next round of activity.*

Important People and Things around 1770

Samuel Adams
Samuel Adams was born in Boston on September 27, 1722. He graduated from Harvard in 1740. After college, he worked as a law student, then a clerk in a countinghouse, next a merchant, and then a partner in his father's business. He was active in politics, and in 1756 he was elected as Boston's tax collector, a position he held for eight years. In 1765, he was elected to the lower house of the Massachusetts General Court and in 1766, he became the clerk of the house until 1774. Adams strongly opposed the taxes like the Stamp Act and Townshend Acts that were passed by British parliament on the American colonists. He organized resistance to these taxes and formed the secret organization known as the **Sons of Liberty**. In 1770, he planned the protest that led to the **Boston Massacre**, and he was involved in the Boston Tea Party in 1773. Adams was a member of the Continental Congress and was one of the signers of the Declaration of Independence. He was lieutenant governor of Massachusetts from 1789 to 1793 and governor from 1794 to 1797. Samuel Adams died on October 2, 1803.

The Sons of Liberty
The Sons of Liberty were a secret organization formed by Samuel Adams and made up of colonists who opposed the taxes like the Stamp Act that were passed by British Parliament on the American colonists. The Sons of Liberty, or "Liberty Boys" as they often called themselves, wanted to keep people from paying these new taxes. They used scare tactics to threaten those who obeyed the tax, and if that did not work, they used violence and stirred up mobs and riots. The Sons of Liberty usually met at night by "Liberty Poles" or "Liberty Trees" to plan their attacks. Their willingness to use violence to fight against British oppression helped lead to the Revolutionary War and the fight for American independence.

The Stamp Act

This law was passed in the British parliament in the summer of 1765. It put a tax on all printed material in the American colonies, such as newspapers, pamphlets, legal documents, licenses, and even playing cards. The British prime minister, George Grenville, proposed this tax in order to help pay for the cost of keeping military defenses in the colonies. When the new law passed, many of the American colonists were very angry. The tax was on things that most of them needed to carry on business and run their daily lives. They thought it was unfair for the British government to tax them like this without their representation in parliament or their agreement to the law. The Stamp Act caused quite a stir in the colonies. Violent riots broke out, and secret organizations like the **Sons of Liberty** were formed to resist the new tax. The colonists slogan was, "No taxation without representation." The Stamp Act Congress was also formed to protest the Stamp Act, and a group of New York merchants signed the Nonimportation Agreement, in which they agreed not to import British goods. Because of the colonists' protest, The Stamp Act was finally repealed, or taken back, in March of 1766.

The Townshend Acts

The Townshend Acts put taxes on things like lead, glass, paper, paint, and tea in the American colonies. They took effect in 1767 and were named for their sponsor, Charles Townshend, the British finance minister. The British government wanted to remind the colonists they were still in control even though they had repealed the Stamp Act taxes. But the Townshend Acts only caused more anger among the colonists. British troops had to occupy the colonies to enforce the taxes and in Boston, this led to the **Boston Massacre**. Because of all the violence and boycotts in protest to the Townshend Acts, they raised very little money, and Parliament repealed them in April of 1770. Their damage was already done, though, and they helped pave the way for the Revolutionary War.

The Boston Massacre

The Boston Massacre happened on March 5, 1770, between British troops and a group of angry colonists of Boston. The British troops were occupying Boston to enforce the **Townshend Acts** and to discourage violent protests by the colonists. The troops were stationed at Boston Common, where colonists would constantly harass them. During one protest, attacks on the troops caused them to open fire into the crowd and shoot five colonists. Crispus Attucks, Samuel Gray, James Caldwell, and Samuel Maverick were killed, and Patrick Carr was seriously hurt and died later. The eight British soldiers who opened fire and their commanding officer were charged with murder but were given a fair trial in Boston and were defended by John Adams, who later because President of the United States, and Josiah Quincy. Two of the soldiers were found guilty but the rest were acquitted, or found not guilty. The Boston Massacre was used by **Sam Adams** and the **Sons of Liberty** to create even more anti-British feelings in the colony.

History in Perspective Timeline

1752—Benjamin Franklin invents the lightning rod.

Summer, 1765—The Stamp Act is passed by British parliament and takes effect on American colonists.

March 5, 1770—The Boston Massacre occurs in Boston, Massachusetts.

December 16, 1773—The Boston Tea Party takes place in Boston, Massachusetts, when colonists protest the British tax on tea imported to the colonies by dumping the tea from three British ships into the Boston Harbor.

April 18, 1775—Paul Revere makes his famous midnight ride to warn colonists of the coming of the British troops to start the Revolutionary War.

1775–1783—The American Revolution takes place between the thirteen North American colonies and their parent country, Great Britain, as the colonies fight for their independence.

July 4, 1776—The Declaration of Independence is approved and adopted by the Second Continental Congress in America.

June, 1783—Joseph Michel and Jacques Étienne Montgolfier became the first human beings to fly in their invention of a hot air balloon in France.

September 17, 1787—Final draft of the U.S. Constitution is presented and later approved as the law of the land for the United States of America.

April 30, 1798—The United States Navy is established.

Kate and the Spies: The American Revolution

Vocabulary Words

apothecary—a pharmacy
*"We'd best get back to the **apothecary**."*

apprentice—someone who learns a trade by working for someone skilled in that trade
*"My other **apprentice**, Johnny, left Boston with his family."*

babble—excessive, meaningless talk
*A **babble** of voices answered him as a number of men all spoke at once.*

bayonet—a steel blade, like a knife, attached to the muzzle of a rifle
*"I was polishing my **bayonet**," the Redcoat said, "and it slipped."*

cloak—a loose-fitting outer garment, similar to a cape
*Kate stood on tiptoes and pushed back the gray wool **cloak** from her blond curls,
but she could still only see the backs of the people ahead of them.*

constable—a public officer responsible for keeping the peace, a police officer
*"Where are the **constables**, or the night watchmen, or the marines?"*

deserter—a person who leaves military service without permission
*"I know you! **Deserter!**"*

flint—a dark quartz material that makes a spark when struck by steel
*Harry reached in his pocket for a **flint** to light a candle.*

handbill—a printed flyer
*They'd been printing **handbills**, or posters, for the Sons of Liberty.*

lobsterbacks and **redcoats**—names American colonists called British soldiers, based on
the color of their uniforms
*Still, part of her couldn't help but find it exciting to have the streets, shops, and common
filled with soldiers in the bright red uniforms that made people call them "**lobsterbacks**"
and "**redcoats**."*

Loyalists—colonists who preferred to remain subject to British rule
*Her parents were **Loyalists**, who believed the Patriots should do as Parliament
and the king said, even if what they said was wrong.*

mobcap—a woman's fancy indoor cap
*A lace-edged **mobcap** topped it all off.*

musket—a long gun, loaded from the muzzle (the firing end)
*Kate watched as Harry went back into the parlor and took down
the old **musket** that hung over the fireplace.*

Patriots—American colonists who wanted to break away from British rule
*"If the ships are unloaded here, we **Patriots** will do it ourselves."*

petticoat—an underskirt
*In her long skirt and **petticoat**, Kate couldn't keep up.*

silversmith—a person who makes items out of silver
*Was that Paul Revere, the **silversmith** who stopped at the
printing shop to talk with Harry so often?*

stoop—a small porch or entrance stairway to a house
*There was no one on the door **stoop**.*

treason—disloyalty to an existing government
*"Before we can be hung, we must be brought to trial and
found guilty of **treason** against Britain and the king."*

wharf—a structure built along the shore that allows ships to dock and load and unload
cargo and passengers
*"We're headed toward Griffin **Wharf** at Boston Harbor," Colin shouted.*

wits—senses
*"You'll need to keep your **wits** about you all the time."*

IMPORTANT PEOPLE AND THINGS AROUND 1775

Samuel Adams
Samuel Adams was born September 27, 1722, in Boston, Massachusetts. After earning
his Master of Arts degree from Harvard College in 1743, he entered private business
as a clerk. He later joined his father's business, but eventually lost all the money his
father had given him. When his business failed, he became a full-time politician, and
was elected to the Massachusetts legislature in 1766. Adams was a vocal opponent of
the Stamp Act and other taxes that the British government placed on the colonists.
He helped organize the **Sons of Liberty** and was a participant in the Boston Tea
Party. Adams was a member of the first and second **Continental Congresses**, and
was governor of Massachusetts from 1793 until 1797. His cousin, John Adams, would
become the second president of the United States. Samuel Adams died October 2, 1803.

First Continental Congress
The First Continental Congress met in Philadelphia from September 5 until October

26, 1774. The delegates, from every colony except Georgia, met to protest the "Intolerable Acts" placed on the colonies by the British Parliament. The leaders of the Congress were Samuel and John Adams from Massachusetts and George Washington and Patrick Henry from Virginia. The delegates voted to stop all trade with Great Britain unless Parliament abolished the Intolerable Acts. They also voted to advise the colonies to begin training their citizens for war with Great Britain; tried to define the rights of America and its citizens; voted to place limits on Parliament's power; and agreed on tactics for resistance against the British acts. By the time the Congress was over, armed conflict with Great Britain had already begun.

John Hancock

John Hancock was born January 12, 1737, in Braintree, Massachusetts. Orphaned as a young child, he was adopted by a wealthy, childless uncle. After his graduation from Harvard College, John Hancock joined his uncle's business and became very successful. Though his background might have drawn him to the Loyalists, Hancock was involved in revolutionary politics, including the Boston Tea Party. He served in the **Continental Congress** and was governor of Massachusetts twice, his last term being from 1787 until his death in 1793. John Hancock's signature is the first—and biggest—on the Declaration of Independence. About his famous signature, he is quoted as stating, "The British ministry can read that name without spectacles." John Hancock died October 8, 1793.

Sons of Liberty

The Sons of Liberty began in Massachusetts in the early summer of 1765 as "The Loyal Nine." Led by **Samuel Adams**, they were a group of shopkeepers and artisans organized to oppose the taxes—including the Stamp Act—the British Parliament had placed on the colonies. The Nine grew and became the Sons of Liberty, and by the end of 1765, every colony had Sons of Liberty branches. The Sons often tried to frighten people away from paying their taxes. At times, they even used violence to convince people to stop obeying British law.

Paul Revere

Paul Revere was born January 1, 1735, in Boston's North End. He learned silversmithing from his father, and took over his father's business when the elder Revere died. When times were tough, he also worked as a dentist to help support his family. Paul Revere became involved with the **Sons of Liberty** in 1755. With excellent skills as a rider, he carried messages between Patriot groups in Boston, New York, and Philadelphia. His engraving of the Boston Massacre stirred up revolutionary feelings in the colonists. He participated in the Boston Tea Party, and was the only participant to keep his promise never to tell of his involvement in the Tea Party. During the night of April 18–19, 1775, Paul Revere took his famous ride to Lexington, Massachusetts, to warn **Samuel Adams** and **John Hancock** that the British were on their way to arrest them. Paul Revere died on May 10, 1818.

HISTORY IN PERSPECTIVE TIMELINE

January 12, 1773—The first American museum is opened to the public in Charleston, South Carolina.

January 17, 1773—Captain James Cook becomes the first European explorer to cross the Antarctic Circle.

1774—Oxygen is discovered by Joseph Priestley.

1775–1783—The American Revolutionary War fought between the thirteen American colonies and Great Britain. It would end on September 3, 1783, with the signing of the Treaty of Paris.

March 23, 1775—Patrick Henry delivers his "Give Me Liberty or Give Me Death" speech in Williamsburg, Virginia.

1776—*E pluribus unum* ("from many one" in Latin) is chosen to appear on the Great Seal of the United States.

January 10, 1776—Thomas Paine publishes *Common Sense*.

September 3, 1777—The American flag known as the "Stars and Stripes" flies in battle for the first time, at Cooch's Bridge in Maryland.

July 6, 1785—The dollar is chosen as the American monetary unit—the first time a government selects a decimal-based currency system.

September 17, 1787—The U.S. Constitution is completed; it will be officially adopted on March 4, 1789.

BETSY'S RIVER ADVENTURE: THE JOURNEY WESTWARD

VOCABULARY WORDS

aplomb—self-confidence
*With all the **aplomb** she had, a muddy Betsy walked tall and regally toward the street that lined the river.*

badger—to annoy or tease
*"I don't want to go. I don't want to be constantly **badgered** by George. He delights in embarrassing me."*

cajole—persuade or coax with flattery
*Betsy watched him **cajole** and plead with Jefferson, but it did no good.*

canter—a smooth, gentle run
*Betsy let Silverstreak **canter**.*

contraption—a strange object or machine
*Johnny dropped a wooden **contraption**, which Betsy guessed was supposed to be a miniature flatboat, into the river.*

foundries—workshops for casting metal
*Boats, of course, but there are a lot of **foundries** for ironwork, too.*

impetuous—acting without thinking
*"He's **impetuous** and doesn't always think before he blurts out something."*

impress—to take control of for public service
*Hundreds of American young men had been **impressed**, as they called it.*

melancholy—sad or depressed
*Time passed slowly, and she felt herself slipping back into that **melancholy** mood again.*

mercantile—a store or market
*They paused to glance inside the brick **mercantile** stores that lined the streets.*

rambunctious—full of energy and uncontrolled enthusiasm
*Surely he wouldn't have been the **rambunctious** type like George, whose curiosity and eagerness were always making him the center of attention.*

recitation—reading or repeating out loud, especially publicly
*His **recitation** sounded as if it were his side of a discussion that had been held earlier.*

satchel—a small bag that usually has a shoulder strap
*The driver came out of the stagecoach office with a **satchel**.*

schooner—a type of ship with two or more masts
*"We've booked passage on the **schooner** Columbia from Boston Harbor and up the Delaware River to Philadelphia."*

shanties—crudely built huts or shelters, usually made of wood
*Clotheslines sagging with laundry were strung between the **shanties**.*

skiff—a type of small rowboat
*They climbed back into the **skiff**, and Marley rowed them to the flatboat.*

solace—comfort in the midst of distress or disappointment
*She found **solace** in her music, and she prayed that she would find a happy life in Cincinnati.*

stillborn—dead at birth
*Betsy's three **stillborn** brothers had been buried in the churchyard.*

swindler—a cheater
*"I've heard there are many **swindlers** who sell boats that use inferior wood or who don't caulk the joints correctly."*

tack—to change a ship's course by turning its head to the wind
*Father had told her they would **tack** many times, or they would go too far out to sea.*

valise—a small suitcase or traveling bag
*She doubted she could get it into George's **valise** without someone seeing her.*

IMPORTANT PEOPLE AND THINGS AROUND 1808

Thomas Jefferson
Thomas Jefferson was the third president of the United States. He was born on April 13, 1743, in Virginia, where he inherited his family's estate at the age of fourteen. He graduated from William and Mary College in Williamsburg, Virginia, in 1762, and then became a lawyer. Jefferson became involved in politics and was active in the events that led to the American Revolution. In 1776, he wrote the Declaration of Independence, his best known work. He became President of the United States in 1801, during which he sponsored the Lewis and Clark Expedition to explore the West and made the famous Louisiana Purchase, buying the huge territory between the Mississippi River and the Rocky Mountains that greatly expanded the United States. His work as president also included the **Embargo Act**. After his term as chief executive, Thomas Jefferson returned to his famous home at Monticello and pursued his interests in music, architecture, science, religion, philosophy, law, and education, founding the University of Virginia in 1825. Thomas Jefferson died on July 4, 1826, exactly fifty years after the adoption of his Declaration of Independence.

Aaron Burr
Aaron Burr was Vice President of the United States from 1801–1805 under President **Thomas Jefferson**. He was born in Newark, New Jersey, on February 6, 1756, and went

on to graduate from the College of New Jersey (now Princeton University). From 1775–1779, he fought with the colonial army in the Revolutionary War. In 1782, he became a lawyer and then involved himself in politics, holding offices in the New York state legislature and as attorney general. He later served in the U.S. Senate and as vice president. Burr ran for governor of New York in 1804 against Alexander Hamilton, but lost. Later, Burr took part in a famous duel with his political opponent; Burr shot and killed Hamilton but was never arrested for murder. After his term as vice president, Burr was involved in many questionable activities including a possible plot to take over the southwestern frontier of the United States. After being found not guilty of treason, Burr traveled in Europe for several years, then came back to the United States to practice law again. Burr died on September 14, 1836.

The Embargo Act
The Embargo Act was a law proposed by **Thomas Jefferson** and passed by the United States Congress in 1807. This law stopped all ships from entering or leaving American ports, to force Britain and France, which were fighting the Napoleonic Wars, to respect the United States' decision to remain neutral. This law also helped stop the British from impressing, or kidnapping, American sailors to serve in the British navy. Unfortunately, it also put many Americans out of business and out of work because all trade between the countries was halted. The U.S. economy was badly hurt, forcing many people to start new lives in America's frontier areas, like Cincinnati, Ohio. The Embargo Act lasted only fourteen months.

HISTORY IN PERSPECTIVE TIMELINE

September 3, 1783—The Treaty of Paris ends the American Revolution, and Great Britain recognizes the United States of America as an independent nation.

1793—American inventor Eli Whitney creates the cotton gin.

November 9, 1799—Napoleon Bonaparte takes control of France.

1799–1815—The Napoleonic Wars are fought between France and other European nations.

March 4, 1801—Thomas Jefferson is inaugurated as President of the United States.

March 1, 1803—Ohio becomes the seventeenth state.

July 11, 1804—Alexander Hamilton is killed in a duel with Aaron Burr.

December 1807—The Embargo Act is passed by Congress.

1812–1815—The War of 1812 is fought between the United States and Great Britain.

1816—German inventor Karl D. Sauerbronn invents the bicycle.

1830—The first railroads are opened in England and the United States.

GRACE AND THE BULLY: DROUGHT ON THE FRONTIER

VOCABULARY WORDS

balustrade—a row of repeating posts that support the upper part of a railing as on a staircase or porch
*Halfway up the stairs, she hung out over the **balustrade** to gaze again at the empty space on the carpet where the piano would be placed.*

buckboard—a four-wheeled vehicle with a floor made of long, springy boards
*The **buckboard** had two sets of seats up front with a long bed in back and high sideboards.*

chandler—a maker or seller of wax candles
*At least the packinghouses would be busy, which meant the tanners and the **chandlers** and soap makers would soon have work.*

commencement—the ceremony for giving out academic degrees or diplomas
*"Mama," she said, "you'll never guess what—I'm going to sing at the school **commencement** exercises!"*

dandy—a man who gives extra special attention to his looks
*"Dapper Drew! Dresses up in pretty clothes! Looks like a **dandy**!" Raggy called out in a singsong voice.*

dapper—neat and trim in appearance; very stylish
*He wasn't a **dapper** Boston dandy anymore.*

delicacy—something pleasing to eat that is considered rare or rich
*There were **delicacies** there, such as his mother's rhubarb pies, which he doubted he'd ever taste again.*

dillydally—to waste time by hanging around or lagging behind
*"See that you are," Mama answered. "Don't **dillydally**."*

ecstatic—extremely excited
*A summer feast! Grace was **ecstatic**.*

exuberance—extreme joy and enthusiasm
*"Please, Lavina," Samantha said, "don't apologize. We love Grace's **exuberance**."*

indigent—very poor
*"Papa says the city voted to pay the way for a few **indigent** children to attend as well as those of us who can pay the subscription to go to school."*

jig—a lively, springy dance
*Grace rolled up the carpet and danced a **jig** as she'd seen the swarthy boatmen do.*

keelboat—shallow-covered riverboat that is usually rowed, poled, or towed and that is used for freight
*Sure enough, three **keelboats** were at the landing.*

larder—a place to store food
*With the new stock of foodstuffs in the **larder**, Papa was sure they could make it through until things turned around, which he believed would be very soon.*

mercantile—a type of market or store
*The heavy door of the **mercantile** was propped open, but the fresh spring air couldn't soften the strong mixtures of aromas inside the store.*

petrified—very afraid
*"If I had to stand before the entire city to sing, I'd be **petrified**," Amy said.*

ruddy—having a healthy reddish color
*Where he used to be pale and wan, he was now **ruddy** and sunburned.*

ruffian—a rough person, a bully
*"Why do they allow **ruffians** like him to attend our school?" Drew wanted to know.*

schooner—a large type of sailboat with several sails
*The shape was that of a sleek cod-fishing **schooner** such as those docked in Boston Harbor.*

stanchion—a device that fits loosely around the neck of an animal so that it can't move too far backward or forward
*Drew lifted the tether out of the ground, and they led the goat to the **stanchion**.*

stern-wheeler—a steamboat driven by a single paddle wheel at the stern
*Drew stopped beside her to study the river. "Why is the **stern-wheeler** out so far?" he asked.*

stevedores—one who works at or is responsible for loading and unloading ships in port
*Then Grace watched as the **stevedores** guided the crane that lifted the crate containing her piano.*

tanner—someone whose job is to make animal skin into leather
*When Carter had first arrived in Cincinnati, he'd worked at the boatworks for a short time but then decided to go out on his own as a **tanner**.*

watchman—a person who keeps watch or guards
*"Give that back," Grace demanded. "That's my mama's cloth. I'll call the **watchman** on you."*

IMPORTANT PEOPLE AND THINGS AROUND 1849

Arthur St. Clair
The United States Congress appointed Arthur St. Clair, a general in the Revolutionary War, as first governor of the Northwest Territory, which included present-day Ohio. On January 2, 1790, St. Clair made an important visit to a settlement called Losantiville. He did not like the name Losantiville, so he ordered it replaced with the name Cincinnati, in honor of the Society of the Cincinnati, an association of former officers of the Continental Army, of which St. Clair was a member. Thus, St. Clair is credited with naming the modern-day city of Cincinnati.

The Stites Party
In November of 1788 a party of twenty-six men, women and children, led by Benjamin Stites, established a settlement called Columbia inside the present-day city limits of Cincinnati. The members of the Stites party are known as the very first settlers of the city of Cincinnati.

The Panic and the Banking Crisis of 1819
In 1819, the United States' economy was in a serious economic downturn. This event was known as the Panic of 1819. It partly resulted from the Bank of the United States, as well as state and local banks, extending credit to too many people. Mostly, these people used the loans to purchase federal land in the American West. As the economic downturn got worse, the Bank of the United States continued to demand repayment for loans. The various banks' actions resulted in the Banking Crisis of 1819.

The Panic of 1819 and the Banking Crisis left many Ohioans destitute, or extremely poor. Thousands of people lost their land because they couldn't pay off their loans. United States factory owners also had a difficult time competing with earlier-established factories in Europe. Many American people could not afford the factories' goods. The United States did not fully recover from the Banking Crisis and the Panic of 1819 until the mid 1820s.

Henry Wadsworth Longfellow

Henry Wadsworth Longfellow (1807–1882) was a famous American poet, one of the most popular of his time. He is well-known for his poem "Paul Revere's Ride." Though many proud citizens of Cincinnati were calling their home "The Queen City" or "The Queen of the West" as early as 1819, Longfellow helped make the nicknames official with his poem "Catawba Wine" in 1854.

HISTORY IN PERSPECTIVE TIMELINE

March 1, 1803—Ohio becomes the 17th state in the United States of America.

1804–1806—Captain Meriwether Lewis and Second Lieutenant William Clark, of the U.S. Army, lead the Lewis and Clark Expedition to explore the American Northwest.

1812—Jacob and Wilhelm Grimm publish a collection of authentic German fairy tales.

1812–1815—The War of 1812 is fought between the Unites States and the British Empire.

September 13, 1814—Francis Scott Key composes The Star-Spangled Banner, which later becomes the national anthem of the United States.

1816—The American Bible Society is founded with a goal to put a Bible in every American home.

1816—A German man named Karl von Drais creates the first model of a modern bicycle.

1819—Cincinnati becomes a city.

March 6, 1820—President James Monroe signs the Missouri Compromise to regulate slavery in the western territories.

1826—The first photograph is taken by French inventor Nicéphore Niépce.

February 18, 1827—The Baltimore and Ohio (B & O) Railroad becomes the first U.S. railway chartered for commercial transportation of freight and passengers.